The
Tainted Relic

THE
TAINTED
RELIC

An Historical Mystery

By

The Medieval Murderers

Simon Beaufort
Bernard Knight
Ian Morson
Michael Jecks
Susanna Gregory
Philip Gooden

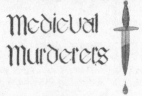

POCKET
BOOKS

First published in Great Britain by Simon & Schuster UK Ltd, 2005
This edition first published by Pocket Books, 2006
An imprint of Simon & Schuster UK
A CBS COMPANY

3 5 7 9 10 8 6 4 2

Simon & Schuster UK Ltd
1st Floor
222 Gray's Inn Road
London WC1X 8HB

www.simonandschuster.co.uk

Simon & Schuster Australia
Sydney

A CIP catalogue record for this book is available from the British Library

ISBN: 978-1-84983-118-5

Typeset in New Baskerville by Palimpsest Book Production Limited,
Polmont, Stirlingshire
Printed and bound in Great Britain by
CPI Cox & Wyman, Reading, Berkshire

'THE MEDIEVAL MURDERERS'

A small group of historical mystery writers, all members of the Crime Writers' Association, who promote their work by giving informal talks and discussions at libraries, bookshops and literary festivals.

Simon Beaufort is the pseudonym under which Susanna Gregory writes her *Sir Geoffrey Mappestone* series of twelfth-century mysteries.

Bernard Knight is a former Home Office pathologist and professor of forensic medicine who has been publishing novels, non-fiction, radio and television drama and documentaries for more than forty years. He currently writes the highly-regarded Crowner John series of historical mysteries, based on the first coroner for Devon in the twelfth century; the tenth of which, *The Elixir of Death*, has recently been published by Simon & Schuster.

Michael Jecks is the author of the immensely popular Templar series, all set during the confusion and terror of the reign of Edward II. The most recent novels in the series are *The Butcher of St Peter's* and *A*

Friar's Blood Feud. Michael was the Chairman of the Crime Writers' Association in 2004–5.

Ian Morson is the author of an acclaimed series of historical mysteries featuring the thirteenth-century Oxford-based detective, William Falconer.

Susanna Gregory is the pseudonym under which she writes the Matthew Bartholomew series of mystery novels, set in fourteenth-century Cambridge, the most recent of which, *The Tarnished Chalice,* has just been published in hardback. She also writes historical mysteries under the name of 'Simon Beaufort'.

Former schoolmaster **Philip Gooden** is the author of the Nick Revill series, a sequence of historical mysteries set in Elizabethan and Jacobean London, during the time of Shakespeare's Globe theatre. The latest titles in the series are *Mask of Night* and *An Honourable Murder.*

medieval
murderers

The Programme

Prologue – In which Simon Beaufort records dire events in Jerusalem in the 1100th year of Our Lord.

Act One – In which Bernard Knight relates dark deeds in Exeter during the reign of Richard Coeur-de-Lion.

Act Two – In which Ian Morson offers a labyrinthine tale of Oxford in the thirteenth century.

Act Three – In which Michael Jecks spins a web of intrigue in the county of Devon in the year 1323.

Act Four – In which Susanna Gregory recounts strange events in Cambridge in the middle of the fourteenth century.

Act Five – In which Philip Gooden takes the stage in London at the time of Will Shakespeare.

Epilogue – In which Bernard Knight comes up to modern times.

PROLOGUE

Jerusalem, July 1100

Jerusalem had fallen to the Crusader armies, and the Holy City was in Christian hands at last. Already, even though only two days had passed since the infidel had been defeated, messengers were riding hard northward to take the momentous news to the Pope and the western kings, proclaiming to the world that God had delivered a great victory into the deserving hands of the invincible, glorious soldiers of His holy war.

Sir Geoffrey Mappestone, one of few English knights to join the Crusade, did not feel much like a conquering hero. Months of starvation, disease, foul weather and hardship had sapped his enthusiasm for the venture. When the towering walls of the Holy City had finally been breached, and the gates flung open to admit the rest of the army, the Christians had slaughtered their way through the civilian inhabitants like avenging angels, and Geoffrey had been sickened by it. The killing had continued for an afternoon, and then a night, so that when the first rays of sunlight lit Jerusalem from the east, it was to illuminate a vision from Hell.

No quarter had been given to any Muslim or Jew,

so that the corpses of small children and old women lay next to those of able-bodied warriors. They had been massacred in their houses, doors and windows smashed by men frenzied by the stench of blood and the thought of plunder; they had been cut down in the streets when they had tried to run to safety; and, worst of all as far as Geoffrey was concerned, they had been murdered in their mosques and synagogues, where they had believed they would be spared.

Geoffrey's liege lord, Prince Tancred, had seized the land surrounding the mighty Dome of the Rock, and had placed his banner over the Temple, promising those inside that they would be spared – in exchange for a handsome ransom, naturally. But the Crusader leaders despised each other as much as they did their enemies, and Tancred's promise of clemency was ignored by his rivals. When Geoffrey visited the Temple the following day, he was forced to wade through piles of corpses that reached his knees. The Jews in their chief synagogue fared no better. They were accused of helping the Mohammedans, and the building was set alight, burning to death all inside.

When there were no citizens left, and when every house, animal, pot and pan had been seized and divided among the invaders, the sacking came to an end. The princes led their proud, blood-soaked warriors in solemn reverence to give proper and formal thanks to God in the Church of the Holy Sepulchre. Geoffrey did not join them, and instead went to stand on the city walls near the Dome of the Rock, wanting no part of the pious gloating that was taking place among the victors.

With the Crusaders at their devotions, and most

of the population dead, the city was quiet. A goat bleated from a nearby garden, and a light, hot wind whispered from the desert and caressed the ancient walls. Eddies of dust stirred in the abandoned courtyard, and patches of dry-yellow grass trembled here and there. Geoffrey went to the battlements and looked out across the barren hillside, to where the Crusaders had camped before their final assault. Empty tents snapped and fluttered, and the odd retainer could be seen here and there, left behind to guard his master's treasure. Behind him, smoke rose in a greasy grey pall; the looters' fires still smouldered among the ruins.

Geoffrey rested his arms on the wall and closed his eyes. The sun beat down on his bare head, and he felt sweat begin to course down his back. Some knights had dispensed with the mail and thick surcoats that had protected them during the battle, but Geoffrey felt uneasy in this alien city, with its minarets and pinnacles, confused jumble of alleyways and lanes, and cramped houses. His armour stayed where it was, and would do so until he felt safe.

'What happened here will live in infamy for many centuries to come,' came a quiet voice at his elbow.

Geoffrey spun around in alarm. His sword was out of his belt and he had it pointed at the throat of the man who had spoken almost before he had finished turning.

The man who stood next to him made a moue of annoyance, and pushed the weapon away. He was old, with a mouth all but devoid of teeth, and the deep wrinkles in his leathery skin suggested he had spent most of his long life under the scorching Holy Land sun. His clothes comprised a shabby monastic habit, worn leather sandals, and a waist-band made from the braided sinews of some animal. His eyes were not the faded, watery blue Geoffrey usually associated with the very ancient, but were bright and clear, so that they looked as though they belonged in a younger, less feeble body.

'You should be more careful,' said Geoffrey irritably, glancing around to ensure the fellow was alone before sheathing his sword. 'It is unwise to slip up behind soldiers so softly – especially now.'

'Especially now,' echoed the old man, regarding Geoffrey sombrely. 'You mean because your friends are so engorged by bloodlust that they strike first and only later demand to know whether we are friend or foe?'

'Yes,' replied Geoffrey, turning away from him and leaning on the wall again. 'You should stay at home and wait for some semblance of order to be established. Until then, Jerusalem is a dangerous city for anyone without a sword – even for monks.'

'I have important matters to attend to,' stated the old man indignantly. 'I cannot linger indoors, when I have so little time left. But you can help me.'

'I can, can I?' said Geoffrey, amused by the presumption.

The old man looked across the courtyard to where the massive octagonal structure dominated Temple Mount, with its smooth, gleaming dome and its walls of brightly coloured tiles. Inside was a stone where, according to tradition, Abraham had prepared to sacrifice Isaac, and where the Jews believed the First Temple's Holy of Holies had been located. Muslims thought it was the spot from where Mohammed had ascended on his Night Journey, and Geoffrey supposed it would now become a Christian shrine. Red-brown smears on the ground and an ominous splattering on the pillars still bore witness to where those under Tancred's protection had been murdered just two days before.

'You did not like what happened here, Geoffrey Mappestone. You did not take part in it.'

Geoffrey regarded him warily. 'How do you know my name?'

The old man shrugged. 'I watched what happened, and I heard you arguing with the murderers who came to spill Mohammedan blood. I asked Sir Roger of Durham who you were, and he told me.'

'Are you Mohammedan?' asked Geoffrey, thinking that if he were, then he would indeed be wise to remain hidden until the killing frenzy was properly over. His friend Roger was a good man, but even he had joined in the wave of violence.

'I am Peter,' replied the old man enigmatically. 'Will you help me, or not?'

'What do you want me to do?'

'Take this,' said Peter, rummaging in the greasy scrip that was attached to his belt and withdrawing a leather bag. 'I want you to make sure it reaches the Pope in Rome.'

'I cannot,' said Geoffrey, refusing to accept it. 'I may be here for years serving Prince Tancred, and the life of a knight in the Holy Land is precarious, to say the least. However, there are plenty of monks leaving for Rome now that Jerusalem is taken. One of them will take it.'

'But that is my problem,' said Peter. 'I do not know your monks, and I cannot tell which ones I might trust and which – and that is most of them, I imagine – I should not.'

'You do not know me, either,' Geoffrey pointed out.

'I know enough,' said Peter softly. 'A man who tries to save enemy civilians when he could be looting speaks for himself. But you *must* help me. What this bag contains is important.'

'I am sorry,' said Geoffrey firmly. 'Ask William Pichard – he is in the Pope's service and plans to travel to Rome soon. He is honest and will take your . . .' He paused, since he did not know what was in the bag that Peter considered so momentous.

'He will die,' claimed Peter authoritatively. 'Are you sure he can be trusted?'

'Why will he die?' asked Geoffrey suspiciously, wondering what he had let the hapless monk in for by so casually offering his services. 'He was healthy enough this morning.'

'That is irrelevant,' said Peter dismissively. 'Very well, since you will not help me, I shall speak to this Pichard instead. He can carry my relic to Rome.'

'A relic? And it belongs to you?' Geoffrey wondered whether the Crusaders were the only ones who had taken the opportunity to practise their thieving skills during the last two confusing days.

Peter kissed the bag with considerable reverence. 'In this pouch is a fragment of the True Cross. I rescued it from the Church of the Holy Sepulchre before your comrades got to it.'

'You stole a relic from a church?' asked Geoffrey, horrified. 'But that is sacrilege! You should put it back before you are struck down.'

'It is too late for that,' said Peter matter-of-factly. 'Far too late.'

'That is not true,' said Geoffrey, resisting the urge to back away from Peter and his dangerous booty. He was not a particularly superstitious man, but only a fool tampered with things he did not understand, and the potency of holy relics most definitely came into that category. 'You should put it back before—'

'I told you, it is *too late*,' insisted Peter sharply. 'This holy thing has been in the Church of the Holy Sepulchre for centuries – always under the care of an Arab keeper. But the events of the last two days have put an end to that.'

'Why an Arab?' asked Geoffrey, curious despite his better judgement, which warned him to have nothing more to do with the matter. 'If it really is a piece of the True Cross, then it will be one of the most sacred things in the Holy City, and should be guarded by Christians.'

'Most Christians are too frightened of its power to serve it properly,' said Peter impatiently, as though Geoffrey should have known this. 'And this Arab family has been looking after it devotedly for hundreds of years. The last member was called Barzak.'

'I suppose we killed him,' surmised Geoffrey, 'not knowing that he and his ancestors had served the Church faithfully for so long.'

'Worse,' said Peter. 'You murdered his family – here, at Temple Mount. When Barzak heard what had happened, he snatched the relic from its shrine and put a curse on it: anyone who so much as lays a finger on it will die.'

'Even more reason to put it back—' Now Geoffrey felt perfectly justified in taking a step backward, and did not care that it made him a coward. At least he would be a live one.

Peter did not seem to notice his unease, and continued with his tale, a faraway look in his blue eyes. 'Moments after Barzak had screamed his oath, the Crusaders burst into the church, and killed him. I saw and heard everything, and only just managed to rescue the relic from Barzak's dead hand before it was trampled and destroyed for ever.'

'If it is really cursed, then the only place for it is in the Church of the Holy Sepulchre,' said Geoffrey, thinking that Peter should have allowed the thing to be crushed so that it could do no one any harm. 'Take it back, and tell the priests what you saw. Perhaps they can—'

'They can do nothing!' spat Peter. 'In this world, there is nothing more dangerous than a holy relic that has been cursed by a good man. It cannot stay in Jerusalem, because who knows what might happen if it fell into the wrong hands? Evil men may use it for their own ends, and all manner of chaos may ensue. No, there is only one place where it will be rendered harmless, and that is Rome, near the tombs of the holy fathers. Are you sure you will not help me?'

'I cannot abandon my duties here,' said Geoffrey reasonably. 'But if this relic is as dangerous as you say, then you should tell the Crusade's leaders. They will know how to keep it from the wrong people.'

Peter gave him the kind of look that indicated he thought him an imbecile for putting any faith in the hard, greedy men who had foisted their hard, greedy troops on the Holy City. 'It will not be safe here, not among these butchers.'

'Then put it back and say nothing to anyone,' suggested Geoffrey. 'The "butchers" will not raid a church now the looting is over – especially not that one – and your relic will be safer here than travelling all the way to Rome.'

'I was wrong about you,' said Peter bitterly. 'I thought you were a man of principle, but you are just like all the others – and a fool into the bargain.'

He turned and walked away, his footsteps echoing across the deserted courtyard in the city that smelled of death.

As soon as the princes' religious obligations had been discharged by way of a lengthy and ostentatious service of thanksgiving, Geoffrey found himself busy for the next week helping them restore law and order in the city. Fires needed to be extinguished, soldiers fed and billeted, horses stabled, and loot divided in a manner that was considered fair by the majority. The damage caused to the walls during the attack had to be repaired, and plans drawn up to strengthen them in the event of a retaliatory attack.

When their day's work was over, and the sun was setting in a ball of fiery red, Geoffrey and Roger of Durham strolled back to their temporary quarters on the Street of the Holy Sepulchre. A civilian curfew had been imposed, so the streets were already mostly empty. An ancient black-garbed

Greek hobbled along one dusty alley, while a man with a donkey cart loaded with fruit travelled briskly in the opposite direction. Two monks hurried towards the Church of the Holy Sepulchre, where a bell was ringing to announce the beginning of compline.

Geoffrey had been too busy to think much about his strange conversation with Peter, but he recalled it in a guilty rush when he recognized one of the monks as William Pichard. Pichard was wearing his Benedictine habit, he carried a pack over his shoulder, and a stout staff was gripped in one of his strong hands. The second monk was someone Geoffrey did not like – a small, weasel-faced fellow from Normandy by the name of Julius. Julius had been involved in an unsavoury incident involving the theft of a gold crucifix some months previously, and, although nothing had ever been proven, Geoffrey had grave doubts about the man's honesty.

'We leave at dawn tomorrow,' said Pichard, after the customary greetings were exchanged. 'I have been away for three years now, and I doubt the Pope can manage without me much longer.' He gave the two knights a genial wink, clearly looking forward to going home.

'God speed,' said Roger, reaching out to grasp the monk's shoulder affectionately. 'Ride light and fast, and do not drink any water your horse will not swallow. My mother told me that, and it is advice that has always served me well.'

'Are you going to Rome too?' asked Geoffrey of Julius, thinking uneasily that he would not make an ideal travelling companion for Pichard, especially if the monk had acceded to Peter's request to take the cursed relic with him. Julius was secretive and unreliable.

Julius shrugged, and a crafty expression crossed his face. 'Part of the way, perhaps. It depends on what opportunities arise as we go.'

Roger was disparaging. 'Not many, I imagine. We looted the best of it on the way here, and I doubt there is much left for the return journey.'

'I have no time for such diversions, anyway,' said Pichard soberly. He lowered his voice confidentially, glancing around him as he spoke, to ensure he was not overheard. 'I have been charged with taking a relic to the Holy Father in Rome. I do not want charge of such a thing longer than absolutely necessary, and intend to travel as fast as possible.'

'A relic?' asked Julius in a way that made Geoffrey uncomfortable. 'I heard a lock of the Virgin's hair is still unaccounted for, and we all chipped a bit off Abraham's Rock in the Temple Mount.' He tapped his scrip, to indicate he carried his piece with him.

'Not *all* of us,' said Geoffrey pointedly.

'I have a piece of the True Cross,' said Pichard softly. 'One that is stained with the most precious blood of Our Lord Jesus Christ.'

Julius's interest quickened visibly. 'Does such a thing exist?'

'It exists,' said Roger, confidently knowledgeable. 'My father is the Bishop of Durham, as you know, and he told me about the True Cross. For many years, no one knew what had happened to it, and it was assumed it rotted away on that hill over there.' He indicated where he thought the site of the crucifixion might be with a vague wave of his hand. 'But then it became known that the Virgin Mary

11

had taken it home, chopped it into pieces, and given each of the disciples a lump.'

'On her own?' asked Julius sceptically. 'These crosses were said to have been very large.'

'Oh yes,' said Roger carelessly. 'She was a strong lady.'

'I am not sure that is right,' said Geoffrey, wondering whether the Bishop of Durham had really told Roger such a story, or whether he had heard something quite different and had embellished it to make it more interesting. 'No one knows what happened to the cross, but the Emperor Constantine was said to have had a piece.'

'My order has known for centuries that a part of it was here in Jerusalem,' said Pichard. 'Therefore, I was not surprised when I was asked to take a fragment to Rome.'

'Where is it?' asked Julius curiously.

'Safe,' replied Pichard. 'In a place that only I know.'

Julius looked disappointed, and Geoffrey wondered whether he should advise Pichard against taking the man with him when he travelled. But Pichard was no fool, and Geoffrey supposed he knew what he was doing.

'I am glad we met, Geoffrey,' Pichard went on, 'because I want you to do something for me. I am clumsy with a pen, but your writing is clear and neat. Will you act as scribe for me?' Without waiting for an answer, he rummaged in his scrip for parchment, ink and quill, which he laid out on a low wall.

Geoffrey stepped forward obligingly, and took the proffered pen, dipping it in the ink and raising his eyebrows questioningly as he waited for Pichard to begin the dictation. It was not the first time he had been asked to write letters on the Crusade. A literate knight was unusual and, although most of his military comrades considered his education anathema, some nevertheless demanded his help on occasion. He bent over the parchment as Pichard started to speak in a low voice.

'This is a fragment of the True Cross, stained with the blood of Our Lord Jesus Christ, which was preserved for safe-keeping in the Church of the Holy Sepulchre in Jerusalem . . .'

Roger leaned over to watch the words forming on the parchment. 'Aye. A relic needs a bit of writing with it, so everyone will know it is real. Sign it with your name, too, to make it look official.'

'And include the date,' added Julius helpfully. 'That will tell everyone it was found after the rescue of the Holy City from the infidel. No one will question its authenticity then.'

'And a seal,' suggested Roger. 'It needs a proper seal.'

'I do not have one,' said Geoffrey, whose hands were devoid of the heavy rings many men used to imprint the letters they had composed. He finished writing the Latin words in his neat round-hand, and waited for the hot evening sun to dry the ink.

'Use mine, then,' offered Roger, pulling the massive ring from his middle finger. 'My father gave it to me after he bought himself a larger one.'

Roger could not write, and had never needed to append a seal to any kind of document, but the ring was gold so he was fond of it. It comprised a disc similar in circumference to a silver penny, and was decorated with a cross surmounted by a mitre, to represent the Bishop of Durham's office as prelate. Geoffrey took it and jabbed it in the middle of the heavy wax that Julius was dripping on to the bottom of his parchment.

'There,' said Julius in satisfaction. 'Now it carries the seal of a powerful Norman bishop. No one will ever dare question its authenticity.'

Geoffrey was not so sure, given the dubious reputation of many bishops – and Roger's father in particular – but he held his tongue, and concentrated on waving the parchment until the wax had set. He handed the completed document to Pichard, who took it and secured it in his scrip. The compline bell jangled again, and Pichard began to move towards the Church of the Holy Sepulchre. The others followed.

'Did you hear what happened here?' asked Roger, gazing up at the church's odd mixture of towers and domes as he walked. 'Miles of Clermont, who was in charge of subduing this particular area, came across an Arab who claimed he was a faithful servant of our Church – and who demanded that he and his family should be spared because of it. But Miles taught him what happens to infidels who soil our sacred things with profane hands. What did the priests imagine they were doing, allowing an Arab inside such a place?'

'Tradition,' said Pichard softly. 'Barzak's family had looked after the relic for years. He *was* a loyal servant of the Church, and Miles should not have killed him.'

He nodded a farewell to Geoffrey and Roger, and entered the building. Julius scurried after him, and Geoffrey watched them with a troubled expression. He wished Pichard had not told Julius about the relic, and wished even more that Julius was not travelling with the monk the following morning. He also wondered whether he had been right to tell Peter that Pichard was someone who could be trusted, fearing that Pichard's willingness to take the relic to Rome might bring him a great deal of trouble.

He watched the two monks aim for the chancel, then followed, intending to cut through the building to reach his temporary lodgings in a lane on the other side. The evening office was already under way, and the heady scent of incense wafted along the nave. The priests clustered around the high altar, chanting a psalm, and their voices echoed through the various chapels that comprised the complex little church. It was cool inside, after the heat of the day, and Geoffrey wanted to linger, to savour the peace, but Roger had other ideas, and began regaling his friend with descriptions of a new brothel he wanted them to visit that evening. He tugged on Geoffrey's sleeve when the knight paused, urging him to hurry.

They left through the back door, heading for the narrow alley where their room was located, with Roger waxing lyrical on the delights to be sampled at Abdul's Pleasure Palace. Geoffrey listened with half an ear, more concerned with Pichard and Julius than with Roger's analysis of Abdul's prostitutes. He was jolted from his worries by an expletive from Roger as they were elbowed roughly out of the way by someone wearing a brown habit. Geoffrey's first thought was that the fellow was Peter, but this man was younger and had more hair. He watched him dart towards a pile of rags, where he dropped to his knees and began a low, keening moan of distress.

Geoffrey felt an acute sense of unease when he saw that the pile of rags was actually a second man in a brown robe, and that he was dead. He strode over to the grieving man and peered over his shoulder. Peter lay there, his face waxy white, and his blue eyes staring sightlessly at the darkening evening sky.

'There is no blood,' said Roger, inspecting the body with the professional eye of a man who had seen more than his share of corpses. 'He must have had a seizure.'

'He said he would die,' sobbed Peter's friend. 'As soon as he rid himself of . . .' He faltered, as if realizing that he should keep his silence.

'The relic?' asked Geoffrey, watching the man scramble to his feet and back away in alarm. 'The piece of the True Cross?'

'How do you know about that?' He glanced around fearfully.

'Peter asked me to carry it to Rome,' said Geoffrey. 'I declined, and someone else is taking it. But who are you?'

'Marcus,' whispered the man. 'Peter and I belong to an Order called the Brotherhood of the Cross, and we devote ourselves to worship of the Holy Rood.'

'Not to who actually died on it?' asked Geoffrey, thinking their priorities were muddled.

'The cross is a sacred thing, imbued with great power,' said Marcus, wiping his eyes on his sleeve and sounding as though he was reciting something he had been taught by rote. 'It is worthy of our complete devotion, just as some orders pay homage to a particular saint.'

'How much of the True Cross exists in

Jerusalem?' asked Geoffrey. 'I was under the impression that there was only a fragment.'

Marcus glanced down at Peter and tears welled in his eyes again, but he answered the question anyway. 'The fragment here, in the Holy Sepulchre, is more sacred than the rest, because it is stained with Christ's blood. But there are other pieces in the city, too, and they are also worthy of our prayers and devotions.'

'There is a huge lump in St Catherine's Church,' said Roger, gesturing with his hands to indicate something the size of a water butt. 'Splinters are being broken off it and sold to anyone with five gold coins.' He patted his purse in a way that made Geoffrey assume he had purchased one for himself.

'That particular piece is not recognized by my Order,' said Marcus, sniffing and wiping his nose on his sleeve. 'But it may be genuine, I suppose. However, it is not as holy as the one that was here.'

His statement made Geoffrey suspect that some unscrupulous cleric had hacked a piece of wood from a building, and was making his fortune from gullible buyers. He imagined that the splinters would make their way to churches and monasteries all over Christendom, where they would be revered and credited with miraculous cures. There was a lot of money to be made by religious foundations that possessed sacred relics, and most would give a great deal to own one. He sensed the business at St Catherine's was probably the first in a long line of hoaxes that would result from the Crusade.

'Poor Peter,' said Marcus, beginning to cry again. 'He said he would die, and he was right.'

'Why did he say that?' Geoffrey recalled Peter

saying that Pichard would die, but he had not mentioned his own demise, as far as he could recall.

'The curse,' whispered Marcus. 'Barzak's curse.'

'Curse?' asked Roger, backing away quickly. 'What curse?'

'Barzak said that anyone who laid a finger on the relic would perish.' Marcus sniffed miserably. 'Peter touched it, in order to give it to a monk to take to Rome – and he claimed that as soon as he relinquished it from his keeping, he would die. I hoped Barzak's curse would not work, but Peter was certain it would – which was why he would not let any of us touch the relic but him. He sacrificed himself to spare the rest of us.'

Geoffrey bent to inspect the body more carefully. There was no wound that he could see, and running his fingers across the man's scalp revealed no evidence of a blow to the head. As far as he could tell, Peter had died from natural causes.

'And he met his maker as soon as he passed the thing to Pichard?' asked Roger, regarding his own scrip with its newly purchased splinter uneasily. 'Lord save us!'

'That was part of the curse,' explained Marcus. 'That once you have set fingers on it, you must keep it about you, if you want to live. Pichard will die, too, once he relinquishes it to the Pope. And the Pope will die after he places it in his vaults.'

'Peter probably believed in the curse so strongly that when he gave the relic to Pichard he lost the will to live,' said Geoffrey practically, knowing the power of the human mind in such situations. 'It seems to me that he brought about his own death.'

'He did believe,' agreed Marcus. 'But so would

you, if you had heard Barzak's curses. They came from a terrible grief, and a deep fury at his betrayal. That relic is tainted, and I am glad it will soon be gone from my city.'

The relic and its curse played on Geoffrey's mind all evening, to the point where he abandoned Roger to his merry pleasures and left Abdul's Pleasure Palace early. He thought about Peter's belief that he would die as soon as he relinquished the relic to Pichard, and reasoned that the old man had perished simply because his heart had stopped beating. Such things happened to the elderly, and it was simple coincidence that he had died on the day he happened to give the relic to Pichard. Or he believed so strongly that he would die, he had frightened himself into doing so. When Geoffrey slept that night, however, it was uneasily.

He awoke the following day before dawn, disturbed by Roger's thundering snores, and went to mass at the Church of the Holy Sepulchre. There were few Crusaders present, because the religious fervour of the previous week was already a thing of the past. He wandered around the building with its many alcoves while the priests recited the office, and eventually discovered a small chapel devoted to the Holy Rood. He entered it quietly, not wanting to interrupt the prayers of the two brown-robed priests who knelt there.

Geoffrey looked at the altar, and saw that it was adorned with a substantial gold cross. In the middle of this splendid item was a recess, complete with a tiny glass window and a minute hinge. One of the priests, who seemed more inclined to talk than to complete his devotions, told Geoffrey that a piece of the True Cross had been kept in it – until Barzak had snatched it out and screamed his terrible curse. It was now empty, and the Brotherhood of the Cross was bereft of its most sacred relic. Some brave man, the monk whispered, had offered to carry it to Rome, where it was hoped the curse would be lifted by St Peter's holy bones.

When the mass was over, Geoffrey went outside to a city that was coming awake. A cockerel crowed, and the sky was beginning to brighten. Within an hour the sun would have risen, and Jerusalem would bake under its scorching summer heat. Carts were starting to rumble along the narrow streets, carrying provisions to the marketplaces, and the few surviving citizens – spared either because they were Christian, or because they had managed to hide until the murderous slaughter was over – were hurrying nervously about their business. Knights swaggered here and there, victors in the defeated city, while a group of foot-soldiers reeled drunkenly towards the Citadel, their night of drinking and whoring done.

Since the gates were still closed, and anyone wanting to leave the city that day would not yet have been allowed to do so, Geoffrey decided to visit Pichard. He wanted to ask why he was prepared to take such a dangerous relic on the long journey to Rome, and had decided to tell him that he could do better in his choice of companion than the light-fingered Julius. He walked to the small inn near St James's Church where Pichard was staying. A large Benedictine lounging lazily on a bench outside told him that Pichard had not left yet, but that he intended to do so within the hour.

Geoffrey climbed the uneven wooden steps to the upper floor and knocked on Pichard's door. There was no reply, so he knocked again, harder this time. When a third hammering went unanswered, he drew a short dagger from his belt, grasped the latch and opened the door.

Pichard was inside, lying fully clothed on the bed. At first, Geoffrey thought he was dead, because he lay so still and his face was an odd grey-white colour. Then he detected a slight rise and fall in the monk's chest. He glanced quickly around the room, to ensure that Julius was not lingering in the shadows with a weapon poised to strike, but it was empty. Two packs lay ready on a bench, and Pichard's travelling cloak was folded neatly on top of them. Pichard, it seemed, had been on the brink of leaving.

Geoffrey strode to the bed and took the monk's wrist in his hand, to feel the fluttering life beat under his fingertips. It was stronger than he had anticipated, so he grabbed him by the shoulders and shook him firmly. The Benedictine opened eyes that were glazed, then licked his lips and managed a faint smile.

'Geoffrey! I thought I would never see a living face again.'

'What do you mean?' demanded Geoffrey. 'There is nothing wrong with you – no wound, no sickness. You were fit yesterday, and I know of no disease that can kill a man with quite such speed.'

It was not true. He had encountered several nasty sicknesses that could reduce healthy men to corpses within a few hours, but most were contracted in damp, unhealthy air or were caused by drinking poisoned water. Pichard was a seasoned traveller, and knew how to avoid such risks.

'The relic,' said Pichard in a soft voice. 'I had it in a bag around my neck last night, but when I awoke this morning, someone had taken it. And now I will die.'

'You will not,' said Geoffrey firmly. 'Healthy men do not simply die.'

'The curse,' whispered Pichard. 'Barzak's curse. He said that anyone who touched the relic and gave it up would die.'

'Rubbish,' said Geoffrey, trying to pull the monk into a sitting position. Pichard was like a dead weight, and flopped back again. 'Barzak may have made such a claim, but rational men of God cannot put faith in that kind of thing. The infidel cursed us all the way from Constantinople to Jerusalem, and we took no notice of them. Why should this Barzak be any different?'

'Because of the True Cross,' said Pichard. 'I felt my strength ebb away as soon as the bag was taken. I was powerless to prevent it from going.'

'If you believe all this nonsense, then why did you agree to take it to Rome in the first place?' demanded Geoffrey, exasperated.

'Because it was my sacred duty,' whispered Pichard. 'It belongs in Rome, where it can be placed somewhere it cannot be used for evil. I knew I would die if I undertook the mission – Peter was honest with me in that respect – but I thought I would be safe until I reached home.'

'I suppose Julius robbed you,' said Geoffrey, disgusted. He wished he had stayed with Pichard the previous night, and then invented some excuse to prevent Julius from going with the monk. But he had not believed Julius would steal the thing quite so soon.

'It was not Julius,' said Pichard. 'It was Peter's friend – Marcus. I saw his face quite clearly in the moonlight. I suppose the Brotherhood changed its mind, and decided to keep the relic here instead of sending it to Rome, as Peter wanted. I cannot blame them.'

'I was under the impression that they considered the thing dangerous now, and better out of their city.' Geoffrey thought about the talkative monk with whom he had chatted that very morning. He had certainly not seemed sorry to see the cursed relic gone.

'Peter did, but perhaps not all his brethren agreed. Regardless, my role is over now. I was to have carried it, but now I am doomed.'

'No,' said Geoffrey. 'If you allow yourself to be overcome by this, then you may well die. But you can fight it. There is no reason you should not see Rome again.'

'I should like to see the Tiber,' whispered Pichard. 'There is no river in the world like the Tiber.'

Geoffrey slipped an arm under his shoulders and hauled him to his feet. 'Then come outside with me. See the sun and the sky, and you will feel better. Your time to die is not yet.'

He began to drag him across the room, staggering under his huge weight. He struggled down the stairs, and hauled him into the open air. Pichard raised his head and squinted up at the lightening sky, and a smile touched his lips. He took his arm from Geoffrey's shoulders and leaned against the wall.

'You may be right,' he said. Geoffrey noticed that colour was returning to his cheeks. 'I do feel better out here.'

'Breathe deeply,' suggested Geoffrey. 'And sit on the bench next to your colleague.'

The fat monk obligingly shifted along so Pichard could rest, muttering about those who drank more than was good for them the morning before long journeys. Pichard did not correct him, but sat with his eyes closed, savouring the rising sun on his face and the strength returning to his limbs.

Geoffrey soon grew restless, and wandered the short distance to the end of the lane, where he watched the sunlight slant in dusty shafts along the main road. Bells chimed across the city, and the streets were becoming busy. Suddenly, a cart thundered around the corner, spilling fruit in its wake. There was no driver, and a small crowd of people ran behind it, yelling for those ahead to bring it to a standstill. But there was little Geoffrey could do to halt a stampeding horse, and he was unprepared to risk life and limb leaping for the reins, when there was a danger of being crushed beneath hoofs or wheels. He flattened himself against a wall and the cart clattered past him. Then, just as it reached the bench where Pichard and the fat monk sat, an axle snapped.

The cart tipped, then fell to one side with a tearing scream of wood. The horse stumbled from the impact, and dropped to its knees, whinnying in pain and terror. Pieces of fruit bounced everywhere, and people raced towards them, aiming to gather as many as they could before the owner arrived to claim them. Geoffrey ran towards the bench, then stopped in horror.

Part of the cart had sheared off into a vicious spike, and this had been driven clean through Pichard as he had basked in the sun. Next to him, his fat friend sat in stunned shock, his mouth agape and his fleshy face covered in a sheen of sweat. Geoffrey quickly ascertained that he was unharmed, then turned his attention to Pichard.

The Benedictine was quite dead. He sat as Geoffrey had left him, with a smile of contentment on his face and his eyes closed. The knight backed away, his thoughts reeling. Was it just a terrible coincidence? Or was Barzak's curse really working? He rubbed an unsteady hand across his face, not sure what to believe. Pichard was dead. Peter was dead. But the relic was gone, back into the care of the Brotherhood, and Geoffrey hoped they would keep it safe, so it would never blight the lives of good men again.

In a small house in what had been the Jewish Quarter of the city, Marcus took a small leather bag from around his neck and handed it to Julius. Julius accepted it with a smile, and loosened the strings of the pouch so he could look inside. He shook it gently, and a piece of wood about the length of his middle finger dropped into the palm of his hand.

'I will ensure this reaches Rome,' he said, slipping it back into the bag and placing the whole thing inside his scrip. 'Pichard was greedy and corrupt, and would have sold it to the first unscrupulous relic dealer who offered him a bargain, but I am not subject to such weaknesses.'

'Be sure you are not,' warned Marcus, sinking to his knees as a curious lethargy came over him. The relic was about to claim its third victim, and he knew that unless Julius could take it to Rome and ensure it rested in the Vatican's deepest vaults with the bones of holy men, then more would follow. Barzak's curse was to be taken seriously, and Peter had been right to organize its removal from the city. He had simply chosen the wrong man, and it was fortunate that Julius was on hand to advise and help. 'Leave now.'

'I am already gone,' said Julius, taking up his travelling pack and heading for the door. 'Finish the wine I brought before you go to tell your brethren of our success. It will fortify you, and you are looking pale.'

Julius took the proffered cup and drained its contents. By the time he had finished, Julius had slipped out of the door and closed it behind him. Marcus was rather startled to hear the sound of a key in the lock. He pulled himself to his feet and staggered towards it, pulling ineffectually until he realized that it would not open. He wondered why Julius had done such a thing, when he had just instructed him to tell his brethren what he had done. He swayed uneasily, feeling dizzy and a little sick, and went to the table, where Julius's goblet of wine stood untouched. And then he understood.

Julius had poisoned him, and had locked him inside this remote hovel so that no one in his Order would know what had been done. But why? Marcus had given Julius the relic in good faith and willingly. Why had it been deemed necessary to kill him? He slumped to the floor as his legs became rubbery and unable to hold his weight. The answer to that question was clear, too: it was not Pichard whose motives and character were questionable, but Julius's. Julius intended to use the relic for his own ends.

Shadows clouded Marcus's vision, and he could not feel his legs. Would he have died anyway, if Julius had not killed him? He had touched the relic – to make sure it was the right one when he had stolen it back from Pichard – and had resigned himself to his fate. But would it have happened? Barzak's curse could have nothing to do with Julius's decision to commit murder. Or could it? As he closed his eyes for the last time, Marcus wondered how many more people would die before the relic reached Rome. He smiled. Julius would be one of them, because he had laid his profane fingers on it. But how many more?

Then darkness claimed him.

ACT ONE

Devonshire, 1194

The cargo boat glided up the last half-mile of the mirror-calm river, its single sail tightly furled, the flood tide being sufficient to drift it to its mooring against the quay. Short and stubby, the *Mary and Child Jesus* sat low in the water, her hold full of casks of wine from Anjou and kegs of dried fruit from Provence. The weather on the return voyage from St-Malo had been kind, unlike the outward trip, when the master had wondered whether he would ever reach harbour alive, with his load of Devonshire wool and Exeter cloth. Thorgils the Boatman, who owned the vessel, as well as being its captain, swore that this was going to be the last trip of the season. November was really too late to be risking the long Channel crossing from the mouth of the Exe to Brittany. After they had discharged their cargo at Topsham, he would take the *Mary* back the few miles to Dawlish and haul her out on the beach for a refit, then spend the time until Easter in his fine new house with his young blonde wife. The thought warmed him in spite of the cold mist that hung over the river, though the ache in his joints told him that he was getting old – twenty years older than the delectable Hilda.

The boat rode sedately along on the tide and Thorgils leaned on the steering board to make sure that her bow would nudge against the quay at exactly the right spot. He glanced to port and saw the flat marshland stretching away to the low hills in the distance. If he were to look back a little, he would almost be able to see Dawlish, the better to imagine Hilda's warm embrace.

Ahead was the river, which rapidly narrowed to reach Exeter five miles upstream. A few yards to starboard was the village of Topsham, with its welcoming alehouses and brothels, though he had no need of the latter.

The master looked down into the well of the boat, where his crew of six were assembling along the bulwark to sing the traditional hymn of thanksgiving to the Holy Virgin for deliverance from the perils of the sea, this time joined by their solitary passenger.

This Robert Blundus was a strange fellow, mused Thorgils, as the singing reached its crescendo when the blunt prow of the *Mary* nudged the quay. He had arrived at the last moment, just before they sailed from St-Malo. The shipmaster had noticed that Blundus kept looking over his shoulder at the bustling throng on the quay-side and seemed relieved when a widening gap began to appear between the ship and the shore. Thorgils suspected that he was either a fugitive from the law or had unpleasant acquaintances who were hunting him down. But it was none of his business, and the coins of mixed English and French silver that Blundus offered as his passage money were genuine enough for the master to accept him aboard without any questions.

The stem-post bumped against the wharf and willing hands ashore lashed a bow-rope around one of the tree stumps buried along the quay-side. Thorgils let the incoming tide push the stern of the *Mary* right around in a half-circle, so that the port side came to rest against the rough stone wall, the steering board left safely out on the starboard side. As the stern ropes were thrown ashore, the passenger moved to stand impatiently at the gap in the bulwarks where the landing plank would be pushed through. His large pack was already strapped to his shoulders, and Thorgils assumed that he was a chapman, one who hawked goods such as thread, needles and ribbons, around towns and villages. It was unusual, though not unknown, for one to cross the Channel in pursuit of such trade, and the shipmaster wondered whether he had family in Brittany.

The moment the gangplank was slid ashore, the traveller hurried down it with only a perfunctory wave of farewell to the crew. The quay-side of Topsham was a short length of stone wall, with muddy banks stretching away on either side. Ships could ride upright at high tide to discharge their cargo, but the rest of the time they lay canted over on the thick mud that extended for miles down to the sea at Exmouth.

Robert Blundus had never been here before, and he surveyed the little port with some disdain, being more used to large harbours such as Southampton or King Richard's new creation at Portsmouth. He saw a line of buildings straggling down the east bank of the river, ending in huts and sheds on the quay. A church tower in new stone rose above the centre of the long main street, and where there was a church, there was always an inn or two.

This turned his mind to the need for a meal and a bed for the night, as the short November day was coming to a close. He humped the heavy pack higher on his shoulders and set off through the cold mud of the wharf towards the high street. An icy east wind made his cheeks tingle and reminded him that he had left the warmer climes of France far behind. At least his ears were warm, as he wore a woollen cap pulled down over his forehead and neck, the pointed top flopping over to one side. His leather jerkin was bulky, belted over a pair of thick serge breeches, cross-gartered above wooden-soled clogs. As he strode purposefully towards the village, a dew-drop formed on the end of his fleshy nose and his rather prominent blue eyes watered as they scanned the motley collection of buildings. Some were stone, but the majority were either wood or cob, a mixture of mud and straw plastered over a wooden frame, with roofs of reeded thatch.

The narrow street was busy, especially with porters lugging large bales of wool or pushing handcarts laden with goods from the quay-side. The usual throng of loungers and tradesmen mixed with wives and grandmothers around the striped canvas booths that lined the edges of the muddy street. Beggars and cripples hunched against walls, and at the gate of the churchyard a leper swung his rattle and hopefully held out his bowl for alms. Some more permanent shops were open behind the flimsy stalls, their shutters hinged down to form counters displaying their goods.

But Robert Blundus was not looking to buy anything except a night's lodging, and his gaze was turned upward to seek the icons of the local inns. Given that only one person in a hundred could read, the taverns advertised themselves by signs hung over their doors. Looking along the street, he picked out several familiar devices – there was a Bush, an Anchor and a Crown. He chose the latter as looking slightly less dilapidated than the others and, ducking his head under the low lintel, went inside.

The large room that took up the whole of the ground floor was lit only by the flames from a large fire burning in a pit in the centre, a ring of large stones embedded in baked clay separating it from the rushes strewn over the floor. A bench ran all around the walls and a few stools and more benches were scattered around the hearth. The room was filled with men, though in one corner he heard raucous laughter coming from a pair of whores who were cavorting with some travellers. The air was thick with wood-smoke, sweat and spilt ale, the normal atmosphere of a busy tavern.

Blundus made his way towards the back of the taproom, ignoring the blasphemous abuse of a young serving-maid who bumped into him with a tray of ale-pots. He found the innkeeper, a surly man with a face badly scarred by old cow-pox, and negotiated for accommodation and food. For a penny, he was promised supper, two quarts of ale and clean straw in the loft. The landlord pointed to a wide ladder in the corner and Blundus shrugged off his pack and manhandled it up the steps. Here he found a dozen hessian bags stuffed with bracken or straw, laid out in rows under the rafters of the thatched roof. He chose one nearest to a dim tallow-dip that flickered on a shelf and dumped his backpack alongside it. The loft was deserted at that time of day, but the pedlar was wary enough to remove a small package wrapped in kid leather and put it for safe-keeping in the scrip on his belt.

Downstairs, he was served his promised meal on a rough table under the ladder, alongside a row of casks of ale and cider. An earthenware bowl of mutton stew was banged down in front of him by the foul-mouthed serving-maid, together with a thick trencher of stale bread on which was a slab of fat boiled pork. A spoon crudely carved from a cow's horn was supplied for the stew, but he used his own dagger to attack the pig meat. A half-loaf of rye bread and a lump of hard cheese followed, and he considered that the food was adequate in quantity, if not quality – though after days of shipboard tack, he was in no mood to complain. After two large pots of passable ale, he felt ready to sleep, as it was now dark outside.

Climbing back up the ladder, Blundus felt both his advancing age – he was almost fifty – and the effects of three days rolling across the Channel on a small boat, so he was glad to flop down on to his bag of straw. He opened his pack again to pull out a woollen cloak to serve as a blanket, then could not resist another look at his most prized acquisition. In the dim light, he groped in his belt pouch and unwrapped the soft leather bundle, revealing a small wooden box, small enough to lie across his hand, intricately carved and partly covered in gold leaf, though much had worn off to reveal the dark rosewood underneath. Blundus opened the hinged lid and looked again at the glass vial that lay inside. He took it out, pulled off the gilded stopper and tipped the contents into his palm. Though he had examined it several times before, the thing still intrigued him – a grey stick-like object, a few inches long, composed of dried wood, as hard as stone. The surface was dark brown in places, which he assumed was the alleged staining with the blood, though Blundus neither believed nor cared whether it had genuinely come from the cross of Jesus Christ. As a connoisseur of relics, however, he knew that it must have considerable value, given its unusual authentication.

Cynically, but realistically, he knew that if all the alleged fragments of the True Cross revered in abbeys, priories and cathedrals across Europe were assembled together, they would not reconstitute a cross, but a small forest! Similarly, most of the bone fragments of the saints and martyrs owed their origin to sheep, swine and even fowls. Still, no religious establishment that wished to attract the lucrative pilgrim trade could afford to be without a relic or two – and the more extravagant the claims of origin, the more valuable they were.

Robert Blundus slipped the relic back into its tube and replaced the wooden plug. Though ostensibly he was a common chapman, this was a cover for his real trade, as a dealer in religious relics. He travelled the roads of England in his search and often went to France, Spain and even Italy to seek sanctified artefacts. He prided himself on dealing in a better class of relics than the many pedlars who hawked homemade or obviously spurious objects about the countryside, and he had built up a reputation for procuring good material. This particular relic was such a prize addition to his stock because it had a certificate of provenance. He felt in the little box and took out a folded strip of parchment, bearing a short sentence in Latin. He could not read it, but for a silver coin a clerk in Fontrevault Abbey had translated it for him. *This is a fragment of the True Cross, stained with the blood of Our Lord Jesus Christ, which was preserved for safe-keeping in the Church of the Holy Sepulchre in Jerusalem.* It was signed by Geoffrey Mappestone, Knight – and, most important of all, bore a small wax seal carrying an impression from his signet ring over the date, July 1100.

Blundus grinned to himself as he carefully put away the vial and parchment and wrapped up the wooden box. Thankfully, the Crusader's certificate of authentication made no mention of Barzak's curse, which might well have reduced the value of the relic to almost nothing.

As he lay back on his pallet, trying to ignore the influx of strange fleas that entered his clothing to breed with his own French mites, he sleepily went over in his mind what the abbey clerk had told him. The man was a priest in lower orders, employed in the chancery of Fontrevault, the famous abbey in Anjou, and was thus well acquainted with the gossip and legends of that place. Sweetened by his translation fee and several cups of red wine, he told Blundus that the relic had been brought to the abbey over ninety years earlier, in the first years of the century. It had been sold to the then abbot by one Julius, who had travelled from Marseilles, where he had landed by ship from the Holy Land.

He was paid for it in gold, on the basis of Sir Geoffrey's authentication, but that evening, on his way to the nearby Loire to take a boat down to the coast, Julius had been struck by lightning in a sudden violent thunderstorm that had appeared from a clear blue sky. The clerk was happy to relate the gruesome fact that when the blackened corpse was found, the gold had been fused into a molten mass which had burned into Julius's belly!

The abbot had had a special gilded box made for the relic, which was placed in an ornate casket upon the altar of the Chapel of the Holy Rood, off the main nave of the great abbey. Though originally vaunted as a most important acquisition, it soon fell out of favour, as pilgrims and cripples who came to pray and supplicate before it either gained no benefit or actually became worse. Within a few years, the relic was shunned and ignored, especially after ominous rumours began circulating about the curse, brought back by knights and soldiers returning from the First Crusade, especially some of the newly formed Templars. The chancery clerk had told Blundus that the present abbot had plans to remodel the chapel and either consign the relic to a remote corner of the crypt or even send it to Rome for others to deal with the unwelcome object as they saw fit.

Robert Blundus had been making his way back through Aquitaine and Anjou to reach the Channel ports to return home after his autumn forage for relics as far south as Santiago de Compostela in Spain. He had called at Fontrevault on the off-chance of picking up a final bargain, perhaps from one of the other relic hawkers trying their luck at selling to the famous abbey. He followed his usual practice of seeking out and bribing some servant of the religious house who knew all the local gossip, and this time struck lucky with the abbey clerk. On the basis of what he learnt from him, Blundus hired a thug from a low tavern to steal the fragment, the side chapel being virtually deserted at certain times of the day. The thief easily levered open the reliquary with his dagger and removed the gilded box. It could well be days or even weeks before anyone noticed that the shunned relic had vanished – and according to the clerk, the abbey authorities might well be relieved at its disappearance.

Without opening the box, the incurious thief had promptly handed it over to collect his reward, and by nightfall Blundus was well on his way north astride his pony. He kept a wary eye open for pursuit, in case the ruffian had given him away, but he reached St-Malo without incident and here sold his steed and took ship for England.

Now he settled back on his bag of straw and contentedly looked forward to going home to his house and his wife in Salisbury. Once he had sold the relics he had acquired, he could live in comfort on the proceeds throughout the winter, until the spring sent him off again on his travels.

Blundus set out soon after dawn, buying a couple of mutton pastries and a small loaf at a stall in Topsham High Street. He ate as he trudged along, well used to long journeys on foot – he felt it was not worth haggling for another pony on this side of the Channel. He was aiming for Glastonbury in the next county of Somerset, before turning eastward for home, but there was no great hurry. He reckoned on covering at least fifteen miles before each nightfall, even during the shorter days of late autumn.

He had enquired of the best route at the inn and

the tactiturn landlord had directed him as far as Honiton, beyond which the man had no idea of the roads. The chapman was told that the village of Clyst St Mary was his first landmark, and within an hour he had passed through the small hamlet, the manor of which belonged to the Bishop of Exeter.

There was the usual straggle of people on the rough track beyond the village, a man herding goats to market, an old woman with a pig on a rope and a number of pilgrims in their wide-brimmed hats, on their way back from Canterbury. An ox-cart rumbled past him, filled with turnips, then the road was empty as it curved through a dense wood of tall trees, their browned leaves fluttering to the ground in the east wind. It was hardly a forest, as just around the bend behind him the strip fields of Clyst St Mary ran up the slopes on either side of the road, but it was a substantial wood, a westerly extension of the forest that stretched eastward for miles towards Ottery St Mary and Sidmouth.

Robert Blundus was not a nervous man and he was used to tramping alone along the tracks of several countries. He had no sword, but carried a stout staff which was mainly for support. He reasoned that a common chapman was hardly worth the attention of highway robbers, though when he could, he tried to travel in the company of others for safety.

Today there was no one going the same way on this part of the road and he stepped out along the empty avenue of trees with no particular apprehension, thinking more of the pitch he was going to make to the Abbot of Glastonbury, to get the best price for his notable relic. It was therefore all the more of a shock when suddenly he heard a rustle in the undergrowth at the side of the track, and before he could turn he was grabbed from behind and violently thrust to the ground. He had a quick glimpse of two ragged figures tearing at the straps of his pack, before he managed to swing his staff and strike one of them on the shoulder. With a bellow of pain, the ruffian raised a club made from a twisted branch and struck Blundus on the head. Cursing, he repeated the blows, and when the pedlar had fallen senseless, gave him some heavy kicks in the ribs and belly for good measure. Pulling the large pack free and rifling the pouch on his belt, the two footpads made off into the trees, leaving the injured man unconscious on the verge.

Perhaps somewhere in Heaven – or maybe Hell – the spirit of Barzak the Mohammedan was content that his curse was still as potent as ever.

High up in the narrow gatehouse tower of Exeter's Rougemont castle, the county coroner was sitting in his cramped and draughty chamber, painfully mouthing the Latin words that his bony forefinger was slowly tracing out on a sheet of parchment. Sir John de Wolfe was learning to read, and at the age of forty was finding it a tedious process. His clerk, former priest Thomas de Peyne, sat at the end of the rough trestle table that, with two stools, was the only furniture in the room that the sheriff had grudgingly allotted them. Thomas watched covertly as his master laboriously mispronounced the words, wishing that he could help him, in place of the stupid vicar who was ineptly teaching the coroner. The clerk, once a tutor in the cathedral school of Winchester, was a fluent reader and a gifted calligrapher – it pained him to see the slow progress that Sir John was making, but he knew the coroner's pride prevented him from asking for help.

On a window sill opposite the table sat a giant of a man, staring out through the unglazed slit through which moaned a cold wind. He had wild red hair like a storm-tossed hayrick, and a huge drooping moustache of the same ruddy tint. Gwyn, a Cornishman from Polruan, had been de Wolfe's squire and companion for almost twenty years, in campaigns stretching from Ireland to the Holy Land. When the Crusader had finally sheathed his sword a couple of years ago, Gwyn had remained as his bodyguard and coroner's officer. He lowered the hunk of bread and cheese that he was chewing and focused his bright blue eyes on the road that came up from the High Street to the gatehouse drawbridge below.

'There's a fellow riding up Castle Street as if the Devil himself is on his heels,' he announced, speaking in the Cornish Celtic that he used with the coroner, who had a Welsh mother from whose knee he had learned a similar language.

'Why can't you speak in a civilized fashion, not that barbaric lingo!' whined the clerk in English. He was a runt of a fellow, his excellent brain betrayed by a poor body. He was small, had a humped shoulder, a lame leg and his thin, pinched face had a long pointed nose and a receding chin. The fact that he had been unfrocked as a priest over an alleged indecent assault on a girl pupil in Winchester made him not the most eligible of men. Gwyn ignored him and, wiping the breadcrumbs from his moustache with the back of his hand, addressed himself again to John de Wolfe.

'I know that man, he's the manor-reeve from Clyst St Mary. I'll wager he's coming up here.'

The coroner pushed his parchment aside in disgust, glad for some excuse to give up his lesson.

'We've had nothing from that area for weeks,' he growled. As the first coroner for Devon, appointed less than three months earlier, he was responsible for looking into sudden deaths, murders, accidents, serious assaults, rapes, fires, treasure trove, catches of royal fish and a host of other legal situations. This was mostly with the object of drumming up revenue for King Richard, to help pay for his costly wars in France, as well as paying off the massive ransom owing to Henry of Germany, after Richard's capture on the way home from the Crusades.

Gwyn was soon proved correct, as there was a clatter of feet on the narrow stairway that curled up from the guardroom below. The sacking that hung over the doorway as a feeble draught excluder was pushed aside to admit two men. The first was a man-at-arms in a thick leather jerkin and a round iron helmet, the other a thin man with a harelip, his serge riding mantle covered in road dust.

'You're too late, Gabriel, the ale is all gone!' mocked Gwyn, grinning at his friend, the sergeant of the castle's men-at-arms. The grizzled old soldier touched his hand to his helmet in salute to de Wolfe, who he greatly respected as another seasoned warrior.

'This man wants to report a violent death, Crowner. Aylmer is his name, the reeve from Clyst

St Mary.' A reeve was the overseer of a manor, who organized the work rotas for the bailiff and was a kind of village headman. This was the first time he had had dealings with this new-fangled business of coroners, and he looked at the new official with curiosity and some unease.

He saw a forbidding figure sitting behind the trestle, a man as tall as Gwyn, but not so massively built. He was dressed in a plain tunic of black, a colour that matched the abundant jet hair that curled down to his collar and the dark stubble on his long, lean face. Heavy black eyebrows overhung deep-set eyes and his big hooked nose and slightly stooped posture gave him the appearance of a great bird of prey. Aylmer had heard gossip about him and saw now why his military nickname had been 'Black John'.

'Well, what's it all about, man? Don't just stand there with your mouth hanging open,' snapped the coroner.

The reeve was jerked into activity and quickly described how a man had been found that morning at the side of the road, with injuries from which he died in less than an hour. He had been discovered by a couple of villagers who were on their way to repair sheep pens on the other side of the woods. One had run back to Clyst to raise the hue and cry, but nothing had been found anywhere and the bailiff had sent Aylmer post-haste to Exeter to notify the coroner.

'We have heard that we must tell you straightway of all deaths, Crowner,' he said earnestly. 'Not even to move the body, so we understand.'

He said this as if it were a totally incomprehensible command, but de Wolfe nodded. 'You did the right thing, Reeve. Do you know who this man might be?'

Aylmer shook his head. 'A total stranger, walking the high road. God knows where he was coming from or going to. Not a local, that's for sure.'

At the moment when the reeve was telling his story, a small group of men were squatting around a dying campfire in a forest clearing, a couple of miles from Clyst St Mary. All were dishevelled, some were dressed in little better than rags, and none looked well fed – a pathetic band of outlaws, bound together only by their hatred of authority and their fear of the law officers of Devonshire. Each one of the nine had a different reason for being outcast in the forests – some had escaped from gaol, either before trial or after they had been convicted, and were waiting to go to the gallows. Gaol-breaking was common, as every prison guard was open to bribery, and often the local community was eager to save the expense of feeding them until they were hanged. Others had sought sanctuary in a church after some crime, then chosen to abjure the realm. The coroner would have taken their confessions, then sent them dressed in sackcloth to a port to get the first ship out of the realm of England – but as soon as they were around the first bend in the road, many such abjurers would throw away the wooden cross they had to carry and melt into the trees to become outlaws. The remainder had just run away when accused of some crime, whether guilty or not. Many did not trust the rough justice meted out by the manor, shire or King's courts – others knew they would be convicted and, as the penalty for most crimes was death, they chose the leafy refuge of the forest or the wilderness of the moors. If such suspects failed to answer to four calls at the shire court, they were declared outlaw and henceforth were 'as the wolf's head' – in other words, any man could legitimately slay them on sight and, as with the wolf bounty, claim five shillings if they took the outlaw's head to the sheriff. This particular group eked out their existence by preying on travellers on the roads between Clyst St Mary and Honiton, though they also stole sheep and poultry from neighbouring villages. One or two even earned a few pence by working in the fields of certain villages, where the reeves turned a blind eye to outlaw labour when the need arose. They lived rough in the forest, sleeping in shelters of woven branches or holes dug in hillsides or river banks, stealing food from isolated crofts or buying it with money thieved from passers-by.

Today, they clustered around the two men who had assaulted and robbed the chapman on the high road, to see what they had stolen.

There was no communal spirit among these men, no sharing of booty, and, unlike the larger gangs, they had no proper leader. Each man kept what he had stolen, and those who failed to make a hit went hungry. But curiosity was a powerful thing, and they all wanted to see what Gervase of Yeovil and Simon Claver had managed to get today.

'We had to beat the bastard quite hard,' grunted Gervase. 'He fought back well enough.' As he spoke, he untied the straps on Blundus's pack and tipped the contents on to the ground.

'What in God's name is this rubbish?' snarled Simon, stirring a collection of small boxes and packets with his foot. Apart from a moderately clean spare tunic, a couple of undershirts and some hose, the packets were the only things in the pack.

'I thought you said he was a chapman?' sneered one of the other outlaws. 'Where's all his stock, then?'

'He had twenty pence in his purse,' countered Simon defensively, aggrieved at the critical attitude of his fellows. 'I took that and Gervase here snatched his pack.'

'You came off best, then,' cackled the other man. 'What he's got doesn't look worth a ha'penny!'

Gervase was looking thoughtfully at the collection of oddments on the ground, and began sorting through the packets and rolls, mostly wrapped in bits of leather or parchment. One particular object, a small wooden box wrapped in soft leather, caught his attention, and he unwrapped it and studied a small piece of parchment with interest, Simon looking over his shoulder suspiciously.

'I might get a few pence for some of this stuff, if I can get into the city,' he said with false nonchalance. He threw the clothing at Simon as he stuffed the other objects back into the pack.

'Here, you can take these, you could do with some clean clothes, the way you stink!'

Simon, a tall, sinewy man of thirty, with a nose horribly eroded by some disease, looked suspiciously at his fellow-robber, afraid that he was being outwitted.

'What's that stuff, then? It was me that hit the pedlar the hardest, maybe I should be getting a share of it?'

To appease him, Gervase, a stockier older man, unrolled one of the packets and displayed a shrivelled piece of skin in a glass vial.

'Some lucky charm to peddle to a gullible widow, no doubt. Probably claimed to be St Peter's foreskin! Worth tuppence, if I'm lucky!'

Though Simon continued to look suspiciously at Gervase, the others soon lost interest in this mundane collection and, after kicking the last glowing embers of the fire into extinction, drifted away, leaving Gervase to shoulder the half-empty pack and wander off deeper into the trees, headed in the general direction of the road to Exeter.

As he walked, he again gave thanks for the fact that he was better educated than these dolts among whom cruel fate had thrown him. He had plans to escape the outlaw life as soon as he could, and this might be the opportunity he had been seeking for over a year. Gervase knew that many other outlaws had unobtrusively slipped back into normal life after an interval, usually at a place well away from their original haunts. One had even become a sheriff, until he was found out several years later.

To escape this miserable existence, it was essential for him to have money, to tide him over until he could build a new life. Until two years ago, he had been a parish priest in a hamlet near Yeovil, where he was born. He had never been a good priest, having been pushed into becoming a choirboy at Exeter Cathedral, after his shoemaker father died and his mother could no longer support five children. At eighteen, he progressed to becoming a 'secondary', an apprentice priest in the household of one of the cathedral canons. In due course, at the requisite age of twenty-four, he was ordained as a priest, and served the canon as one of his vicars, attending most of the endless services each day while his master stayed at home taking his ease. Dissatisfied and disgruntled, he eventually obtained a living at a parish near his home town and, though it was a poor one, at least there he was his own master. A fondness for wine and occasional trips to a brothel in Exeter, however, made him discontented with his miserable stipend, and he was driven by debt to sell a chalice and plate from his own church, claiming that they had been stolen. He was soon exposed and the bishop's Consistory Court expelled him both from his parish and from the priesthood. It was only by claiming 'benefit of clergy' that he avoided the Shire Court, which would surely have hanged him, as all thefts of objects worth more than a shilling were felonies and inevitably carried the death sentence.

Thrown out of his living, Gervase turned to petty crime to survive and, following thefts from various villages, he was soon was on the run from the 'hue and cry'. The only place left was the forest, and for the past year or so he had been living rough with this handful of crude companions. He was careful not to let them know that he had been a priest; his tonsure had grown over before he became outlaw and he never revealed that he could read and write, a legacy from his days in the cathedral school that he had attended as a choirboy. Gervase was not quite sure why he had hidden his background, except to avoid possible ridicule from their jealous tongues, but now he was glad, as they would not realize that he recognized that at least one of the relics in Blundus's pack was of some value.

The band of outlaws usually split up each day, going about their own nefarious business, but meeting either that evening or the next at some pre-arranged rendezvous in the woods. This time, the former priest hoped that, with luck, he would never see them again, if the plan that was fermenting in his mind was successful.

Early that afternoon, Gervase was resting up in a thicket just inside the edge of the forest, a few hundred paces from the Exeter road. The next part of his plan required the cover of darkness, so he was dozing under a ragged blanket that he usually wore wrapped around his shoulders, trying not to shiver in the late autumn chill.

He was unaware of someone passing on the muddy track who had much in common with him – another unfrocked priest. Thomas de Peyne was jogging by on his pony, sitting side-saddle like a woman. He was following the rest of the coroner's team and the reeve from Clyst St Mary as they rode to inspect the body of Gervase's victim. A mile farther on, they saw a small group of men standing at the edge of the track, under a canopy of red- and brown-leafed trees.

'They are my men, guarding the corpse,' announced the reeve, and when they dismounted and approached the sentinels, they saw a still figure sprawled face down in the grass and weeds. Gwyn and the coroner squatted alongside it and de Wolfe tested the stiffness in the arms and legs. 'Been dead at least a few hours,' he grunted, then ran his fingers over the back of the cadaver's head, where he felt dried blood in the hair and a pulpy swelling covering half the top of the head

'Not much doubt how he died,' said Gwyn, with grim satisfaction, as he laid his own fingers on the scalp. 'He's had a good hammering on his head – come and have a feel, Thomas!' The big Cornishman could never resist teasing the clerk, as he knew how squeamish Thomas was about such matters.

John de Wolfe looked down at the body, taking in the sober but good-quality serge breeches and leather jerkin, with a stout pair of clogs on the feet.

'Not a yeoman nor a journeyman,' he mused. 'Neither does he look like a pilgrim or well-to-do merchant.'

'He'd do for a chapman, I reckon,' said the reeve. 'Though he's got no pack.'

Gwyn heaved the body over on to its back. 'He still has a scrip on his belt,' he grunted, opening the flap of the purse attached to the dead man's belt. 'Empty! Whatever was in it has gone the same way as his pack.'

Though not mistrusting his officer, John felt obliged to look for himself, and he frowned as his finger picked up some glinting specks as he poked into the corners of the pouch.

'Strange! Looks like shards of gold leaf.'

'Maybe he was a goldsmith?' hazarded Gwyn. 'Though they rarely travel alone, given the value of their wares.'

One of the villagers, who stood forming a silent audience, spoke up.

'Plenty of bloody outlaws in these woods. Damned menace they are, stealing from us all the time. I lost three chickens last week – and it weren't no fox, neither.'

'They don't usually kill, though,' admitted the reeve.

'He was just unlucky, this fellow,' said the coroner. 'They must have hit him harder than they intended.'

Even with the body face up, no one recognized the man. His face was discoloured from the death staining that had run downward into his skin, except where the nose and chin remained pale from being pressed into the ground.

'Stranger, he is!' remarked another bystander. 'Not from round here.'

Between them, Gwyn and the reeve pulled off the jerkin, undershirt and breeches and examined the rest of the body.

'Some nasty scratches on his chest and loins – and big fresh bruises as well,' observed the coroner's officer, pointing to some pink-red discolorations on the victim's trunk. He felt a couple of broken ribs crackling under the pressure of his big fingers.

'Been kicked, no doubt,' grunted de Wolfe, an expert on all manner of injuries after two decades of fighting in Ireland, France and the Holy Land. He looked up at the reeve.

'You said he was still alive when he was found?'

One of the villagers, an older man with grey bristly hair, answered.

'Only just, Crowner! I found him and he lasted no more than half an hour after that before he passed away, God rest his soul.'

'He said nothing about who attacked him?'

The man shook his head. 'Anyway, he wouldn't

recognize some bloody forest thieves, especially as he's a stranger. All he got out with his last gasps was "Glastonbury" – and then something about some curse.'

De Wolfe glared at the villager. 'What sort of curse? Was he just cursing those who attacked him?'

'No, there was some name he called it . . . what was it, now?' The elderly villein scratched the grey stubble on his face as an aid to memory. 'Yes, strange name it was, stuck in my memory . . . Barzak, that was it!'

It was dusk by the time John de Wolfe got back to his house in Martin's Lane, a narrow alley that joined Exeter's High Street to the cathedral Close. It was a tall, narrow building of timber, one of only three in the lane, facing a livery stable where he kept Odin, his old warhorse. He was in good time for the evening meal and so avoided a sour face from his wife Matilda, who was forever complaining about the irregular hours that resulted from him being the county coroner – though it was she who had pushed him into the post several months before, seeing it as a way to claw her way farther up the social ladder of the county hierarchy. Her brother, Sir Richard de Revelle, was the sheriff of Devon, and to have a husband who was the second-most senior law officer was another feather in her snobbish cap.

Matilda was a short, heavily built woman, four years older than her husband. They had been pushed into marriage by their parents sixteen years earlier, and both had regretted it ever since. Until he gave up warfare two years previously, John had

managed to stay away from his wife for all but a few
months of those sixteen years, at endless
campaigns in Ireland, France and in the Holy Land
at the Third Crusade.

Their meals were usually silent affairs, as each sat
at the far ends of the long table in the hall, the only
room apart from Matilda's solar built onto the back
of the house, reached by wooden stairs from the
yard behind. Tonight, John made an effort at
conversation, telling Matilda of the unknown
victim of outlaws at Clyst St Mary. She showed little
interest, as usual, and he thought sullenly that if
the dead man had been a canon or a bishop she
would have been all ears, having a morbid fascination with anything to do with the Church. She
spent much of her time at her devotions, either in
the huge cathedral a few yards away or at her
favourite little parish church, St Olave's in Fore
Street, where he suspected that she had a crush on
the fat priest.

He pressed on doggedly with his tale, telling how
he had held an inquest in the tithe barn of the
village, getting Gwyn to gather as many of the male
inhabitants over twelve years of age as a jury. They
had to inspect the body and the First Finder, the
old man, had to relate how the corpse was discovered. As he was a stranger, it was impossible for the
village to 'make presentment of Englishry', to
prove that he was a Saxon and not a Norman,
though as well over a century had passed since the
Conquest, this was becoming more and more
meaningless as the races intermarried. It was
another ploy for the King's Council to screw more
money from the populace, however, as without
such proof the 'murdrum' fine would be imposed

on the village, as a redundant penalty for Saxons assassinating their invaders.

There was little else the inquest could achieve, he concluded to the inattentive Matilda. The only possible verdict was 'murder by persons unknown', and there seemed little chance of ever finding the outlaws in those dense woods that threaded through cultivated land all over the county.

When they had finished their meal, boiled salmon with onions and cabbage served on trenchers of thick stale bread, their maid Mary came in to clear up and bring a jug of Loire wine, which they drank seated on either side of the blazing log fire in the hearth. John had made one concession to comfort in the high, bare hall by having a stone fireplace built against the back wall, with a new-fangled chimney going up through the roof, instead of the usual fire-pit in the centre of the floor, which filled the room with eye-watering smoke.

They sat in silence again while they finished their wine, then his wife predictably announced that she was retiring to her solar to have her French maid Lucille prepare her for bed. John sat for a while with another cup of wine, fondling the ears of his old hound Brutus, who had crept in from the back yard to lie before the fire. Some time later, the dog rose to his haunches and looked expectantly at his master, part of a familiar routine.

'Come on, then, time for our walk.' With Brutus as an excuse that fooled no one, least of all Matilda, John took his wolfskin cloak from a hook in the vestibule and stepped out into the gloom, heading across the close for the lower town. Here, in Idle

Lane, was the Bush Inn – and its landlady, his Welsh mistress, the delectable Nesta.

At about the same time that the coroner was loping through the ill-lit streets of Exeter, the outlaw Gervase was committing yet another felony in the village of Wonford, just outside the city. By the light of a half-moon, seen fitfully through gaps in the cloud, he crept up to the village church. It was deserted in the evening, as the parish priest had no service until the early morning mass the following day. When Gervase trod quietly up to the church door, he knew from his own experience that the parson would be either sleeping or drinking after his supper in the small cottage at the far end of the churchyard. Gently opening the door, he made his way in almost pitch darkness to the back of the building, below the stubby tower that had been added when the old wooden church from Saxon times had been reconstructed in stone twenty years earlier.

Here he groped about and was rewarded by the feel of a coarse curtain which hung over an alcove, a space for a birch broom and a couple of leather buckets as well as ecclesiastical oddments, such as lamp oil, candles and spare vestments. Gervase pulled the curtain aside and felt around the walls inside until his fingers found some garments hanging from a wooden peg. Taking them down, he went back to the door and waited for the moon to appear again, so that he could see what they were. With a grunt of satisfaction, he found that he had a broad-brimmed pilgrim's hat and an old cassock, a long black tunic that reached to the ankles, as well as a thin white super-pelisse, usually called a 'surplice'. This last was of no use to him and he took it back to its peg, then made off into the night with his spoils.

After sleeping under a bush just within the forest's edge, he rose late and ate the remnants of the food he had saved from the gang's last meal. In the daylight, he saw that the cassock was patched and threadbare, but still serviceable. His next task was to take his small knife and, after honing it well on a piece of stone, use it not only to rasp three weeks' growth of stubble from his face, but also from the crown of his head, roughly restoring the tonsure that he used to have before he was ejected from holy orders. It was a difficult task to perform on himself, but with patience and determination he made a fair job of transforming himself back into a priest, especially after he had stuffed his own meagre clothing into his pack, put on the stolen cassock and jammed the battered hat on his head.

Around what he judged to be noon, he went back to the road and with his ash staff in his hand, set off boldly towards Exeter. He decided that it was highly unlikely that he would be recognized by someone from his past life in distant Yeovil, especially as the drooping brim of the pilgrim's hat helped to obscure his face. There were a few others on the track, going both to and from the city, but the main traffic of people going into Exeter with produce to sell had long since dwindled, most entering the city as soon as the gates opened at dawn. To those whom he passed he gave a greeting and sometimes raised his hand in a blessing. After a while he began to feel as if he really was a priest again, and he became more confident as he approached the South Gate. He slowed his pace so that he entered together with a group of country folk driving a couple of pigs and carrying live ducks and chickens hanging by their feet from poles over their shoulders. The porter on the gate was too interested in munching on a meat pie to give him even a cursory glance, and soon Gervase was striding up Southgate Street, past the Serge Market and the bloodstained cobbles of the Shambles, to reach Carfoix, the central crossing of the four main roads. He had been to Exeter a few times, some years ago, but now had to ask directions from a runny-nosed urchin.

'Where's St Nicholas Priory, lad?'

The boy decided that this cleric was too tough looking to risk some cheeky reply and pointed out the way. 'Not far down there, Father. A rough part of town, that is.'

Gervase entered some narrow lanes and found himself in a mean part of the city known as Bretayne, filled with densely packed houses, huts and shacks, the filthy alleys running with sewage, in which urchins, goats, dogs and rats seemed to survive in squalid harmony. After a few turns and twists, he saw a small stone building, enclosed by a wall that marked off a vegetable plot and a few fruit trees.

There was no porter on the gate and he went along a stony path that led around to the entrance. Near by, a barefoot monk was hoeing weeds between rows of onions, a dark Benedictine habit hoisted up between his bare thighs and tucked into his belt. He straightened up and stared curiously at the visitor, who held up his hand in a blessing and dredged some appropriate Latin greeting from his memory.

'I wish to speak with the prior,' he said, reverting to common English.

'Ring the bell at the door, Brother,' replied the gardener, pointing at an archway.

He did so. A young novitiate appeared and, after enquiring about his business, led him along a short, gloomy passage and knocked at the door of the prior's parlour.

Inside, Gervase found the head of the establishment seated behind a small table, some parchments before him and another pale young brother seated at his side, wielding a quill pen. Prior Vincent was a small man with an almost spherical head. He had no tonsure, for he was completely bald, and his face was moon shaped to match. Given his small eyes and prim, pursed mouth, Gervase felt that he was not the ideal customer for a sacred relic, but he had little choice in the matter.

With the novitiate lurking behind him, the other two monks stared enquiringly at this rather shabby priest who stood before them.

'What can we do for you, Brother? Are you seeking bed and board on your travels?' asked the prior, in a high, quavering voice.

The renegade priest falsely explained that he was from a parish in North Somerset, on his way home from a pilgrimage to Santiago de Compostela and recently landed from a ship at Plymouth. Gervase followed his habit of sticking as close to the truth as possible, as he had once been a pilgrim to Santiago many years before and could fabricate a convincing story about it if challenged. He chose Somerset for his parish as this was in a different diocese from Exeter and it would be less likely that anyone here would be familiar with any of the incumbents from that area.

'I would be grateful for a little food and drink, but I have no wish to impose upon you for a night's lodging,' he said piously.

The prior nodded, relieved that they were spared the trouble and expense of putting up an unexpected guest. 'Young Francis here will see that you get something in the kitchen, before you go on your way.'

He said this with an air of finality and picked up a parchment roll again, but Gervase had not finished. 'There is one thing more which may interest you, Prior. I will admit that after six months' journeying, I am destitute, my last coins being spent on the passage from St-Malo to Plymouth.'

The prior suppressed a groan, thinking that here was another impoverished priest looking for a handout, but his suspicions were dispelled by Gervase's next words.

'I came across a remarkable item on my travels which I felt might interest some religious house in England. I intended taking it to Wells or perhaps Winchester, but as I find myself in Exeter with virtually no funds to continue my journey, I thought to offer it here first.'

Prior Vincent was intrigued, but he was not altogether satisfied with this scruffy clerk who had wandered in from the street.

'Why, then, did you not go first to the cathedral?'

The outlaw had anticipated this question – he had deliberately avoided the cathedral, where the far larger complement of priests increased the risk of his being recognized.

'I had heard of St Nicholas Priory and knew it to be a daughter of Battle Abbey, whose fame is known far and wide. It occurred to me that you might relish the opportunity to secure the object to present to your abbot, gaining his gratitude and respect.'

The flattery was not lost on the prior, who could also benefit from some extra goodwill from his superior at Battle, the abbey near Hastings erected by William the Bastard to commemorate the great victory of the Normans that gave them England.

'What is this remarkable object?' he snapped. 'Not yet another piece of the True Cross, I hope?' he added sarcastically.

Gervase managed not to look discomfited as he admitted that, indeed, it was. 'But with a great difference, Prior, from the usual dross that unscrupulous relic merchants hawk around. This has undoubted authentication.'

He bent to open his satchel and took out the faded gilt box, removing it from its leather wrapping and handing it to the bald monk.

'Pray read the message on the parchment in the box – and be sure to study the seal upon it,' he recommended.

There was a silence as the curious prior, with his even more inquisitive clerk craning his head over his master's shoulder, looked at the glass tube and read the letter from Sir Geoffrey Mappeston.

'I have heard of that knight,' volunteered the clerk. 'He was a famous Crusader earlier this century!'

'So have I, boy,' retorted Anselm testily, fingering the seal attached to the parchment. 'It certainly seems a genuine note. Whether or not the relic is authentic is another matter.' He jerked his round face up towards the visitor. 'How did you come by this?' he demanded. 'Did you steal it from some cathedral in France or Spain?'

'Indeed I did not!' exclaimed Gervase indignantly. 'I bought it at considerable expense from a relic dealer near Chartres, whom I succoured when he was in distress.' He spun an inventive yarn about helping a man whose horse had bolted, leaving him on a lonely road with a broken leg. In return, the dealer had let him have the relic at a reduced, but still substantial, price, which accounted for Gervase's present poverty.

'For the good of my soul, I would sell it for no more than I gave for it, at no profit,' he said piously. 'Such a relic would be a valuable acquisition for any religious house and repay its cost a thousandfold from the offerings of the pilgrims that it would attract. One only has to look to Glastonbury Abbey to see what riches they have amassed since they discovered the bones of King Arthur and his queen there!'

He said this with a sly grin, in which the other men joined with conspiratorial smirks of disbelief at the enterprise of their Somerset brothers. Prior Vincent turned over the ancient tube thoughtfully and stared at the contents with a mixture of reverence and scepticism. Then he reread the faded words on the parchment and studied the seal more closely.

'How much do you want for this?' he asked eventually, peering pugnaciously at the man opposite.

'What I paid for it, the equivalent of thirty marks,' lied Gervase.

The prior put the vial on his table as if it had suddenly become red hot.

'Twenty pounds! Impossible, that's more than a year's income for this little place. You should be willing to donate such a sacred object to us for the good of your mortal soul, not trying to extort such a huge sum from your own brothers!'

Gervase was in no mood to start bargaining with the very first customer he came across.

'Would that I could afford to, Prior – but I sold all I had to fund my pilgrimage and now have nothing in the world. My living in Somerset has been given to another in my absence and I am not sure of finding a new stipend on my return. I have to recover this money in order to live!'

The rotund priest opposite was not impressed by this plea. He pushed the box, tube and parchment back across the desk towards Gervase.

'Then you had better give this to your bishop as a bribe for a new living – I certainly can't afford a third of that price, much as I would like to present it to my own abbot.'

As the outlaw retrieved his property, he concealed his disappointment philosophically, consoling himself with the knowledge that this was the first attempt at a sale and there were several other opportunities.

As he left the room, the prior seemed sorry enough for this penurious priest to repeat his offer of hospitality, and Gervase was taken by the young probationer for a plain but hearty meal in the small refectory. Here he tucked into a bowl of mutton stew, followed by a thick trencher of stale bread bearing a slab of fat bacon and two fried eggs, all washed down with a quart of common ale. After foraging and often going hungry in the forest, this was the first decent meal he had enjoyed in a couple of years, and he uttered not a word until he had finished. Then he spoke to the young lad, who had watched in awe as Gervase wolfed down the food.

'What other religious houses are there in these parts?' he asked.

The novitiate shrugged. 'Apart from the cathedral, nothing that is likely to afford such an expensive relic. There's Polsloe Priory just north of the city, but they have only have a handful of nuns. On the road to Topsham is St James' Priory, but again there's but a few brothers there. Your best chance would be at somewhere like Buckfast Abbey, but you must already have been there, as it's on the road from Plymouth.'

Gervase nodded vaguely, not wanting to reveal that he had been nowhere near Plymouth or Buckfast. He knew this large abbey on the southern rim of Dartmoor by repute, and decided to try his luck there next, as it was a rich Benedictine establishment famous for its huge flocks of sheep and herds of cattle. They should easily be able to afford his price for the trophy he had for sale.

When he left St Nicholas, he walked back into the centre of Exeter and went into an alehouse on the high street. He felt suddenly weary and bemused at being among crowds of people after his years of furtive hiding in the woods. In spite of his claims of destitution, he had a purse full of pennies stolen from various places, and he sat savouring the novelty of drinking in an inn. Though it was not a common sight to see a priest in an alehouse or a brothel, it was far from unknown. Some parish priests, and even vicars and canons from the cathedral, were well known for their dissolute behaviour. Gervase was careful not to flaunt his stolen cloth and sat in a darkened corner of the large, low taproom, keeping his hat on to mark him as a pilgrim to any curious eyes. After a few quarts, he became sleepy, as the warmth and smoke from the log fire in the fire-pit in the centre of the room overcame him. When he awoke, he saw that the day was declining into dusk and, stirring himself, he enquired of the potman whether he could get a penny mattress for the night.

'The loft is full, Father, I'm afraid. But you'll probably get a place at the Bush in Idle Lane.'

He gave directions and, in the cold twilight, the renegade priest made his way down to the lower part of town and negotiated for a night's lodging with the landlady of the inn there. After a couple of years of enforced celibacy, he eyed the attractive red-haired Welshwoman with covert lust, but her brisk, businesslike manner discouraged him from any lascivious overtures. He spent the rest of the evening drinking and having another good meal of boiled pork knuckle with onions, before taking himself up the ladder to the large loft. For the first time for several years, he luxuriated on a soft pile of sweet-smelling hay enclosed in a hessian bag, with a woollen blanket to cover him. Unlike in the other inn, there were few other lodgers and, oblivious to the snores of two other drunken patrons in the corner, he soon slipped into a deep sleep, from which he was never to awaken.

*   *   *

A couple of hours after dawn the next day, Lucy, one of the two serving maids at the Bush, climbed up the wide ladder at the back of the taproom, clutching a leather bucket of water and a birch broom. Her morning task was to clean up the loft after the overnight lodgers had left – all too often, those who had drunk too much had thrown up their ale over the floor or their pallets.

This morning, however, it was a different-coloured fluid that required scouring from the bare boards. As soon as Lucy reached the top of the ladder and started to move among the dozen rough mattresses laid out on the floor, she gave a piercing shriek that brought the landlady Nesta and her old potman Edwin running to the foot of the ladder, together with one or two patrons who had been eating an early breakfast.

'That priest that came last night!' wailed Lucy from the top. 'He's had his throat cut!'

Edwin, a veteran of the Irish wars in which he lost one eye and half a foot, stumbled up the ladder to confirm the maid's claim, and a moment later he reappeared beside Lucy.

'She's right enough, mistress! I'd better go for the crowner straight away!'

Within half an hour, Sir John de Wolfe and his officer and clerk had arrived on the scene, any problem at the Bush being a great spur to their keenness to attend. Before climbing the ladder, John slipped an arm around Nesta's slim waist and looked down anxiously at her. At twenty-eight, she was still attractive, with a trim figure and a heart-shaped face crowned with a mass of chestnut hair.

'Are you very upset, my love?' he murmured in the Welsh that they used together.

His mistress was made of sufficiently stern stuff not to be shocked by a dead body.

'I'm upset for the reputation of my inn!' she replied pertly. 'It's not good for business to have customers murdered in my beds.'

She had experienced an occasional death in the tavern, always the result of some drunken brawl, but to find a guest lying on his pallet with his throat cut was an unwelcome novelty.

'Let's see what this is about, Gwyn,' snapped the coroner, leading the way up the ladder, at the top of which Edwin awaited them. With Gwyn close behind and Thomas de Peyne a reluctant third, he trooped across the wide floor of the loft. Apart from one remaining lodger, who had drunk so much the previous night that he was still snoring in a far corner, the high, dusty loft was empty. Two rows of crude mattresses lay on the bare boards, the farthest one in the second line occupied by the corpse. The place was poorly lit, as there was no window opening in the great expanse of thatch above them, but a little light filtered up from the eaves and through the wide opening where the ladder entered. Edwin had had the forethought to light a horn lantern, and by its feeble light de Wolfe bent to examine the dead man.

A great gash extended from under his left ear across to the right side of his neck below the jaw, exposing muscles and gristle. A welter of dark blood soaked his ragged shirt and the blanket, running down into the straw of the palliasse, and there was a patch of dried pink froth over the centre of his neck.

'A single cut, right through his windpipe,' observed Gwyn, with the satisfied air of a connoisseur of fatal injuries. 'No trial cuts either – so he didn't do it himself.'

'Hardly likely to be a suicide, if there's no knife here!' sneered Thomas sarcastically, always keen to embarrass his Cornish colleague. He pointed to the crown of the dead man's head, where bristly tufts of hair remained on the bared scalp, together with some small scratches. 'That's a strange-looking tonsure, master. Freshly made with a very poor knife.'

John had to agree with him, but saw no particular significance in it.

'Let's have a look at the rest of him, then.'

They went through their familiar routine of pulling up the rest of the clothing and examining the chest, belly and limbs, but apart from the massive throat wound there was nothing to find.

'His clothing is poor, even for a priest,' grunted Gwyn. 'The shirt is little better than a rag and his shoes are worn through.'

'The cassock is a disgrace, too!' complained Thomas. 'I wonder if he really is a priest?'

The coroner looked up at Edwin. 'How many were sleeping here last night?'

'We only had three besides him,' quavered the old man. 'Apart from that drunken sot in the corner.'

De Wolfe loped across the loft and shook the man awake, but could get no sense out of him, as he was still totally befuddled.

'Who were the other three?' he demanded, frustrated at the lack of witnesses. Edwin shrugged and Nesta answered from where she stood on the ladder, halfway into the loft.

'They were travellers, who went on their way soon after dawn. They took pallets in the first row just here, so can't have noticed this man lying dead over there in the darkness.'

'Somebody must have come up here to kill him, so maybe it was them,' reasoned Gwyn.

Nesta shrugged her shapely shoulders. 'We were even busier than usual late last night. People come and go all the time. I can't watch every move they make.'

'He doesn't look as if he had anything worth being robbed for,' objected Gwyn, prodding the corpse with his foot.

'His scrip looks empty, but you'd better make sure,' ordered de Wolfe, indicating the frayed leather purse on the man's belt.

Gwyn pulled it off and squeezed it, feeling nothing inside. He opened the flap and upended it over his palm. 'That's odd!' he boomed. 'Let's have that light a bit nearer, Edwin.'

As they stooped over the lantern, they could see small flecks glistening in its light.

'Shreds of gold leaf, just like we found on that fellow robbed at Clyst St Mary! Bloody strange, that!' observed Gwyn.

De Wolfe rubbed at his stubble thoughtfully, but could make no sense of the coincidence. He decided to leave his inquest until the afternoon, giving Gwyn time to round up as many of the previous night's patrons as he could find, to form a jury. Meanwhile, they adjourned down to the taproom for some ale and food, while they discussed the matter. As soon as Nesta's maids had scurried in with bread, cold meat and cheese, and Edwin had brought brimming pots of the best brew, they sat around a table and tried to make sense of this violent death. Thomas seemed very pensive as he sat picking at his breakfast.

'I've been thinking about what the other dead man said before he passed away,' he offered timidly.

Though Gwyn was playfully scornful of the little clerk, John de Wolfe had learned to respect the ex-priest's learning and intelligence.

'What's going through that devious mind of yours, Thomas?' he asked encouragingly.

'This gold leaf – that must surely link them, it's not a common thing to find in poor men's pouches. And gold leaf is usually applied to valuable or sacred objects.'

'How's that connected with whatever that robbed fellow said in Clyst?' asked the sharp-witted Nesta.

'It comes back to me now – the old man in Clyst said the victim had uttered the words "Barzak" and "Glastonbury".'

'If he was walking northward through that village, he may well have been making for Glastonbury, so what's the mystery?' grunted Gwyn.

'It's the oldest abbey in England – Joseph of Arimathaea and perhaps even the Lord Jesus himself may have visited there,' said Thomas, crossing himself devoutly. 'But it's the other word he uttered that intrigues me – Barzak!'

'What the hell's a barzak?' growled the big Cornishman, determined to deflate his little friend.

'Not what, but who?' retorted Thomas. 'I recollect the legend now, it's been told around our abbeys and cathedrals for many years. It's a curse, which again the old man in Clyst mentioned.'

Nesta, Edwin and even Gwyn were now intrigued, but de Wolfe was his usual impatient self.

'Well, get on with it, Thomas! What are you trying to say?'

'The Templars brought this story back long ago, of a tainted relic from the Holy City.' He crossed himself yet again. 'It seems that a fragment of the True Cross was cursed by a custodian called Barzak and anyone handling it died a violent death as soon as it left his possession. The relic has been virtually hidden away somewhere in France for many years – I seem to have heard it was in Fontrevault, where old King Henry's buried. It was useless as an attraction for pilgrims, as they learned to shun it.'

The coroner pondered this for a moment, as he supped the last of his ale. 'So why should this thing turn up in Devon?' he asked dubiously.

Thomas shrugged his humped shoulder. 'Perhaps the man in Clyst had brought it from France – he could have been coming from the port of Topsham, if he was on his way to Glastonbury.'

'Sounds bloody far fetched to me!' mumbled Gwyn through a mouthful of bread and cheese.

De Wolfe stood up and brushed crumbs from his long grey tunic.

'It's all we've got to go on so far. Thomas, you're the one with the religious connections, so go around and see if you can find any rumours about a relic. And you, Gwyn, round up as many men who were drinking in here last night as you can and get

them down here before vesper bell this afternoon.
I'll go and tell our dear sheriff we've had a murder
in the city.'

The coroner's brother-in-law, Sir Richard de
Revelle, was busy with his chief clerk in his
chamber in the keep of Rougemont when John
arrived. He sat at a table, poring over parchments
that listed tax collections, ready for the following
week's visit to the Exchequer at Winchester. More
concerned with money than justice, the sheriff was
supremely uninterested in the death of a lodger in
an alehouse, until he heard that the man was a
priest. At this news, de Revelle sat back and stared
at de Wolfe.

'A priest? Staying in that common tavern, run by
that Welsh whore?'

John resisted the temptation to punch him on
the nose, as he had suffered this particular provo-
cation many times before.

'My officer and clerk are about the town now,
trying to find out more about him,' he replied
stonily. 'There may be a connection with the
murder of a chapman yesterday – probably by
outlaws.'

De Revelle was more concerned about the man
being a cleric, not out of any particular concern for
the welfare of priests, but because he was a political
ally of Bishop Henry Marshal in their covert
campaign to put Prince John on the throne in
place of Richard the Lionheart. De Revelle was
always on the lookout for any opportunity to
further ingratiate himself with the prelate, so he
felt it might be worth stirring himself to catch the
killer, if it raised his stock with the bishop. He

demanded to know the details of the crime and John explained the circumstances of both deaths, but held back Thomas's suggestion about the cursed relic.

Richard leant back in his chair and stroked his neatly pointed beard thoughtfully. He was a small, dapper man, with a foxy face. Fond of showy garments, today he wore a bright green tunic with yellow embroidery around neck and hem, with a cloak of fine brown wool trimmed with squirrel fur thrown over his shoulders against the chill of the cold, dank chamber.

'A gang of outlaws could hardly have cut the man's throat in the upstairs of a city alehouse – even though that Bush is a den of iniquity!' he sneered, determined to taunt his sister's husband with reminders of his infidelity. 'Far more likely that your doxy turned a blind eye to some local robber who preys on her guests.'

Once again, John refused to rise to the bait and suggested that a squad of soldiers should be sent to clear the outlaws from the woods around Clyst St Mary. De Revelle dismissed this idea with a wave of his beringed hand.

'A waste of time! Every bit of forest in Devon is crawling with these outcasts. Trying to find them is like looking for a needle in a haystack. But I want to catch the killer of this priest, for the bishop will be on my neck as soon as he hears about it.'

John decided to keep Thomas's doubts about the genuineness of the priest to himself for the moment, else Richard's interest would rapidly evaporate. With a muttered promise to keep the sheriff up to date with progress, he left his brother-in-law to continue his embezzlement of funds from the county's finances and went back to his own bleak office in the gatehouse.

With both his assistants out on the streets, de Wolfe felt obliged to occupy himself and reluctantly turned back to his reading lessons, slowly tracing the Latin script with a forefinger and mumbling the words under his breath. An east wind whistled through the open window slits and he huddled deeper into his cloak as the morning wore on. In spite of the discomfort, which he had learned to endure after twenty years' campaigning in a range of climates from Scotland to Palestine, he eventually fell asleep from the sheer boredom of his lessons, and jerked himself awake only several hours later when Thomas de Peyne limped up the stairs and pushed through the sacking over the doorway.

'I've found who he was, master – and where he came from!' squeaked the little ex-priest excitedly, proud of himself for being able to be of help to this grim man to whom he owed so much for giving him a job after his disgrace. John, still half asleep, glared bleary eyed at his clerk. 'Tell me about it,' he grunted.

'I went first to the cathedral and made enquiries among the vicars and secondaries, but no one had any news of such a priest. Then I went down to St John's Priory on the river, but again they had seen no one like that. I tried a couple of the city churches with no result, then ventured into Bretayne to call at St Nicholas Priory.'

John groaned. 'You're getting as bad as Gwyn for spinning out a tale! Get to the point, man!'

Unabashed, Thomas dropped on to his stool and gesticulated as he spoke. 'One of the younger brothers there told me that a rough-looking priest had called yesterday and had talked with Prior Vincent. I asked to see the prior, but he refused to talk to me. However, his secretary told me that the man said he was Gervase of Somerset and that he tried to sell a valuable relic to the prior, but wanted far too much money for it.'

'Did he say where he was going after leaving St Nicholas?' demanded the coroner.

The clerk shook his head ruefully. 'No, but he muttered something about other great abbeys being glad of the offer, like Buckfast or Glastonbury.'

De Wolfe reached out a long arm and clapped Thomas on the shoulder.

'Well done, young man! I don't know what I'd do without you.'

The clerk glowed with pride at such rare praise from his master.

'The secretary didn't tell me how much the man wanted for the relic, sir – but it must have been many pounds, by the indignation in his voice. Well worth killing for, I'm sure.'

The coroner jumped up from his table and strode to a window slit, staring blankly down over the city as he pondered. 'But where is it now? And who the hell knew that this Gervase possessed it? And who is this priest, anyway? Where did he get the relic?'

Eager to please, Thomas applied his sharp mind to the problems. 'If he really was a priest! I've got my doubts, he looked much too rough. And as to where he was going, then the two abbeys he spoke of seem the most likely places to raise money on a religious relic.'

De Wolfe turned from the window. 'Well, he's not going anywhere now, other than a pauper's grave! But his killer must be trying to sell the thing in his place.'

He was interrupted by Gwyn lumbering into the chamber, to report that he had found a score of men who were in the Bush the previous night and had warned them to assemble as a jury in the back yard of the inn later that day. Thomas proudly repeated his story for the Cornishman's benefit, and the coroner's officer tugged at his long ginger moustaches as an aid to thought.

'Then we'd best get those monks from St Nicholas down to the inquest,' he suggested. 'At least they can identify the dead 'un.'

De Wolfe agreed and told Gwyn to go up to the priory after his dinner and summon them to the Bush. 'Better take Thomas with you, he might be more tactful with a bunch of Benedictines than you. They can be an awkward lot, if they're not handled right.'

His warning was all too prophetic, for when he came back to the gatehouse after a silent meal with Matilda in Martin's Lane, a glowering Gwyn reported that Prior Vincent had refused point blank to come to any inquest and forbade any of his monks to attend. 'He said you had no authority over men of God and if you didn't like it, you could appeal to the Pope!'

John cursed all intransigent monks, but failed to see what he could do about it. He was not sure how far a coroner's powers stretched, as the whole system had been set up on the strength of one paragraph in the Articles of Eyre at Rochester in September.

For once Thomas, usually a fountain of knowledge on all matters ecclesiastical, was unable to help him. 'I know the cathedral precinct is outside the jurisdiction of both the city burgesses and the sheriff, as well as yourself, master,' he offered. 'But the Lord Bishop has voluntarily handed over his rights in respect of killings or other serious crimes of violence within the Close.'

'I know, but that doesn't help us in respect of monks inside a closed community like St Nicholas,' grunted de Wolfe. 'I'll have to seek the advice of your uncle.'

Half an hour later, he was sitting in the house of the Archdeacon of Exeter, one of the row of canon's dwellings that formed the northern boundary of the cathedral Close. John de Alençon was a thin, ascetic man with wiry grey hair around his shaved tonsure. His face was lined and care-worn, but relieved by a pair of bright blue eyes. The two Johns were good friends, though de Wolfe had little love for many of the other twenty-four canons, who, like the bishop himself, tended to be supporters of Prince John. De Alençon was fervently loyal to King Richard, as was the coroner, and this contributed to the bond between them. De Wolfe explained the situation, as they sat over two cups of good Poitou wine.

'So can I insist that this prior and his secretary appear at the inquest? They are the only ones who met the fellow before he was killed.'

The lean canon rubbed his nose thoughtfully. 'Like you, I have no idea of the powers of this new office of coroner. It seems to have been dreamed up by Hubert Walter to squeeze more money out of the populace for our sovereign's benefit.'

Hubert Walter was the Chief Justiciar and virtually ruler of England, now that the King had gone back to France, never to return. Hubert was also Archbishop of Canterbury and had been second-in-command of the King's armies when John was in the Holy Land.

'If they were your vicars in the cathedral, would you order them to attend?' persisted the coroner.

De Alençon shook his head. 'That's a different matter, John. St Nicholas is not only a priory, outside the control of this cathedral – it's also a daughter establisment of Battle Abbey in Sussex, a powerful institution. Only their abbot could decide the issue – and it would take you the best part of a fortnight to get an answer there!'

De Wolfe swore under his breath. 'Is there nothing we can do?' he asked testily.

The archdeacon smiled and downed the last of his wine, before rising.

'We can both take a walk up there and try a little gentle persuasion. I should leave that big sword at home, John – this requires diplomacy, not brute force!'

As the cathedral bells tolled for the late afternoon vespers, a crowd began assembling behind the Bush tavern in Idle Lane. The muddy back yard was big enough to accommodate them between the cook-shed, the brewing hut, the pigsties and the privies. Gwyn made them shuffle into a half-circle around one of the trestle tables brought from the taproom, on which lay an ominously still figure covered with a couple of empty barley sacks.

The big Cornishman used his stentorian voice to formally open the proceedings, as he bawled, 'All ye who have anything to do before the King's coroner for the county of Devon, draw near and give your attendance!'

As de Wolfe waited at the head of the makeshift bier, he noticed that the sheriff had just arrived with Canon Thomas de Boterellis, the cathedral's precentor, whose duties were to organize the many daily services. John tried in vain to think of some reason why they should have taken an interest in a lowly tavern death. The pair, one gaudily dressed in a bright green tunic and a cloak, the other in a cowled black cassock, pushed their way through the onlookers to stand alongside the prior's secretary from St Nicholas. When John and the archdeacon had gone to the priory, they had received a frosty reception from Anselm, but after some placatory words from de Alençon, he had softened enough to come to a compromise. He still refused to leave the priory himself, but agreed that his secretary, Brother Basil, could attend to confirm the identity of the victim.

Now de Wolfe stepped forward to begin the inquest and glared along the line of jurors, who were as much witnesses as judges, as they were the ones who were in the alehouse the previous night.

'We are here to enquire into the death of a man thought to be Gervase of Somerset, though that may or may not be true. Anyway, it's certainly true that he's dead!'

There were a couple of dutiful titters at his attempt at levity, which brought another fercious scowl to the coroner's face. Then he called forward the maid Lucy, who was the First Finder of the body. She briefly described how she had come across the corpse and had screamed out for the potman and the landlady. Strictly speaking, the First Finder was supposed to raise the hue and cry, by knocking up the nearest four households and starting a hunt for the killer. That might be possible in a village, but in a city it was impracticable.

'The man had been dead for some hours,' declared de Wolfe. 'The body was cold and stiff when I examined it early this morning, so there would be no point in seeking the killer, who would have been long gone.'

John noticed that the sheriff's eyebrows had risen in a supercilious smile and he had the uneasy feeling that de Revelle was there to make trouble. He had to press on, however, and deal with the next issue, that of identity. He asked Brother Basil to step forward, and the thin young man, enveloped in a black robe too large for him, came hesitantly to the front. At a sign from John, Gwyn whisked one of the sacks off the corpse and, to a chorus of gasps and oaths from the audience, exposed the upper half of the body. The white face contrasted ghoulishly with the dark red blood clot that filled the gaping wound in the neck and spread over the adjacent skin and clothing.

'Brother, is this the man who came to the priory of St Nicholas yesterday?'

The young monk took a few tentative steps nearer the cadaver and stared at the face, then moved slightly so that he could inspect the ragged tonsure on the top of the head. With a face as pale as that of the corpse, he nodded, and replied in a tremulous voice.

'That's the man, Crowner. He gave his name as Gervase and said he was a parish priest from

Somerset, returning from his pilgrimage to Santiago de Compostela.'

He explained about the offer of the relic of the True Cross and the rather unusual fact that he had a genuine letter of authentication signed and sealed by a crusading knight.

'Were you satisfied that this man was truly a priest?' demanded de Wolfe.

The monk hesitated. 'It was hard to decide, sir. He wore a cassock, as you see, but it was in a poor state, even for one who had endured the hardships of a pilgrimage. And his tonsure was strange, though again, he may have just restored it after having been on such a long journey.'

'You seem doubtful, Brother. What did Prior Anselm think?'

The young secretary shuffled his feet uneasily. 'He shared my concerns, he told me later. But the man could read the parchment he brought and he spoke some Latin to one of our brothers in the garden. Who else but a priest could have done that?'

Nesta was called to confirm that the dead man had arrived at the tavern the previous evening and had paid for a meal and lodging for the night, but could add little else.

'Did you think it strange that a priest should need to stay at an inn?' asked John, trying to keep his voice as gruff as with the other witnesses, though everyone present was well aware of his relationship with the landlady of the Bush.

'It was a little unusual, though I have had travelling clerics lodge here before, when all the cathedral accommodation was full. He said that the morrow he was promised a bed at Buckfast Abbey and just needed a mattress here for the night.' She further agreed that she had noticed nothing suspicious going on in the loft the previous night and said that people lodging there came up and down the ladder at will, so she would have no reason to take notice of them on a busy evening.

There was no other evidence to be gained, so de Wolfe made the jury file past the corpse to inspect it more closely. Some were hesitant, others avidly curious, and when they had finished the coroner barked his instructions at them.

'You must come to a verdict about this yourselves, but I see no alternative to you declaring that this man, said to be called Gervase of Somerset, was unlawfully slain by a person or persons unknown.'

He glared along the line of sheepish men and boys, as if challenging them to contradict him – and a moment later, after some hurried murmuring among themselves, one stepped forward and mumbled their agreement. John was just about to wind up with a final formal declaration for Thomas to write on his parchment roll when an unexpected and unwelcome interruption took place. Richard de Revelle strode forward and officiously held up a hand to halt the proceedings.

'Not so fast, Coroner! There's a witness you've not heard.'

His thin, foxy face wore a smug expression which he failed to restrain, as de Wolfe glowered angrily at this intrusion.

'What are you talking about? This is my inquest, you've no right to interrupt.'

'I am the sheriff! I can do what I please when it comes to the administration of justice,' sneered de Revelle. 'You claim this was a killing by persons unknown, but I see little effort on your part to discover who it was.'

He swung round and beckoned to someone at the back of the crowd. Reluctantly, a thin, middle-aged man came forward; John recognised him as a patron of the Bush, a servant from one of the canons' houses in the Close.

'What can this man tell us that we don't already know?' demanded de Wolfe, glowering at his brother-in-law, who stood with a self-satisfied smirk on his face.

The sheriff ignored the question and addressed himself to the man, who stood before them, obviously ill at ease.

'You are Martin Bedel, a servant of Canon de Boterellis?'

The older man, dressed in a plain brown tunic over cross-gartered leggings, bobbed his head. 'Yes, sir. I am the precentor's bottler.'

This was the servant that attended to the drink in the house.

'And you frequent this inn?' snapped de Revelle.

'Aye, I often come for company and a gossip, when my duties allow. Sometimes I come to break my fast in the morning, for their cooking is the best in the city.'

There was a snigger from the crowd, quickly suppressed when the sheriff glared around at them. De Wolfe frowned across at Gwyn, who shrugged to indicate that this must be one of the customers he had failed to round up for the inquest.

'And were you here last evening – and again this morning?' persisted Richard.

The coroner's impatience and foreboding got

the better of him. 'What is the point of these questions? If he knows anything, he should have come forward before.'

'Well, he's coming forward now, thanks to the orders of his master, the precentor,' replied the sheriff complacently. He turned back to the bottler. 'What did you see last night?'

'Well, it was as usual, sir. Many people inside, comings and goings up the ladder to the loft. Some I knew, some I didn't. Mistress Nesta herself climbed up a few times.'

'What of it?' snarled de Wolfe. 'She has her sleeping-room up there.'

'Yes, I'm sure you're well aware of that!' said de Revelle, sarcastically, this time ignoring the suppressed snigger from the audience. 'But Martin, you were also here this morning for your breakfast, so what did you see then?'

The wizened servant shuffled his feet as he gave an abashed glance at both Nesta and the coroner. 'I saw the landlady coming down the ladder, looking pale and shaken. There was blood on her apron, sir.'

A buzz of concern ran around the crowd assembled in the yard. But de Wolfe gave a derisive bark. 'For God's sake, she had just been up to see if she could aid the man! Look at him, he was weltered in blood, of course she would get soiled!'

'The other maid had no blood upon her!' retorted the sheriff.

'Then she probably kept well clear of the corpse!' roared de Wolfe.

'Probably? You make assumptions, Coroner.' The sheriff turned back to the discomfited Martin. 'Was this before or after the alarm was raised by this other "unsullied" maid?' Richard emphasized the word sarcastically.

The bottler looked more embarrassed than ever. 'I feel pretty sure it was before, sir.'

'Pretty sure?' snarled de Wolfe. 'What sort of evidence is that? De Revelle, you are wasting my time!'

Now Thomas de Boterellis pushed forward and stood alongside the sheriff. He was a heavily built, podgy man, with a waxy complexion to his face, from which two rather piggy eyes looked out coldly upon the world.

'My servant told me this early this morning, de Wolfe. I felt it my duty to notify Richard de Revelle, as it was a matter relating to a serious crime.'

John snorted in disbelief. 'Since when does a cathedral precentor go running to a sheriff over a death in an alehouse?'

'Sir Richard is a particular friend of mine. We had business this morning and I happened to mention the matter,' retorted the canon pompously.

'And cockerels may happen to lay eggs!' snapped de Wolfe. 'Did the pair of you just happen to be coming all the way down here to the lower town this morning?'

The sheriff blustered his way back into the acrimonious conversation.

'The fact remains that this man was done to death in this woman's tavern. She sleeps within a few yards of where he was killed, she was seen to go up and down repeatedly, she denied any knowledge of the death, apparently a valuable object is missing – and she was seen by a reputable witness to have blood on her clothes!'

'All of which means absolutely nothing!' roared John. 'This stupid man can't even remember if he saw the blood on the lady before or after the body was discovered!'

'I seem to recollect that it was before,' bleated Martin, trying to claw his way back into his master's favour.

Now de Wolfe completely lost his temper. 'Listen! My inquest is over, my jury has agreed the verdict and that's the end of it, until we find the real culprit!' he roared. 'So clear off, all of you, and attend to your own affairs!'

The crowd, hugely intrigued to see this public row between their betters, stood gaping at the performance until Gwyn started to shoo them away, but de Revelle and the precentor stood their ground.

'Unless you produce this "real culprit" very soon, John, the execution of my own duty to keep the peace by arresting malefactors might not be to your liking!'

With this parting threat, he took the arm of de Boterellis and pushed through the dispersing crowd, leaving the coroner to stand fuming with rage, tinged with a little apprehension.

An hour later, a council of war was held in the Bush, with all the staff of the inn and the coroner's team clustered around a table, food and ale before them. John was concerned at the naked threat that the sheriff had made against Nesta.

'That bastard's got it in for you, Crowner,' said Gwyn, through a mouthful of bread and cheese. He was feeling a little crestfallen for having failed to track down the precentor's bottler to include him in his inquest jury, but his master had no blame for him, realizing that it was impossible to identify everyone who might have visited the alehouse the previous night.

'As usual, de Revelle's trying to get back at me for antagonizing him over his support for Prince John,' growled de Wolfe. 'That damned precentor is the same way inclined, currying favour with the bishop, who was one of the main players in the last revolt.'

When Richard the Lionheart was imprisoned in Germany, his younger brother John had made an abortive attempt to seize the throne, and many of the barons and senior clerics who supported him were still covertly plotting another uprising.

'How can we protect dear Nesta?' broke in the ever practical Thomas, who worshipped the Welshwoman for her unfailing kindness to him.

'As the bloody sheriff said, by finding the real killer,' replied de Wolfe. 'And quickly, for I suspect that de Revelle is keen to cause me as much trouble as possible, may God rot him!' He turned to his mistress, who was looking defiant, but apprehensive. 'Let's get the story quite clear, *cariad.* Lucy screamed out when she found the body, so you ran up to the loft and went to look at it. That's when you got blood on your apron?'

'Of course! I bent down to make sure he was dead and got blood on my hands from the edge of the blanket. I wiped them on my apron, which was also soiled at the hem from blood on the floor.'

'We need to find the bastard who did this, that's the best way of getting Nesta off the hook,' grunted Gwyn. 'I'll get back on the streets and find every man-jack that was in here last night and this morning – and every whore, too! I'll shake them all until their teeth rattle, to get 'em to tell me all they know!'

As good as his word, he swallowed the last of his ale and lumbered out into Idle Lane, leaving Thomas de Peyne to continue the debate.

'We know now how that gold leaf got from Clyst St Mary to this place,' he declared. 'This man Gervase must have stolen it from that chapman.'

'Which surely means that he was no priest, but a robber – probably an outlaw,' observed Edwin.

'Or had been a priest once, like me,' added Thomas sadly. 'But who would have known that he was carrying a valuable object, worth killing for?'

'He wasn't flashing it around in here, was he, Nesta?' asked John.

She shook her head emphatically. 'No, he sat and had his food at that table over there, then drank a quart of ale and went up to bed. I hardly noticed him. Certainly he had no conversation with anyone else, as far as I remember.'

Edwin, Lucy and the other maid agreed, confirming that the murder victim seemed a shadowy figure who met no one else that evening. They talked a while longer, but nothing new came to mind, and with considerable unease at having to leave Nesta behind at the inn, John reluctantly left for Martin's Lane and another cheerless supper with his wife.

Two hours before noon the next day the coroner, together with his clerk Thomas, were at the gallows field on Magdalene Street, half a mile outside the South Gate. Executions took place once or twice a week, depending on how many felons had been sentenced by the Shire Court or the Burgess Court.

When the royal judges came to the city, either as Commissioners of Gaol Delivery or at the very infrequent Eyre of Assize, the gallows was busier, but this morning there were only three customers to be dispatched into the next, and hopefully better, life. The coroner had to be present, as he was responsible for confiscating all the worldly goods of the victim for the King's treasury and recording the event on his rolls.

Though mutilation, either cutting off a hand, castration or blinding, was a common penalty for serious assault or minor theft, murder or stealing anything worth more than twelve pence was a hanging offence, as was the capture of anyone previously outlawed. One of today's felons was such an outlaw, another being a tanner who had beaten his wife's lover to death on catching them in flagrante delicto and the third a boy of fifteen who had stolen a pewter jug worth twenty pence.

A small crowd had assembled to watch the proceedings, some of them relatives of the condemned, the others spectators who came regularly, regarding the executions as a form of entertainment. These were mainly old men, housewives and grandmothers, with a horde of toddlers and urchins running around them. A few pedlars and pie-men always attended, making a reasonable trade as the spectators waited for the show to begin. Even the town beggars and a couple of hooded lepers lingered on the edge of the crowd, rattling their bowls and crying for alms.

The gallows was a massive beam supported at either end by two tree trunks. Five rope nooses dangled from it and ladders were propped at both ends. There were a number of hangmen in Exeter, all part time, as they also followed other trades. Today a slaughterman from the Shambles was officiating; he favoured the use of an ox-cart, rather than pushing the victims off a ladder. Hands lashed behind them, the victims were stood together on a plank across the cart, directly underneath the gallows. The executioner climbed up, put a rope around each neck, then gave the ox a smart smack across the rump, though it was so used to the routine that it hardly needed such a signal. As it trundled forward, the three poor wretches were left hanging momentarily in space, their screams abruptly cut off as the strangling rope cut into their throats. Immediately, members of the families of two of the condemned rushed forward and dragged down violently on their legs to shorten their suffering, but the outlaw, who had no one to see him off, was left to kick and twitch for several minutes until death mercifully overtook him.

John watched the proceedings impassively, as violent and sudden death held no novelty for him, after more than twenty years on the battlefields of Ireland, France and the Holy Land. Thomas de Peyne was not made of such stern stuff and always turned his head away as the ox-cart began to move. As soon as the bodies had stopped dancing on their ropes, the crowd began to drift away, except for the wailing families, who lingered with their handcarts to claim the bodies for burial.

The coroner waited for his clerk to gather up his writing materials and stow them away in his shoulder bag, then began walking back towards the city walls. It was hardly worth saddling up his stallion Odin for such a short distance, and within a few minutes they were approaching Exeter's massive South Gate, where they saw a large figure coming towards them with a familiar rolling gait.

'Here's Gwyn. What's he want?' demanded Thomas.

The usually phlegmatic Cornishman was agitated. 'I've found a man who saw something in the Bush last night,' he boomed. As they hurried back towards Idle Lane, the officer explained that he had managed to round up another dozen men who had been drinking in the tavern, and one of them remembered seeing a hooded man coming down the ladder late that night. 'He says he wasn't in a priest's garb, but the hood was over his face and he had no cause to make any effort to recognize him.'

'At least it lessens the threat against Nesta, if we have a new possibility,' muttered John. 'Have you kept this man at the Bush?'

'They're all there, Crowner. I told them they must wait until you came.'

The new witnesses were in the taproom when they arrived, taking advantage of the wait to drink more ale. John questioned the man Gwyn had found, but he was unable to add any more to his recollection that the hooded man had come down the steps and vanished out of the front door.

'His robe was grey and dirty, Crowner. I can say no more about him than that he was tall.'

John questioned all the other men, but none of them had noticed the mysterious figure, and he became frustrated that there seemed no way of identifying the fellow.

'He may have nothing to do with it,' cautioned Thomas tentatively. 'Perhaps he was one of the other lodgers from the loft.'

Nesta shook her head as she stood listening. 'None of those travellers was particularly tall – and none wore a dirty grey robe,' she said firmly.

John de Wolfe snarled again at the men, trying to force someone to remember more details, but they all shook their heads sadly, despite the fact that they would have liked to help both the coroner and his popular mistress.

Then suddenly there was a voice from behind him, a sing-song piping that came from a vacant-faced youth who had been squatting in a corner.

'I know who he was! I begged him for a ha'penny for ale when he came out of the door.'

There was a sudden silence as everyone turned to look down at the ragged boy. Though not an idiot, he was 'simple', as the tolerant locals called him, a loose-lipped, runny-nosed lad with an abnormally big head. Nesta, who gave him spare food almost every day, crouched down beside him and spoke to him gently.

'Peter, did you see his face? Who was he?'

The boy looked at her and then at the expectant men with an almost pitying expression.

'Don't you know? It was Simon Claver, him with the rotten nose that used to live in Smythen Street.'

At this, there was a babble of voices from the surrounding men, cut short by de Wolfe's harsh voice.

'Who in hell is Simon Claver?' he demanded.

'He was a smith, from just up the road here,' answered the potman.

'Simon beat up his brother-in-law more than a year ago, half killed him!'

There were murmurs of agreement from the others. 'He escaped the hue and cry and secured sanctuary in Holy Trinity,' continued old Edwin, who knew all the local scandals. 'Then he abjured the realm, but ran away before he got ship at Topsham, so he was outlawed.'

The coroner looked across at Gwyn and nodded. 'Sounds as if he could be our man – but where the hell do we look for him?'

De Wolfe's desire to lay his hands on the killer of Gervase was multiplied a thousandfold by that evening, as while he was sitting at his cheerless supper table with Matilda, Gwyn arrived in a state of extreme agitation to report that the sheriff had arrested Nesta on suspicion of murder.

'The bastard sent half a dozen men-at-arms to the Bush and they've dragged her off to Rougemont!'

Though Gwyn was unwelcome in the house because of his wife's antipathy to what she called 'Celtic savages', the urgency of the situation made both him and his master careless of her antagonism.

'There's even talk of putting her to the ordeal of water,' roared Gwyn angrily. This was a primitive test for guilt reserved for women, whereby they were thrown bound hand and foot into deep water. If they sank, they were innocent; if they floated, they were guilty and hanged. Men were forced to run barefoot over nine red-hot ploughshares or pick a stone from the bottom of a cask of boiling water – if burns developed, they were judged guilty.

John leapt up from the supper table, his stool crashing over behind him.

'She can't be put in those foul cells under the

keep!' he yelled. 'Not with that evil pervert Stigand as her gaoler.' He glared across at his wife. 'Your damned brother is doing this out of sheer malice, Matilda! No woman should be kept in Rougemont at the mercy of that fat swine!'

Matilda looked back impassively at her husband for a long moment, and John wondered whether she was going to use this as a way of punishing him.

Then she too rose from her chair and came around to him.

'Call Lucille to bring my mantle. I'll come with you to see Richard – but only to keep that woman from the cells. I'll not interfere in anything else.'

The next morning saw John de Wolfe at the castle at the crack of dawn, after an almost sleepless night worrying about Nesta and the implacable resolve of Richard de Revelle to blame her for the killing at the Bush.

In the cold morning light of his gatehouse chamber, he told Gwyn and Thomas what had transpired the previous evening when he had confronted the sheriff.

'Thank God my wife had enough compassion to persuade her brother to lock Nesta in an empty chamber on the upper floor of the keep, rather than in that hellhole in the undercroft. Gabriel's wife will attend her and at least see that she is fed until I can get her released.'

'What about the bloody sheriff?' growled Gwyn. 'Is there no chance of him coming to his senses over this?'

John shook his head. 'He has the bit between his teeth, aided by that damned precentor. This is a heaven-sent opportunity for them to get even with me for hounding them about their treacherous sympathy for Prince John.'

Thomas looked even more miserable than usual, hunched on his stool, wringing his hands in anguish. 'How can we save dear Nesta, Crowner? I fear for her very life, now that the sheriff is set upon making her a scapegoat.'

'Find the real killer, this Simon Claver! I tried to persuade de Revelle last night that this was the obvious way, but his mind is as closed as his ears. He refused even to countenance a search for the man, saying that the word of an imbecile lad was no grounds for looking for anyone other than the landlady of the tavern!'

'But where the hell would we start looking, Crowner?' observed Gwyn glumly.

'That stolen relic is of no value to the thief until he can sell it,' pointed out Thomas. 'He has to find a buyer, and the only people interested would be religious houses.'

De Wolfe drummed his fingers on his table. 'He may first have gone back to his outlaw gang in the forest. I couldn't persuade the sheriff to lift a finger against them, he claimed it was a waste of effort.'

Gwyn scratched a few fleas from his unruly red thatch as he thought.

'Gabriel told me that de Revelle was leaving this morning for his manor at Tiverton, to spend a few nights with his wife, God help her. Maybe we can persuade Ralph Morin to take out a posse while the sheriff's away?'

The 'posse comitatus' was an invention of old King Henry, who authorized each county to mount bands of armed men to seek out wrongdoers when necessary. The idea appealed to the coroner, and he went off to the keep to seek his friend the constable, who commanded all the men-at-arms of the castle garrison. Though Ralph had no love for de Revelle, he was at first uneasy about going against his wishes, but John persuaded him that the sheriff had not actually prohibited a search, only shown a lack of enthusiasm.

By the tenth hour, a score of soldiers, led by Morin and Sergeant Gabriel, were marching over the drawbridge of Rougemont and meeting up at the South Gate with the coroner, his officer and another twenty volunteers from the Bush. These had rallied around to try to help the plight of their favourite innkeeper, and with a motley collection of swords, pikes and daggers, they tagged on behind the column of soldiers. All were on foot, as horses were of no use for combing the woods for fugitives.

In less than two hours, the posse was in position, half the men forming a line that entered the forest from the side where the chapman had been killed, the rest two miles away, approaching from the main track to the north. The men-at-arms, dressed in partial battledress of iron helmets and boiled leather jerkins, alternated with the city volunteers.

De Wolfe and his officer were with the southern party, the constable and his sergeant with the others. They had little hope of catching all the scattered outlaws, who infested every patch of forest, but within three hours their pincer movement through the almost bare trees and scrub managed to grab two men, one found cowering in a bramble thicket, the other up a tree. The latter betrayed his presence when the branch broke and he fell with a scream and a crash within fifty yards of the nearest soldier. With a twisted ankle, he was unable to make a run for it, and when the two lines of searchers met up, de Wolfe and Morin decided that, given the failing light, they had done all they could that day.

The two captives, desperately frightened, ragged wrecks of humanity, were forced to their knees inside the wide circle of their hunters. As outlaws, they were well aware that their lives were forfeit and it was only the means of their deaths which lay in the balance.

John stood over them, sliding his great sword partly out of its scabbard, then slamming it back again.

'We are entitled to strike off your heads here and now!' he rasped. 'The men I appoint to do it will be pleased to earn an easy five shillings' bounty. So is there anything you have to say that might delay that moment?'

Nothing could have been more effective in loosening their tongues than the sight and sound of that sword, and within a few moments John learned that Gervase and Simon Claver had indeed been members of their outlaw band.

'Simon reckoned he was entitled to a bigger share of Gervase's loot, so he said he was going after him in Exeter,' quavered the older captive, a toothless scarecrow with some pustulous disease of his hands and neck.

'Just before he left, Gervase let slip the fact that some relic in a little box might be valuable,' croaked the younger man with the injured leg.

'That set Simon thinking and he left us the next day.'

The cavalcade set off for Exeter, the older man

half supporting, half dragging the other along the track, both destined for the cells in Rougemont until they were dispatched on the next hanging day.

As the four leaders marched at the head of the column on the four miles back to the city, they discussed the results of their expedition.

'It's clear what happened now and we know the identity of the two villains,' growled de Wolfe. 'Ralph, there's no reason now why Nesta should be kept locked in that damned chamber!'

The constable pulled at his beard, worried at his own position in all this. 'I agree, John, but I can't let her out until de Revelle gets back. I'll be in enough trouble with him as it is, taking a troop of soldiers out of the city against his inclinations.'

'He'll be back in a couple of days, Crowner,' said Gabriel, soothingly. 'My wife will see she's comfortable until then.'

John gave an angry grunt and Gwyn tactfully changed the subject.

'What about finding this bastard Simon Claver? That would really put Nesta in the clear.'

De Wolfe rasped a hand over his black stubble as they walked faster in the gathering dusk, anxious to get to the South Gate before it closed at curfew. 'Nesta said that this Gervase claimed he was going to get a bed at Buckfast Abbey the next night, though I wouldn't trust anything he said.'

'As your clerk mentioned, he has to sell the relic to a bunch of monks or priests to realize any profit on his theft,' added Ralph Morin. 'But from the direction that chapman was going, he could have been aiming east, to sell it somewhere like Wells Cathedral or Glastonbury Abbey.'

Gwyn nodded his shaggy head. 'That old fellow in Clyst reckoned the dying man mentioned Glastonbury just before he passed out.'

With this information as the only clues they possessed, the coroner and the constable agreed to search in both directions as soon as the city gates opened in the morning.

'You and Gwyn go east towards Somerset,' suggested Ralph Morin, 'and I'll send Gabriel and a couple of men down the Plymouth road towards Buckfast. This fellow is on foot, so horsemen should catch him up, even though he may have had two days' start.'

John spent a restless night, even though he knew Nesta could come to no harm in the castle, with the sheriff away and the sergeant's wife pledged to look after her. Matilda was as surly as usual and made no mention over supper of her unexpected intercession on the Welshwoman's behalf. Once again, John realized how little he understood Matilda, who was capable of surprising him with acts of kindness, even though she maintained her grim façade most of the time.

After a quick but substantial breakfast in his maid Mary's cook-shed in the yard, the coroner went across to the stables opposite, where the farrier was saddling up the patient Odin, and a few moments later he rode out to meet Gwyn at Carfoix. They had agreed to leave Thomas behind, as his reluctant efforts at riding side-saddle on his miserable pony would only slow them down – and he was needed at Rougemont to write down the confessions of the two outlaws now incarcerated in the foul cells below the keep.

Gwyn was waiting cheerfully on his big brown

mare, ready for anything the day might bring. As they trotted out of the South Gate and along past the empty gallows on the Honiton road, the coroner's officer debated their chances of finding Simon Claver.

'If he went westward, then he would have reached Buckfast by now, even on foot. But Gabriel and his men should still get news of him there.'

'We have the better chance, if he's making for Glastonbury or Wells,' called de Wolfe, over the clip of the hoofs. 'Few men will cover more than fifteen miles in these shortening days.'

Their fear was that, after Honiton, Simon might have turned off towards Bridport and Dorchester, if he was aiming for the abbeys and cathedrals of the south-east. But Somerset was still the best bet, thought John, and they kept on doggedly for the next few hours. The rutted track of the high road was in its best condition in this cold, dry weather, and they were able to put a good many miles behind them before dusk fell. They found an alehouse in a village beyond Ilminster and endured a poor meal there, before finding a heap of hay in a nearby tithe barn for a night's sleep. The coroner and his officer had slept in far worse places during their campaigning days and were quite content with their accommodation.

The next morning, after some stale bread and hard cheese from Gwyn's saddlebag, they were on their way again, John still anxious about Nesta, now that Richard de Revelle might have returned to Rougemont from his marital duties at Tiverton. They passed the usual thin stream of travellers going in both directions – pilgrims, merchants, ox-carts, flocks of sheep and a few pigs and goats, as well as the occasional chapman and pedlar to remind them of the relic dealer's fate. An east wind now blew a fine powdering of snow on to the grey countryside, and John huddled deeper into his wolfskin cloak and pulled the hood up over his head. Gwyn now sported a leather shoulder cape with a pointed cowl, under which he wore an old barley sack wrapped around his neck.

They trotted on for another couple of hours, staring suspiciously at every traveller they passed, trudging along the highway. At an alehouse in a small hamlet, they stopped for some bread and meat, warming themselves with a pot of ale which the landlord mulled with a red-hot poker. They enquired whether any man with a rotted nose had called there in the past day or so, but no one had seen such a traveller.

When they went on their way again, under a leaden sky that promised more snow, Gwyn voiced a question that had been in de Wolfe's mind.

'How long are we to keep going, Crowner?' he asked.

'Until nightfall. We'll turn back in the morning,' grunted John. 'By then we'll have outdistanced him on foot. If we don't see any sign of the swine, it means he must either have gone west or turned off to Dorchester.'

'Then let's hope Gabriel had better luck at Buckfast,' prayed the Cornishman. But a mile farther on, the luck turned out to be theirs.

Here the road passed between dense woods on either side, the trees coming right down to the edge of the track. A cart laden with straw passed them in the opposite direction, and on the empty road ahead, they saw a lone figure trudging along, a long staff in one hand. As they came nearer, they saw that he wore a shabby grey mantle with a hood and that he was limping slightly. From the back, he looked little different to scores of others they had encountered, but on hearing the clip of their horse's hoofs, the man turned his head. Being an Exeter man, living near the Bush, he recognized the coroner immediately. Throwing down his staff, he ran for the shelter of the trees, only a few yards away. With a roar, Gwyn spurred his mare after him, but he was too late to reach him before the man vanished into the undergrowth that choked the spaces between the tall trees.

De Wolfe was only inches behind, and with a curse he slid from Odin's back as Gwyn leapt from his own saddle and plunged into the forest after the fugitive. Though most of the leaves had fallen, there were tangled masses of bramble and bracken between the first trees, but once they were in deeper, the ground was almost bare and the three men pounded along, weaving between the trunks. Though Gwyn had a start, he was heavier than the wiry coroner and de Wolfe rapidly caught him up.

The man ahead seemed to have forgotten his limp, as fear of inevitable death gave him wings, but the long legs of the coroner defeated him in the next hundred yards. With a final yell, de Wolfe threw himself at the man's back and brought him down, with Gwyn hard on his heels to make sure that he stayed there.

Panting with exertion, John drew his dagger and held it at the fugitive's throat as soon as Gwyn turned him over. The grotesque corrugations on one side of the man's nose removed any doubt that they had caught Simon Claver, who stared up at them in abject terror and the firm expectation that he was about to die.

The coroner reached Exeter around noon the next day, having pushed his heavy warhorse as fast as he could, though Odin was no sprinter. In his haste to get back to secure Nesta's safety, de Wolfe had left Gwyn to ride back more slowly, as he had Simon Claver walking behind his mare, his bound wrists roped to the saddle-horn. It would be another day before they arrived, but de Wolfe wanted to get his mistress out of custody as soon as possible. His task was not helped by the fact that Simon had stoutly denied killing Gervase, even though they had found the faded gilt relic box in a pocket of his mantle.

On arrival at the castle, he hurried to the keep and found Ralph Morin in the constable's chamber off the main hall.

'He's in a foul mood, John,' were his first words as the coroner entered. 'Lady Eleanor must have given him a bad time and he's highly incensed that we took a raiding party into the forest against his wishes. You'll have a hard task persuading him to release Nesta.'

De Wolfe told him of their successful capture of the outlaw and the recovery of the holy relic. 'But the bastard resolutely refuses to confess to killing Gervase – he says he met him after he had been to St Nicholas Priory and Gervase agreed to let him take the thing to Glastonbury to sell, whereupon they would split the proceeds.'

Ralph gave a cynical snort. 'A likely tale! But de Revelle will seize upon it, never fear!'

He was right, for when John went down the hall to the sheriff's chamber, he was met with a mixture of anger, sarcasm and sheer spite.

'The man is to hang whatever happens, so why should he tell anything but the truth? I'll certainly not release the prime suspect on such flimsy grounds. This Claver is obviously an outlaw and a thief, but that doesn't mean he killed that man in the inn.'

Nothing would shift the resolve of John's obdurate brother-in-law, and the coroner left in a towering rage, promising to get the whole truth from Simon when he arrived, even if he had to torture him to within an inch of his life. On his way back to Martin's Lane, he met his friend the archdeacon, and he poured out his problems to John de Alençon.

'In some ways, this could be considered to be a matter for the Church,' said the priest gravely. 'I have heard of this relic and, given the provenance offered by that letter from Sir Geoffrey Mappestone, it has a good claim to be a genuine piece of the True Cross.' His hand automatically strayed to his head, heart and shoulders, reminding de Wolfe of his clerk's almost obsessive habit. 'Even though apparently tainted, it is still a part of our Christian heritage and this outlaw should be made to fully confess how he came by it.'

When John suggested that Simon Claver should submit to the *peine forte et dure*, even the usually compassionate archdeacon agreed. When he heard that the sheriff was reluctant to get at the truth for reasons of his own, de Alençon declared that he would call upon de Revelle and make his own ecclesiastical demand that they extract the truth from the outlaw.

The next day, when Gwyn tugged the exhausted and footsore Simon up the drawbridge into Rougemont and across to the stinking undercroft below the keep, he found that preparations were already in hand to persuade the outlaw to speak more eloquently.

Stigand, the evil custodian of the gaol, was waddling across from an alcove with some thick plates of rusty iron, each about a foot square. With a loud clatter, he dropped these into a pile in the centre of the dank cellar, panting with the exertion, as his grossly obese body was not meant for heavy work. When the coroner's officer arrived with the new prisoner, Stigand shackled his wrists to the barred enclosure that led through into the half-dozen cramped cells.

'They're coming at noon to listen to this fellow sing!' lisped Stigand through his slack, blubbery lips. He kicked the prisoner, who had sunk exhausted to the floor, and received a heavy clout across his head from Gwyn.

'Leave the man alone, you evil sod!' snapped the big man. 'Give him some water and a couple of crusts.'

As he left, Gwyn wondered briefly why he should be at all solicitous to a man they were shortly going to torture, then hang in a few days, but there was something about the hopeless captive that reminded him of a beaten dog.

When the cathedral bell announced the middle of the day, a small crowd assembled in the undercroft to view the proceedings. The reluctant sheriff was there, as was the coroner, his officer and clerk, the constable, and the Archdeacon of Exeter. Sergeant Gabriel, who had returned from his fruitless search in the west, was in charge of a trio of men-at-arms brought to handle the prisoner. Now partly recovered from his trek across the countryside behind Gwyn's horse, Simon was dragged to the centre of the large space, struggling and mouthing obscenities. Two soldiers manhandled him to the ground and shackled his outstretched arms and legs to rusty rings set in stones in the damp earthen floor.

As the sheriff stood aloof, with his arms folded under his bright green mantle, John de Wolfe took over the proceedings. Though he was no keen advocate of torture, it was part of the judicial process, and with Nesta's freedom at stake he had no compunction in applying it to this evil man.

'Simon, you have a last chance to tell the truth. You are well aware that as a captured outlaw, your life is already forfeit, so you have nothing to gain by being obstinate.'

All John got for his words was a further stream of curses and denials, so he nodded at the gaoler, who stood by expectantly. Stigand bent with difficulty over his fat belly and lifted a metal plate, clutching it to his stained leather apron as he turned to the prisoner, crucified on the floor. With much puffing, he bent and placed the slab of iron on Simon's chest. His breathing restricted, the man began to wheeze, and his curses became muffled as he ran short of air.

'Speak now and ease your suffering!' pleaded John de Alençon, making the sign of the cross in the air over the man.

Laboriously, the gaoler lowered another plate,

this time on the man's belly, preventing him from using his stomach muscles to draw in air. His oaths and obscenities became mere gasps and his face began to turn purple.

'Speak, man, you have nothing to lose!' shouted de Wolfe, as the outlaw's lips became almost black. 'Nod your head if you submit!'

As Stigand puffed over with yet another plate ready to load on to the man's chest, Simon's stubborn wilfulness cracked. Blood spots had begun to appear in the whites of his eyes.

'Relieve him, before he dies on us!'

Somewhat reluctantly, the sadistic gaoler pushed the plates from the sufferer's chest and belly, then took a leather bucket filled with dirty water and threw it over him. A few moments later, after his ravaged face had returned almost to its normal colour, Simon Claver began to speak, still pinioned to the floor. He now admitted everything, his jealousy at Gervase having the best part of the chapman's loot, his following him to Exeter, finding him in the Bush and cutting his throat.

'I didn't mean to kill him,' he croaked. 'But as I was pulling that golden box from his pack, he started to wake and I panicked!'

Leaving Thomas to crouch down and write the confession as a record for his inquest rolls, de Wolfe went across to his brother-in-law and confronted him.

'Satisfied now, Richard? You arrested my woman out of sheer spite, damn you! You've heard the confession from this man, so I hope you'll not only order her immediate release, but go and give her a personal apology. Then I may not need to write every aspect of the matter in my presentment to the royal justices when they next come to Exeter!'

Richard began to huff and puff, but he knew that he was beaten, and after a few more heated words, he turned on his heel and marched stiffly up the steps out of the undercroft.

'And good riddance, I say,' muttered Gwyn in his master's ear, as they watched the sheriff vanish. Suddenly, there was a commotion behind them and the voice of Thomas squeaked above the hubbub.

'He's having a fit! What's wrong with him?'

They turned and hurried over to the group around the staked-out prisoner. Simon's back was arched and his arms and legs jerked spasmodically, rattling the chains that held him. As John dropped on to his knees beside him, he saw that the man's eyes had rolled up so that only the whites were showing, then there was a final great convulsion and he sank down, immobile.

'He's bloody well dead!' boomed Gwyn, in a voice that expressed more incredulity than concern. 'Why should he corpse himself now, and not when he was being squeezed?'

Thomas de Peyne looked up, his face paler than usual as he crossed himself.

'The fool must have handled the relic – it's Barzak's curse once again.' His troubled eyes rested on his master. 'Crowner, for the Blessed Virgin's sake, don't open that tube, whatever you do!'

During the following week, life gradually returned to normal for the coroner's team and the folk at the Bush. Nesta seemed none the worse for her sojourn in Rougemont, though climbing into the tavern's darkened loft at night made her uneasy for a while. The sheriff remained distant and aloof, never referring to the matter again in John's presence. His sister was as surly and resentful as ever with her husband, ignoring his halting thanks for keeping Nesta out of Stigand's clutches.

The matter of the tainted relic still had to be settled. After John had taken it from Simon Claver, he had left it on the ledge in his chamber in the gatehouse, where Gwyn kept his bread and cheese. Though still sceptical about Barzak's curse, he thought it as well to humour Thomas's concerns and leave the tube unopened.

After a day or two, he decided to give the thing to John de Alençon to dispose of as he thought fit. The archdeacon seemed to take a more serious view of the relic's powers, and at a meeting of the cathedral chapter, following which Bishop Marshal granted his consent, it was decided to offer it free to Glastonbury Abbey. This venerable church always seemed keen to collect relics and the pilgrims that they attracted. Letters were exchanged with the abbot, but the generous offer was gracefully declined. It seemed that Glastonbury was equally aware of the sinister history of the relic and decided not to risk taking a viper to its bosom. More letters passed across the country and eventually a home was found for the suspect relic at Tewkesbury Abbey, whose abbott apparently considered the holiness of his institution more than a match for an ancient curse.

John de Alençon could not resist a sigh of relief when he watched the gilded box and its sinister contents vanish into the scrip of a pilgrim travelling to St Cuthbert's shrine at Lindisfarne, who had promised to deliver it to Tewkesbury en route.

He said as much to his friend the coroner, as they sat over a jug of Anjou red that evening.

'Let's hope they hide it away securely,' replied John de Wolfe sombrely. 'I'd hate to think that some other poor devil reawakens Barzak's curse.'

'Amen to that!' replied the archdeacon, raising the cup to his lips.

ΛCT TWO

Oxford, 1269

When the fat boy was found huddled inside the sanctuary of St Frideswide in Oxford, there was a furore. Discovered by Brother Richard Yaxley, the feretarius or guardian of the shrine, in the early hours of Sunday, it was at first thought he was dead. Brother Richard's immediate concern was that there would be disastrous consequences for the earning potential of the priory. And right at the start of St Frideswide's Festival as well. He concluded that rival establishments in the competition for the attention of the pilgrims had somehow contrived to sully the sacred location. Outraged, he hurried out to raise the alarm. Soon the stone shrine was surrounded by worried monks, who peered in disbelief through each of its six narrow apertures, three set evenly in each side. The prior, Thomas Brassyngton, looked in through one of the apertures, which was in the shape of an ornate cross carved within a circle. He expressed the thought on everyone's mind.

'How on earth did he get in there?'

There was a buzz of conversation as the brothers mulled over the puzzle. The apertures were very small, and the body inside the shrine was very large. Brother Richard was by now beginning to look embarrassed. As feretarius, it was his responsibility to keep watch over the shrine during the feast period, when the public were to be granted access. The shrine was located in the feretory – the area behind the high altar – on a raised stone platform. The previous night Brother Richard had been elsewhere, and did not wish his prior to know where. Staring at the huddled form draped across the gilded coffin housing the bones of the saint, he gave voice to the next obvious thought.

'And how are we going to get him out?'

At that moment, a voice piped up from within the sacred spot.

'Hello, Brother Richard. What am I doing in here?'

A puffy, round face emerged from the bundle of rags that formed the impediment to the monks allowing pilgrims into the shrine that morning. There was a look that was a mixture of puzzlement and simple joy on the unlined features. Richard Yaxley gasped, recognizing the miscreant for the first time.

'Will Plome! What are you doing in there?'

The fat boy giggled.

'I said it first. You tell me.'

'Will!'

Plome may have been a simpleton, but he recognized when someone meant business. He had once been part of a troupe of jongleurs and players, and had learned to distinguish the different tones of voice which actors such as John Peper and Simon Godrich used. The feretarius's voice was now very like the one Simon used for God. Or sometimes the Devil. He screwed his face up in a way he hoped would convey contrition.

'I'm sorry, Brother Richard. I just wanted to get close to her blessed presence. I came late last night, and as you weren't here . . .'

Will missed the piercing look of disapproval that the prior gave Brother Richard at this revelation. And Richard's downcast glance. He was too simple to know he had got the feretarius into trouble. He went on with his story.

'I knelt before the shrine, and prayed. I prayed for good weather for the sheep, because they have to be out in the fields. And I prayed for the fish because they have to be in the ponds where it's wet all the time. And I prayed . . .'

'Let's not go through all the beasts you prayed for, Will Plome.' Brother Richard's words were sharply rebuking. A reflection of the difficulty in which he found himself.

'Oh, and I prayed for you too, Brother Richard.'

The assembled group of brothers sniggered at the simpleton's unintentional association of the feretarius with the beasts of the field. Brother Richard's face reddened. The prior took over the gentle encouragement of the progress of the fat boy's story.

'And did you pray for the saint to make you thin, Will? So that you could climb inside her shrine?'

Will Plome giggled.

'No, Father Prior. That would be silly.'

It was Thomas Brassyngton's turn to blush.

'Then how did you get in there?'

'That's what Brother Richard just asked me.'

The prior saw this was going to require patience, a commodity he had little of at present. The day was progressing, and the pilgrims outside the church would soon be clamouring for access. Not only had he the saint's bones to display, but more recently he had acquired a phial of St Thomas Becket's blood. That would be an added attraction. After all, he could not rely on old saints ad infinitum. Their attraction and efficacy would inevitably wane, and he needed to add new vigour occasionally. New blood – literally so in this case. He noted with approval that Brother Richard had at least remembered to put out the large oak collecting boxes at the entrance to the shrine. The church was in need of improvement and repair, and the pilgrims' contributions were a valuable source of revenue. But the fat boy was stopping it all from flowing. The prior put on his severest voice.

'Will Plome. Unless you come out of there immediately, I shall bar you from all the sacraments of the church.'

'Oh, all right, Father. You only had to ask,' grumbled the simpleton. He slid round behind the saint's coffin and disappeared from view. A miracle in its own right for one so large. The prior stared in astonishment at the trick. Then he felt the stone slab under his feet start to move. He stepped back sharply in alarm, thinking the very foundations of the church were crumbling. Then he watched in trepidation as the grey slab rose an inch or two, and slid sideways. From the mouth of the dark space below the slab emerged the round and hairless head of Will Plome. The prior laughed at his own gullibility.

'Of course, I had forgotten about the Holy Hole.'

In years gone by, pilgrims had been allowed

closer proximity to the saint by crawling from the retro-choir under the reliquary and into the shrine itself through a so-called Holy Hole in the shrine's floor. It had been eighty years since its usage had been stopped owing to the damage caused to the saint's coffin. Too many hands rubbing away the gilded ornamentation. The closest veneration available now was by putting a hand through the pierced apertures in the sides of the shrine. The apertures through which everyone had thought Will Plome had inserted his obese body. Whereas the simpleton had merely found the old access, and used it. Perhaps the saint had spoken to him after all. Thomas could not be sure. So it was with a little more respect that the prior took Will Plome's arm, and helped him out of the gloomy pit.

The rest of the day passed well enough for the fere-tarius and the prior. Freed of its encumbrance, the shrine welcomed its numerous visitors, and the coffers started to fill. Beyond the press of the enter-tainers, pardoners and memento sellers who milled around the close in front of St Frideswide's Priory, the town too benefited from the swell of pilgrims. Running north–south through Oxford, Fish Street was far busier than normal. The towers of St Michael's at Southgate, and St Martin's over-looking Carfax, marked the two ends of the busy street. In all, they were but two of some thirteen parish churches within the walls of bustling Oxford town. At the bottom end of the street, around South Gate, the firewood sellers were soon replen-ishing their wares. Farther along, the fishmongers rolled out more stout, stinking barrels of salted fish. Then, closer still to Carfax – the central cross-roads – the stalls of the tanners and glove-makers, their narrow shop frontages hiding the tradesmen's workshops behind, drew crowds like flies on meat.

By the early evening, the bustle at the heart of Oxford had died down somewhat. And as darkness fell, the tradesmen were deserting the streets, and securing their narrow shop frontages with shutters and bars. Honest English citizens retired behind their stout oaken doors. As did the equally honest members of the considerable Jewish community living on the eastern side of Fish Street, whose good sense told them to avoid confrontation by staying off the streets at night. For as night descended, another population stirred. The first to invade the streets was the army of rats and mice that fed off the leavings of the humans. But these scurrying denizens of darkness were comparatively harmless. Unfortunately, they did not have the night to themselves. The long winter evenings dragged on interminably for the young men studying at the university that formed the heart of the town. Boredom and the easy availability of drink provided a heady combination for those seeking to keep warm on a cold night before the curfew bell rang. Half the householders of Oxford brewed and sold beer, and drinking appeared to be an inevitable accompaniment to each step in a university man's career.

That night, the watch, led by the town constable, Peter Bullock, plodded wearily along the broad aspect of the High Street. As they passed St Mary's Church, Bullock saw a man he recognized as the feretarius of St Frideswide's in earnest conversation with an Augustinian canon. In fact, it looked as though the conversation was getting a little heated, as Yaxley began waving his fist at the canon. The latter was a short, fat man with a lined face and little hair, and was unfamiliar to the constable. The monks of Oseney Abbey were not frequent visitors to the town. Bullock tensed, expecting to have to prevent an altercation. Then he was distracted by a group of raucous students in fine, but somewhat dishevelled, attire who burst from the church doors. Bullock shook his head in disdain as the youths staggered across the path of the watch, obscuring his view of the altercation, and down Grope Lane opposite. Guen's bawdy-house was obviously in for some drunken customers, he opined. Straight from the sacred to the profane. The refrain of a familiar, taunting song drifted back up from the narrow alley.

Juvenes sunt lepidi,
Senes sunt decrepiti.

Bullock could not help but grin, taking in the wrinkled faces of his fellows. He himself was a squat man, with a bent back and a permanent scowl for a face. He was also well advanced in years – as were his colleagues of the watch. The students' ribald song was appropriate. Youth is all charm, old age decrepitude. If his time as a foot-soldier had taught him one thing, it was the eternal truth that life was brief, youth exhilarating, old age a burden, and death a certainty.

'Enjoy it while you can, boys,' was his muttered benediction. When he looked back at the steps where the two monks had stood, they were gone. So he put the incident out of his mind. The watch proceeded towards East Gate, the last gate it had to secure to make the town safe for the night.

Just as they were swinging the gate closed, a figure on horseback slipped through the narrowing gap. The man, sitting astride a jaded palfrey, was tall and well built. He rode straight backed despite the signs of a long journey shown by the lather on the horse's flank, and the splashes of mud on the man's cloak. Bullock reckoned him to be a soldier of some sort from his bearing. But he could not see his face because of the hood that was pulled well forward to protect the traveller from the cold of the winter's evening.

'You are just in time, my friend,' called the curious Bullock.

As he passed, the man eased round in his saddle, placing a gloved hand on the well-worn bags that hung across his thighs.

'I hope so,' was his enigmatic reply.

Bullock saw a flash of sharp, steadfast eyes set in a bronzed face that suggested the man had recently lived under hotter skies than the soft, misty climate of southern England. He had a feeling he knew the man, but could not place him. Then the rider was spurring the tired horse on. Bullock was left with the sight of a broad back, the clatter of hoofs on the stones of the street, and a sense of impending danger.

The second day of the festival was, if anything, even busier than the first. But all this activity created an unpleasant taste in the mouth of Brother Robert Anselm of Oseney Abbey. The tall, rangy monk with his gaunt face was every inch an ascetic. His dark, worn robes hung badly on his spare frame, as though he had lost a lot of weight lately. Which in fact he had, as he worried incessantly about the worm he saw boring into the soul of the abbey that had been his home for more than thirty years. This was the year of Our Lord 1269, the fifty-third of the reign of King Henry III. And despite the King's virtuous translation of the body of St Edward the Confessor into a golden shrine for the greater glory of God, evil was rampant in England.

By the afternoon, the mayhem in the grounds of St Frideswide's had got too much for him. It was not that the rival establishment to the abbey was drawing greater crowds, and therefore more income than his own Augustinian foundation. That mattered little to him. In fact he was glad that the current Abbot of Oseney, Ralph Harbottle, was elderly and reluctant to indulge in the unseemly battle for vulgar approval of the mob – the *plebis frequentatio*. No, what truly appalled him was the unholy marketplace full of sellers of wax effigies – used as offerings – purveyors of souvenirs, pilgrim badges and foodstuffs operating right at the doors of the church. Had not the Lord Himself driven the money-changers from the Temple? What was happening in the grounds of St Frideswide's was a mockery of His actions. St Augustine's own words came to his lips. 'Business is in itself an evil, for it turns men from seeking true rest, which is God.'

Muttering, he turned up Northgate Street, past the weavers and corn merchants, and out through the gate where the Bocardo prison was incorporated into the walls of the town. Some unfortunate wretch hung his arm out of the narrow slit of a

window in the prison, begging for food. Anselm
ignored him. Outside the walls, the taint of sin was
even worse than around St Frideswide's. The
ramshackle buildings there housed the *sordidissimi
vici* – the stews of loose women, and the thieves'
kitchens of Broken Hays. Robert Anselm was glad
finally to be free of it all, and hurried over the two
bridges that crossed the fast-running streams that
fed the Thames to the west of the town. The second
bridge was rickety, without a handrail, and he
walked over with caution. Once over, however, he
strode out more certainly along the westerly
causeway towards the abbey.

Oseney Abbey was one of the glories of Oxford,
perhaps of all England. Even from the outskirts of
the town, the pinnacled buttresses and stately
towers of its new church dominated the water
meadows above which the abbey stood. On cold,
damp days such as this October one, its yellow
stone fabric rose out of the bone-chilling mists that
hung low over the marshy ground, criss-crossed
with the narrow channels of water that ran into the
Thames. Behind its imposing gateway lay the world
of court and cloister, infirmary and dormitory. The
fine lodgings of the abbot and the canons could
not be bettered anywhere in the region. And in the
abbey grounds stood mill and tannery, orchards,
arbours, dove-houses and fish-ponds.

But it was the church which was its centrepiece.
An earlier abbot had begun rebuilding it and the
monastic buildings some twenty years previously.
The church was nearing completion, but elsewhere
building work continued. Brother Robert Anselm
had to skirt around the master mason's crude
lodge in the centre of the unfinished cloister court,

trampling over the residues of stone-cutting. He ignored the lime mortar dust that clung to the folds of his robe. A building site was a noisy place, and he was eager to seek the quiet sanctuary of the church.

At three hundred and thirty feet long, it was one of the largest churches in England, with a central and western tower and twenty-four altars. But it was more particularly the carefully wrought pattern on the tiles that decorated the floor at the core of the church which attracted him. A series of twelve apparently concentric circles was divided into four quarters representing the four Gospels and the four stages of the mass. Closer examination revealed that the circles were actually a single serpentine pathway with seven abrupt turns in each quarter, leading to the central rose, which bore six bays or petals. Seven, if the very centre was included. This pattern mirrored the great rose window in the western wall of the abbey church, and was the same distance horizontally from the main entrance as the window was vertically above it. So, if the base of the wall had been a hinge, the bright and colourful window would have folded perfectly over its darker image on the floor. Numbers and symmetry mattered to Brother Robert in ways he could not fully explain. And the pattern on the floor tiles was his sanctuary and his contemplative conduit.

It was a holy labyrinth, and for the rest of the day, after his unpleasant experience in a festive Oxford, Anselm sought calm in its serpentine pathways.

'So, you don't know who the man is, but you think his arrival in Oxford bodes ill?'

William Falconer smiled wryly at his friend's perplexing announcement. Bullock, for his part, pursed his lips and outstared the big, raw-boned man who stood before him. Falconer was a Regent Master at the university, teaching the seven liberal arts to a motley band of clerks who formed part of the student body. His only acknowledgement of his status was the threadbare black gown he wore. Eschewing any tonsure or master's biretta, he went about bare headed, letting his thinning, grizzled hair grow naturally until it was time to hack the tangled length short again. His coarse, ruddy face and hands were those of a labourer, and misled an observer into thinking the man before him was uneducated. Until they saw the sharp, piercing intelligence behind Falconer's pale blue eyes. It was a look that had scared many a recalcitrant student into submission.

The two men were standing in Falconer's private solar in Aristotle's Hall, the student lodgings that Falconer ran to supplement his meagre teaching income. It had been two days since Bullock's disturbing sighting. He had spent the previous day trying to convince himself that he was being ridiculous. After all, the traveller had been just one more arrival among many in the town for the festival. And nothing untoward had occurred yesterday. But in the end he trusted his instincts, and on this third morning of the festival he had hurried over to Aristotle's Hall to test his fears on his friend.

The two men stood because, though the room was of sufficient size to accommodate them, it also contained the books and experiments that occupied Falconer's enquiring mind. They afforded little space for any of the comforts of living. To the left of the chimney breast was a toppling stack of his most cherished books and papers, including the prized works of al-Khowarizmi, the Arab mathematician. To the right of the fireplace were several jars of various sizes, containing potions and pastes exuding strange and exotic odours. Falconer no longer noticed the smells, and had in fact mostly forgotten the reason for some of the concoctions lurking in the pots. A truckle bed was hidden in one corner, for the bulk of the room was taken up by a massive oak table that was both eating surface and workbench. On it there were animal bones, human skulls, carved wooden figures, stones that glittered, and lumps of rock sheared off to reveal strange shapes in their depths. Peter Bullock was used to the chaos.

'I tell you who he reminded me of. That Templar, Guillaume de Beaujeu.'

Falconer considered this for a moment, then shook his head.

'No, that cannot be. The last I heard of him, he was in France, and well on the way to becoming the next Grand Master of the Order. His responsibilities would not allow him to travel incognito to Oxford just at the onset of winter. You must be mistaken, Peter.'

Peter's grunt carried a clear indication of his lack of conviction as to Falconer's estimate of the man. He hadn't seen him, and the air of authority and calm that enveloped him more certainly than the warm cloak he had draped around him. True, it was over a year since either man had seen the Templar. And everyone had been preoccupied by the presence of the heathen Tartars in England at the time. He had then been a great help to

Falconer in solving a murder. But Bullock wasn't
convinced that this meant they would always be on
the same side. The Templars were a secretive
bunch, who followed their own devious course
through Christendom. On the surface, their duty
was to escort pilgrims safely to the Holy Land. In
the process they also acted as reliable bankers,
ensuring money entrusted to them in the West
could be drawn in the East. But everyone reckoned
there were deeper currents beneath the surface.
So, in Bullock's mind, if your journey was along a
similar route to the Templars, then you could
profit from an alliance. But if your paths crossed,
you needed to take care. Especially if there was
something of value to the Order of the Poor
Knights of the Temple in the offing.

'Well, you may think what you wish, William. But
I am prepared to wager that something unpleasant
is about to happen.'

As if in response to Bullock's prophecy, the door
of Falconer's sanctuary was flung open to reveal
the dishevelled figure of Miles Bikerdike, one of
Falconer's newest students. He had obviously run
some distance, as he stood in the doorway gasping
to catch his breath. His face shone with excitement.

'Master . . .'

'Take a deep breath, Miles Bikerdike, and tell me
what's afoot,' rebuked Falconer. With each passing
year, his students seemed to get younger, and more
prone to childish behaviour. Falconer could not
fathom why. Miles, with his round, fat face and
wispy, blond hair, could be taken for a babe in
arms. The babe managed at last to blurt out his
message, however.

'Master Falconer. There has been a murder. They say his head has been struck quite off his body.'

Brother Robert Anselm liked to walk the labyrinth. The symmetry pleased him, comforted him, when his mind was in turmoil. It was in turmoil now, and he shuffled round the serpentine route of the labyrinth, striving to concentrate his mind on the four elements of the mass as he moved from one quarter to another.

Entrance into Evangelium. Three turns and into Offertory. A turn back on himself and it was Evangelium again. Then three loops and back into Offertory. Two loops and he was walking Consecration. Like devotion, the route was never straightforward. Two more and he was in the final quarter – Communion. The dizzying, looping walk inward represented the first step of the threefold path.

Purgation.

It was not true to say that the monk's head had been removed from his body. Rumour, after all, was always a precursor to exaggeration. When Peter Bullock and William Falconer saw the body, however, they realized that in this case the rumour had not much outstripped the reality. But first, they had had to be brought to where the body lay. Miles Bikerdike had taken them to John Hanny, another of Falconer's students, who was sitting in the cold, cavernous hall on the ground floor of Aristotle's. Hanny was pale faced and shivering. It was he who had found the body. Still more than a little scared, he agreed to lead the two men to where he had seen the supposedly decapitated corpse. They set off down the High Street, and at Carfax, Hanny was about to turn up to North Gate when Bullock stopped him.

'Where did you say the body was, boy?'

'Beyond Broken Hays stews in the lower water meadows.'

'Then we shall go through the castle, and take the postern gate into the Hamel.'

Bullock was referring to the thoroughfare that the canons of Oseney Abbey used to get to the Chapel of St George inside the castle walls. It would be quicker that way than skirting round the town walls. He led the other two down Great Bailey and into the castle precinct, to which he held the keys. Once through the postern gate, they were out into the water meadows close by Oseney Abbey faster than by taking the normal route. Bullock questioned the boy as they walked over a bridge and along Oseney Lane.

'And what were you doing here, when you should have been preparing for your lessons?'

The boy blushed, and began to bluster. Before he could say anything foolish though, Falconer stopped him with a raised palm. Bullock's questioning was pertinent, because anyone in the vicinity of a murder could be a suspect. And at the very least should have started a hue and cry on discovering a body. If the boy was caught out lying, he would be in even deeper trouble. Falconer had an inkling what he had been about, and prompted Hanny to tell the truth.

'I am sure Peter Bullock will forgive you a small sin, if you tell us the truth.'

Dumbly, the boy looked at his feet, bound warmly in a thick layer of sacking.

'Master, I was up before dawn to fish for eels. I have been so hungry of late, and have no money for food.'

The eels were the property of the abbey, and to take them was tantamount to poaching. Falconer silently cursed his own oversight concerning the welfare of those in his charge. Why had he not seen that John Hanny was going hungry? Not all the students at the university were from rich families. Many were poor and allowed licences to beg in order to remain at the university. For such as they, an education was their only hope for a future, and a means of advancement. Hanny earned his keep by serving meals to the richer students, and feeding afterwards on the leftovers. Obviously not enough had been left for him. For the first time, Falconer also noted how patched the boy's outer tabard was. He would not have missed such signs of distress a few years ago.

'Go on,' he said gruffly, to conceal his own sense of guilt.

'I stayed outside the gates last night, and slept in an empty hut on the edge of Broken Hays. It was cold, but dry enough. I was intending to wake up in the night to fish, but I slept on.' Suddenly his face lit up. 'I suppose, then, I didn't really break the law, did I? As I overslept.'

'Your intention is crime enough for me, John Hanny. Continue.'

Hanny's face fell again, as he saw the steeliness in Falconer's eyes. He might have known the master would not allow him to escape so easily. It was going to be a case of memorizing vast swathes of Priscian's *Grammar* for the foreseeable future. He sighed.

'In the end, something woke me up. It was like the howl of a dog. At first, I thought it had been part of my dream. But then I heard it again. I thought maybe a fox had been caught in a snare, so I went out on the meadow to see.' His voice began to tremble. 'That's when I saw him.'

Falconer put a large, firm hand on the boy's shoulder, and squeezed hard.

'Is it far from here?'

The boy shook his head, and pointed mutely across a small stream at a raised bank on the other side. At first, the scene looked peaceful enough. Cattle were grazing on the land below the bank, steam forming around their nostrils, as their hot breath plumed out into the cold air of the morning. On the edge of the bank lay a huddled shape resembling a pile of rags.

'Stay here, John.' Falconer reinforced his command by squeezing Hanny's shoulder again. He beckoned Bullock to follow him. The two men continued on along the raised causeway that was the lane until they were close by the shape on the edge of the dyke. They had to scramble down from the lane into the field, where the cattle grazed on, unconcerned by the human activity. The ground was thankfully firm under foot. Falconer's boots were old and cracked, and inclined to leak. Closer to, the bundle revealed itself as the body of an Augustinian monk. The robes were those of a canon, not a lay brother. He had to be from the nearby abbey. And he had to have been murdered. For the monk's throat had been slit, and blood soaked the top half of his robe, and the ground around his shoulders. But what was truly strange was the attitude of the body.

'What do you make of that, William?'

'A pious murderer?'

The monk lay on his back, his legs stretched out, as though he had lain on the ground to sleep. His hands were arranged one over the other on his chest, and a rosary was linked round the fingers. He resembled a recumbent statue from the top of a tomb. Moving round the body, they could clearly see the man's face. From his features, now soft and flaccid in death, they could still discern that the man was old. The face was lined, and his sparse, white hair was restricted to a tuft over each ear. His empty eyes were staring blankly up at the pale, blue winter sky.

From a pouch at his own waist, Falconer drew a V-shaped metal device. At the end of each arm was a circular ring in which was set a convex glass lens. He held the point of the 'V' to his forehead, and looked at the body through the two lenses. Falconer's eyes were not as piercing as he liked his students to think, and the eye-lenses, especially crafted for him, allowed him to see more clearly close up. Particularly useful when clarity of vision was of the greatest importance.

It did not matter to the constable what his friend could see through his eye-lenses, though. Bullock had recognized the monk immediately. It was the man with whom Brother Richard Yaxley had been arguing the previous night. What was it Falconer had said in reply to his question just now? A pious murderer. Maybe he had been jesting, but Yaxley fitted the bill exactly.

'Look here, Peter.'

'What's that?'

Falconer pointed at something under the monk's

clasped hands, half hidden in the folds of his robe.
He delicately lifted one cuff.

'It's a blade. A curved blade.'

Falconer drew the implement from its hiding
place. Immediately, he knew what it was. Weren't
they surrounded by the abbey fields where the lay
brothers toiled to put provender on the canons'
table? It was the wrong time of year now for any
reaping to be in progress. But the curved blade
would have found a use some weeks earlier. It was
a hand sickle. Now it had been used to reap the
harvest of this unfortunate monk's life.

His sun-burned face stood out like a sore thumb
amidst the pale-faced tradesmen setting out their
wares in the streets of Oxford. When the man
chose to, however, he could blend with shadows,
and disappear into the background. He had the
uncanny ability to seemingly appear out of
nowhere. A skill he had learned from his deadly
enemies, the Hashishin, or hashish-eaters, of the
East. The more popular term for them nowadays,
under their current leader, the Old Man, was
Assassins. But today there was no need for him to
hide away, and sneak down alleys. Today he could
be his more natural self, upright soldier and Poor
Knight of Christ and the Temple of Solomon. As he
entered the North Gate of the town, Matthew
Syward, the watchman, having only just opened the
gate, observed the tall man of military bearing with
interest. Syward's wife was a termagant, and he
often dreamed of living the life of a soldier. He
imagined that this one was probably returning
from a night roistering in the stews of Broken Hays.
He tipped a knowing wink at the soldier as he

passed. But the man ignored him, and began to weave his way through the growing press of people. Oxford was always busy at the time of St Frideswide's Festival, the normal bustle of the town being swollen by the presence of the blind, the lame and the scrofulous come for a cure. And by the unwelcome presence of beggars and pick-pockets. The watchman cursed the haughty soldier for his high-and-mighty attitude, hoping he would lose his money to a cutpurse. Matthew Syward didn't like people who thought they were a cut above him, even if in truth they were. He would remember the man.

Unaware of the unfortunate impression he had created on the watchman at the gate, the Templar returned to the Golden Ball Inn, where he was staying. He had been lucky to find a room at such a busy time, but then good gold coins had helped. He suspected the sour-faced merchant who now sat in the corner of the inn, atop his bags, had been evicted from his room owing to the Templar's own generous offering to the innkeeper. The sight gave him a twinge of guilt as he sat down to a breakfast of bread and ale. After all, his monastic vows had included that of poverty. But then again, he had experienced a tiring journey, and his quest was at the behest of the Grand Master, no less. That it contained a secret and personal element too he had divulged to no one. Yesterday had supplied a promising start to his search. And this morning might have seen its culmination. His early morning errand had been unsatisfactory, however. Nevertheless, he relished the taste of the freshly baked bread the serving-maid had provided. Later, his body and mind refreshed, he would continue his search. Absently, he rubbed at a fresh brown stain on his sleeve.

Falconer left the constable, Peter Bullock, brooding over the corpse, and after telling the pasty-faced John Hanny to return to Aristotle's and eat something from the Master's own supplies, he carried on towards Oseney Abbey. Bullock had been unusually excited since seeing the face of the dead monk, but would not tell his friend what bothered him. Falconer knew better than to press him on the matter. He would find out soon enough, no doubt. For now, he had to break the news to someone at the abbey that one of their canons had been murdered in quite unusual circumstances. After that, he would unburden himself of the affair. He did not relish getting embroiled in the jurisdictional arguments that would ensue over who should prosecute the case. The monk had probably been killed by someone from the town, and Bullock would expect to play his part. But the land on which he was killed belonged to the abbey. Moreover, the monk probably taught at one of the university schools, so the Chancellor would no doubt become involved too. Falconer would be well out of this nightmare.

As he crossed the raised causeway leading to the abbey, he startled some magpies in the field to his right. They rose in a clatter of wings, their tails held stiffly behind them. They reminded him of the story of the founder of the abbey, Robert d'Oyly, whose wife, Editha, had seen some magpies chattering in the selfsame fields. Only she had seen them as souls in purgatory crying out for prayers. Her vision had resulted in the founding of the abbey. He counted these magpies as they flew up. There were seven of them.

Entering the abbey through its main gate, Falconer hesitated, pondering who to talk to first. As it was well past dawn, the abbot would no longer be in the chapter house. And the service at prime was over. In years past, the monks would now have been occupied with manual labour. But times had changed for the abbot and his fellows. The lay brothers did that sort of work, while the canons devoted themselves to prayer and contemplation. The old aphorism that the world divided itself into three classes – those who fought, those who laboured and those who prayed – had a great deal of truth in it. Especially within the walls of an abbey.

As he made his way through the cloisters, he saw a familiar figure approaching him. Brother Peter Talam was the bursar of Oseney, occupying himself with all its external affairs, especially the rebuilding work that was still in progress twenty years after its initiation. He was a large man with a severe mien, and his steps were as short and as stiff as his manner. This always gave him the appearance of someone in a hurry. Indeed, he was so preoccupied that he almost ran into Falconer, rearing back like a charging horse only at the last minute.

'Master Falconer. I did not see you. It has been a long while.'

Falconer recalled that when they had last spoken some years earlier, he had been investigating the strange affair of the death of the papal legate's cook. That had been an unpleasant time for the abbot and the bursar. It appeared that now he was in danger of being embroiled in a similar business.

'Brother Peter. I imagine you are busy.'

Talam's life was one of bustle, so it was no surprise when he averred that he was indeed so.

'Yes, I am. La Souch is not in evidence, and his men are just sitting around awaiting his instructions.'

Falconer wondered whether this missing La Souch was the monk he had found in the meadows. But then, why would Talam refer to 'his men'?

'La Souch?'

'La Souch. Eudo La Souch. He is the master mason in charge of our building works. A surly fellow from the Low Countries who thinks he can come and go as he pleases.'

Falconer saw the glint of battle in Brother Peter's eyes. He felt sorry for this Hollander, if he thought he could best Brother Peter. Many a wily tradesman from the town had tried, and lived to rue the day. Still, if he was a master mason, then he was a person of no small intelligence, who had progressed through a training no less arcane than that endured by any master of philosophy at the university. And he would possess secret knowledge of formulae as complex as those of any mathematical savant. If anyone could give Talam a run for his money, maybe it was Eudo La Souch.

By now, the bursar was dancing on his toes, unable to contain his staccato little trot any longer. He was bothered by more than the missing master mason apparently.

'What is more, Brother John Barley did not appear for prime this morning. The abbot, being charitable, is fearful for his health, seeing that he and Brother John are of an age. So I must seek out an errant brother, as well as La Souch.'

The bursar sounded exasperated at being required to run around tracking down missing canons who should know better. But Falconer thought that perhaps Brother John Barley had a very good reason for his non-attendance. Before Talam could race off about his errands, he grabbed the monk's arm. He knew the abbot was quite elderly. So the missing John Barley would be so too.

'Tell me, Talam. Brother John – is he bald? With little tufts of white hair at his ears?' Falconer demonstrated the tufts he had seen on the corpse by bunching up his own fingers at the sides of his temple, and jabbing them back and forth.

Talam's lips formed into a downturned curve. If Falconer had not known him, he would have thought it was a grimace. In fact it was Talam's severe version of a smile. It was the closest he came to showing amusement.

'That is Brother John. Let's just say he has no longer any need of the barber to maintain his tonsure.'

'Then I think I have some bad news for you.'

Oseney Abbey was soon awash with rumour. Including a scandalous suggestion of self-harm. Though how Brother John could have cut his own throat then lain impassively with his hands crossed on his chest was not fully explained by the instigator of that rumour. It served only to make Brother Robert Anselm more agitated, and he resorted once more to the little pilgrimage of the labyrinth. A turn into Evangelium to begin. Three turns and into Offertory. A turn and back into Evangelium. Three turns and into Offertory again. Two turns and into Consecration. Two turns and into Communion. The holy path led hypnotically back and forth, calming his soul. Until Brother Robert reached the Holy Jerusalem in the centre of the labyrinth, there to enter the second step of the threefold path.

Illumination.

As Falconer approached the abbot's offices, he heard raised voices. Or more exactly, one raised voice interspersed with the weary tones of Ralph Harbottle, the abbot.

'You must find more money, or the supplies of stone will run out. Then the work for my men will dry up, and I will be forced to find them work elsewhere.'

The foreign tones were guttural and peremptory, the talk of building work. It had to be Eudo La Souch, the master mason. In reply, Harbottle's voice betrayed a man run ragged, and weary of the distraction.

'In truth, Master, you should speak to Brother Peter about this. He is the bursar.'

'And he tells me he cannot conjure funds from the air. He says you need to attract more pilgrims. The priory in the town not only has its saint, now it has the blood of St Thomas the Martyr too.' The Hollander paused, then continued in more wheedling tones. 'I was told my predecessor knew something about a relic . . .'

'No!' Ralph Harbottle's voice was suddenly firm and peremptory. 'No, I forbid you to speak of the matter. If we have to delay the work begun by Abbot Leech, then so be it. The new buildings have been twenty years in the making already, another twenty will not matter greatly. You have only been in charge for two years. There is plenty of time ahead of you.'

'Not if you cannot pay me.'

Falconer stepped back as a stocky, well-built man stormed out of the abbot's office. His weather-beaten face betrayed his outdoor occupation, as did the knotty muscles of his arms protruding from the rolled-up sleeves of his dark blue tunic. He scowled at the Regent Master in his path, and Falconer stepped aside. The mason pushed past, and stomped off down the passageway. It seemed Eudo La Souch was not a man to be crossed when he was in a temper.

'Ah, Master Falconer. Thank you for coming. A bad business this.'

Falconer turned to look at the tired abbot, Ralph Harbottle, standing in the doorway to his inner sanctum. The man seemed even older than when Falconer had seen him last. His skin was ashen, and parchment thin, his grey hair hung lankly on his forehead, and in thin wisps over his ears. Falconer imagined that if he hadn't been holding on to the door frame, the abbot might have collapsed.

'The murder, I mean.'

Falconer hadn't imagined it had been anything else that Harbottle was ruing. But perhaps his mind had still been on the row with the master mason, and the shortage of funds. Falconer was also curious about the reference to a relic, but he put it out of his mind owing to the pressing matter of the murdered canon. At Talam's insistence, he had reluctantly agreed to see the abbot. Though unwilling to get involved, he agreed he should at least tell Harbottle face to face what he had seen.

'Indeed, Abbot.'

'I have arranged for the body to be brought back here. Though I have no doubt that the constable will want to interfere, and ask questions of all the brothers. You know the sort of thing. "Where were you last night?" and "Did you murder Brother John?"'

Harbottle threw his hands up in a gesture of disgust at the idea. Prompted by such thoughts of Bullock blundering in, Falconer spoke without further consideration. At the same time cursing himself for breaking his own resolve not to become involved.

'You cannot think of a reason why anyone at the abbey should have had cause to envy or dislike Brother John Barley, can you?'

Harbottle looked shocked.

'I knew it! Master Falconer, this is a house of God, a place of prayer and contemplation. There is no room for envy or hatred, nor any of the vices that might occasion such intemperate feelings.'

Falconer refrained from reminding the abbot of the scandalous murder that had previously taken place at the abbey, and who the perpetrator had been. It looked as though it would not take much more to crush the poor man totally. He was clearly at the end of his tether over the changing fortunes of the abbey. But Harbottle was also a perceptive man. He would not have risen so high in his order if he had not been so. And he could see the clouded look in Falconer's eyes. For a man of uncommon piety, he was also a realist. He sighed, and flopped down on to the hard, wooden seat behind him.

'I am sorry, Falconer. I am beginning to fear that being in charge of the abbey is getting beyond me.

During my novitiate I never dreamed of having to face such complicated . . . secular issues. As a novice, my day was filled with labour and the contemplation of God. Now all I am allowed to think about is the difficulty of getting supplies of stone. And the passing of fellow canons of my generation. There have been too many of them of late, I fear. First there was Brother Benedict, then the unfortunate accident suffered by Brother William . . .'

Falconer interrupted the abbot's ramblings.

'Brother John. Was he a contemporary of yours too?'

'Yes, we entered the novitiate together. Virtually on the same day. And I can assure you no one even disliked him, much less hated him enough to . . . to try and hack his head off. He was inclined to pranks, but never malicious.'

The abbot shuddered, and bowed his head in prayer. After a few moments, Falconer slipped silently out of the room. There appeared to be nothing to be gained by questioning the abbot further. He would return to Oxford, and see what Peter had dug up.

The bustle of St Frideswide's holy day market was at its height. The environs of the church thronged with sellers of candles and insignia, pilgrim badges and tempting victuals. Many of the faces in the crowd belonged to robust young men. They were *peregrini*, professional pilgrims who hired themselves out for pay. They performed pilgrimages and penances on behalf of those rich enough to want to avoid the discomfort of wandering from shrine to shrine in the inclement weather England threw at them. Peter Bullock elbowed his way through the throng, his ears impervious to the blandishments of the stall-holders. He wanted to speak to Brother Richard Yaxley about his altercation with the dead canon before the murder became too widely talked about. He didn't want Yaxley to have any time to prepare a story.

Mounting the steps of the church, Bullock ignored the mumbled complaints of the line of pilgrims waiting their turn at St Frideswide's shrine. They probably thought he was trying to push in ahead of them. But when they turned round and saw his stony face, all their cavilling ceased. Instead, the pilgrims looked furtively at their feet, at the intricately carved stonework, at their neighbours in the queue. Anywhere to avoid the constable's implacable gaze. Inside, the church was a blaze of light. Extra candles and tapers lit the interior, especially the rear of the high altar where the shrine stood. The scene did not inspire Bullock. In fact, it was an irritant to him. He knew the two chaplains who scurried back and forth, and that many of the tapers were paid for out of a grant forced on the Sheriff of Oxford by King Henry after his spat with the barons five years earlier. The town had favoured the barons, and when the King had ultimately triumphed, the town had paid the price. To the tune of one hundred shillings annually. The tapers burned night and day for the soul of the King, in an attempt to neutralize the curse said to fall on any monarch entering the confines of the town.

Bullock spotted Yaxley standing at the side of one of the many large, iron-bound boxes strategically placed along the pilgrims' route to the shrine. He was glowering at an elderly, lame man in rags who had had the temerity to pass without making an offering. Yaxley bent down, and whispered in the cripple's ear. The man gulped, and extracted a small coin from his battered purse. It was probably all he had to buy a scrap of food later. No doubt Yaxley had advised him that miracles did not come cheap. And that hunger was temporary.

'Brother Richard, might I have a word?'

Bullock was pleased that his unremarked approach surprised Yaxley. In fact, a guilty look flickered across the monk's features before he could wipe it out with feigned anger.

'I am doing God's work, Constable. There is no time for idle chit-chat.'

Bullock snorted in contempt.

'I am sure God will not begrudge a few pilgrims remission from their sins without charge.'

He grabbed Yaxley's elbow firmly, and propelled him away from the cripple, who gratefully slid the coin back into his purse. He led Yaxley into a quieter side chapel away from the main hustle and bustle. The monk's face was ashen, but still he preserved his façade of aggrieved innocence.

'Really, you should speak with Prior Thomas first. I will not be bullied in this way. You have no jurisdiction over me.'

'Shall I then get him to ask where you were last night? And the night when Will Plome found his way into the shrine?'

Yaxley began to shake, and his bluster disappeared.

'How do you know about that?' He and the prior thought they had kept the incident with Plome quiet. Bullock just smiled wolfishly, forcing Yaxley to speak first. 'Look, what is all this about? I . . . fell asleep when I should have been alert. That is all.'

'And last night?'

'I was here all night. You don't think I would be so foolish as to fall asleep again, do you?'

'Presumably, there is no one who can verify that?'

'Why should there be any need to be?'

Bullock could tell from years of experience that the monk was being evasive. He didn't believe his excuse that he had fallen asleep the night that Will Plome had gained access to the shrine. Moving the slab at the entrance to the Holy Hole would have made a dreadful noise in the stillness of the church. Yaxley had definitely not been carrying out his duties as feretarius that night. The question was, where had he been? And had he been absent last night also, when Brother John Barley had been murdered? Bullock decided on an all-out attack to keep the man off balance.

'Why? Because Brother John Barley was murdered either last night, or in the early hours of this morning.'

The feretarius looked horrified.

'And you think I killed him? Why?'

'Why? Because I saw you arguing with him two days ago. What was that all about?'

Yaxley went pale, then tried to cover his discomfort with a sneer. 'Because I am certain it was he put Will Plome up to sneaking inside the saint's shrine in order to discomfit the priory. The simpleton could never have found the old entrance without help, and Barley is of an age to recall stories of its use. The canons at Oseney are jealous of the shrine's popularity, and would stop at nothing to spoil that.'

'And why blame Brother John specifically?'

'Because he . . .' Yaxley paused, framing his words carefully. 'Because I had heard tell that Barley was claiming he would soon do something to the great benefit of Oseney Abbey. That he had a rare gift to give. When I asked him about it that day, he laughed and just asked about Will Plome. I could see that was his "rare gift" to the priory – a cruel prank. If he had not been the instigator, how would he have known about the incident?'

'Maybe he knew the same way I did. From Will Plome himself. Will has been telling everyone that the prior thought he had become miraculously thin in order to gain access through the viewing holes. He thought that very funny. As for the slab, anyone who treads on it can see it rocks. Will was probably just curious, and investigated what was underneath. If you had been there, you might have seen that.'

Yaxley ignored the implication that Bullock doubted his claim of being asleep at his post. He merely stuck to his story.

'As for last night, I was here attending to my duties. Now you must forgive me, as I must attend to them now.'

Bullock knew that as yet he could do nothing to undermine Yaxley's assertion. Though he did wonder whether John Barley had really had something to offer the feretarius. If so, what could it have been? Without any more information, however, he would have to let the feretarius go. For the time being.

Falconer had got no farther than the open yard of the cloister in Oseney Abbey. In its centre stood the timber-and-thatch affair that was the master mason's lodge. More than just a shelter, underneath which the mason carved his stone, it stood as a symbol of the man's arcane skill. Scattered on the table underneath the thatch were La Souch's instruments. With a mason's square, compass and straight edge, he mapped out the geometry that defined the symbolism of the church. The floor plan was based on three squares set in diamond formation, each overlapping the other. Three squares – Father, Son and Holy Ghost. Where the two outer squares overlapped, at the centre of the central square, was the most sacred place in the church. Ultimately, the whole building was a symbolic rendition of the Heavenly Jerusalem. But equally a master mason was a practical man, and used mathematics to calculate the strains and stresses of the construction. La Souch was architect, structural engineer, mystic and building contractor rolled into one.

At the moment, he was preoccupied with restoring the Oseney Ring of bells to the new west tower. He was scrambling like a monkey up the rickety framework of timber, rope and pegs that surrounded the tower, giving out orders as one of the bells began its precarious ascent on the end of a rope pulley. Falconer wondered which one it was. The bells were named Hauteclere, Douce, Clement, Austyn, Marie, Gabriel and John. There were seven in all. At one point the bell caught on a projecting timber, and La Souch swung out over the void, maybe forty feet in the air, to free it. Falconer held his breath. He himself was fearful of heights. But La Souch seemed oblivious to the danger. He freed the bell, and swung back nonchalantly on to the scaffolding. Falconer looked away as the man clambered ever higher.

That was when he saw the oddest sight. Inside the church, by the dappled light of a stained-glass window, a tall, skinny monk described a weaving path in the centre of the nave. His movements veered arbitrarily left and right, and sometimes the monk turned back on himself, appearing to retrace his path. Gradually, though, he moved from the periphery of the nave towards a central point. There was a look of fierce concentration on his face. At the centre of his ramblings he stopped, and turned slowly round in a complete circle. His face, coloured by the broken light from the window, now looked ecstatic, and was quite unheeding of Falconer observing him. The Regent Master began to feel a little embarrassed at spying on the monk's devotions, but was drawn towards him. He wandered into the church, and stood in the shadow of a pillar. From there, he could see the pattern on the floor of the nave which the monk had been following. It looked like a maze. Or more strictly speaking a labyrinth. A maze had dead ends, whereas the labyrinth ran circuitously but inexorably in one direction.

'It describes a contemplative journey. A pilgrimage.'

The gentle voice was that of the tall monk, addressing Falconer from the core of the labyrinth. His face was radiant in the coloured light, his smile one of peace.

'You start at the western end. There.'

He pointed at the entrance to the labyrinth, clearly inviting Falconer to walk it. The Regent Master complied. He could do with a little contemplation on his existence. The twists and turns meant the journey could not be hurried, and Falconer slipped into a steady rhythm. His pacing brought him tantalizingly closer and closer to the centre, while still circling round it. Round and round the monk, who turned slowly to observe his new tyro. Finally, the two men stood in the centre, and the monk grasped both of Falconer's shoulders in approval.

'There. That part of the journey is a purging, a letting go. Do you feel it?'

Falconer was not sure what he felt. He was not a man accustomed to feeling the mystical. But somehow he did experience a relief from the pressures of his normal life. Students and their diet. The monk offered his name.

'Robert Anselm.'

'William Falconer.'

'Ah, yes. I have heard of you.'

Falconer guessed the monk was thinking of the previous murder that had brought him to Oseney. Now a second one had occurred, and here he was again. Albeit reluctantly.

'Here in the centre is an opportunity for insight, and illumination.'

Falconer reckoned he also needed that right now. Not least to sort out his doubts about his continuing vocation. Anselm went on to describe the symbolism of the six petals around the central core of the labyrinth. Mineral, plant, animal and so on – all the elements of the world were there represented.

'And the very centre is the seventh symbol. In the person of the Trinity. Here, beneath this stone.'

He pointed a reverential finger at the carved

stone in the centre. Falconer could not see it clearly without using his eye-lenses. Too embarrassed to take them out before a stranger, he bent down to examine the carving. It was of God as a master mason, or architect, wielding a giant set of compasses.

'Does it provide you with any insight, Master Falconer?'

'About what?'

'The death of Brother John, of course. Do you see it?'

Falconer shook his head.

'I am afraid I rely on facts, Brother Robert, and there are precious few of those at present.'

'You will see it, if you only look. I am sure.'

Falconer was not as confident as Anselm seemed of his ability to see the killer. It was time for him to go, and to pay better attention to John Hanny's needs. He thanked the monk, and left. Anselm winced as Falconer ignored the twisting outward labyrinth, and crossed the floor in a direct line to the doorway.

The Templar, once refreshed by the morning bread and ale, ventured out into the throng of pilgrims making their way to St Frideswide's Church. The skinny, dark-haired maid who had served him his food both days was also the maid who had plumped up his straw mattress for him on arrival. When he left the Golden Ball Inn, she was hovering by the door, a sly look on her pinched face. He admired her persistence, which flew in the face of her lack of comely charms, but it was wasted on him. His order demanded chastity, as well as obedience and poverty. And he had never had any difficulty obeying the rule of chastity. Nor that of poverty – the order provided him with all he wanted. It was obedience which was most irksome to the Templar, and which provided him with the greatest struggle. If he had chosen to obey the Grand Master strictly, he would probably have given up his quest by now. But he hadn't. He had not come this far to give up so easily. Last night's little setback needed to be overcome, and he could not do that by scuttling back to Occitania. He would have to return to Oseney Abbey and the mason.

If he could find the man in charge of the building work there, he might succeed where he had failed with the monk. Not knowing the short cut that had taken Falconer, Bullock and the boy Hanny out on to the water meadows, the Templar exited the North Gate and followed the well-trodden northern track to the abbey. So it was that he missed Falconer, who was returning to Oxford by the postern gate in the castle wall.

On his way to the abbey, the Templar talked to the ragged *peregrini*, who were seeking to double their fortunes by adding the power of the relics at the abbey to that of St Frideswide. He asked casually whether anyone had heard of a portion of the True Cross in the vicinity. Suddenly he was surrounded by shining faces, eagerly demanding that, if he knew of such a relic, he tell them of its location. It was of inestimable importance to them. One man with a boil-ravaged face would not let go of his sleeve. He was convinced that the Templar knew more than he was admitting to, and begged to be let into the secret. He was desperate for a cure. The Templar broke free of his clutches only with some difficulty. Thereafter, he refrained from revealing his intentions to his fellow travellers.

At the abbey, the Templar cast around until he saw a man carving a diamond pattern on the surface of a cylindrical piece of stone. Each piece, piled on its companion, would make up one of the pillars to the entrance to the nearly completed church. The Templar stood and marvelled at the man's skill as he worked on in silence. Every blow was precise and controlled, leading to a groove that spiralled up the pillar section. Could this be the mason he sought? He had supposed him to be older. He tested the ground with a question.

'Did you know that a pillar, being the synthesis of a circle and a square, represents the marrying of the spiritual and the material worlds?'

The man smiled coolly, and chose his reply carefully.

'Yes. And that the pillars named Jachin and Boaz stood either side of the entrance to Solomon's Temple.' La Souch stopped chipping at the stone, and squinted into the sun, studying the dark-skinned stranger.

'You are a Templar?'

The man briefly inclined his head. It was barely an acknowledgement, but enough. The mason set his tools carefully on the floor of the lodge where he sat.

'Some people say you lot have more secrets to hide than we poor masons. Have you been to the Holy Land? The darkness of your skin suggests you have, and recently.'

The Templar grimaced.

'Alas, I got no farther than our fortress near Famagusta on the island of Cyprus. I leave the honour of having once freed Jerusalem from its yoke to one of my ancestors, Miles de Clermont. I have to be content with the Heavenly Jerusalem embodied in the structure of churches such as this one you have constructed.'

'Me and my predecessor, God rest his soul. I have only been working here for two years, myself.'

That was not what the Templar wanted to hear. He had come all this way because of a story concerning the mason working on Oseney Abbey in England. Certain knowledge had been conveyed to the Templar Grand Master. Knowledge of a particular relic that the Order had been seeking for years. At one time they had traced it to Tewkesbury Abbey, but it was no longer there, and the trail had gone cold. Then a story about a mason working in Oxford had reached the Grand Master. It now appeared that story had been too long in surfacing. The old mason was dead. There perhaps remained a slight chance that the knowledge had been passed on, though.

'But you work to plans laid down by the master mason who came before you?'

Eudo La Souch produced a snorting laugh that had his labourers working on the site looking in his direction. They were curious as to what had amused their normally sour taskmaster. But he waved his hand at them, and they hastily returned to what they were doing. La Souch examined the Templar, lounging in the shade of the lodge roof. Despite the man's relaxed posture, he could see that his muscular legs held his body in perfect balance. His arms, crossed nonchalantly over his chest, were actually tensed and ready for an assault from any quarter. He wondered whether the man ever truly relaxed.

'If you think there were any plans, then you do not understand how we work.' By 'we', he meant the secretive guild of master masons. 'We have no need for drawings. It's all in here.' He tapped his head. 'The closest you would come to plans are those.'

He pointed at a large area of plaster on the ground in the centre of the cloister. It was criss-crossed with faint marks – lines scored in the surface of the plaster.

'What's that?'

'It's a pattern floor, where I can draw up full-size templates for the construction.'

'Then you have no records of work carried out by your predecessor?'

La Souch shook his head. The Templar was dejected. His search for the relic had come to a dead end again.

'And when you started you didn't hear of any rumours of a relic that might have had a special place constructed for it?'

'Relic? What sort of relic?'

'A piece of the True Cross.'

La Souch tried to keep calm, and not to show this Templar he knew anything about such a relic. He was afraid to speak in case his voice quavered. He shook his head, and picked up his stoneworking tools again. He began chipping at the stone, though he knew he was ruining the block with shaking hands. Out of the corner of his eye, he watched the Templar sigh, push himself away from the wooden post he had been leaning against, and walk away. La Souch made sure he was well out of sight before he downed his tools. He hurried over to the fabric rolls that held the accounts of the building work for the last twenty years. He would need to redouble the effort of his search now he knew for certain. Previously, the existence of the relic had only been a story hinted at by the workmen he had inherited from his predecessor. The Templar had now confirmed its reality.

'Have you seen John Hanny? I told him to come back here, and wait for my return.'

The three students who sat companionably at the table in the communal hall of Aristotle's shook their heads in unison. It was late afternoon, so they were about their supper, a pan of bean potage, which sat steaming in the centre of the plain trestle table. Edward Bygrave, a wealthy student dressed in fashionable parti-coloured tabard and scarlet hose, spoke up for them all.

'Please, Master Falconer. He fetched the potage for us, and we invited him to eat also. But he said he could not. And truthfully, he did look ill. Sort of pale.'

Falconer didn't like the boy's truculent tones, nor the way Miles Bikerdike grinned at Bygrave's report. He doubted they had so readily offered poor Hanny his share of the food. Despite the fact he had earned it by serving his wealthier fellows. Hanny would have fetched the potage from the bakery oven, where those who lacked the where-withal for cooking had hot meals prepared for them. It should have entitled him to his share. Even at the expense of his pride.

'Very well. But no-one thought to ask him where he was going, I suppose?'

Again the little group shook their heads solemnly. Falconer sighed heavily, wondering whether he was still up to teaching his students. The Seven Liberal Arts were all very well. He could still pound those into their skulls. But it seemed that common decency was an increasingly difficult attribute to impart.

Though he wanted to talk to Bullock to see whether the man had any further news on the monk's death, he knew he would have to ensure that John Hanny was found first. That would be his penance for ignoring the boy's plight until now. In fact, some deep concern was beginning to gnaw at his stomach. He had unquestioningly accepted Hanny's version of why he had been outside the walls that night. What if he had not been eeling, but was somehow embroiled in the death of the monk, after all? Falconer shuddered at the thought that he might have completely misread the boy. He turned back towards the front door of Aristotle's and the darkening streets. The three students were already beginning to reach for the ale jug, and joking with each other. Hanny's plight was already forgotten as far as they were concerned. Angry that they did not share his worries, Falconer decided to leave them with a severe command.

'You are to speak Latin, and only Latin, to each other. These are the rules of the university, after all.'

Their groans cheered him up somewhat.

Outside, the narrow lanes were dark and silent. Almost everyone would be at supper, but still the quiet was unusual. Oppressive even. Suddenly he was on the alert, his senses sharpened as if on the eve of battle. He had been a soldier in his youth, and his awareness of danger had never left him. If something was afoot, then it was doubly important to find John Hanny, and keep him safe. He decided to avoid the open thoroughfare of the High Street, choosing instead to go down Kibald Street, and into Grope Lane. He didn't think Hanny would be in one of the bawdy houses there. Though the girls cost only a few pennies, that was more than the boy possessed. But there were also some low taverns in the street, feeding Grope Lane's customers' other appetite. He poked his head in a few doors, but here too there were few people. And those there were had fallen into a drunken stupor. At the bottom of the lane, he turned into St John's Street, then up Shidyerd Street into Little Jewry Lane. He was now approaching the back of Jewry, and could hear a dull rumbling sound. At first it puzzled him, as he could not make out what was causing such a noise. Then he distinguished the sound of splintering wood, followed by a surge in the noise. He could now hear individual voices calling out in triumph. It was the sound of a mob.

As if on cue, a bell began to toll wildly. It was the unmistakable note of St Martin's Church. The bell that called the town to arms. Falconer had heard it tolling before, often to be matched by the resonant sound of St Mary's. That was the warning bell for the university. He wondered whether something – the death of the monk perhaps – had sparked off a riot between town and gown. But the bell of St Mary's Church remained silent, and the sound of the mob appeared to be restricted to Fish Street, along which were ranged the homes of the Jews of Oxford. Falconer hoped that his old friend, Jehozadok, was safely indoors. The old rabbi was too frail to stand up to the mob, and he knew it.

But some of the younger Jewish men would probably not be so circumspect.

Only the other day, Falconer had seen one youth who he knew as Deudone accosting the pilgrims making for St Frideswide's. He was pretending to limp, then uttering an oath and suddenly walking freely. Then he had thrust out his hand, saying the pilgrims should give him alms as his miracles were just as genuine as the saint's. Fortunately the pilgrims had turned away in disgust. On another day, his contemptuous behaviour could have got him into trouble. A riot such as was boiling up now would be an admirable opportunity for Deudone to think of showing his mettle. The boy was an ardent suitor of Hannah, daughter to the apothecary Samson. Her raven-haired beauty had turned his head, and he would do anything to earn her admiration. It was too much to hope that he would hide away from the mob. Moreover, he was the ringleader of a larger group of hotheads.

All thoughts of John Hanny temporarily shelved, Falconer hurried down Jewry Lane, hoping to reach the home of Deudone's mother, Belaset, before the mob did. Belaset was a widow who had taken over her late husband's business very successfully. Her financial acumen was the equal of, if not greater than, her husband's. Sadly, the skill seemed not to have passed on to the son. Deudone was impetuous, with little aptitude for hard work. If Falconer knew Hannah's mind as he thought he did, she would not be impressed by any of the boy's wild behaviour. But he still needed to be prevented from confronting a mob of angry people intent on causing mischief.

As he emerged from the end of Jewry Lane on to

Fish Street, Falconer could see that the mob was busy at the top end of the street, where it joined La Boucherie. The houses of some of the more prominent members of Jewry were located there. But then they could withstand the efforts of the mob. They were built of stone, and had sturdy oak front doors. With one eye on the milling crowd, lit by flaming torches and resembling a scene from Hell, Falconer eased along the shop frontages at the lower end of Fish Street. Jehozadok, Hannah and Samson lived in neighbouring houses close by. And Belaset lived below them next to the cloisters of St Frideswide's Church, just beyond the synagogue. Sometimes the songs of the Talmudic scholars would mingle strangely with the sounds of a religious procession on its way to the shrine of the saint. Tonight, the only sound was the unpleasant and dissonant roar of angry people intent on causing damage. And the racket was getting nearer.

He knocked quietly on Belaset's door, hoping the woman would realize it was not the mob outside yet. A panel slid back, and Falconer could see a pair of brown eyes behind the grille set in the opening.

'Belaset. It's me, William Falconer. You need not let me in. I only wish to know that everyone is safe. Have you seen Jehozadok?'

The woman's deep, dark eyes stared out through the grille calmly.

'You need have no fear for him, Master Falconer. He is here with me. And so is my son. I have told Deudone that he is to stay inside and protect us.'

Falconer saw the flash of amusement in her eyes. They both knew it was she protecting her son, not the other way round. He saw the outer edges of her eyes crease up, and imagined the smile on her lips.

'It helps that Samson and Hannah brought the rabbi here, and have stayed with us too. Thank you for your concern, but you should look after yourself now.'

'Have you any idea why these people are on the rampage?'

Falconer could hear the heavy sigh despite the thickness of the door.

'Do they need a reason, when the greatest in the country treat us so badly? But Hannah said she did hear from the cutler who rents his shop from them that there was some talk of a ritual murder near Broken Hays. Whoever found the body has accused us, of course.'

'A ritual murder . . .?' Falconer was appalled. Since the ridiculous story of a child murder in Lincoln some fifteen years previously, horrific tales of Jewish rituals abounded. It needed only some incautious remark to set off a vicious attack on local Jews. Could it have been John Hanny who had unleashed this current riot? And had he done it unwittingly, or with malice in his heart? Either way, the boy needed to be found.

In the dying light of the candles in the nave, Robert Anselm stood at the centre of the labyrinth, far from the turmoil of Jewry. Around him on the floor of the nave were ranged six hemispheres. They resembled rose petals, with the end of the labyrinth walk as the stem of the flower. Each hemisphere was a symbolic representation of the attributes of the world. He turned round slowly on the spot, meditating on each portal individually. The first was Mineral, the next Plant. Then came Animal followed by Human. The last two were Angelic and the Unnameable. The seventh point was the central slab at his feet. Here was Illumination.

He recalled a time more than thirty years earlier, when he had desperately needed illumination, to resolve the great tribulation that had confronted him with the arrival of the relic. The relic was supposed to have been the answer to Oseney Abbey's prayers – its saviour. The rumours of its arrival had begun three days before, and had caused a great stir among the brethren. Even the young Anselm had welcomed the news at first. The abbey took a great deal of money to maintain, and resources had dwindled of late. A new focus for pilgrimage could make all the difference. Robert Anselm could see that.

Brothers Petroc and Peter had been overcome by the majesty of the relic. They had twittered on after nones, finishing each other's sentences as they had a habit of doing.

'Is it not a wonder to behold, young Robert. A piece . . .'

'. . . of the True Cross, here in . . .'

'Oxford. At our abbey.'

It was not long, however, before the abbot was cautioning everyone to remain silent on the matter. And Robert Anselm no longer felt elated. No, he had felt only oppressed. By then he had learned a deadly secret, so that, rising from his knees after prayers one evening, he had had to fight for breath. Petroc and Peter had helped him out of the chapel into the fresh air, where he took in great lungfuls of the sweet-scented air. It nevertheless tasted bitter on his tongue. He had retched. He had then hidden his true emotions, by dipping his head between his legs, and moaning. A non-committal sound that the two brothers took as disappointment that the relic was not to be. They had left him to regain his composure. The following morning, though, Anselm had numbly risen from his cot before the third hour of the morning. No great task, because he had not slept all night, and his duties called him to the kitchens. But it had been with a heavy heart that he had begun his daily tasks.

Daily tasks that had absorbed him ever since. This night, thirty years on, he began to tread the route towards the exit of the labyrinth. This journey out represented Union, and action in the world.

Falconer crossed Fish Street, and stood in the doorway of St Aldate's Church opposite Belaset's house. The mob was rampaging down the street, led by some massive brute of a man with a thick ginger beard. His face was red, though whether this was due to exertion, drink or the light of the flaming brand in his fist was difficult to tell. One eye was clouded dead white, which gave him the look of one half dead. But his actions were lively enough. He charged up to the door of the Jewish synagogue, and thumped on it with the butt of his firebrand. Sparks flew into the air.

'Kill the Jews. Kill the child-killers. Kill the monk-killers.'

His cries were echoed like a litany by the jostling crowd of angry people behind him. They were largely men of the town, though there were a few women on the fringes, who by their ragged looks were perhaps there for any pickings from the riot rather than out of conviction. Falconer also spotted the gaudy robes of a few clerks in the midst of the more sober dress of the townspeople. He screwed up his eyes to try to commit their faces to memory, cursing his poor vision. The lenses he had were only of use at close quarters. So the faces of those farthest away were no more than a blur. But then he did see someone he recognized skulking on the edge of the mob. It was unmistakably John Hanny, and he looked distinctly uneasy.

Falconer eased from under the shadow of the church porch, and skirted round the crowd, closer to where Hanny stood. Ginger-beard was having no success with his assault on the synagogue door, and those at the back of the mob were beginning to drift off down Pennyfarthing Street, and Jewry Lane. All but the most hotheaded would soon begin to realize that their shouts, and the noise of their attack on the Jews' houses, would bring the constable and his crew to the scene. And Falconer knew he should get John Hanny away before that happened. Peter Bullock was no respecter of university privileges. In fact they irked him, despite his friendship with Regent Master Falconer. He would cheerfully incarcerate an errant clerk in the Bocardo, if he could catch him at wrongdoing.

As the pent-up emotions of the individuals in the mob began to leach away, and they began to disperse, Falconer reached his guilty student clerk. He grabbed his arm tightly.

'John Hanny, you will come with me. Now.'

The boy's face, as it turned to Falconer, was a

picture of shock, and shame. He stammered a sort of lame excuse, but his teacher was not in a mood to listen. He strode off down Little Jewry Lane, dragging the youth stumbling and groaning behind him. Turning swiftly left and then right, he hurried down the unsavoury alley accurately named Schitebarne Lane, and back towards Aristotle's Hall.

In the quiet and safe atmosphere of the communal hall, he sat Hanny down beside the embers of the fire. The other students had retired to their shared dormitory rooms, carelessly leaving a cold mess of potage on the hearth. Falconer, towering over Hanny, demanded to know what the boy was doing starting a riot. Hanny's face was as white as a sheet, and his words came in little gasps.

'I swear I did not actually say it was the Jews. That was the fault of that wall-eyed giant. He said it must have been the Jews, as they were always killing Christians for their rituals.'

Falconer snorted in disgust. He would let Bullock know about the wall-eyed man, assuming that the constable hadn't manage to grab him off the street anyway. The boy had been foolish, and incautious like any young man with a story to tell. But what was it he had said that had excited the crowd so? There was nothing in the details Hanny had given him and Peter Bullock which could have done that. Had he held something back?

'I think you had better tell me everything, John.'

John looked glumly at the ground, where a careless spillage of bean potage had left a dark brown stain. He pushed at the mark with his foot, spreading it in the straw.

'You will not believe me, if I told you.'

Falconer smiled gently. Young men like this student often imagined that they had seen wonders. When their vision was clouded with drink, and all they had been witness to was something unusual, that nevertheless had a perfectly rational explanation. The Regent Master's guiding star was Aristotelean logic, which demanded scientific observation and comparison of facts. Occasionally in the past, he had been incautious enough to express opinions openly about others' beliefs. And that had put him at odds with the Church and the university establishment. More than one chancellor had hinted at heresy, and threatened him with an appearance before the Black Congregation. It had not helped his position in the university, and his reputation was tarnished as a consequence. Lately, he had grown more circumspect, more compliant, which did not entirely please him. But he was weary of conflict and controversy, and not for the first time questioned whether he should even be teaching at all. But, at his lowest ebb, he would encounter such a lost youth as John Hanny, and his commitment was renewed.

'I might just surprise you, John Hanny. I am old enough to have seen many things, and few, if any, have given me cause to marvel. Except for the gullibility of student clerks.'

John blushed, and began a stumbling revelation.

'I did go eeling that night. That was the truth. And I did fall asleep in the hut, and was awakened by a noise. But I saw more than I told you or the constable.'

The boy paused, a fearful look in his eyes.

'Go on. You must tell me everything now.'

'When I crawled out of the hut to see what had made the noise, I saw him.'

'The dead monk?'

'No. Him. The murderer. He was bending over the body with something in his hand. A curved blade. It looked like a sickle. I watched as he turned the body over and straightened the legs. He did something else that looked like a sort of magical pass with his hands over the body. Then he laid the sickle under the monk's hands, folding them across the body. What could he be doing else, but conducting some Jewish ritual over the man he had killed?'

Falconer wondered too, but was not inclined to think Hanny had seen a ritual of any sort. It was more likely the killer had been searching for something the monk had in his possession. But who had the boy seen who had him so scared he dare not at first reveal this knowledge?

'Tell me who you saw.'

The boy screwed up his face in fear.

'I thought it was the very Devil, sir. Or if not him, some Jew. He was big and dressed all in black, and I saw his face when he turned away from the body. It was dark-complected, and the eyes burned like coals. I swear that is the truth. He actually reminded me of that youth Deudone, who is always mocking Christians, and bragging about how much richer he is than us.'

'You didn't mention him by name to the mob?'

'No, master!'

Falconer held in his anger at the boy's unthinking demonization of the Jews. But it was doubly worrying, if Hanny imagined he had seen Belaset's son at the scene of the murder. Most people would not want any further proof of the guilt of a Jew.

'I want you to think most carefully, use your brains to think about what you really saw. Perhaps you will make more sense in the morning. We will tell the constable then.'

Hanny subsided on to his stool, and looked incredulously at his master.

'Master. Don't you believe in the Devil?'

Falconer grunted. How could he explain it to this callow youth in a way that did not sound like heresy?

'The Devil? Put it this way, John. I do believe in the ability of man to create infinite evil.'

Peter Bullock yawned, and kneaded the small of his back. He had had a frustrating night with nothing to show for his discomfort but cold feet, and a nagging ache at the bottom of his spine. After being hauled from his bed to a disturbance in the Jewish quarter that had turned out to be something and nothing, he had decided to make use of the disruption to his sleep. He had sneaked into the precincts of St Frideswide's Church, and found himself a hiding place behind one of the empty vending stalls there. He could see the tapers still burning inside the church, and the shadow of someone moving about. It had to be Brother Richard Yaxley, carrying out his duties as fere-tarius. During the festival, the monk remained in the church at night to guard the shrine. Or rather, he should do so. Bullock was sure he had deserted his post the time Will Plome inserted his fat frame into the shrine. And he suspected Yaxley was also absent when he murdered Oseney Abbey's Brother

John Barley. But suspicion was not enough. Bullock needed proof. Last night he had been determined to gather the evidence by spying on the man.

He found that by perching on a wall he could observe Yaxley moving around inside the church, going from offertory box to offertory box. He was collecting the coins in a bag, which was soon heavy with the bounty. He then moved towards the high altar. For a while he disappeared from Bullock's limited view. In fact, he was out of sight for so long that the constable was on the verge of entering the church, thinking Yaxley had given him the slip. Then he reappeared, unencumbered by the bag of coins. Bullock watched as Yaxley climbed to his watching loft at the level of the triforium windows. There, he settled down on a straw-filled mattress, and lay back. Disappointed, Bullock observed in envy as the monk spent a comfortable night resting in the warmth of his station above the shrine.

It was a grey dawn that saw Bullock easing his aching bones, and slipping away for a cold breakfast of bread and ale. Frustrated at being none the wiser about Yaxley's earlier activities, he almost didn't hear his old friend, Falconer, calling from behind him.

'Peter. Peter. You're abroad very early.'

Bullock slowed his pace to allow Falconer to catch up with him, and they walked together towards the castle.

'I might say the same for you, William. But I have been on business. What's your excuse?'

Despite his determined tread, Bullock was finding himself hurrying to keep up with the taller man's loping stride. Fortunately for him, Falconer stopped abruptly in response to his question, and stood at the corner of Fish Street and Pennyfarthing Lane. He watched distractedly as the early-rising tradesmen opened the shutters of their shops and began setting up their stalls. They had to profit when they could. And it would be another lucrative day meeting the needs of the pilgrims who thronged into Oxford for the Feast of St Frideswide. The lanky Regent Master turned his gaze on his stockier companion.

'Business? What business? The riot that took place across the street from here yesterday? I was coming to tell you about that. It was a wall-eyed man with ginger hair who was the ringleader . . .'

Bullock smiled grimly.

'Ah. William Lawney. That makes sense. He owes a lot of money to the Jews. Money he borrowed for a business venture that failed. Thank you for that. I was on the scene too late to do anything about the commotion. All the excitement had evaporated by the time I arrived, and everyone seemed to just disappear down convenient alleys before I could employ my sword to good effect.'

The constable was renowned for his huge but rusty sword which hung at his hip most of the time he patrolled the streets of Oxford. He no longer bothered about the sharpness of its edge, because, if he ever drew it, it was to employ the flat of the blade. That was far more effective a deterrent, when laid across a clerk's buttocks, than a cutting edge. And more forgiving. Last night, the crowd had dispersed without even the need for that.

'I will deal with Master Lawney. But no, that was not the business I was thinking of.'

'The murder, then.'

'Yes. I have been observing my suspect.'

Falconer frowned, and looked at the salted fish seller rolling his barrels of produce out on to the street. It reminded him again of the starving John Hanny, and what the boy had seen that night.

'You have a suspect? Who is that?'

Bullock bubbled with the satisfaction of putting one over on his erudite friend. It was not often that he got to the truth before the Regent Master.

'Why, Brother Richard Yaxley, of course. I saw him arguing with the dead man the night before he was killed. He claims over some trifling incident concerning young Will Plome, but that is a red herring.'

Falconer knew Plome, who had come to Oxford with a troupe of travelling players. There had been a murder that had almost been laid at the door of the fat youth. Until the Regent Master had solved the puzzle. The jongleurs had moved on, but Will had stayed behind. He now made a living running errands for kindly people who pitied his simplicity.

'What did Will have to do with it?'

Bullock waved a beefy hand dismissively in the air.

'Oh, nothing really. It was a trifle. But I do think he was put up to embarrassing the feretarius by Brother John Barley. You know how some of the monks at Oseney envy the popularity of the saint's shrine. Especially at this time of year.' The constable rubbed his finger and thumb together to signify the lucrative nature of the shrine. 'And haven't you always told me that money is an excellent motive for murder? Yaxley also said that the monk had something of great value to offer, but had then played that trick on him instead.'

Bullock was prepared for his old friend to pour

scorn on his conclusion. And was surprised when Falconer merely responded with a tilt of the head, and a little grunt. If he hadn't known him better, Bullock would have thought the Regent Master had actually agreed with his analysis. Without demur. But in reality, Falconer just seemed distracted, and not at all full of the usual enthusiasm he exhibited over a murder. He appeared to be more interested in the mundane activities of the fish seller, Luke Bosden, setting up his stall across the street. Bullock narrowed his eyes, and peered at Luke as he rolled out another barrel of salted fish. If his actions were so interesting to Falconer, then maybe there was some deep riddle to be solved by observing them.

In fact, Falconer was not really looking at the fish seller. He was merely worried about the state of John Hanny's mind. And his belly. The description of what he had seen the night Brother John Barley was murdered had left Falconer half inclined to admit to the very real existence of the Devil. And to consider taking holy orders to seek expiation of all the heretical scientific ideas he had held heretofore. Anything rather than think Deudone was involved in the death.

Yet Falconer had always relied on observation to guide his thinking. And it was a very real world which bustled around him now. The mundane life of real toil that a man like the fishmonger Bosden pursued in his effort to feed himself and his family. If there was anything spiritual in this world, it was the relentless optimism that sustained such men as Bosden. By comparison, Falconer, who did nothing more than cram a few notions into the heads of boys more often than not reluctant to give them room, felt himself worthless. He took a deep breath, and tried to concentrate on what Bullock had been saying. There was a connection. Suddenly it came to him. The conversation he had overheard between Harbottle and the master mason.

'What was that you said about something of value? Could it have been a relic?'

Bullock sighed, realizing that Falconer had not been listening to a word. A relic? There had been nothing of the kind, only a trick played on Yaxley that had badly misfired. But at least this was more like his old friend. Off on a sidetrack, when the obvious was staring him in the face. He went over his conversation with Yaxley again, asserting that no mention had been made specifically of a relic. This obviously did not put Falconer off, for now he had a request for Bullock.

'It could be that you are right, Peter. But we need to go and talk to the abbot. Will you send one of your men to Oseney to ask the abbot if he will see us? There is something I must do first. Oh, and will you ask him to arrange for us to talk to the master mason, La Souch, also?'

Bullock nodded in agreement, though he didn't know why they needed to talk to a mason. Nor was Falconer forthcoming about the urgent errand he had to attend to first. Such mysterious behaviour was typical of his friend, and he had long given up trying to fathom him out. He turned to go down Pennyfarthing Street towards St Ebbe's Church, and the castle postern gate, while Falconer turned the other way. His resolve momentarily reinvigorated, Falconer could not help having a final dig at his old friend.

'You have discounted our mysterious Templar, then?'

Bullock grunted in a non-committal fashion. In fact, he had forgotten all about him.

If Peter Bullock had known that the Templar was already abroad, and had exited the town while Master Falconer was brooding over the fate of fish-mongers, he might yet have included him in his reckoning. For the Templar was returning to Oseney Abbey, convinced it was the goal of his mission. When he had last spoken to the master mason, he had been sure that Eudo La Souch knew more than he was telling. He had mentioned the possible existence of a piece of the True Cross somewhere in the abbey, and the mason had all but screamed out he too knew of it. His face had paled, and sweat had broken out on his temple. La Souch had tried to mask his reaction by picking up his tools, and chipping away at the section of stone pillar he had been working on. But the new chis-elling had been a mess compared to the work he had carried out before. His hands had trembled, and he couldn't wait to be rid of his inquisitor. The Templar was sure he knew something. But did he know the actual location of the relic? Or, like himself, was he still searching?

He had decided there and then not to press the man to reveal what he knew. With his skill at persuasion, learned from his old adversaries, the Assassins, he could easily have extracted what infor-mation the mason had. But then he might have found himself in another dead end like the one he had encountered with the monk, John Barley. Far better to let the man pursue his own searches, and uncover the truth. Then the Templar could intervene, saving himself a lot of work. Today, he was planning to find out how far the mason had got. The Templar strode cheerfully along the roadway towards Oseney Abbey, crossing the two streams that marked the edge of the water meadows. In passing it, he hardly gave the place of Brother John Barley's murder a second glance.

When William Falconer and Peter Bullock met up at Northgate, the Regent Master looked pleased, but was no more forthcoming about his errand. Instead, the two men walked in companionable silence towards Oseney. A trickle of pilgrims preceded them through the entrance to the cloisters of Oseney Abbey. Normally, no-one but the canons and lay brothers would be allowed access to this part of the abbey. But today the church entrance was blocked by a mesh of scaffolding that hung on the western façade. Eudo La Souch's work was progressing despite the financial straits of the abbey. And because of that, the cloister was open to give access to the church for pilgrims. Bullock looked up and marvelled at the size of the new church. Over their heads rose flying buttresses topped with pinnacles, and the two magnificent towers, the western one of which housed the Oseney Ring of bells. He tipped his head back, and admired the soaring bulk of the tower. It was impressive, even clad as it was in wooden scaffolding, and it stood square and solid against the scudding clouds and pale blue of the morning sky. He thought he saw a bird swooping round the topmost pinnacle, and screwed up his eyes to identify it. It was large, and on reflection appeared to be diving hawk-like towards the earth rather than spiralling round the tower. Its wings were thin and flailed at the air, though, unlike those of any hawk that might stoop for its prey in this fashion. In fact, it was far too large for any bird. Bullock cried out and clutched at Falconer's sleeve. The Regent Master turned his gaze up to what Bullock saw just as the figure resolved itself into the shape of a man.

'God in Heaven!' cried Bullock, just before the flying man crashed through the thatch of the master mason's lodge, and thumped into the earth below.

Falconer and the constable raced across the cloister, and through the scatter of pilgrims fleeing in the opposite direction. Inside the devastated lodge, lying flat out on the plaster pattern floor, lay the broken body of the master mason, Eudo La Souch. A thin trail of dark red blood leaked from the back of his head following the tracks of the templates scored in the floor. It slowly described the outline of a curved section of a clerestory window.

The cloister suddenly seemed to fill with people. Those pilgrims who had fled the plummeting body were now drawn back inexorably. The gruesome sight of the broken mason was a sharp reminder of the frailty of the human body. And would no doubt act as an additional spur for the pilgrims seeking remission of their sins before the master mason's fate became their own. Bunched together in the crowd was the gang of workmen and apprentices who until that moment had been employed by Eudo La Souch. Their faces were strained and pale. Unless another master mason was found, and quick, they were out of work. One older man among them, dressed in an apron and blue shirt flecked with spatters of lime mortar, stepped forward from the crowd to get a closer look at his erstwhile employer. He pulled a tattered brown hat off his head, crushing it in his calloused hands. After convincing himself that the body was indeed that of La Souch, and that he was without doubt dead, he turned to the tall, black-clad figure of William Falconer. As far as he could tell, this was a man of authority, who needed putting straight.

'Impossible,' he grunted, in an accent as thick as that of his dead master.

'What's impossible?' Peter Bullock cut in quickly, asserting his own control of the situation. The man merely looked up at the tower, and down at the body. Then snorted, shaking his head in disbelief. It was Falconer who answered Bullock's question, however.

'I think our friend here is suggesting that it is impossible that the master mason could have fallen accidentally. And I would tend to agree. I saw La Souch shinning up the scaffolding when the bells were being replaced, and he was as nimble and sure footed as a squirrel.'

Satisfied that his opinion had been heard, the builder nodded, stuffed his battered hat back on his head, and went back to his comrades to confer. Falconer saw Robert Anselm pushing through the crowd of pilgrims, some of whom were now on their knees praying. Whether for the soul of the dead man, or their own salvation, Falconer could not quite determine. For a brief moment he also thought he saw a familiar, sharp-featured dark face at the back of the crowd. Then Anselm stood in his way, and the face was gone. The monk gasped when he saw the state of the body, broken by the fall from one of the highest towers in the country. He crossed himself.

'May God receive his soul. Poor man. There have been accidents before, of course. But nothing as . . .' He waved his hand at the horrific sight, apparently unable to find words to describe it adequately. '. . . as this.'

Falconer took the shocked monk's arm, leading him away from the unpleasant sight.

'I'm afraid, Brother Robert, that this was probably no accident. La Souch was a master mason, as at home at height as on the ground.'

Anselm frowned, tapping at the earth nervously with his sandalled foot.

'But wouldn't that perhaps make him careless? If he truly regarded working at the top of the tower as safe as working below, could he not have tragically misjudged his footing?'

'It's possible, I suppose, Brother Robert.'

Falconer was reluctant to concede as much to the monk. But his mind was brooding on the thought that, just when he wanted to see the mason about a mysterious relic, Eudo La Souch had unfortunately plunged to his death.

'And you think this relic is the key to what is happening here?'

Falconer nodded in response to Peter Bullock's question. The two men were sitting in the scriptorium of Oseney Abbey, currently devoid of the monks who would normally be taking advantage of the morning light to copy texts for the abbey library. The two rows of high stools stood unoccupied, though the burnished wooden desks were still scattered with papers, and the horn boxes filled with quills. The distant sound of plainsong was all that betrayed where the scribes had gone. A song for the soul of Eudo La Souch. Light streamed in from the scriptorium's high windows, and across the floor to the men's feet.

'It has to be. Firstly, Brother John Barley is murdered after offering what we think may have been a relic to the feretarius of St Frideswide's Priory, then . . .'

Bullock interrupted.

'Though that may have been a cruel jest on Barley's part. We don't know that for sure.'

'If it was a prank, then it went horribly wrong. From Brother John's point of view. No, I am inclined to think it was genuine. What else was the murderer doing, when John Hanny saw him, as he put it, "making passes" over the monk's body? What else but searching for something.'

'Then, do you think he found what he was looking for? If so, why did La Souch die? Unless . . .' Bullock's face suddenly lit up, as a thought struck him. 'Unless La Souch killed Barley for the relic, took it, and was himself killed in his turn!'

Falconer pulled a face, dousing Bullock's enthusiasm with cold scorn.

'Hmmm. I don't think so, unless we have a string of relic thieves, all queuing up, and prepared to murder in turn for its possession.'

Bullock was disgruntled by Falconer's careless dismissal, and eager to defend his proposition.

'Is that so far fetched? A holy relic is a worthy prize indeed, and many would give a fortune for possession of one.'

Falconer suddenly bent forward at this point, tapping Bullock on the knee with a bony finger.

'And that is what is worrying me about this whole affair.'

Bullock reared back, brushing the offending digit away with the back of his hand.

'What?'

'If the holy relic – whatever it is – is so great a prize, then why do we not know of it? Why does the abbey not display it with joy and attract a multitude of pilgrims? And why did John Barley wish to offload it on to the feretarius of St Frideswide's? With whom he did not have an exactly fraternal relationship.'

'That is a very good question, Regent Master Falconer.'

Another voice cut into the men's conversation. Falconer looked over Bullock's shoulder to see Peter Talam, the bursar of the abbey, entering under the soaring archway that led into the scriptorium. His bustling walk raised dust motes that sparkled in the shafts of light crossing the room.

'I heard a whisper of just such a relic a number of years ago. Apparently the translation from Tewkesbury to the abbey was effected over thirty years ago. Well before my time, I might say.'

Falconer invited Talam to sit on the stool next to himself and Bullock. But the restless bursar paced backwards and forwards, continuing to raise dust around his heels.

'Being responsible for the funds of the abbey, I was of course intrigued by the story of a relic in our possession. Especially as it was said to be a piece of the True Cross with Christ's blood on it. I even asked the abbot about it. This was more than ten years since. But he would say nothing. Neither confirming nor denying the story. And I could tell by his look that I was expected never to raise the question again. So I didn't.'

Falconer could well believe in Talam's discretion. He was stiff, but a dedicated servant to the abbey.

'But someone else did, and recently.'

Falconer recalled the brief snatch of conversation between Abbot Harbottle and the master mason that he had overheard. La Souch had clearly heard the story about the relic himself. He had also got the same short shrift from Harbottle that Talam had received ten years earlier, when he had asked about it. But the effect on the abbot had been devastating, as Falconer himself had witnessed. He realized that Bullock was looking at him with curiosity etched on his face. It was Talam who spoke, however.

'Eudo La Souch asked the abbot about the relic?'

Falconer nodded.

'So the mason did know about the relic, but did not possess it.' Bullock was chagrined he hadn't seen it. 'Could he have known its location?'

'I think not. Or he would not have still been here. He would have ... what is the expression? ...' Falconer smiled contemptuously. 'Translated it.'

Talam pursed his lips in disapproval. The translation of a saint's remains or any other such relic was in some people's eyes a euphemism for theft. But those holy people who effected the removal of such relics, sometimes without the owner's approval, were seen to be merely responding to the demands of the saint to be relocated. To be carrying out a *furta sacra* – a holy theft, or translation. But he had to admit there was truth in the man's deduction. If Eudo La Souch had somehow located the relic's hiding place during the rebuilding work, he would have disappeared as soon as he had been able to remove it. It did still leave the question as to why such a valuable relic had been hidden in the first place, though. The same difficulty had occurred to the constable too.

'But why hide such a venerable object?'

Talam sighed, and for a moment ceased his endless pacing.

'Only the abbot knows that. And he's not telling. If only we knew who the monks were who trans . . .' He looked Falconer squarely in the eye, and chose his next word carefully. '. . . brought the relic here. Unfortunately, Brother John Barley was the last of that generation. Apart from the abbot himself.'

Falconer suddenly recalled the abbot lamenting the deaths of several of his colleagues. Now it had a meaning. Sitting as they were in the vast room where texts were copied, and records of the abbey's life were written, Falconer had an idea.

'Tell me, Brother Peter, did all those of John Barley's age die a natural death? I mean, due to advanced years?'

Talam looked puzzled.

'I don't know what you mean, Master Falconer. Over the years, many canons have passed over to the Heavenly Jerusalem after a full life of prayer.'

'But, in recent years, have there been deaths among the older canons not due to the natural process of time? Apparent accidents, perhaps?'

'There have been some, of course. Just before I came here, I believe there was a brother who ate a poisonous plant accidentally. As for others, I cannot say. Brother Thomas was killed by robbers on the road returning from Glastonbury seven years ago. But these are perfectly normal occurrences in the dangerous and lawless world in which we live.'

'Perhaps, Brother Peter. Perhaps. But if John Barley was killed for the relic, perhaps others have died because of it. Would you be so kind as to show me the abbey chronicles anyway?'

'Going back how long?'

'Let's say twenty years. To start with.'

Falconer was soon settled down with the records that Talam provided. But, though he seemed content to plough through them, Bullock could not face the thought of sitting with dusty tomes for hours on end. Reading old documents concerning past history was not his idea of pursuing a murder case. Future success required vigorous and decisive action. Besides, he still had his suspicions about Yaxley, the feretarius. He decide to return to Oxford, and winkle the truth out of the man.

And if that didn't work, there was always the Templar.

It was taking Falconer a long time, but a pattern was beginning to emerge. Starting with a monk twelve years earlier who had died as a result of falling masonry occurring during the building of a section of the great abbey church. The appropriately, if unfortunately, named Brother Benedict Mason had died instantly. One year later it was the turn of the monk Talam had recalled, who had died shortly after eating his dinner. Brother Ralph Durward had been found stone cold, and blue lipped, when he had failed to answer the call of the first bell of the day. The cook had been mortified when it had become apparent that an excess of digitalis had found its way into the monk's food. He could offer no explanation for the error. And just as Talam had said, Brother Thomas Dyss had been killed on the road just west of Oxford, barely three miles from the sanctuary of his abbey. He had made the long journey to Glastonbury and back without mishap, only to be stabbed to death almost on his doorstep. Robbers on Standlake Common had been blamed. Between these three incidents six other canons had died, though most of old age or disease. The only other death that attracted Falconer's curiosity was that of Brother William Hasilbech. He had been found on the road north of Oxford with the marks of horses' shoes imprinted in the bruising on his body. His head was crushed, as if by the flying hoof of a horse. But this was during the lawless times, when the barons had fought the King. There had been much traffic of armies hurrying thither and yon. It could even have been the King himself, or his son Edward, who had carelessly ridden down the monk one dark evening. Both had been in the vicinity of Oxford at the same time. Falconer recorded it as a possibility in his search for a pattern of deaths.

It was another hour, and by candlelight as night closed in, before he found the final suspicious incident. Brother John Paston had gone into the church during a violent thunderstorm one night a year earlier, and had been discovered only the following morning, with a chewed-up scroll blocking his mouth. He had choked. It had been supposed that Paston, a deeply devout if rather difficult individual, had been emulating the command of the mighty angel in Revelation, who,

to the accompaniment of seven thunders, adjured
John in the following way. Take the scroll, and eat
it. It will turn your stomach sour, though in your
mouth it tastes as sweet as honey.'

Falconer doubted that the soggy paper wedge
had tasted so to Paston in his last moments. By the
guttering flame of the candle stub, he scratched
down the names on a scrap of parchment, left by
the monk whose desk he sat at.

Mason – brained by a stone
Durward – poisoned by a plant
Hasilbech – trampled by a horse
Dyss – stabbed by a robber
Paston – suffocated on a scroll
Barley – throat cut by a sickle

Six monks, all dying in suspicious circumstances,
when viewed from this new perspective. But didn't
these things always come in sevens?

'Don't forget La Souch, flying from the tower,
and dying like Hiram Abiff.'

Falconer stiffened as the disembodied voice whispered an answer from the darkness. He hadn't
known he had uttered his final thought out loud.
Maybe he hadn't. He sat perfectly still, listening and
trying to work out from where the voice had come.
Whoever it was, was referring to the ancient mason
of Solomon's Temple in Jerusalem. Hiram Abiff
had been killed by three apprentices, and tossed
down from the Temple rather than betray the
masonic secrets he was entrusted with. Could the
person in the darkness be a Jew? Deudone, perhaps?
Not to be outdone in esoteric knowledge, Falconer
offered another similarity to test the hidden man.

'Just as James, brother of Jesus, was struck on the head and cast down from the Temple rather than reveal the secret that the two pillars Jachin and Boaz were the gates of salvation.'

The lurker in the darkness gave a little grunt of satisfaction.

'I knew you would understand. So, now you have possession of a secret of your own. What do you think should be done about it?'

The voice was cold, and dispassionate, and it sent a shiver down Falconer's spine.

Bullock was in some difficulty. He had searched high and low but he could not find Richard Yaxley. The feretarius had seen to his duties as normal up until the closing of the church to pilgrims. After that, no-one was quite sure whether they had seen him. The chaplain servicing the tapers was certain Yaxley had gone to take the pilgrims' offerings to the priory chest. But only because that was what he did at this time every day. The bursar thought he had seen him, but then couldn't be certain, as he may have been thinking of yesterday. Or the day before. The upshot was that Yaxley had disappeared, and the night was drawing in. Deeply concerned that a potential murderer might be on the loose, Peter Bullock hurried towards his lodgings in the castle. He had the curfew, and the locking of the town gates, to see to. But at the same time, he would use the crew of the night watch to scour the streets for the missing monk. They were a bunch of old men, but Yaxley was hardly a desperate criminal who would seek to fight his way out of a corner, if found. He was more a lurker in the dark, and a back-stabber.

Crossing Carfax, he was hailed by Matthew

Syward, who kept watch at the North Gate for him. In truth, the man was lazy and unreliable, more inclined to ogle the women who frequented the stews of Broken Hays than attend to his task. But the job was poorly paid, and required attendance when others would prefer to be at home, or in the tavern with comrades. It was well nigh impossible to get someone who could be relied on. Syward was the best Bullock could hope for. So, when the gatekeeper tried to tell him of the swarthy man with the soldierly mien who had once again sneaked out through the North Gate just before curfew, Bullock didn't pay much attention to him. Syward was always taking against someone he thought had slighted him, and making up stories. It was Yaxley Bullock needed to find, before another murder was committed.

The figure glided silently out of the darkness, and rested his hands on Falconer's tense shoulders. He looked down at the list scratched on the parchment before the Regent Master.

'Hmmm. They are all dead, then.'

'De Beaujeu – it is you. I could not be sure. In fact, when the constable reckoned he had seen you, I did not believe him. After all, nothing could be so important as to bring a future Grand Master of the Order of the Poor Knights of the Temple all the way to Oxford. But when I went back to John Hanny's description of the ... apparition he had seen hovering over the body of John Barley, it did set me to thinking. Before I came here today, I spoke to Hanny once more.' He didn't admit that the real reason he had returned to Aristotle's Hall was to ensure Hanny's welfare. That he was getting his fair share of food. His conscience had pricked him hard. 'This time, his story did make me wonder if the dark-skinned man could yet have been young Deudone the Jew. But he said the lurker in the shadows was cool and calm. Such self-assurance shown by taking the time to search the body eliminated the hotheaded youth. He is boastful and would have panicked, whereas you, a Templar . . .' Falconer let the idea hang in the chill air for a moment, remembering too the fleeting glimpse of a familiar face he had seen in the crowd around the dead mason's body. 'If it was you, this relic must be something very special.'

He could still feel the steely grip of Guillaume de Beaujeu on his shoulders. Close to his neck. So close that he was unsure of the man he had once thought of as his friend. He recalled Bullock saying that you couldn't trust the Templars, if your motives did not coincide with theirs. Maybe the constable had been right. One way or the other, he had to know the truth.

'Was it you my young student saw standing over the body of John Barley?'

De Beaujeu's fingers dug into Falconer's flesh. Then relaxed.

'Surely, William, you cannot think I killed him? I thought you knew me better than that.'

'Truthfully, I think I hardly know you at all. You are a very . . . inscrutable sort of man.'

'While you wear your heart on your sleeve for all to see. Talking of hearts, how is the beautiful Anne, by the way?'

Falconer did not respond to the Templar's enquiry about Mistress Anne Segrim. She was and always had been another man's wife. That was the end of the matter.

'I see.' De Beaujeu took his hands from Falconer's shoulders, and slid down on to the stool next to him. 'Well, you were right about the apparition this boy saw searching the body. It was me, and I was looking for the relic. I was also aware the boy had seen me. That's why I left before I could be dragged into the whole sorry mess. I was following a rumour about this particular relic when I heard of the monk John Barley offering just such a one in the town, and arranged for him to bring it to me. But I was too late. The murderer got to him first, and there was no sign of the relic on the body. All I could do for poor Barley was to arrange his body more sympathetically than the killer had left it.'

Falconer recalled remarking to Bullock, when they had found the body, about the piety of the arrangement of its limbs. That had been De Beaujeu, then, and not the murderer. He believed the Templar when he averred he was not the killer. For if he had been, then Hanny would have been dead too by now. The Templar would not have left a witness alive.

'This relic must mean a lot to you.'

The Templar lowered his gaze, and his voice became slightly muffled and tremulous.

'You are right. I came here to find the relic on behalf of the Order. But I have a personal reason for tracking it down also. Let me explain.'

In the gathering darkness, De Beaujeu related to Falconer a story of death and despair appropriate to the gloomy surroundings in which they sat. He told a tale of a fragment of the True Cross, stained with Christ's blood, which had passed from hand to hand for one hundred and fifty years, leaving mayhem in its wake. He told of the curse that tainted the relic, causing the death of anyone who touched it. How the Muslim guardian of the relic had laid the curse before being slain by a Crusader simply for being an Arab in Jerusalem.

'That Crusader was Miles de Clermont. And he was my ancestor.'

Falconer could hear in de Beaujeu's tone of voice the burden this placed on the Templar. His Order wished to hide the tainted relic from the world. But it seemed de Beaujeu felt personally responsible, not only for the action of his ancestor, but for every death caused by the tainted relic ever since. Falconer, however, still refused to accept the sorcery.

'I don't believe in such nonsense as curses. Why, if I did, I would be shrivelled to nothing by now from all the curses laid upon me by my students down the years. They have cursed me a-plenty for the work I have set them.'

De Beaujeu shook his head sadly.

'This is too deadly to be taken so lightly, William. If you could only hear the tales that down the years have accompanied this relic . . .'

Falconer abruptly interrupted.

'Exactly. That is what they are. Just tales, recited to please a gawking audience of fools.'

'And the deaths of these six monks?' De Beaujeu tapped the scrap of parchment with the six names on it. 'Did they not appropriate the relic, and in so doing tarnish their souls, so that their deaths were inevitable? Is it not the way they died which has led you to assuming these six names are those of the monks who have touched the relic?'

Falconer was trapped by his own logic. That

indeed had been his thinking, he had to admit to the Templar.

'But they were killed by a human agency, not by the relic in some mystical way.'

'Does it matter how they died? The fact is they touched the relic, and now they are dead. As is the mason, La Souch.' De Beaujeu paused. 'And with them dies the only hope I had of tracing the relic's location.'

Falconer couldn't help but smile. Something else had just fallen into place for him.

'Not exactly. Unless La Souch was felled by avenging angels, or the ghost of this murdered Arab . . .' He held his hand up to ward off De Beaujeu's incipient protest at his flippant remark. 'Unless some supernatural power is at work here, La Souch was killed by someone other than the six errant monks, who by then were all dead themselves. So someone else knows about the tainted relic, and thought that the master mason had uncovered its whereabouts. That was a secret this person thought worth keeping. And I have an idea how to find out who it is.'

Bullock hurried through the night, hoping he might be in time. His failure to find Yaxley had driven him to seeking out Will Plome. It had occurred to him that the simpleton may have been aware of the feretarius's absence when he made his late night visit to the shrine. Even Will could have assumed that Brother Richard would stop him climbing down the Holy Hole to gain such close proximity to the saint. The boy had lodgings in Sleying Lane outside the town walls, charitably provided by no less a person than the Jewess

Belaset. It was no more than a simple room, but Belaset charged nothing for it. Getting Will's eager, if unreliable, services in return. Businesslike she might be, and better at it than her husband or son, but she was also a mother. And she could not bear to see somebody's son reduced to begging in the street. Few were aware of her kindness to the simpleton, as she cared for none to know. But Peter Bullock knew, and though it was late, he called on Belaset. He wanted her help when he confronted Will.

Belaset agreed to accompany him, though she was herself worried about her absent son, Deudone. He had gone off into the night about some mission of his own. Belaset was afraid he would get himself into trouble, and hoped he had merely gone to press his suit with Hannah. But in the meantime, she couldn't refuse to help the constable coax the truth out of Will. So, having roused the sleeping guardian of South Gate, and berated him for his laxity, Bullock, along with Belaset, slipped quietly through the wicket gate set within the massive town gates proper.

It did not take long to rouse the bewildered Will Plome, and soon he was lighting a cheap tallow lamp to illuminate his quarters. The yellow glow revealed a little room that was surprisingly neat, though spartan. The furniture amounted to no more than a low bed, a stool and a table. On the table lay some gaming boards, one a circular tablet with holes bored in it in a sort of pattern. Most of the holes were filled with pegs. Bullock recognized it as a board to play the Solitary Game on. The other board he couldn't figure out. It looked like two chessboards linked together, and on it were arrayed gaming pieces, some of which were circular, some triangular and some square. Bullock took it for a child's toy, to pleasure Will's simple mind. The boy saw him looking, and explained.

'It is a game I was taught by Master Falconer. He calls it the Philosopher's Game. He gets angry when I beat him at it.'

Bullock smiled, imagining his friend allowing the simpleton to win, and feigning annoyance as part of the game. But Belaset put him right.

'Will is very good at the game. And I suppose William Falconer is annoyed at Will's skill because it requires a high understanding of mathematics, such as the Regent Master fancies is only reserved for himself. Will has the beating of me at it too.'

Bullock coughed in embarrassment, not understanding how a simpleton could have a greater mind than both this clever Jewess and his best friend. It didn't make sense, unless the woman was having fun at his expense. He would have to ask Falconer later. But first he needed to know all about Yaxley, and his nocturnal activities.

'Will Plome, you must tell all you know about what Brother Richard at St Frideswide's has been doing these last few nights. You do know something, don't you?'

Will looked anxiously at his friend, Belaset. 'Brother Richard committed a mortal sin . . .' He faltered. The olive-skinned woman looked deeply into the boy's soul with her big brown eyes.

'Tell him the truth now, Will.'

The truth, when it came out, did not surprise the constable one morsel.

*   *   *

Falconer stood at the edge, contemplating the pilgrimage before him. He knew he would find enlightenment in the labyrinth. The path was tortuous, twisting back on itself, taking him through the four stages of the mass. He stepped forward and entered into Evangelium. Three turns and he was in the segment representing Offertory. A turn back on himself and it was Evangelium again. Then three loops and back into Offertory. Two loops and he was walking Consecration. Like any pilgrimage, any seeking for purgation, the route was never straightforward. Two more turns and he was in the final segment. Communion. He stood right in the centre of the labyrinth, surveying the six petals at its core. And the seventh point under his feet at the centre of the labyrinth. He knew that here lay Illumination. Under a slab with a carving of God represented as a master mason. The perfect hiding place for a cursed relic. The slab under him rocked slightly.

'Has it been vouchsafed to you yet?'

The voice was quiet, and deliberately held low. But Falconer could detect the tremulous undercurrent in it.

'Illumination? Yes, it has.'

He looked across the void that was the labyrinth to where the figure stood, tall and angular, between the pillars at the back of the nave. The rose window hung over his hooded head, lit only by the cold rays of the full moon. The colours were dulled and leaden.

'We all touched it, you know. The relic. And so our fates were sealed on that day so long ago.'

'There was nothing inevitable about the deaths of your fellow monks, Brother Robert.' Falconer was still clinging to the idea of his rational world. 'That was in your hands, not fate.'

'In one sense you are right, Regent Master. But there was some inevitability about how they died, don't you think?'

'No, Brother Robert. You arranged that yourself to fit into your little world of the labyrinth.' Falconer slowly circled the central core of the maze, listing each of the contemplative elements around its edge. 'Mineral – Brother Benedict Mason killed by masonry. Plant – Brother Ralph Durward poisoned by a herb. Animal – Brother William Hasilbech trampled by a horse. Human – Brother Thomas Dyss killed, apparently by a robber, though that was you too, wasn't it?' Falconer stared through the gloom at the hooded figure. Robert Anselm did not move a muscle, so Falconer continued his litany. 'Angelic – Brother John Paston suffocated by a scroll as in Revelation. And finally, the Unnameable – Brother John Barley reaped by a sickle, just like the actions of our Lord in Revelation.'

Anselm nodded with apparent satisfaction at the symmetry of the deaths. But Falconer had not yet finished. He began to wind his way out of the labyrinth, walking first directly towards the monk, but then turning left into Communion. A complete about-turn then brought him back on his outward track, only for him to turn left again around the rim of the labyrinth. He talked as he circumnavigated the course to Union. Action in the world.

'What I don't understand is how you fitted into this group. They were all old men, and had brought the relic here a very long time ago. You could only have been a boy at the time.'

'I was seven. I worked in the kitchens here, and the canons were so used to seeing me around that they didn't see me any more. If you know what I mean. When the six canons – Mason, Durward, Hasilbech, Dyss, Paston and Barley – came back with a piece of the True Cross, I overheard their conversation. I crept into the chapter house where Hasilbech was showing Abbot Leech their *furta sacra*. It seemed nothing at first sight. Just a small wooden box. Then Brother Thomas Dyss opened it up, and removed something. It seemed to shine of its own accord, though no doubt it was just a reflection of the light shining on it through the windows. It was a glass bottle. For some reason Brother Thomas opened it, and slid the contents out on to his palm. The canons passed it around. Only the abbot refrained from touching it. It was only later I knew how lucky he had been. He was reading a small strip of parchment that had lain at the bottom of the box. When he finished reading, his face drained of blood, and he urged Ralph Durward, who was holding the contents of the bottle in his hand to return it to the vial immediately. Then he commanded the canon to put the bottle back in the box, which lay on the seat of his chair. Finally, in the face of all the protests from his six canons, he ushered them from the chapter house. It was only when they had gone that I realized they had left the box behind. I could not resist it.

'Risking being caught in the act, I sneaked over, and opened the box. Inside lay an old glass vial with a gilded stopper. It was difficult to see what was inside because the glass was clouded. So, like Brother Thomas, I picked the vial up, and unstoppered it. As I tipped the vial, a greyish piece of wood slid out on to my palm. On its surface was a dark brown stain. Somehow, I knew immediately what it was, and I was awestruck. I cannot describe the feeling to you, even now.'

As the monk spoke, Falconer's progress out through the maze was leading him inexorably to Anselm. He could see how the monk's eyes glittered in the darkness at the recollection of holding the True Cross stained with Christ's blood in his hand.

'Of course, then I did not know of the curse on those who touched the relic. That only emerged in rumours at the abbey the following day, when the relic, so newly acquired, disappeared, never to be seen again. Abbot Leech had read the warning enclosed in the box, and enjoined the community not to mention its existence. He hid it away himself, then later had it immolated by the mason rebuilding the abbey. No-one knew that the kitchen boy had touched it also. The dire consequences of the curse filled me with horror. I was only a boy, yet my careless curiosity had apparently doomed me. In the same way it had doomed the six canons.'

Falconer now faced Anselm at the very exit to the labyrinth.

'But you later also learned that those who touch the relic only die when they relinquish it from their possession, didn't you?'

Anselm's hooded head dipped in acknowledgement.

'Yes. And that is why it must remain in the abbey. The others couldn't see that. But they were very old, and had no reason to fear death. John Barley would have given it to Yaxley merely to be rid of it, if I had not stopped him. He felt he could sacrifice what was left of his life to rid the abbey of the cursed thing. But I still wanted to live.'

'And Eudo La Souch?'

'The mason had discovered where his predecessor had finally hidden it at Abbot Leech's behest. The other day, I came upon him rocking back and forth on the slab. He pretended to be just checking on the security of the tiles, but I knew what he was doing. So when he next ascended the tower to check the bells, I pushed him off. You see, the relic cannot leave the abbey, or I will die.'

'That's nonsense. You of all people must see that. It was you who killed your six fellow canons, not the relic. Or its curse.'

The hooded figure shook its head, and lifted a trembling hand up.

'Then by what agency am I afflicted with what plagues me?' He swept the hood away from his head, and Falconer gasped at seeing how gaunt and grey Anselm's features had become. The man was wasting away before his eyes.

'It is as if a rat gnaws at my vitals, giving surcease neither night nor day. I don't think I will stand it much longer.'

Indeed he looked like a living skeleton already, consumed from the inside out. But he was a spectre with a purpose. He pulled a knife from under his robe and, summoning all his failing energies, sprang at Falconer. But he was too weak already. He almost fell into de Beaujeu's arms as the Templar stepped out of the shadows, where he had been hiding. Despite his failure to achieve his aim, the monk's face still bore a beatific smile.

'I have lost, then. But if I were to have the chance once again to hold the True Cross in my hand – to touch Christ's blood – I would take it willingly.'

Abbot Ralph Harbottle lifted the small wooden box out of the exposed hole in the floor at the centre of the labyrinth. Seeing for the first time what the abbot before him had taken such care to hide away. It was made of rosewood, carved and gilded, though the gilding was largely worn away. Cautiously, he lifted the hinged lid to reveal the contents to the three men standing with him. William Falconer and Peter Bullock peered into the box, where lay a small glass vial atop two battered strips of parchment. It seemed far too insignificant to be such a powerful and revered relic, with such a weighty and gloom-ridden history. Bullock was disappointed. As disappointed as he had been to discover from Will Plome that Brother Richard Yaxley's only crime was to have become enamoured of Matthew Syward's wife. On learning the truth, the constable had rushed from Will's hovel to catch the two adulterers in the act. In the end, his only satisfaction had been to see the pompous feretarius turned into a grovelling penitent. Belaset had returned home to find Deudone moping over his rejection by Hannah. It had still been Falconer who had uncovered the real murderer.

Harbottle touched the two pieces of parchment. One averred the authenticity of the relic. The other, slightly less ancient document warned of the curse. It was the latter Abbot Leech had read on the fateful day the box had been brought to Oseney. Harbottle closed the lid of the rosewood box, and passed it to the third man. The Templar, Guillaume de Beaujeu, hesitated only a moment before taking it from the abbot. Possession of the box represented the culmination of a long and tortuous pilgrimage for him.

'I promise to keep it safe, and henceforth prevent it harming anyone else. What my ancestor, Miles de Clermont, brought about, I will bring to an end. No more deaths will be occasioned by this relic.' But then he realized the implications of his actions. He looked up to meet Harbottle's lugubrious stare. 'What of Brother Anselm?'

The abbot shook his head. Anselm was not yet dead, but it was inevitable anyway, whether the relic was removed from the abbey or not. His end was not far away, and his dying would be a painful journey. There were many deaths besmirching his immortal soul. De Beaujeu took a deep breath.

'Then let him be the last that dies because of this curse.'

ACT THREE

South Witham, Lincolnshire, June 1323

It was twilight, and the rough door scraped on the packed earth of the floor. The sudden gust of wind made the cheap candle gutter. It sparked and hissed malevolently on the table.

Luke peered inside and had to quash the urge to recoil when he caught sight of the corrodiary's[1] eyes. In the gloom Luke thought they they had filled with blood, as though old Johel had died of a fit. The flame's reflection glittered balefully in them. Brother Johel looked like a demon, squatting there on the other side of the chamber, his elbows leaning on the bare boards of the table while he glared fixedly at the doorway.

Luke had to force himself to cross the threshold, his knowledge of the man's crimes making his progress reluctant.

'Godspeed, Luke.'

Well, his voice hadn't changed. Still powerful,

---

[1] Often retired monks or members of the King's or a wealthy magnate's entourage, the corrodiary was the recipient of a 'corrody' or pension. The monastery would take a lump sum and then give food, lodging and sometimes spending money to the pensioner.

with a rough edge; like that of a man who'd spent his life bellowing at others. Which he had, of course.

Under his threadbare and stained tunic, once white, now filthy grey, the corrodiary was ancient, with swollen and arthritic joints looking out of place on such withered limbs. He was probably sixty to five-and-sixty years old, and each of those years had taken its toll. Tracks of pain were carved about his brow and into the flesh on either side of his slit-like mouth. His flesh was so lean that, although it was leathery from long days in the saddle in the Holy Land, it yet showed the tracery of fine veins underneath. Livery blotches marked his face and his crabbed hands. Scrawny jowls dangled from his jaw; his cheeks were prominent, but served only to add to the impression of gauntness.

He would soon be a corpse. His eyes alone held remnants of the vitality that had once set the seal on his character. The near-madness gleamed in them still.

When Luke had first met Brother Johel, they had been as sharp as a falcon's, but over the last four years they had lost much of their brilliance. Forced to accept that he could never avenge his slaughtered comrades or the destruction of his life's efforts, there was little softness left in them. His own torture was one stage of his suffering, but more poignant to him was the failure of his dream of a fresh Crusade to free the Holy Land. Only misery remained – and fear. Johel knew as well as any that he was dying, and Luke felt sure that it was this knowledge which had turned him into an old man in a matter of days. Luke should feel sympathy, but compassion was scarce in these terrible times. God had forsaken the realm, and all must look to themselves.

The candle was one of the manor's own: small and thin, made of foul-smelling mutton fat that burned slowly and unevenly. It illuminated a scant few feet, and in Luke's eyes it made the room hellish. All about was dark, but in the middle of the room the reeking flame made the monk's face appear still more awful than Luke had expected. It could have been the face of a tormented soul.

'You came.'

Luke nodded and cleared his throat. Stupid comment, it was obvious, wasn't it?!

'Why, though? Just because an old corrodiary called for help.'

Luke felt a spark of irritation. 'If you don't want me . . .'

'I do. Come closer.'

'Just tell me what you want, old man.'

'I want you here, where I can see you.'

The voice was weaker; the devil was not long for the world, Luke told himself. He should respect a man like this, one who had commanded earls and lords. He might seem feeble, but he was entitled to respect. Probably his mind was going. Luke felt a fleeting sadness to think that Johel would soon be gone.

Reluctantly he stepped forward. 'Well?'

A hand snaked up and gripped his rough habit, hauling Luke forward fiercely. '*Don't treat me like an imbecile, boy!*'

Luke felt dazed with shock. The man was supposedly close to death, aye, but he had power in those wretched hands. The suddenness of the attack made Luke dizzy; nausea washed through him, and he felt close to puking.

Johel continued in a malevolent whisper, 'You can shit yourself now, boy, and you can laugh at me when I'm dead, but for now you have only me here. And I have only you!'

The contempt was like poison. It trickled through Luke's pride, eating it away. He wanted to defend himself, but couldn't. 'Let me go!'

'Shut up! You know who I am?'

'Johel of Acre.'

'And what was I?'

'A brother in the Order.'

'Yes. The Poor Fellow Soldiers of Christ and the Temple of Solomon,' Johel said with grave emphasis. He coughed, the spasm making his fingers twist in Luke's tunic. 'Remember that name, boy, if you value your soul! And serve the Order.'

'What do you want with me, old man?' Luke asked. Anger was beginning to flare, and he added snidely, 'The Order's gone, you remember? The Pope declared it . . .'

'We answer only to God, then!' Johel looked at him fiercely, but gradually slouched and released Luke. His hand fell to the table as though lifeless. 'But you're right. I have a *request* to make of you.'

'What do you mean?'

My God! Johel thought again, peering at the lad, aware, so aware, of his own impending doom. This was a matter too weighty for a dying man, but he had a last duty to perform for the defence of all. He was a Templar, a proud warrior-monk in the service of God, but he was so weak. Yet this matter was too important to be left unresolved.

Christ Jesus, why have you done this to us?

Johel let his eyes drop. All they had tried to do was perform God's will on earth. They had ignored all the snares and politics of the secular world, and that omission had brought them down. Many were already dead, and he would soon join them. Yet there was still a task that he had to complete.

He reached under his tunic and brought out a small box. And then, as Luke's eyes widened, he explained about the marvellous relic within.

Bishop's Clyst, Devonshire, November 1323

The famine was over, true enough, but that wasn't much help to a body. Not when a man had an empty belly and no money in his purse to fill it. Not that Will Hogg was unused to that. He had plenty of experience of hunger. Everyone did.

This was a busy little vill. He was standing by the trunk of a great beech whose upper branches reached out over the trackway and shaded it. To his left was a gurgling little river, quite fast flowing just here, between steep, muddy banks, while behind him lay the long and damp path that led to the city.

It was a good spot here, at the ford. The rain had poured down recently and the River Clyst had swollen and burst its banks, flooding the whole plain. Even in the height of summer the boggy ground here was sodden, but today it was much worse. People would have had to have tramped through the soggy marshland to get here, feet already soaked and chilly, and their senses would be as numbed as their toes by the time they reached the bank. And here they'd have to contemplate crossing the river itself, and would pause while they sought the best route. Although the passage of many feet had tramped a ramp into the bank just here, that was no proof that the best route was straight through the water to the other side. A traveller must spy out the shallowest passage. That was when they would make their attack.

There were plenty of ruts in the damp soil to show how many carts had come this way to go to Exeter's market. The great city sat safe behind its massive red walls some two miles west and a little north. They were hidden from view down here in the Clyst Valley, but Will knew that they would be gleaming up there in the morning sunshine over the bend in the River Exe. He stared up that way with a strange sense of longing. He was aware of a curious wistfulness as he brought to mind the picture of the great city walls, dwarfed by the two massive towers of the Cathedral of St Peter within. There was safety in there.

Exeter was full of wealthy people who lived in comfortable houses drinking wine from silver or pewter goblets with their friends. If his father hadn't died for the King, Will could have had a life like that himself. It wasn't his fault he was like this, a broken-down man with no occupation, making do as best he could. At least he had a small corner to sleep in, out of the rain and away from the cold. After the last few years it felt like a palace to him, especially with winter approaching. He'd had his share of sleeping under hedges in winter.

The others were spread about. Andrew had some space at the inn; Rob had his in Elias's stable, just over the way from his brother. Those two were often the source of news about travellers, essential in this work.

Adam was more reliable. That was why Will had agreed to share his room with him. The others were good companions, but Will wasn't so sure about them. Andrew was bright enough, and he had that edge of hardness, but Rob was a fool. Always worried about the risks. He was the one who counselled caution when the others wanted to try their luck.

If it was up to him, they wouldn't be here now, sod him. He wanted them all to wait. Said it was too soon after their last attack. Feeble cretin! They wanted money, and the way to get it was by boldness.

There was a low whistle, and he dropped to his knees as he heard voices, a jingling of chains, a creaking of harness, and he made out two figures, one slumped man on a large rounsey[1], one younger-looking fellow on foot. Both were clad in black, the walker appearing to be wearing clerical garb, a heavy-looking satchel over his shoulder, the rider looking more like a down-at-heel knight. God alone knew, there were enough of them just now, since the King had taken his revenge on the barons who'd threatened his authority. With their lords executed, the men-at-arms had to seek new masters. A man was nothing without patronage.

The horseman was tired, head nodding, perhaps asleep already. Yes: these two should be easy targets.

*　　*　　*

[1] A fair-sized horse of reasonable price, rounseys were used for almost any work apart from pulling carts. They were used as pack animals, but also as general riding horses by travellers or as war-horses by men-at-arms.

The outlaw rode along slowly, jogging easily in his saddle. At the sound of a bird by the roadside, his head snapped around. He stared, gradually relaxing as the noisy clattering of wings disappeared into the distance. It was only a wood pigeon, he saw, and that was cause for comfort. No pigeon would stay if there was a man about the place. There would be no ambush here if a pigeon was roosting.

A fugitive must always be on the lookout for danger. Any man could make an attempt on his life now, capture him and remove his head, declaring him to be outlaw without fear of punishment. He had to be on his guard at all times. It was fortunate that he was at least a knight and used to seeking out ambushes. He'd learned his skills well when he lived at my Lord de Courtenay's household as a child and youth. That was four-and-thirty years ago. Much had happened since. He had travelled the world, seen the destruction of so much that had been good – and finally renounced his past life of service and hope. Now all he had was his oath, and he would be damned before he broke that.

His chin rested on his breast again. Yes, he had learned to be alert when it was necessary, but here in the sleepy flatlands on the outskirts of Exeter, there was less need. He wasn't in France evading the King's damned officers, nor in the Holy Land, where an ambush was to be expected at any moment. He was in England, in one of the most peaceful parts of the kingdom, and God's Wounds, but he was tired. His head moved with the horse's steady amble, and he felt his eyes closing once more. The journey had been long, and they were nearly at their destination.

There was a change in the gait of his mount, and he opened his eyes to see that the beast was favouring his front right hoof.

'Wait!' he called.

'What is it?'

'My horse is lame.'

The clerk nodded, but then looked ahead again. 'You can catch me up, Sir Knight. I'll get on. I am so desperate for ale I think my belly thinks my throat's been cut.'

The outlaw nodded. There was surely no danger up here. He jerked his head and the clerk continued. Meanwhile the outlaw swung himself down, lifted the offending hoof, and saw the large pebble caught there. He pulled out his dagger and inserted it, twisting it gently, all the while talking to the beast to keep it calm. If you could keep them quiet and confident, they were twice the animals.

So it was by the merest chance that he wasn't caught and slain in the first moment when the trap was sprung. A stone in the hoof saved his life for just a little longer.

A raucous din. He was startled by the explosion of noise, and he looked up to see a blackbird cackling out its warning cry. Then he heard the shrill shriek.

He levered the stone from the hoof, thrust the dagger back in the sheath, then leaped on to the horse's back. There came another scream, and he clapped spurs to the beast's flanks. The brute reared, whirling as though preparing to bolt away, but he jerked the head around and galloped off after the clerk, riding towards Exeter.

As he rode through a small stand of trees, he saw the clerk lying on the ground, a man over him.

Roaring his rage, the outlaw drew his sword and pelted along the road at the man, but as he approached he felt, rather than saw, the figure rise from a crouch with a long staff in his hands, saw the iron tip swing towards him. He ducked, but the heavy metal butt still caught him over the ear, and he nearly fell from the saddle. Waving his arm for balance, he turned the horse, and rode back, fury overwhelming his sense of duty.

That was the cause of the deaths. If he had continued and ignored the assault, so many lives would have been saved, he later realized, but at that moment the only thought in his mind was avenging this blow.

And that was how the curse came to be laid once more on Exeter's population.

Exeter, Devonshire, November 1323

Brother Joseph yawned and scratched at his beard as he ambled happily from the little garden where he grew his medicinal herbs. He was a round-faced man, and his chin was forever rough and stubbly, no matter how often he asked the barber to scrape it. The damned fool never saw to his razors properly, that was the problem.

It was already late, and he was looking forward to the end of the final service of the day so that he could go to his cot and sleep. Funny how, as a man grew older, he craved earlier nights. When he had been a lad, he had been keen to stay up most of the night and drink as much ale as he could, while also befriending attractive wenches; later he'd been more interested in staying up to pray to ask forgiveness for those nights of dissipation.

The days when he would stay up all night were long gone, and with them the guilt of a young novice. He was contented now, happy to look to his bed with gratitude that it was lonely. When he was younger, he would have been sad at the thought of the cold blankets and palliasse being empty when he went to them. In those days the only bearable bed was one in which young Mags or Sara was already waiting; now his bed was for sleeping, and my God, how delightful that was!

He could smile to himself at the thought. Mind, the chance of misbehaviour would be a pleasant thing. Even if he'd grown a paunch and didn't need to worry so much about shaving his tonsure since most of his hair had disappeared, his brown eyes were still attractive to women; but he believed that they mostly saw him as a pleasant old soul, rather than a risk to their virginity. So be it. They were probably right.

Not old at some four-and-forty years, Joseph was that rare creature, a man who was entirely satisfied with his life. He knew his position in the world: he was a monk in the hospital of St John, with responsibility for the treatment of sick travellers. Normally this wasn't a particularly arduous task, of course, but there was a steady trickle of people coming through the city asking for attention. Since the famine there had been fewer people passing through, but Joseph didn't care. He had the garden to keep him busy. There was always something to do.

Whistling as he walked to the little lean-to shed beside the priory's wall, he heard a call. Glancing over his shoulder, he saw a man up at the gate with the porter, then more men behind him in the gateway, and he frowned a little. They were carrying something – a heavy sack or bundle. Or body.

Dropping his tools, he started to run to the gate.

Rob kept starting and staring at the door, but whenever it opened, there was never any sign of Andrew. 'Where is he?'

'Sit down and shut up. We've got the stuff to split up.'

Adam nodded. 'Will's right, Rob. If Andrew didn't want to come and get his money, that's his lookout.'

'But where is he? He ought to be here.'

Will leaned back easily until his back was against the wall. He was a good-looking lad in a bold way. Only two and twenty, he had fine fair hair, somewhat lank, which constantly drooped over his grey eyes, concealing the fact that there was a slight cast in his left. He wore a cheap and faded grey fustian tunic and dull green hose, and he pulled at a loose thread at his knee as he gazed at Rob. 'Look, he's not here. We can either wait, or divvie it all up now. Right?'

Rob frowned. 'I'll take his share, then, and . . .'

'Oh no,' Will said smoothly. 'I'll keep his share safe. We'll see what we do with it later. For now, we'll just make four shares. Tell him to come to me later and we'll work it out.'

Not for the first time, Rob wondered what he was doing with these two. There were other men he could have worked with, but no, Andrew had said that these two were safer for them.

'There's strength in numbers, Robbie, boy,' he'd said. 'We're half the gang, and while we're half, we're safe. If I ever disappear, though, you look to yourself.'

And now Andrew wasn't here. Rob had seen Will knock the cleric down, and it was as he was grabbing the bag from his shoulder that the madman appeared, howling and screaming at them, waving his sword wildly like a berserker. Rob had fled in the face of that lunatic, and he'd thought the others had too. But there was no sign of Andrew when he got back to the stable, and although he'd waited there for an age, there was still no Andrew when he came here to the alehouse for the sharing.

Will took his silence for agreement, and leaned forward over the rough table. The bag had a purse inside, and in it were a few coins, carefully counted into piles and passed about the table. There were some clothes, a shirt which Will claimed, a spoon which Adam took, and a little knife, which Will thought Andrew would like, and which he placed with the pile of coins ready for Andrew to collect. He glanced at Rob challengingly as he did so, but Rob didn't care. His mind was on his brother, wondering where he was.

The fear was like a cold trickle of water running down his back at the thought that Andrew may not have survived. Sweet Jesus, don't let him be hurt, Rob thought. The only man he knew and trusted in the world surely couldn't have been taken from him.

'Marge, bring us ale!' Adam shouted to the woman at the bar. She brought jugs, ignoring the fact that the three were concealing their booty on the table. Will stared at her with empty eyes as she set drinking horns on the table, the blankness a threat. She met his look with contempt, curled her lip and returned to the bar.

'What's this?' Will muttered as he reached into the bottom of the satchel, a frown darkening his brow.

Rob watched as he brought the thing out. It was a bag of purple material with a draw-string loosely tied. Will untied the string. Inside was a package wrapped in fine pigskin. When he unfolded the leather, he revealed a small box.

It was an attractive little casket of dark wood. There were intricate carvings over it, and metal glinted in the recesses. Yellow metal. Instinctively all three men leaned forward, their heads almost touching as Will pulled the lid open and stared inside.

There was a fine felt cloth, again in purple. And on it lay a glass vial, much marked and dirty. The glass was scratched and grey, as though ancient, with a greenish tinge. There were two pieces of parchment beside the vial. Will plucked them up and glanced at them for a moment, but he had no use for scribbles. He threw them on the floor irritably so that he could stare more closely at the vial. Picking it up, he pulled the stopper free, upending it into the palm of his hand.

A sliver of silvery-grey wood fell out. The three gazed at it, then at each other.

Adam was the first to break the silence. He picked it up and began to chuckle, his voice a hoarse rasp that was somehow shocking in the tavern. 'A piece of turd! I like that!'

'It's not that,' Will said, and he too was grinning. He took it and studied it. 'I think it's old wood.'

'Throw it on the fire, then. The box should fetch a few pennies, though,' Adam said, and reached for the casket.

'No, we'll leave it as it was,' Will said, putting his hand on the box. He carefully inserted the piece off wood back in the vial and stoppered it, putting the vial back in the box and closing it.

Adam pulled a face. 'Let me have a look at it.'

'Leave it, Adam. There are other things to worry about. Look at Rob there, worried about his brother. You should be thinking more of his feelings.'

Rob glanced at Will, and saw a cynical, cold expression on his face, and was suddenly sure that he would have to protect himself against Will. Andrew had been right, as usual. Together they had been half the gang – now he was only one member of a larger band, and no longer held the balance of power.

There was something else, too. Will sat quietly, one hand upon the box. Adam's hand was near the box. It was as though Will was challenging Adam to try to take it from him. Adam saw the expression in Will's eye, too, and wasn't sure he wanted to accept the challenge. He lowered his head with displeasure. 'I want the thing.'

'Then buy it,' Will said. 'You want it, you give me back all your coins from tonight, and then you can have it.'

'When Andrew gets here, he'll make you two give it to him anyway,' Rob said.

Will didn't look at him. 'You think so? Perhaps it's too late for that. I've taken a fancy to this box, and I will keep it.'

'You aren't the leader of our group yet,' Adam snarled.

'I think I am.'

Will, having spoken, drew the box towards him. Adam said sneeringly, 'You take the thing, then. It's nothing to me. But remember this, it's not yours or anyone's – it's ours – and you don't have the right to do anything with it.'

'Then I'll buy it from you,' Will said easily. He took half his money and then hesitated. 'No, we're here to drink, and Andrew isn't. We'll sell this thing to him.'

He took Andrew's money and divided it equally between them, then put the box in its wrappings on the table beside him. 'If Andrew gets here, he can have it.'

'No!' Rob protested. 'I'll look after his stuff. Give it to me!'

'What if he doesn't come back, Rob?' Will said easily.

Rob blurted, 'He'll be here soon!'

But even he did not believe it.

A woodsman found the body some little while later. Old Hob was out with his dog, and while crossing the common on the Exeter side of the ford, his dog ran off, then stopped dead in a clump of brambles, and growled, low and menacing.

This was no cattle dog, it was a good rache, a hunting dog that could chase its quarry by smell, and the woodsman knew better than to dispute its sense. He hurried after it, wondering whether there could be a deer hiding away there, hopeful that a good blow with his axe (without a witness) could result in food for some few days.

'Sweet Jesus!' he breathed when he saw the face staring at him from among the bushes. The face of a dead man, blue-grey in the twilight, with his throat cut from ear to ear.

*   *   *

Much later, Will belched and grabbed hold of the doorway as he left the alehouse. It was dark already, and the city was all but deserted, but there was a man being smothered by Moll the whore at the street's corner as Will stood on the threshold and peered up and down the street.

Adam thought he was clever, but it was Will's brain which was going to lead them now. It was obvious enough even to Rob that his precious brother wasn't going to come back, and now it was up to Will to take over. He already had his plans, and it wouldn't take him long to implement them.

He'd never asked for more. Rob was an old woman when it came to planning and choosing a target, but Adam was reliable enough. His only problem was, he tended to believe, touchingly, that he had a brain. He didn't. As far as Will was concerned, Adam had less intelligence than a stook of wheat.

Take his reaction tonight. As soon as he had been faced down by Will, he went into a sulk, and it was only later that he recovered his equanimity, when he'd beaten several barrels of crap out of that poor sod at the bar. Who was it? Oh yes, Tad. 'Tad the Bad', they called him, because of his flatulence, but tonight he was 'Tad the Trampled'. Yes, Will thought with a cheerful gurgle. Tad the Trampled. That was good. He'd been so thumped by the infuriated Adam that it was a miracle he was still able to whine and crawl away.

Will wouldn't have done that. He had no argument with Tad. No, if Adam had insisted and tried to take the box, Will would finally have let him have it. But then, later, he'd have made sure that

Adam never crossed him again. That was the trouble with a small band like theirs. It was impossible if there was a second man trying to get to the top. Will was the top man now, and he wasn't going to let anyone, let alone a shite-for-brains moron like Adam, take his position.

Shame that Rob was so upset. It was his brother, but in God's name, even brothers had to separate some time. And there was no shame in Andrew dying at the hand of a knight. That was plainly what Rob would think, that the man on the horse had ridden his brother down.

Will set his jaw. The trouble was, if the knight was about the city now, it would be possible for him to cause some problems. Who could have foretold that the bastard would hang back and reappear at the gallop only when the pathetic little cleric had already been taken care of? No one could have foretold that that would happen, but if Will had been in charge, he'd have set one man to keep an eye on the cleric, and left the other three watching and waiting to catch the knight, pull him from his horse, and kill him as well. Still, Andrew wouldn't make that mistake again. Or any other, for that matter, the cretin.

He paused. The knight had been too far away to get a good look at any of them, hadn't he? Could he have caught a clear view of their faces? Not Will's, surely. Will had been over the other side of the clearing. He could have seen Rob, though, or maybe Adam. If he had, that was their problem, not his.

Most importantly, the box was nice and safe. Adam had tried to grab it, but Will had kept it. Later he would take it to a man he knew behind

Exeter's Fleshfold, above a small butcher's shop, who would sometimes deal in little trinkets. Judging by the box, it must be valuable, although why a splinter of timber in a vial should be, Will didn't know. He suspected it might be a relic, which was why he had pulled it out, in case it brought him luck, but there was no magical tingling in his fingertips as he handled it, no spark of excitement in his belly or fire in his bowels. It was just an old chip of wood. Probably sold to some gullible trader with more money than sense. Well, with any luck, Will could find another one with a purse bigger than his brains. He wondered fleetingly what the two pieces of parchment had been, but the idle thought was soon lost as he lurched down one alley, then turned into a narrower one.

This wasn't his way home, but Moll lived down here, and he had some business with her. She'd been all over that man like a cheap tunic, and Will had a sudden urge to know who he was. There was something unpleasantly familiar about the man. When she came home, Will would be waiting for her.

It was late when the outlaw finally managed to sleep; the body in the alley haunted his thoughts, and as he settled himself he would see again that appalling face, the spilled guts, all that, and his sword befouled with gore and blood. Although he was used to bloodshed – Christ's bones, he'd been a warrior for too long not to be accustomed to it – yet the murder made him feel tainted, as did his furious attack on the corpse.

Marching through the alleys afterwards, he came

to his inn. It was a poor place, this, but it had one attribute: the master and his wife were uninterested in him or anyone else. All they wanted was the money that people brought. They didn't care what men might have done. It was all the outlaw could have desired.

He gave them a curt nod as he closed the door behind him, and the pair eyed him silently. They were sitting at their fire, a mean thing in the middle of the room impounded within a ring of stones like stray sheep.

'Are you staying in the rest of the night?' the old woman demanded.

The outlaw looked at her. She appeared little better than a beggar, and her husband had the appearance of a cur who had just been whipped. 'Why? Do you wish to follow me about my business?'

'No, Lord, no!' the man interrupted hastily. 'Just . . . the watchmen will be about, and you could be hurt.'

'I'll not be at risk,' the outlaw said softly, but with menace in his tone. He walked to them quietly, his soft Cordovan leather boots making little sound on the earthen floor, until he was standing before them, his hand resting on his sword hilt. 'I am not in danger here, am I?'

'Of course not, master,' the man said.

The outlaw's eyes weren't on him, though, they were on the vixenish features of the man's wife. She was the sort who'd cut a man's throat without thinking, the bitch. A man couldn't trust a woman like her. Any man who had been celibate all his life could see the type: one who would lead her man into danger for the gratification of her own lusts.

Women always hankered after money or things. The outlaw had been warned of their wiles while he was a monk.

'I'll stay here, then,' he said softly.

She had set out a palliasse for him on the floor near the fire, but he ignored it and walked out behind the bar. There was a small cellar out there, and he peered about him with satisfaction.

'What do you want in here?' she demanded, following him.

'Peace,' he said shortly, and ushered her from the place. He closed the door and slid a heavy barrel in front of it to block it. There was no other entrance, nor a window. Satisfied, he drew his sword, wrapped his cloak about himself, and sat on the floor facing the door.

He was safe enough. God Himself was watching over him, and those whom He protected needed fear nothing from the maggots who inhabited this miserable world. His sword was dedicated to God's service.

The dream came to him more often the older he grew, as though his heart were ensuring that his memories could not fade.

Baldwin de Furnshill was eighteen at the time, and the noise of the siege had never left him: the roars and shrieks of men, the thunder of massed kettledrums, the ringing clash of sword against scimitar, the appalling damp sucking sounds of weapons impaling bodies. All was terrifying.

He had sailed there full of hope. His stout English companions would soon put paid to these subhuman creatures with their dark skin and weird war cries. The ship's master had told them of other glories, how English Crusaders had evicted the infidels before. Richard of England had come this way, he said, and pointed to an island to the north.

'He took Cyprus, because the king of the island tried to ransom Richard's fiancée and his sister. King Richard went through the place like a lance through butter, even though he had fewer men. That's what you'll do at Acre. Go at them and see them off.'

Setting foot on the harbour, Baldwin knew the ship's master had been boosting their morale. He must have known that there was no chance of pilgrims defeating the army that encircled Acre. It was too vast.

They had arrived to find the city in flames. There was a thick pall of smoke over all, and as the English party left the ship, they stood awestruck. All about them was mayhem. Men shouting, women screaming, children wailing. A sudden thud made the ground quake, and Baldwin caught the eye of a man-at-arms who sat on a bale of cloth near by, nursing a stump where his arm had been.

'They have a big bastard mangonel over there. Keep your head down or they'll take it off.'

If at that moment Baldwin felt less certain that he and his comrades could turn the tide and rescue this city, he was soon to be convinced of the inevitability of their failure. It was later that first day, when he clambered up the walls.

Over the wide plain, shimmering in the heat, men moved like demonic ants. The distance made them seem tiny, but their numbers were appalling. Baldwin gaped at the sight, and the sense of fear that had first gripped him at the port now returned and seemed to clamp itself in his throat, making breathing difficult. He felt the sweat start from every pore and gazed about him with terror.

In all that horror, as the boulders pounded the walls and the defenders toppled all about, if there was one thing that maintained men's sanity it was the Temple.

The Order's building was at the south-western-most point of the city. It was a strong fortress, but the knights didn't cower inside. Although the Temple was some distance from the battle, each day the Templars were in the thick of it. As the Moors attacked, Guillaume de Beaujeu, the Grand Master of the knights, would rush there with his men. They would enter the fray with their terri-fying cries, the black and white *Beauséant* high over their heads, hacking and stabbing until the attempt was repulsed. Then they would hurry to the next fight, their resolution and determination a spur to all the defenders of that hellish place.

Then came a day of disaster.

A massive, crushing explosion, and Baldwin had to duck to avoid splinters of rock thrumming past. He was near the aptly named 'Accursed Tower', and the Moors were attacking at every point. Their siege ladders rose, hordes of screeching warriors clambering up the lower rungs before the steps were vertical; arrows pinged off masonry by Baldwin's ear; slingshot bullets rattled from armour; yet over all the din of war he could hear the shrieks to his right. Glancing around, he real-ized with horror that the enemy had reached the tower and were barricading the doors against the city, preparing to create a sally-port in the heart of the city's defences.

Baldwin pressed forward with others, but it was

the Templars who stormed on through the massed bodies. Baldwin saw Guillaume de Beaujeu at the front, exhorting his men to greater efforts, and then he raised his arm, sword already bloody and smeared as though with a fine red oil, only to falter and disappear. The fighting grew more vicious, no quarter given on either side, and then Baldwin was struck a ringing blow on his helm which knocked him all but senseless. He was helped to safety by a weeping man.

'I am all right,' Baldwin gasped after a few moments. His head still rang, but the worst of the pain was already abating. He thanked his rescuer, but the fellow didn't seem to hear. He was staring after a group walking away slowly, carrying a body.

'Did you see it? Did you hear him? There's no hope for us now.'

'Who?' Baldwin demanded.

'Beaujeu! He said: "I can do no more. I am dead. See, my wound."' Suddenly the man sobbed. His beard was scorched away from one side of his face, the flesh raw from sunburn. He stared up and shook a fist skyward. 'Christ in Heaven, why won't you help us? We're defending *Your* lands!'

'Baldwin?'

The kick to his foot made him grunt with annoyance, but Baldwin opened one eye and peered upward without enthusiasm. 'What do you want now? Can a man not enjoy a moment's peace, Simon?'

His assailant was a tall, lean man in his mid-thirties. Simon Puttock had strong features. His face was sun- and wind-burned, and his hair was beginning to turn to grey at the temples, but for all that he looked like a man many years younger. His dark grey eyes held a mischievous amusement as he looked down on his friend.

For the last seven years this square-faced, rugged man had been bailiff at Lydford Castle, and the daily riding over the moors to negotiate with the miners of the Stannaries in their disputes with each other and with the local population had given him the leanness of a trained whippet. Now, however, he had been granted a new post by his master, Abbot Robert of Tavistock. He had become the abbot's official as Keeper of the port of Dartmouth, a position that he found much less attractive.

'The Keeper of the King's Peace must be exhausted after too many strenuous days. Once upon a time he would have woken with the dawn.'

'Some of us have to work for our living, Bailiff. I have sat and decided too many fates in the last few days to want to listen to chaff from lowly officials.'

'Oho! Lowly, am I?' Simon chuckled, and then reached for the blankets covering Baldwin's body.

'You forget yourself, Bailiff!' Baldwin growled. 'I am a Keeper of the King's Peace and this week I am one of His Majesty's Justices of Gaol Delivery. I have power of life and death, so do not vex me.'

'I shouldn't dream of it,' Simon said innocently, choosing a stool and sitting near by.

Baldwin grunted, eyeing him doubtfully, a tall, broad and thickset man, running a little to fat now. He was over fifty years old, but the years had been kind. He had dark brown hair and eyes, and a beard that neatly followed the line of his jaw. Once, when Simon had first known him, that beard had been black, but now it was pickled and spotted with white. There were sparkles of white on his head, too, and Simon was suddenly aware that his companion was in fact an old man. It was an alarming realization. He had lost too many friends already, and the thought of losing Baldwin too was somehow sickening. He could feel a heaviness in the pit of his stomach at the mere idea.

'I don't trust you,' Baldwin declared, and reluctantly rose from the bed. He shivered a little in the coolness and pulled a linen shirt over his nakedness. 'This week has been grim. Too many men hanged.'

'They've received their justice.'

'Aye, true enough, but sometimes a man would prefer to leaven the justice a little,' Baldwin said absently. In his mind's eye he could see one man's face as he confirmed the decision of the other two justices and sent the fellow to the gallows. Most peasants exhibited little emotion. For them death was the end to a life of toil, perhaps. Or they were prepared for death, having seen so many friends and relations die during the famine. Misery and suffering were so common that even a sentence of death could seem like a release.

But this man was young. At his wife's side was their child, a toddler who stood sucking a thumb and watching wide eyed as his father's case was dispatched. The peasant glanced at them, and Baldwin had seen tears well in the man's eyes. There was no wailing or howling to accompany the tears, just the sudden trickling that made Baldwin pause and think, and then the wife started to sob, a racking, tearing noise, and her baby began to bawl, and Baldwin's heart felt as though it must break.

The verdict was just; there was no doubt of that.

The fellow had stabbed another man in a tavern. Such things happened all the time, and usually the community would stand together and suggest that it was a foreigner passing through the vill who had committed the act. The sad fact was, though, that the dead man was a King's Purveyor; he was in the vill to collect fodder and stores for the King's household.

It was that which had guaranteed the peasant's execution. No man could strike down one of the King's officers with impunity – but how would another respond if he heard a Purveyor deciding to take all the food set aside for winter?

Baldwin had seen too many men die. In an attempt to lift his own spirits, he said, 'Only a young man would dare to fool with a knight.'

'True. I am not so old as you.' Simon chuckled.

Baldwin nodded, but thinking of the felon's hanging brought to mind his dream again.

The horror of the siege was still fresh in his memory even now, more than thirty years afterwards, and he hoped it would always remain so. It had been the cause of his decision to join the Templars, because he had been saved by the Templars after being wounded. The knights had taken him to Cyprus and nursed him to health. As a result he had lived, and from that day he felt that he owed them his life. To repay the debt he had joined them.

His thoughts were interrupted by a knocking at his door.

'Yes. What do you want?'

'A messenger from the hospital. They've got a man in their infirmary who's been attacked on the road here.'

Baldwin nodded and sighed. Then he ran a hand through his hair and grimaced at Simon. 'I suppose we ought to talk to him.'

The fellow was lying in a cot with a tired-looking monk standing at his side.

'Brother?'

'I am Joseph, the infirmarer. This man was brought to us late yesterday as we were closing the gates.'

'He looks in a bad way,' Simon said with that hushed voice used by people in the presence of the sick.

This was a pleasant little chamber, this hospital. Not far from the East Gate, the Hospital of St John was a small chapel with six beds. Each faced the altar, with the cross prominently in view to all, so that all the poor souls in their beds could see it and pray. Brother Joseph could ease their symptoms, but naturally the actual cure was up to them and the power of their own prayers.

Joseph passed a hand over his tired face. Strange to think that only last night he had been cheerfully looking forward to his bed and congratulating himself on the fact that he took such joy in sleep. It was ironic that he should think so just as this poor fellow was being carried to him.

'He is. His arm is broken, but I think with God's grace it should mend without too much trouble. I think his ribs are broken, too, and his head was badly knocked. It's the stab that worries me most, of course, but I have hope.'

'Why should his assailant beat him so?' Baldwin wondered.

'If you wish to learn that, you will have to speak

to the porter of the East Gate. He had the body brought here on a hurdle.'

'Has he spoken at all?' Baldwin enquired. 'Has he mentioned the attack?'

'No. He arrived in this state and has remained silent. If he recovers, perhaps he can tell what happened, but it will be a close-run thing.'

'Is he from this city or a foreigner?'

'I do not know. Ask the porters. One of them may know him.'

Baldwin nodded and the two left the brother in the doorway to his little hospital, yawning with exhaustion.

At the entrance to the hospital, Baldwin and Simon spoke to the gatekeeper. He was reluctant to tell them anything, other than the fact that he had been in his lodge preparing to lock up for the night when John, the East Gate porter, had arrived with three or four others and the man lying on his hurdle.

Leaving him there and walking the few yards to the East Gate, Simon muttered bitterly, 'You would've hoped the bastard would want to help us find the man's attacker.'

Baldwin shrugged. The system of fines to make sure that men turned up in court often led to their being less than helpful. 'Let us see what we may learn from the porter.'

The lodge was built into the wall, a solid building with a thatched roof set at the back of the two towers about the gate itself, and the porter matched his home perfectly. His face was florid, topped with a messy rick of fair hair, and he was stolid and broad. His face was square, with small, hog-like eyes which held a suspicious leer, as though he doubted the integrity and honesty of any upon whom his eyes might alight. His grim expression was not improved by the sight of Simon and Baldwin. 'What do you want?'

'The man whom you took to the hospital yesterday,' Baldwin said. 'What can you tell us about him? Was he from the city?'

'How should I know? So many come past here each day.'

Baldwin's smile was wearing thin. 'We need to learn who he is.'

'Good. Do it and leave me to *my* work.'

Steel entered Baldwin's voice. 'Your work at this moment is to help the Keeper of the King's Peace. If you do not, I will have you attached and kept in the castle's gaol to contemplate your obstruction until the coroner holds his inquest, and I will ensure that all here know it is because of you that they are to be fined so heavily for finding the body.'

'He's not dead, is he?' the porter demanded, but his arrogance was already dissipated. The First Finder of a body would be forced to pay a surety to guarantee that he would turn up in court at the trial, and if there was no proof that the dead man was English, the hated murdrum tax would be imposed on everyone in the area.

'He wasn't dead when you found him, was he?' Simon pointed out.

'If he was, I'd hardly have taken him to the hospital, would I?'

'How did you find him?' Baldwin asked.

'A brat: Art. He said there was a man in the ditch out there.' He pointed through the gate. 'I wasn't going to believe him, but he was a persistent little sod.'

'Did anyone see how he got there?'

'If they did, they didn't say. Since the famine fewer men are prepared to help each other. No one wants to be First Finder. I dare say several saw him and chose to forget him.'

Simon knew that. Too often people would ignore a body at the roadside; they'd all grown inured to the sight of the dead. Half the population had died during the famine. 'Did this helpful child Art say how he found the man?'

'Someone paid him a penny to tell me. He showed me the coin – it was real enough.'

'The boy, where is he?' Baldwin snapped.

'Art? Up at the market, I expect, the thieving little git. He'll be up there scrounging something, same as usual.'

In Exeter, just as in the smallest vill, orphans tended to be protected. They could count on family or godparents to protect them and look after their property in trust. Masters would see to the needs of apprentices, sometimes neighbours the children of the family next door, with neither hope nor expectation of reward for their kindness, and in Baldwin's experience such children often thrived. Cases of abuse were remarkably rare.

Apparently Art had been orphaned three years earlier. He was a scruffy urchin of twelve, with a shock of tawny hair that stuck up vertically from his head. His face was long, with intelligent brown eyes that considered Baldwin like an equal. The knight reflected that the fellow had probably experienced as much life as many men of Baldwin's age.

'You found a man yesterday, Art?'

'Who says?' he responded quickly.

'The porter of the East Gate.'

'I told him where he was, but I didn't find him.'

'Who told you about him?' Simon asked.

Art stared at him and remained stony faced until the bailiff pulled a coin from his purse.

'Don't know him. He was all in black – black cloak, black hood, the lot.'

Simon sighed. 'How tall? As tall as me?'

Art looked at him speculatively. 'Maybe taller.'

'And I'm almost six feet,' Simon murmured.

'What of his face?' Baldwin tried. 'Was he light haired or dark? Did he have a beard, a scar? Had he lost his teeth, had he all his fingers? Was there anything which could help us?'

'He had bright eyes, and a cold voice. That's all. Never took his hood off, so I never saw his face,' Art said. 'But I suppose he was like you. He had . . . you know.' Art puffed out his chest and drew his mouth down into an aggressive line, scowling, clenching his fists and squaring his shoulders. 'Your build. His arms were like yours. Strong.'

'You saw all that under his cloak?' Simon asked doubtfully.

The lad said scathingly, 'It doesn't take much to see how wide a man's shoulders are, no matter how many cloaks he puts on.'

There was a cry from behind them, which Baldwin ignored as he leaned forward. 'Are you saying he looked like a knight?'

'Yes. But not some rich one like you,' Art said, although with a trace of uncertainty as he took in Baldwin's rather threadbare tunic with the red colouring faded from overuse.

Baldwin was about to defend his clothing when Simon murmured, 'Baldwin!'

A man-at-arms was hurrying towards them with a pole-arm in his hands. 'Sir Baldwin; Sir Baldwin! There's been a murder, sir!'

In the early morning light Baldwin could see that the corpse had been a young man. He had blue eyes, fair to mousy hair, with eyes set rather close together, and a nose that was long; it had been broken. He was clad in dingy grey fustian with green woollen hose, from his leather belt dangled a short knife.

It was the tunic which caught Simon's attention. The fustian was open from breast to cods, and his belly and torso had been slashed in a frenzied attack. His bowels spilled on to the alley's filth, and the stench even so early was already repellent.

'Christ Jesus!' Simon muttered thickly.

'He has been stabbed in the back,' Baldwin said, after rolling the body over and studying the naked back. He saw Simon's expression.

It was endearing to Baldwin that Simon was still squeamish; on occasion it could be annoying. Today, though, Baldwin could all too easily understand Simon's reaction.

'Why would someone open him like that?' Simon demanded harshly.

'A drunken brawl?' Baldwin guessed. 'Rage at some perceived slight? Whoever did this hacked at him like a madman.' He turned to a sergeant. 'Do you know who he is?'

'I think his name's Will Chard. He's got a common fame as a draw-latch, I think.'

'Where's the First Finder?' Simon demanded.

''Tis him over there, Bailiff,' the sergeant said, jerking his chin towards a man slumped against a wall, his face in his hands.

They walked to him. Baldwin said, 'What is your name?'

'Rob, master. Rob Brewer.'

He was in his early twenties, Baldwin guessed, a scrawny lad in a faded green woollen tunic and heavy hose. About his neck was a worn cloak of some heavy but badly worn material. Once it would have been worth a lot of money, but now it showed its age. He looked terrified: his eyes kept returning to the body on the ground, to the blood all about.

'You found this man?' Baldwin demanded.

'I was walking past and almost fell over him! Christ's pain, but I'd have done anything to miss him!'

'It is no surprise,' Baldwin mused. 'The sight . . . Exposing his entrails like that . . .'

'Paunched,' Simon said. 'Like a cony.'

Rob whined, 'Who'd do that to a man?'

'Men will bait traps with rabbit's guts, won't they?' Baldwin said. 'Strew rabbit's intestines about a field and wait, and soon a fox will arrive. Release the hounds and they'll take the fox.'

'You say this is a trap?' Simon asked drily. 'To catch what?'

Baldwin smiled thinly. A figure was hurrying towards them, a rotund shape clad in clerical black – a clerk from the cathedral sent to record their inquiry – and Baldwin beckoned him. 'I doubt this was a trap. This looks like a vengeful rage . . . but revenge for what?'

*　　　*　　　*

'I was up early to fetch bread from the baker's, and found him on my way.'

'Have you seen him before?' Baldwin asked.

'Never!' Rob declared with a shudder. If he admitted he knew Will, they might decide he was a felon and arrest him. He had to protect himself, deny everything.

'Where were you last night?'

'In the Blue Rache,' Rob said without thinking. Christ's balls! He shouldn't have said that! He closed his eyes and swallowed. 'I slipped on his entrails!'

Simon could all too easily imagine him; walking here just after dawn, down a dim alley with little light to show the way, and suddenly coming across this foul corpse. It must have been terrifying – although the lad must have been distracted not to have seen the mess, or smelled it, in even the dullest daylight. He leaned against a door, queasy, and had his weakness rewarded with a long splinter in his thumb. Swearing under his breath, he stuffed his thumb in his mouth.

Rob couldn't help his eyes going to the pool of vomit near a doorway.

Baldwin continued, 'You are sure you do not know him?'

'Me? I . . . no.'

'Which baker's were you going to?'

'Ham's – behind Chef's Street.'

'Where do you live?'

'Out near the corner of Westgate Street and Rack Lane. There's a little yard behind Elias's stables. I live there.'

Baldwin glanced at the clerk and repeated: 'Elias's stables . . . You work there?'

'Yes. I muck out and look after the horses. He lets me exercise them, sometimes.'

Baldwin nodded thoughtfully. He turned his back, staring at the cathedral's towers. The workmen intent on rebuilding the place were like so many bees about a hive. 'What were you doing here, then?'

Rob gazed at him. 'Sir?'

'This alley does head in the rough direction of the Westgate, but it's hardly direct to or from the baker's, is it?'

'I wanted a walk – to clear my head after last night. I'd had a lot to drink, and I needed to clear my head.'

'Were you alone in the tavern last night?'

'Yes.' Rob met Baldwin's disbelieving eye with determination. No good could come from admitting he had been drinking with Will and Adam all night. It wouldn't bring Will back.

Nor Andrew either, he reminded himself.

He looked a fool, Moll thought. Sitting there so forlorn, like a child who'd lost his mother. Telling lies like that was stupid. The Keeper might not know him yet, but as soon as he asked anyone else, he'd learn that Rob and his brother were close confederates of Will, and then where'd he be? In the shit, that's where. He'd already told them he was in the Rache.

She'd not tell *them*, mind. She had enough problems with the law without courting more trouble from felons like Rob and Adam. No, better that the Keeper learned all he wanted from others.

Not that she could help much. She'd been upstairs with that poor bastard when Rob had knocked, and it was only when she saw the state Rob was in that she realized she could have been protecting a killer. References from past clients were all very well, but if this fellow was a killer . . . still, he'd run out like a scalded cat, and she was safe when he was gone, so that was that. Rob, though, he was different. If he wasn't careful, the Keeper would put two and two together and realize Rob had been here earlier and found the body in the middle of the night.

He didn't believe me, Rob told himself.

Christ, save me! When he'd run over that mess last night, he'd almost emptied his own bowels. His foot had stuck on something, and when he looked down he thought it was a lump of pig's liver, until he realized it came from no pig, and that was when he collapsed and threw up. He couldn't think straight.

It was like being in a trance. The First Finder always woke the neighbours to witness the death, and they raised the hue and cry together. Last night he'd banged on Moll's door first because he recognized it.

Shit, she'd scared Rob! She'd had the door open in a flash when he banged on it, and a man pelted into him, running off into the night almost immediately. She told him the sod was nothing to do with this, he was a well-paying bedmate, but it'd embarrass his wife if she learned he'd been here, so Rob agreed to forget him.

Moll was clever. She took charge: he was drunk, as she said, and it would be better if he 'found' the body in the morning. Men had been executed for less than being drunk in the presence of a body, and if the city's sergeants found an easy answer, they'd stop looking for a killer.

Now he thought about it, the man was curious. Strange for him to be up and bolt from a whore's house just because someone knocked. If he feared his wife finding him, why didn't he just hide and let her open the door? Rob wondered who the man was. All he'd seen was the shadow of dark cloak. He'd worn a cowl that covered his face; not that it was needed in the gloom of the alley.

Wandering here today, the previous night had seemed dream-like. Andrew missing, Will dead . . . he came back hoping it was a dream, but there was Will, so he raised the neighbours, and the hue and cry.

Not that it was much help. The neighbours were here now, shivering in the cool morning air. An old candlemaker and his woman, a dyer and a tawyer with a daughter. None of them sharp witted, none of them heard the attack. All denied hearing anything.

Neither had Rob, come to that. And he couldn't have been far behind Will when whoever it was did this to him. The bastard was still warm when Rob fell over him.

Simon drew a small knife and hesitated before running the blade along the splinter's path. It stung, but he inserted the point and levered it out, listening as Baldwin asked his questions.

It should have been the new coroner, Sir Peregrine de Barnstaple, investigating this, but he had left for Topsham after the Gaol Delivery hangings because of a brawl between sailors: three of them had died. In his absence, it was only natural that the Keeper should take over. The Keeper had the right to order the posse and lead it to find a felon.

Even now Simon was sure that Baldwin doubted Rob's evidence. Something had caught his fancy about the ostler, although now he was squatting and frowning at the pooled vomit. Simon left him: he was more intrigued with the young woman.

This Moll was an auburn-haired woman of maybe three- or four-and-twenty, with a dumpy figure but a face that would have been pretty, in a soft, pale, round sort of a way, but for the calculation in her eyes when she looked at a man. From this Simon was convinced she was a prostitute, maybe one of those who inhabited the cheap taverns and alehouses along the South Gate road.

While Baldwin left the puke to talk to the neighbours, Simon wandered to her side. 'What do you think really happened?'

'How should I know? I was safe in my bed.'

'All alone?'

'Why – you jealous?'

'Could be! Did you know this man?'

'Never seen him before,' she said, but her eyes moved away from Simon.

'Who was he?'

'Don't know what you mean.'

'Did he try something on? You called your pander to pull the bugger off you, and he took offence at the fellow's cheek? If your pimp killed him, there'll be no blame attached to you.'

She smiled at him with quick contempt. 'You think my pander would do something like that?

233

He'd shit himself at the thought. It's only women he bullies.'

'Then you're protecting someone else? Who? *Why*? Whoever did this could attack again. Such frenzied butchery – it must be a madman. He could strike again, maid. Maybe he'll attack you next.'

She eyed him a moment. 'No. I think *I'm* safe.'

When they released him, Rob ran all the way from the alley to the place up at the old Friars' Hall, and then ducked down another alley and waited, heart pounding savagely. He'd almost been caught, and his terror was only increased by the sudden approach of heavy feet. It sounded like the city's bailiffs, and he closed his eyes. At any moment the Keeper's voice would rasp out an order for his attachment. He'd be hauled off to the gaol until he could be brought before the justices and hanged. He just *knew* it. Why had he ever . . .

The steps passed by the alley and on down towards the West Gate, and he felt his breath leave him in a sharp gasp, as though it would be his last.

It was awful. He was lost, confused. His brother was gone, Will was dead . . . who could he trust? There was only Annie, no one else. He must tell her what had happened.

He shot off up the lane past the priory of St Nicholas, and on to the shanty town. Once this had been the abode of Franciscans, but recently they'd moved away. In the space of two years nine of the brethren had died because of the foulness of the location, so they'd moved to a new six-acre site outside the walls.

In their place a series of huts had been built. Bays were made from scraps of timber lying about. Wattles were thrust between them and smeared with daub, and thatch was thrown on top to keep out the rain.

None was strong; none was proof against more than a mild wind or shower, and yet people flocked here. It was proof of the misery of life in the outlying areas that so many were keen to come to this place, which was already known for its malodorous air and the illnesses the foul air caused. The friars had been driven away, yet others more desperate were happy to live here.

The place he wanted was up near the northern walls. It was a scruffy place, the daub falling from the walls while the thatch was worn thin and penetrated in many places where birds had made their homes, or stolen the straw for their nests. What remained was green and little use in a storm, but neither was the rest of the house. The door was an old blanket, which fluttered and moved with every breeze.

Rob hesitated, then cleared his throat. 'Annie? Are you there?'

'Of course I'm here. Where else would I be?'

She pulled the curtain aside and he walked in, revelling in the nearness of her body as he ducked under the low lintel.

'What are you doing here?' she asked.

Annie was about twenty years old, as tall as Rob, but better built because during the famine years she had been in the service of a lord who had seen to the well-being of his servants, and bought in food even as prices rose. Fodder prices rose by six times before the end of the first summer, and buying grain for the serfs of his manor finally ruined him. Three years earlier she had been turfed out when the old man died, brought down by fear of God and the struggle to support his people. His wife, the bitch, hadn't the same sense of responsibility, and she'd seen to it that all the 'useless mouths' were evicted.

Rob first met her on the road from the north, up near Duryard, a mile or so north of the city. She had been a waif-like creature, all skin and gangling limbs, with huge eyes in a skull-like face, and he had at once taken pity on her.

'Hello, where are you from?'

'Tiverton.'

'Where are you going?'

'Exeter.'

Each word had seemed as though it must be dredged up, and each time it took a long while for her to mouth an answer, she was so exhausted.

'Do you have somewhere to go?'

'No.'

She was one of hundreds who had come this way seeking employment or merely a roof. At first, when the city had stocks to be shared, people were permitted inside the walls, and the churches thundered the responsibilities of Christian to Christian, but that was seven years ago. When Annie arrived, the same men who had demanded that food and drink should be shared were more cautious. Only those who could help Exeter should be supported, and those who couldn't must return home. Their parishes should shoulder the burden, rather than expecting Exeter to suck in all those without means.

Rob had been lucky. He and Andrew had been orphaned when he was not yet ten. Andrew was already apprenticed with a metal smith, and Rob was accepted into the household, but Andrew was rowdy and unreliable. The smith kicked them out after Andrew fought another apprentice in the smith's hall.

It was Rob's skill with horses which led to his being hired by the stables. That meant good food, a bed and some money, but not enough. He didn't think he received his due, so when Andrew suggested something more profitable, he'd leaped at the chance.

Annie obviously had a clear idea what she could do in Exeter.

'Come with me,' he said as kindly as he could. 'You don't want that game. I know a place . . .'

She was so fragile, like a butterfly; she stirred something warm and protective in him, and Rob responded to it and the hope of companionship it brought. He brought her here to the old friary lands, where a friend lived with his wife, working on the cathedral's rebuilding. She would be safe here, and in return for a little work about the place, and Rob paying a little rent, she could share their board until she found work.

Annie soon filled out, and now she was a buxom maid, with a tunic of red-stained cloth, and a crimson sleeveless surcoat over it. Her apron was faultless, clean and fresh. Her shining dark hair was decorously braided and wound into a thick bunch under her wimple; a pity, for he adored to see it loose. She had once said, laughing, that he only ever liked to see her wanton, and to be honest it was largely true. When she was naked over him, breasts free, her hair hanging on either side of her face like great raven's wings, he felt true happy contentment. Yet it wasn't just lust. No, it was more than that. The sight of her smiling face was enough to send a thrill of pleasure to his heart. To see her content was to fill him with joy.

Her eyes were on him in the gloom, but today there was no delight in them. He hated to see her like this: suspicious and unhappy. Sometimes she could be a little peevish. He only hoped that this wasn't one of those days. He had enough on his plate.

'Annie, have you heard?'

'About Andy?' she said quickly.

Rob gritted his teeth. 'He's missing. I don't know where. And Will – he's dead. I found him last night in an alley, and . . . Christ's Bones, but it was awful. Someone had cut him up.'

'Why do that?' she asked.

There was scant interest in her voice, but that was reasonable. Will had been his friend, not hers. It was one of the things he loved about her, this naturalness and refusal to feign feelings that she didn't have. At no time would she lower herself to pretending affection for someone when there was nothing there. She'd have made a dreadful whore. He was also glad that she didn't harp on about Andrew. It was hard enough for Rob without having to cope with her feelings as well.

'Will had plenty of enemies. A thief who preys on travellers is never without foes. Someone recognized him and killed him,' Rob said, thinking about the tall, dark keeper and his words about catching foxes.

'Did he leave many alive?' she said pointedly.

Rob didn't answer. Confirming what he and the

others had done to win money was unnecessary. She knew what they were. It wasn't as though she wondered where Rob had won the money to keep her happy. He hadn't hidden anything; he could have lived on his stable's income had he not put her up in this shack. It was the money for that which drove him to Will and robbery.

'I'd have thought there were few enough living to take revenge on him,' she said. 'He saw to that.'

Rob knew she was in the right there. There were only a few who wanted to see him dead.

And he had himself been one of them.

When their questioning was complete, Baldwin and Simon beckoned the clerk to follow them, and strode to the Blue Rache.

'What is your name?' Simon asked of the clerk. 'I haven't seen you about the place before.'

'I am Jonathan, Bailiff. I hail from Winchester, and it is only a mere chance that I happened to be here. The good dean asked me if I could attend your inquiry, because he was holding a meeting this morning, and it was a great honour to be able to help you.'

'You mean you have heard of Baldwin and me?'

'No. But it's always an honour to help law officers in their duties.'

'Oh,' Simon said, a little chastened.

The cleric saw his face fall and chuckled. 'But although I have not heard of you myself, Bailiff, Dean Alfred was insistent that I should come. You have helped him in the past, and he wished me to convey his best wishes and begs you will advise him of any aid you need.'

'That's good to know. Why are you visiting?'

'I brought messages to the chapter from the bishop.'

Simon nodded. Bishop Walter had been drawn from his comfortable palace in the service of the King, and now spent much of his time in the King's household travelling about the realm. Naturally he wanted to communicate with his brethren at regular intervals. 'Have you been here before?'

'No. Never. It is a wonderful city. It flourishes under the benevolent eye of Bishop Walter.'

Simon grunted his approval. He knew the bishop quite well, and liked him.'Where are we going now?' Jonathan asked after a moment or two.

'The alehouse where the witness was drinking last night,' Baldwin responded. 'I want to confirm that man's name, and also see why that fellow was so anxious. I think he lied about finding the body.'

Simon waited, but Baldwin was not going to explain his thoughts. For his part, Simon was intrigued about Moll. 'She was convinced she was safe. She had no fear of being attacked herself.'

'Perhaps she guesses the identity of the murderer, then,' Baldwin said.

'So you are going to make sure of the dead man's name,' Jonathan said.

'That and anything else we can,' Simon said. 'I've often found murders were committed in hot blood because of arguments about money or a woman. Perhaps someone from the place can point us in the direction of the murderer.'

'I see. Is that it?'

Baldwin had stopped at a low, thatched, dilapidated building with a tired-looking bush of furze tied to a horizontal pole over the door. The knight turned with a grimace to Simon and rolled his eyes.

'This looks like your sort of den, Simon. I doubt whether they'll have Guyennois wine fit for a knight.'

'Don't judge the ale by the tun,' Simon said loftily.

Jonathan sniggered and, boosted by his appreciation, Simon shoved at the door.

Simon had visited many alehouses and taverns when his father was steward of Okehampton Castle. When he travelled with his father they would stop at places like this to refresh themselves and ensure their road ahead was safe. Alehouses were cheap drinking halls in which a man could consume as much rough ale as he wanted before collapsing. Food was rudimentary if available, and company was of the lowest sort; if a peasant wanted a place in which to sing and dance, however, there was nowhere better, and Simon had fond memories of many small alehouses.

Expecting this to be rough, Simon was not disappointed. It was the sort of hovel where people would assume that a foreigner was worthy of contempt and deserved to be considered an enemy. This was not Simon's city, but that mattered little to the people inside. He could have been a man from one street away and they would have studied him in the same mistrustful manner. Because he was not of their own parish and lane, he was a foreigner to be scorned.

He walked inside and the room's noise was hushed in an instant. Where before there had been excited chatter and arguments, now there was a menacing stillness. Unabashed, Simon strolled to the bar, a simple board laid over two barrel-tops, and leaned on it.

The chamber was perhaps fifteen feet by twenty, and the bar was at the far end. Along the walls were three benches, and in the middle of the room was a fire, which threw up a sullen flame every so often in the midst of a rank smoke. There were two barrels upended to serve as tables, and about these were some rough stools, three of them simple cylinders sawn from large logs. On the floor was a fine splintering of ancient rushes, their stalks long since mashed by the passage of so many feet, and the whole place reeked of urine and sourness.

In all there were some fourteen men in there. Simon took in their faces as he leaned against the bar. Some were vacant with ale even at this early hour, but two or three looked belligerent enough. Simon smiled at them easily. There was a mixture of folk: nearer Simon stood a pair of sailors, who brought the stench of tar and the sea into the place, their hands stained black, their faces burned the colour of old oak. Behind them was a carter, chewing slowly at a straw while he toyed with a jug of ale. Farther back was a group of three men playing at knuckles, rolling the bones enthusiastically and seeming to pay Simon little attention. In short, it was the usual mix of people who had come to Exeter to make use of the market, some to buy, some to sell.

One of the sailors curled his lip and spat, but as he did so there was a shivering ring of steel, and all eyes turned to the doorway where Baldwin stood, his sword held negligently in his fist. Suddenly everyone found merit in a study of the contents of their cheap pottery drinking horns. Jonathan nervously stepped around Baldwin to take his place at a bench, where he smoothed a sheet of vellum and readied pens and ink.

While he prepared himself, Simon faced the ale-wife. 'There's a man murdered up the lane from here. First Finder was called Rob Brewer, who was in here last night.'

She was a pretty girl, perhaps nineteen or twenty years old, and with bright golden hair almost concealed under a cotton cap. Green eyes with hazel flecks met his unflinchingly. She shrugged and cast a glance over the drinkers. 'Loads in here last night.'

'The dead man was young, two or three days of beard, some inches shorter than me, fairish hair cut short, long nose, eyes set close, pointed chin – do you know him?'

'Was he wearing a grey fustian tunic?' asked a man.

'Aye, and green hose,' Simon agreed.

The speaker was thirty or so, with a face scarred from the pox and a great shining burn scar that ran from left to right temple over his brow.

'Did you know him?'

'If it's the same lad, it was Will from Chard.'

'Did he get into a fight last night?' Baldwin called.

'He was here with some friends. They argued a bit. Who doesn't?'

'We have to find his killer,' Simon said. 'Who was he with? What happened?'

'There were two men with him. One was a youngster works up near West Gate. I thought *he* was Rob Brewer. The other's heavier, fellow by the name of Adam.'

Another spat at the floor. 'Bastard should be called Cain.'

'Why?' Simon asked, glancing at Baldwin. He

243

had noticed that name, Simon saw. Brewer had told them he didn't know who the dead man was.

This man was dark skinned with a cast in one eye and a bruise on his right temple. He spoke with a slight lisp, as though a tooth was giving him pain. 'He's dishonest. He'd rob his mother for profit, then beat her if there wasn't enough.'

'Get on, Tad. You're sore 'cos he knocked you down,' commented the first.

'Shut your noise, Ed. You don't know the little shite.'

Simon raised a hand to silence them both. He nodded to the man with the cast in his eye. 'Why did he hit you?'

The man looked shifty, as though he didn't want to discuss his affairs with a law officer. 'He was making trouble.' Seeing Simon's expression, he glowered, then added, 'Look, he was in here with his friends, Rob and Will, and they were making a load of noise. I sort of asked him to shut it. That's all.'

'No, it's not all,' Simon said. He leaned against the bar. 'Where can we find these men now?'

Tad shrugged and turned away. 'Who gives a . . .'

Suddenly the knight in the doorway was in front of him and the sword was under his chin. Tad clenched a fist, but before he could think of swinging, he found himself grabbed by the shirt and thrust back against the wall. The sword's point was pricking the soft flesh of his throat.

Baldwin grinned wolfishly. 'I do, friend: *I* do. And I intend to find out.'

The knight looked as grim as a mercenary. Tad had no doubt that he'd skewer him in an instant, and enjoy doing so.

'Adam, Rob and Will,' Simon said patiently.

'What were they doing; what caused your fight with Adam – *everything.*'

Tad was tempted to tell him to go and swive his horse, but the sword's point was sharp. There was a trickling under his chin, and he had an unpleasant suspicion that it was blood. He daren't move his head in case he impaled himself. Someone had once told him that an easy way to kill was with a thrust under the chin, straight up, through the tongue, the palate, and into the brain. He had a sudden vision of his body on tiptoe, the point of that evil-looking blue blade buried in his skull . . .

'All right!' he gasped. 'But take that sword away.'

To his relief, the pressure subsided a little.

'What do you know of this man Rob?' Simon asked.

'He's a stableman. If it wasn't for his brother, he'd never have started their game.'

'He's pathetic,' Ed agreed. He belched.

'Who is his brother?'

'Andrew. But he didn't come in last night,' Tad said. 'I didn't see him.'

'Wasn't here,' Ed agreed. 'Probably out with his wench.'

'Who is she?' Baldwin demanded.

'How should I know? Thing is, the brothers are always together. There's a reason when they aren't.'

Simon frowned. 'Could Rob Brewer have killed Will of Chard, then?'

'No.' Tad didn't think so. 'He's not a hard man. His brother Andrew could. It's said him, Adam and Will attack people on the way here to market, knock them down and take their purses. Adam is a hard bastard. He's got a room up near the Dominicans. Down Stycke Street. There's a cordwainer's shop – the man lost a lot of money and rents a room over the shop. Adam and Will live there. Well, Adam does now.'

'What of Andrew?'

'Rob's brother? He shares with Rob most nights. A stable's a good warm place to live.'

'What was your argument about last night?' Simon asked.

'Look, Adam was looking for a fight. That's how he is. The more he has to drink, the more he wants a fight. He made some comment about me, and I . . . That's all.'

'He insulted you to your face?' Baldwin said.

'Not to my face, no. He said it to another, and he told me.'

'Tell us what happened.'

Tad could remember the whole evening perfectly clearly. 'I got there before them. I got to the alehouse for a chance to relax, when those three turned up, bought their ales, and sat down in the corner of the room away from the door.'

'Rob was with them?' Simon sought to confirm.

''Course.' In his mind's eye he could see the three sitting with their heads close together, staring at the things in Will's lap. Tad glanced at Simon's face and grimaced. 'Look, they'd robbed some poor bastard, I expect. Probably beat up someone, left him by the roadside and brought all his stuff to be shared out.'

'What did they divide between them?' Baldwin said.

'Will had a little box. I saw Adam try to grab it,' Tad recalled, 'but Will wouldn't let him.'

Simon glanced at Baldwin. 'Will had something Adam wanted?'

'Did it rattle, this box?' Baldwin guessed. 'Did it contain money?'

'I saw him share out coins first, so it wasn't that. No, there was something else in the box itself. Like a glass vial or something.'

'What was it like, this box?'

'Oh, just dark wood. There were some shiny bits on it. Didn't see more than that.'

Baldwin was frowning. 'Did anyone else in the tavern see it?'

'A stranger. I saw him staring.' The sword rose slightly and he spoke more hurriedly. 'Tall, built heavy like a man-at-arms, dressed in black. Good leather boots . . . He was with one of the whores.'

Jonathan's reed was over-full, and on hearing this word he made a large blot on the page. He quickly tried to rectify the mistake by setting his sleeve over the ink and soaking it up, but he was too hasty and knocked his reeds on the floor. Moaning to himself, he bent to retrieve them, and noticed two small parchments under his table. He picked them up with the reeds and set them on the table as he continued writing.

'Christ's bones,' Simon breathed. 'I'd bet my horse that he was the man told Art to fetch help.'

Baldwin's puzzlement grew. 'In which case, was he a companion of the wounded man, or a friend sworn to avenge him? Or does he also seek to steal this box?'

'Did you see any sign of Rob's brother last night or today?' Simon asked.

There was no answer beyond a slow shaking of heads. Baldwin was about to draw Simon aside to talk when there was a loud pounding on the door. The sergeant who had been by Will's body came in, panting. 'Sir Baldwin, there's another body, out towards Bishop's Clyst. Can you come?'

Rob was so forlorn that Annie finally agreed to go for a drink. Neither wanted to go to the Blue Rache, and she suggested a tavern out near the Guildhall.

'I'm worried,' he said when they had a pot of ale each and were sitting outside in the sun. 'Andrew has disappeared. I don't know where he could be. And Will dying . . . I don't want to stay with only Adam.'

'Why not? He's not changed.' Her tone was cold, and she looked pale. Rob thought she was quite distracted . . . it was only to be expected. She had loved Andrew too. He'd been like a brother to her. 'Will's dead, but I expect Andrew will turn up again.'

'No,' he said with conviction. 'If he was going to come back, he would have already. Yesterday we attacked two men, a clerk and a man-at-arms, and I think Andrew was killed by them.'

'It would take much to beat Andrew,' she said. 'He'll come back, you see.'

'If he doesn't, what'll I do? I can't stay with Adam. He's mad – he'd kill me in a moment's rage. The only time he's happy is when he sees other people suffering.'

'Rubbish. He just wants to make money, and stop living hand to mouth all the time.'

'Well, we all do. But there are ways of doing it that are safer.'

'Safer?' she scoffed, and nodded towards St Nicholas Priory. 'I suppose you'd prefer life in the cloisters, would you?'

He was quiet for a moment. 'No,' he said softly. 'I don't want to lose you. I couldn't join the monks.'

'Then stop whining about him. He's part of your life. *Our* life.'

'If I stay with him, I'll end on a felon's rope.'

'Oh, leave him, then!'

He was hurt that she was irritated by his ramblings, yet he had to explain his plan to her. 'Perhaps I could find a new trade.'

'What?' she demanded. 'You have no skills. Everything you've tried has turned sour. You're good with horses, but that won't make you rich.'

'Well, I can't carry on like this for ever,' he said, glancing about them. 'Being a felon has no future. Not if a man wants to be married. I could learn myself stonework, perhaps? There's always a living to be earned as a mason. I could build walls. They can't be that difficult.'

She looked at him. 'Maybe,' she said, relenting in the face of his misery.

Just that was enough to make him grin. She almost expected him to start capering, like one of those bears that would dance at the whistle of his master. He made her want to scream, and the feeling made her hate herself.

This man had saved her when she first arrived, and she was grateful to him for that, but he was so *pathetic*! Rob always moaned and whined, seeing risks or dangers in any plan, never agreeing to any new ideas, not like Andrew. Andrew had always worn that smile of confidence. If he wanted something, he found a way to acquire it.

'We could leave the city and find a new place,' he said. 'We could marry.'

'What, with all the gold we've saved?' she

demanded scathingly. 'Shall we hire a pair of horses to ride to York or London?'

She had nearly died during the famine. Nobody could make her surrender to fate again. Here there was a house, some food and friends. She'd sworn that she would never starve again, no matter what.

'I have something,' he said quietly, and he stole a look over his shoulder before reaching under his tunic and bringing out a leather purse. 'This could make our fortune. Will said it was Andrew's share from our ambush yesterday, but he wanted to steal it. I managed to keep it last night . . . now I don't know what to do with it.'

Annie eyed him doubtfully. Rob had been kind to her when she'd needed help, but that didn't mean she was keen to *marry* him. God! The idea he'd take her away to an uncertain life elsewhere was ridiculous. Andrew maybe, but not Rob. No: she couldn't go with him.

Interesting box, though. She opened it and saw the glass bottle. She stared, wondering what it was.

There were few things that could be worth having a box like this built around them. It was beautiful, like a . . .

Peering closely, she frowned. She'd seen boxes like this, though more richly decorated, in churches. Studying it, she could see fragments of gold leaf adhering to the lid, and she took the vial out and stared at the wood inside, rattling it gently. She touched the plug but didn't pull out the stopper. Something made her stop. Her breath was a little strained, and her heart was thudding painfully as she shook her head and replaced the vial unopened in the box. If this was a holy relic, she didn't want to touch it. It could burn her.

It was worth money, that was certain. Rob wasn't wrong there. Someone would pay lavishly for it. And then there was the splinter inside. She had heard of relics of the lance used to stab Christ on the cross, pieces of iron from the nails which held Him, part of the trencher used in the last supper, all sorts. And then there were the pieces of the original cross on which He died . . .

A splinter of that would be worth a fortune. Plenty there to allow a man to marry. She licked her lips, and grinned to herself. After all, the man who was in love with her would make a good husband.

Baldwin and Simon found a mount for Jonathan and hired horses out to the scene. There was an old woodman there with a good white-and-tan rache, a broad-chested dog with slightly pendulous jowls, but intelligent eyes in a strong face. Always fond of dogs, Baldwin made a fuss of him before turning to the body.

'You found him here?' he asked.

'I'm Hob, from Bishop's Clyst. I was up here to take down a tree for —'

'Yes, I am sure,' Baldwin interrupted quickly. 'You were up here legitimately. And your hound found this man?'

'He was there under the furze, and Gaston found him. I was fair sickened to see him.'

Baldwin crouched at the side of the body. There was no doubt about the death. His throat was opened almost to the spine, and the cartilage and vessels had contracted, making the wound gape still more. Jonathan coughed once before remembering his calling and murmuring a lengthy prayer.

'Do you recognize him?' Baldwin asked the woodman.

'No. He's a stranger to me.'

'There is little enough to distinguish him,' Simon said. 'Brown jack, linen shirt, woollen hose . . .'

'His description would be little help, too,' Baldwin said. 'He's moderate height, brown eyes and hair . . . a little weakly of frame, perhaps. Ach! There's nothing here to help us find his murderer. If he was local, this description would hardly find him.'

'If he's a traveller,' Simon said, 'he would have had a pack with him. There's nothing here, so he was probably robbed.'

Baldwin nodded as he rose to his feet. 'So all we know is that we have the body of a young man here, his throat cut. He could be a local man, could be a traveller. If he's a traveller, his belongings have been stolen.'

'And we know that the trio in the Blue Rache last night had a haul of money and a small box,' Simon said.

'So is it a fair assumption that this man was their benefactor? Perhaps,' Baldwin mused. 'Along with the man in the hospital.'

Simon had another thought. 'Interesting that this man had his throat cut.'

'How do you mean?' Jonathan asked.

'Just that this man had his throat expertly slit, while Will and the man in the hospital were both stabbed in the back.'

Baldwin nodded. 'And a killer will often use the same method of murder. It's what he grows accustomed to.'

'You mean that there might be two murderers?' Jonathan said with sudden alarm.

Baldwin smiled. 'A man might kill in a number of ways. No, there's nothing to prove that there is more than one murderer. In any case, a stab in the back is a common wound when the victim has been ambushed,' he added, suddenly thoughtful.

Simon set his head to one side. 'There is one other aspect to consider, Baldwin. We were told in the Rache that there was another man who was missing, weren't we? Could this be Rob's brother?'

'Andrew?' Baldwin glanced at the body again. 'Andrew was missing last night, as you say, so yes, this could be him. But that means also, perhaps, that the man in the hospital could be him?'

Adam was irritable and nervy as he wandered about the market. The warm morning made him lethargic, but he found himself jumping at strange noises. The bulls were being baited to tenderize their meat before slaughter and butchery, but a shriek from playing children made him start with alarm. He wandered among the stalls, buying a pie and eating it voraciously, suddenly feeling starved. Once that was gone, there was little money left from the cash he had won yesterday, and he rattled the few coins in his palm dejectedly. He wanted some ale.

The Blue Rache was quiet when he entered, and he scowled about him as he crossed the floor. If the shits were angry just because he'd thumped one turd, they'd best look out. He might hit another today.

He beckoned the ale-wife, who glanced about her anxiously before licking her lips and going to him. 'Yes?'

'A jug. Come on!'

She turned the spigot on the barrel and held a jug under it.

When she passed it to him, he turned and glared at them all. There wasn't one who could hold his gaze. All cowards! All weak and shitting themselves. They wouldn't know how to set a good ambush or how to steal a prize from even the most feeble of travellers. No, it took a man like him, someone good with his fists, someone with some courage.

'There was a set of king's officers in here earlier,' Elias said.

'So what?' Adam sneered.

'Will's dead. Apparently they've already got the idea you and him knew each other.'

Adam nodded, took a long pull of his ale, and set the jug down before whirling and catching Elias by the throat. He shoved the squeaking man backward in a rush, scattering drinkers and stools wildly until he reached the wall and thrust Elias hard against it. It was a thin wattle screen, and as he rammed Elias against it, the structure moved, the plaster cracking. 'Who told them about us, Elias? It was you, wasn't it? By the nails and the blood, you little . . .'

'Not me, no!' Elias managed. 'It was that arse-licking sodomite Tad, not me!'

Adam pushed him once more, and this time the crackle was noticeable. The wall gave way at the ceiling and a fine plaster dust fell in Elias's eyes. 'You were always his friend, weren't you?'

The wattles were pushed from their sockets in the beam overhead, and now large chunks of plaster were falling on Elias's head. He had to blink to clear his eyes.

'He was just someone to drink with, that's all. I hardly know him!' Elias said quickly.

Adam's fingers felt like steel pincers, relentless. Elias knew that death must soon overtake him. His breath came with great difficulty; he could feel blood welling in his sinuses and between his eyes. It was impossible to swallow – and then he felt his head crash into the wall one last time, and this time it gave way. There was a roar, and now he was in the midst of a cloud; all was white and choking, and he was cut and scratched by lathes and wattles, suddenly finding that he was looking up from the floor.

The dust was suffocating. It rose thickly, like flour in a mill when the wheel was turning, and it stuck in his mouth and nostrils. Vaguely he could hear voices.

'It wasn't him,' the ale-wife screeched. 'Leave him, Adam.'

'Why should I? He's helped sell me to the King's men.'

'He didn't; Elias said nothing.'

Elias managed to roll on to all fours, coughing and retching. Then Adam's boot caught his belly with all the malice of his frustration. Elias was lifted into the air, and he crashed to the ground in the ruins of the wall, his lungs smothered by the lime plaster, struggling for breath.

Adam studied him with satisfaction for a moment. 'Well, maid. Who did tell them?'

'They came here asking questions, so they already knew Will had been here before they came.'

Adam chewed at his inner cheek. He saw Elias crawling away, and it was tempting to kick him again, but there were too many questions in his mind. 'Who told them to come here?'

'Perhaps someone saw who killed Will?' She held his gaze. 'You lived with him. Did he get home last night?'

'I argued with him last night. You saw us. Over that box. I thought he'd chosen to go somewhere else for the night. Maybe stay with Rob or something. I didn't think he was dead.'

For the first time he felt the loss of Will's help. Never thought he'd ever think that; never thought he'd miss Will's sharp mind. Adam was more used to learning what he wanted without subtlety.

'Marge, if you know something, you tell me before I get angry.'

'You wouldn't hurt me,' she said with certainty.

He moved to reach for her, but as he did she lifted her hand, and in it was gripped a fine-bladed dagger, wickedly sharp and pointed. She ran it over his knuckles, and he yelped as the razor-edge made itself felt. There was no pain as such, only a faint tearing sensation, and then a line of blood as his flesh was parted. He withdrew his hand, then prepared to launch himself at her, crazed with rage. She held her ground, and the knife danced before his eyes.

'I don't know what you want, Adam. Will's dead, and the officers know you knew Will. You lived with him. Don't take it out on us.'

His face was expressionless as he cupped his bleeding fist in his right hand. He didn't know what to do – perhaps he should speak to Rob and see what he reckoned. That would be best. Yes. But he wanted to punch someone first.

She curled her lip. 'Adam, Tad didn't tell anyone

about you. They asked questions, but when they left, Tad ran out the back. He escaped. You should too.'

'What does that mean?'

Her irritation spilled over. He had ruined her wall, badly hurt Elias, and threatened her. What he did to Will outside her alehouse was none of her concern, but when his actions led to a Keeper taking an unhealthy interest in the Rache, she had good reason to be angry. 'You want to know? You killed Will, didn't you, so get out of the city while you can, because that Keeper, he's got the eyes of a demon. He'll find you and he'll hang you. Leave the city while you can.'

Moll was late to rise that day.

The previous night had been largely sleepless, and the interruptions to her business had exhausted her. Then, of course, she'd been woken early by the men clustered about the body, and only returned to her bed after a bite of bread with some potage for her lunch. This time she had slept well, and the knocking at her door made her jerk awake with some alarm. The noise was terribly loud in the silence of her hall, and she sat up with apprehension, an emotion that only faded as she climbed from her bedding and pulled a shirt over her head.

Padding over the packed earth of the floor, she threw some sticks on to the embers of the fire. Punters preferred a warm room – and hopefully she'd be able to warm some leftover potage later, when the man had gone.

She had several clients who visited her in her home, usually the wealthier ones, of course, because only they deserved the advantages of her undivided attention in her own bed. Others could make do with a quick knee-trembler against an alley wall.

The fire looked all right, so when the knocking came again, she walked out to the front door and pulled it open. 'Who is it? Oh! I thought . . .'

'Didn't expect me, eh, Moll?'

And Moll scarcely felt the club smash the side of her skull. The bones fractured as the cudgel's weighted head slammed against them just above the ear, and although she could say nothing, so shocked was she to be attacked, her body refused to collapse. It took two more thunderous blows to force her to her knees, and then she crumpled.

She was long dead before the smashing blows ceased, and then there was little left of her face. Only a bloodied mess of hair and flesh.

Simon and Baldwin arrived back at Exeter just as the cathedral bells were singing out their invitation to the faithful at vespers. It was still daylight, but here in the alley between the hospital and the Dominicans' priory, the sun was all but obscured by the houses on either side. This was a poorer area and few houses had jetties – not many had an upstairs chamber – but the lane was so narrow that it was ever twilight here.

The home to which they had been directed was a shabby place with little to endear it to Baldwin. As he looked at it, his nostrils discerned only the stench of excrement, the sour tang of urine. In the lane itself there were many deposits on the cobbled way, and Baldwin wondered when the scavengers would ever come down here. They'd clear the High Street, sure enough, but a downtrodden backwater like this would probably never see them from one month to the next, and while Simon pounded on the door, Baldwin found himself peering up and down the street, wondering what could tempt a man to live here. He could conceive of nothing worse; at the sight of it he longed to be back at his small manor of Furnshill up near Cadbury.

When the door opened, Simon immediately pushed it wide, and Baldwin followed him inside, Jonathan squeezing in behind him.

'Is this where Adam and Will from Chard live?' Simon demanded.

'They live here, yes.'

The old man was almost petrified with fear. His attention was moving all the time, from Baldwin to Jonathan to Simon and back, and if Baldwin needed proof of the evil of the man who was using his rooms, the terror evident on the man's face was enough to convince him. 'Where is Adam now?'

'I don't know – he wouldn't tell me where he was going, lord.'

The old man's eyes were rheumy and pale, with red rims. He was crabbed and wizened, like a plant that has been deprived of the sun for too long. His fingers were red knuckled and claw-like. His wife was a little taller and better formed, and although her hair was silvery like his, it seemed to hold more vitality. She appeared overwhelmed by Baldwin and Simon's entrance, and she kept throwing little glances at Jonathan, as if pleading that this man in clerical garb should protect them.

Baldwin was not in the mood for a lengthy discussion. 'Where does he usually go at this hour?'

'He sometimes wanders about the city – he never tells us where he's likely to go. Why should he?'

'How did you meet him?' Simon asked more quietly.

The man opened his mouth to speak, but it was his wife who answered, her voice resigned. 'He is my son.'

Rob was working on the horses, grooming two rounseys for the dean of the cathedral, when he saw the shadow in the doorway. He said nothing, for it was the responsibility of his master, the stable owner, to respond to customers.

'Enjoying yourself, are you?' Adam asked quietly.

'Well enough,' Rob said. He glanced at Adam, then looked away again quickly. Adam caught sight of the look and walked around the horses to Rob's side. Rob shot him another look. 'Something wrong?'

'Seems like you think so,' Adam said. 'It's strange to think that only last night we were all there arguing about the box.'

'You've heard about Will?'

'Oh, something's happened to him?'

Rob's hand stopped moving over the flank of the chestnut before him. After a moment he took the brush off the beast and started plucking spare hairs from it. 'I found him, Adam. He was butchered, his belly was slit wide, and his bowels spread to the world.'

'Why? Who could have hated him that much?'

Rob was silent.

Adam turned to him. 'Why're you so quiet?'

'You were arguing with him about that box, and then you left shortly after him. Did you follow him, Adam?'

'I had no need to. I was going home to my bed,' Adam growled.

'You wanted the box, though, and he wouldn't let you have it. Did you kill him?'

Adam bit his lip, turned aside for a moment, and then flew at Rob. Rob ducked aside and darted behind the rounsey. 'Do you mean to kill me too, then?'

'I've killed no one.'

'No one except the traveller.'

'That was Will, not me. I only hit him.'

'He's just as dead. That was why we got the box in the first place.'

'The box,' Adam repeated, and he sighed. 'Well, that's done now. Can't find that. It's gone for good.'

'Yeah,' Rob agreed, avoiding his eyes. He saw the blood on his knuckles and wondered where it could have come from.

Before he could ask anything, Adam said, 'I'm going to see if I can find someone else. You coming?'

'I've got to finish the horses before I do anything.'

'What about afterwards? There's time to find another man,' Adam said with a cold grin on his face. His head jutted forward, and Rob thought he looked like a foul demon, something with no feelings, no sympathy. The idea made him shiver.

He was glad that he could escape this mess. Soon he and Annie would have left Exeter and Adam for ever. She'd come round. There was nothing for either of them here. Not now.

'Your son?' Simon breathed. 'That explains a few things.'

'From my first marriage,' she continued. Her

husband sat on a stool and she stood behind him, her hands on his shoulders. 'When he came back I was pleased, and begged my husband to let him stay.'

Simon asked, 'You have changed your mind now?'

'Look!' the man, Jack, said, and while Sara, his wife, averted her eyes, he lifted the front of his old smock. On his belly and breast were bruises, some violent yellow and orange, others blue and grey. 'When I asked for help with the money, this is how he repaid our kindness.'

'Have you told anyone?'

'Jack didn't tell me about it until two days ago, and by then, what could we do?' Sara asked.

'I couldn't throw him to the watch. They'd order him to behave himself or they'd fine him, and then they'd leave him here with us. And he would kill us,' Jack said forcefully. The passion of his words seemed to exhaust him and he slumped back. 'He's beaten her too. He treats his own mother as badly as me.'

'Let us know when he returns,' Baldwin said, 'and we shall have words with him. I swear that you will be safe from him soon enough.'

'I wouldn't see him killed,' Sara said sadly. There were tears in her eyes.

It made Simon wonder what would make a mother lose her love for her child. Here was a woman who had seen her son beat her husband, who had felt his anger on her own person, and who yet supported and protected him. What could the lad do that would make her lose her love for him?

'I shall order a man to keep watch on this place in case he returns,' Baldwin said when they were outside again. 'He's a violent, dangerous man, this Adam.'

The three stood at the end of the alley for a moment, savouring the air. It was foul with excrement and urine, but seemed much more wholesome than the close atmosphere inside the house.

That held only the smell of fear.

Brother Joseph sat back on his old stool, feeling the sudden weakness where the worm had eaten away the socket of a leg, and rebalanced himself, leaning against the wall. There was no cure for the woodworm. It would keep attacking the place. Beds, chairs, panels, everything was at risk. It might take time, but the things would always get through in the end.

The lad looked little better. If anything he was growing worse. The stab wound was nasty, a deep thrust in the back, and it had made the lad feverish. Poor devil! It would be a miracle if he survived.

There was a soft knocking at the door, and he grunted as he rose and went to see who was there. A red-faced novice stood waiting. 'Brother Joseph, I didn't know what to do. She was so insistent.'

Joseph waved him away and stood in his doorway as the girl approached. 'Yes?'

'May I see your patient, even for only a moment, Brother? I think he is known to me,' Annie said.

It had been a long day for Simon and Baldwin, and the two men repaired to their inn as soon as the light began to dim.

'There is something odd about this affair,' Baldwin said as they waited for their ales to arrive.

A maid bustled up with a tray and two jugs which she deposited on the table between them, and then winked lecherously at Baldwin. He was shocked, and looked at the bailiff, who was grinning broadly. 'What does she think she's doing? Is she a whore?'

'Clearly she doesn't care about fashion, if she's prepared to look at a man like you,' the bailiff said dispassionately.

Baldwin glanced over to where the maid was speaking to another client. She was small, slim, dark haired and attractive, with doe eyes, a tip-tilted nose and freckles. Even as he looked her way, she faced him and smiled straight at him. He hastily returned to face Simon. 'Absurd!'

'Perhaps. Now, how will we find Adam?'

'There is a man waiting for him to return to his house. In the meantime I want to find young Rob again. If it is true that he was with Will's band, perhaps they too argued over this trinket, whatever it was, and fought?' Baldwin sipped ale.

'You were suspicious of him from the first, weren't you?' Simon said.

'There was an inconsistency in his story,' Baldwin admitted. 'He said he found the body and was sick, but when I saw the vomit there on the ground, it was quite cold.'

'You touched it?' Simon winced.

'There is no place for squeamishness when you are investigating a death,' Baldwin stated sententiously.

'Perhaps. But why should they kill him there? Why not out in the open that afternoon?'

Baldwin drank and winced at the flavour. 'Perhaps it was the argument which resulted in the death. If so, better to kill him in a quiet alley than a busy tavern.'

'Why would they gut their old companion?' Simon wondered. 'It sounds like more than a mere argument. Men like them would stab and kill without thinking, but to mutilate the body – that seems more than a dispute over money.'

'Perhaps it was they who attacked the poor fellow in the hospital,' Baldwin said. 'I wonder whether he will recover enough to tell us who attacked him?'

'I pray he will,' Simon said glumly. 'I don't like to think that the killer could remain free, not seeing how he mutilated Will Chard's body.'

Baldwin nodded, but as he did so he caught sight of Jonathan's face. The clerk was reading a small parchment with an expression of horror. 'What is it, man?'

'Christ in Heaven . . . I think I know why they fought over the box!'

Annie was in her room. She had wept herself almost to sleep by the time the quiet knock came at her window, and she wiped her eyes hastily before rising and going to it. All the family were asleep, and she had to step carefully over their bodies as she made her way to the door, twitching the old blanket aside.

'What is it?' she hissed. 'It's late. You'll wake them.'

Rob stared at her with wild eyes in a pale face. 'We have to go. Will you marry me? We'll get away from here, sell this box and make a new life for ourselves.'

'I'm not going anywhere, Rob.'

'It's too dangerous here, though! First Andrew, then Will, and now Adam is saying he wants me to stay with him – he'll kill me if I do!'

She walked away from the shack a few paces so that their voices wouldn't stir the family. 'Why should he?'

'He more than likely killed them both, don't you think? Adam was always jealous of Will and Andrew, and he probably did that to them both just to get them out of the way.'

'A bit foolish, wouldn't you think? Doing that so that he could run a gang half the size?'

'You don't understand him, Annie.'

'No. And I don't want to. Rob, I don't love you, and I can't marry you. I love someone else.'

It was on the tip of his tongue. Rob licked his dry lips, but he couldn't accuse her. He'd always known that she got on with him, of course, but that was different to thinking that she'd willingly give him up for the other. Never, except in those red, ferocious dreams in the middle of the night, had he thought that she'd discard him for the other man.

'I'm sorry, Robert,' she said, and she tried to touch his face with her hand.

He snapped his chin away. 'Don't!'

'I didn't want to hurt you.'

'But he's *dead*! How could you love a man who's dead?'

She smiled then, a lovely, transforming smile that thawed his heart even as her rejection had frozen it. 'But he's not. He's alive and in the hospital. Your brother is alive!'

'What do you mean?' Baldwin said, snatching the parchment from the clerk.

'Can you read it?' Jonathan asked. 'It says, "This is a fragment of the True Cross, stained with the blood of Our Lord Jesus Christ, which was preserved for safe-keeping in the Church of the Holy Sepulchre in Jerusalem", signed by Geoffrey Mappestone, Knight.'

Simon knocked back the last of his drink and belched softly. 'What's it got to do with all this?'

'I found it on the floor of the tavern with this other piece,' Jonathan said, unwrapping the second parchment.

Simon frowned. 'What makes you think that piece of scrawl has anything to do with the casket?'

'They had an argument in there,' Baldwin said. 'We've heard that already. Three unlettered men finding a box – why should they want to keep papers with it? We're lucky that they didn't cast these into the fire. Instead they merely tossed them aside, not realizing their value.'

'What value do pieces of parchment hold?' Simon scoffed.

'If they validate the history of a marvellous relic, they are priceless,' Baldwin said, but as he spoke Jonathan held up his hand, pale and anxious.

'Listen to this!' He read the strip of parchment with a finger running along the old and faded letters. '"I, Guillaume de Beaujeu, found this relic. It was originally bought with innocent blood and is utterly cursed. Any man who touches the fragment of Holy Cross will die as soon as the relic is relinquished."'

Baldwin blanched. He grabbed the parchment and read it himself. He sat back, it seemed to him that in the far distance he heard again those dreadful massed kettledrums, the screams and shrieks, the rattle of sling-stones, the metallic 'ting' of arrows bouncing from walls . . . and saw again in his mind's eye the bold warrior de Beaujeu, sword raised, suddenly overwhelmed. He saw all this and he felt sickened.

'Baldwin?' Simon asked. He had risen and stood at Baldwin's side. 'Jonathan, fetch some wine. Strong, red wine.'

As soon as the clerk was gone, Baldwin murmured, 'I saw him die.'

'Who?'

'Guillaume de Beaujeu. He was the man whom we revered above all others in Acre. Courageous and bold, but wily, he lead the Templars in their defence of the city.'

'But he was superstitious,' Simon said.

Baldwin frowned. 'I should not have thought so. No more than a bishop. He died before the fall of Acre, and his treasurer, Thibaud Gaudin, took all the relics and saved them. When the Order of the Temple was disbanded, all the relics were taken, though. I wonder how this one survived?'

'Perhaps it was simply unregarded,' Simon suggested.

'Scarcely,' Baldwin said.

Jonathan had returned, unnoticed, and he held out a mazer of wine. He looked as though he should have drunk it himself.

'Perhaps it was left alone because it was feared?' he said.

If there was one thing that the outlaw was good at, it was patience. He stood outside the house, listening and watching carefully. There was no sign of his prey, but another man interested the outlaw now. All evening he had waited here, hoping to catch sight of Adam, without luck, but he had begun to notice that he was not alone. There was another man watching the same doorway, a younger man with a good-quality tunic. He looked like a rich man's servant, or maybe an official from the city?

So Adam had upset another man. This could complicate matters.

It was one thing to kill a felon like this Adam, but a different thing altogether to murder an officer in cold blood.

And then he saw the stumbling shape of Adam lurching down the lane. The outlaw quickly shifted his belt, hitching it up so that the hilt lay within easy reach. Then he pushed himself out of the doorway where he had been resting, and set off up the alley towards the door of the place where Adam lived. As he did so, he saw that the youngster had spotted Adam too. Being no fool, he was not going to confront the man. Instead, he turned down the alley towards the outlaw and passed him at a trot. Off, no doubt, to call for assistance. The outlaw smiled to himself. There would be little need for that shortly.

He reached the doorway at the same time as Adam. Nodding to the felon, the outlaw cast a look about him. There was no one. He drew his sword as Adam pushed the door wide, and brought the pommel crashing down on his head. Adam roared with pain, his neck muscles contracting, his shoulders hunching, and he spun to confront the outlaw. The outlaw had completed his blow, drawing the blade back, his right fist at his flank, elbow crooked, ready to stab, his left hand outstretched, palm flat, his weight balanced on his right leg.

Adam saw him, and the outlaw saw the blank incomprehension in his eyes. Then there was only blind rage. He darted back, slamming the door, but it bounced off the outlaw's boot. The outlaw sprang forward into the gloomy interior, and he heard the rasp of steel as he entered. There was a flash, and he parried. A crash of metal, and his arm was jerked with the force of Adam's fury. Then the blade came again, a heavy falchion by the look of it, wickedly curved and deadly. He shoved his fist across his body, and the blades met with a loud ringing. A second glint, and he had the man's measure. Adam was a hacker, preferring to use blunt force to wear down his opponent rather than subtlety.

But the outlaw was a trained warrior, skilled in the craft of swordsmanship and experienced in a hundred battles. He parried once more, fell back, and then stabbed forward, once, his leg straightening, as did his arm. The falchion was swinging at his neck, but he was ready, and caught the flat of the blade with his left hand, knocking it safely up and away even as he felt the gentle resistance of Adam's breast. He pushed on a little farther, and he saw the anger leaving Adam's face, to be replaced by a wondering shock. There was a clatter as the falchion's tip struck the ground and Adam started to stagger backward. His legs struck a stool and he slipped down to sit, dully gazing up at the outlaw.

The outlaw heard a gasp and a sudden sob, and turned his head to see an old man and a woman sitting not far from him. The distraction was enough. Adam flicked his falchion's point up and the outlaw felt it enter his belly, tearing through his bowels and snagging on his lowest rib. There was no pain, not yet. That would come later.

He put his boot on Adam's fist and trampled it as hard as he could, pushing the blade away from himself, and when he was free of its encumbrance, he pulled his sword out of Adam, and whirled it around in a fast, slashing sweep. There was a fountain of blood, and in its midst he saw the uncomprehending expression in Adam's eyes as the head rose as though balanced on a column of crimson, and fell to the ground.

Baldwin and Simon were about to settle on their benches when the man arrived. 'He's back, Sir Baldwin!'

Jonathan was dozing on a bench, and Simon kicked him awake before the three followed the watchman out into the road.

Baldwin was relieved to be out of the tavern and doing something. He had remained there idly for too long after reading de Beaujeu's words, and the memories that his words brought were painful. All those good, honourable men had died, and for what? There was no reason. The Templars had been created to protect pilgrims travelling to the Holy Land. Dedicated, answering only to the Pope, they couldn't believe that the pontiff could betray their trust, but he had. He had sided with the avaricious French king to bring about their ruin, and many had been slaughtered, some tortured to death, others burned on pyres as recusants. Since then the warrior-monks had been given the choice of life in a harsher Order, or eviction. Many finished their days as beggars on the streets of Paris.

271

At least, he reflected, de Beaujeu had not lived to see the destruction of all he had believed in.

Their way took them along the High Street almost to the hospital, and then down the alley. This dark gulley between the buildings was always gloomy, but tonight there seemed to be some excitement. Up ahead there was the noise of many voices, as though there was a gathering of some sort. Baldwin was at first glad, for he thought that the noise would conceal their arrival. But then he realized that the noise emanated from the house where Adam lived, and he felt his optimism fade.

The house was bright with candles. A wailing and sobbing came from within, but the men had to battle their way past the plug of intrigued bystanders in the doorway. Once past them, Simon groaned in revulsion, while Baldwin could only stand and stare in sympathy.

On the floor before them, the old woman lay cradling her dead son's body in her lap, trying to hold his head on the neck, rocking backwards and forwards as though to help him sleep.

Joseph grunted when he heard the knocking. He had just dozed off, and almost fell from his stool. As it was, it gave an ominous creak as he shifted his weight; he must tell the prior and acquire a new one soon. This really was past safe use. Before long the thing would break, and then where would they all be if Joseph broke a wrist or an ankle?

'Yes, yes. I'm coming, I'm coming,' he responded testily as the knocking came again. He pulled the door open. 'Whatever is the urgency at this time of night? I . . . Come in here, my good fellow. What on . . . who did this?'

The outlaw walked inside and limped to the stool. 'It was my own foolishness, I think, Brother. I am a cretin. And I fear that I am dying. Please – would you hear my confession?'

'Not until I've had a look at your wounds,' Joseph said. He helped the man up again, and walked him to a bed before stripping him and helping him to lie back. Fetching water, he bathed the wounds. Seeing how the wound entered the right, lower part of his abdomen, and clearly rose up to exit his body higher, on the left-hand side, he said, 'You were stabbed very cruelly here.'

The outlaw nodded grimly. 'It is a grievous wound. I . . . I feel it. I cannot live.'

Joseph sucked his teeth. There was a lot of blood seeping from both wounds, and there was the odour he recognized, the smell of bile and bowel solids. This was a man who was dying, there was no need to conceal the fact. And better that he make no attempt to do so. A dying man had the right to time to reconcile himself, and prepare himself to meet the Maker.

'I thought so. The man I had brought here. Is he still here?'

'You had . . . you mean the wounded fellow? He is still here, yes.'

'Can he speak yet?'

'Er, no. No, he is still unconscious. I think that the wound was very deep. It is not certain that he will live.'

'Then I have a tale to tell you, Brother. And when I have told it, you can tell him too, and maybe the others who'll ask about me,' the outlaw said. 'Know, then, that my name is John Mantravers, of South Witham,' he began.

*   *   *

Simon and Baldwin had completed their work at
Adam's house when there was another call on the
cool night air, and the two men stared at each
other before running into the alley with the
sergeant and Jonathan.

'What is this call for?' Simon burst out as they
began to run along the alley northward towards the
High Street. They turned left, heading to Carfoix,
listening to the shouts and horns.

'Down here!' Baldwin shouted as they passed
South Gate Street. They ran down this, and then
realized that they had overshot the lane they
needed. Turning back, they found the dim
entrance, and were soon pelting along it. Simon
kept to the rear, so that he could assist Jonathan,
who was suffering from a stitch.

The house looked familiar, and Simon stared at
it. In the dark it was hard to see where they were,
but then he realized: it was Moll's house. This was
where they had found Will's body the day before,
but then they had approached the place from the
other direction.

A man stood in the alley, a towel at his mouth.
There was a pool of vomit near him. 'I knew her,
knew her well, you know? She was always a kindly
wench, if you paid her well. I was due to see her
tonight, but I was late. I couldn't help it. I opened
the door when she didn't answer. I just thought she
was angry because I was late . . .'

The words washed over Simon as he pushed
the man out of the way and followed Baldwin
inside.

The abode was pathetic. There were the tattered
remnants of an old blanket hanging at the window
in an attempt to make the place more homely, but

to Simon it served only to emphasize how mean and unlovely this life had been.

On the floor were plain rushes, moderately recently spread but unfresh. From the beams dangled fresh herbs and some flowers, but their soft perfume couldn't hide the sourness of sweat and sex – nor the metallic odour of blood.

It was that which made Simon want to gag. From the dark and gloomy alleyway they entered this place by the rotten door, which scraped its way over the packed earth of the threshold. The darkness made Simon think of hell. There was a foulness about it, as though the air itself were poisonous, and he wondered whether he would succumb to one of the diseases that bad air could bring. Beyond the uneven planks of the door, there was a short passage. Once this might have been a moderately pleasant house, perhaps even the residence of a wealthy trader or professional, but now it had become rotten, decayed. Walls were cracked and unpatched. The lime wash was all but gone, leached away inside and out. Overhead he could see more sky through the holes in the roof than he could through the window.

After the short corridor was the room itself, but Simon couldn't take stock. His eyes were drawn to the thick spatters of blood on the walls, and then to the ruined body on the floor by the palliasse. He swallowed at the sight. An arm, broken at the elbow, lay oddly twisted. The bodice of her tunic was open, ripped from the neck to her navel, and her blood had run between her breasts. Thick trails ran down her chest and stained her skirts.

Simon had once seen a man's head smashed by a

maddened carthorse's hoof, and this looked much the same. The right side of Moll's head was stove in, with a mess of hair, shards of bone and grey filth filling the cavity. It made Simon sick to see, and the smell added to his deep revulsion.

'She has clearly been beaten savagely,' Baldwin murmured, and Simon was conscious of a curious quiet about him.

'Why would any man do this?' he muttered.

'Why indeed?' Baldwin agreed as he began his study of the body and the surrounding area. 'It is a display of brutality – much like the corpse of Will outside her door.'

Jonathan officiously barged past the group of neighbours huddled at the door and stood near Simon. The bailiff could hear him swallow as though with difficulty, like a man with a mouthful of dry bread and nothing to drink to ease it down. 'The poor soul.'

A sergeant in the doorway hawked and spat. 'She was only a whore, Brother.'

Jonathan turned slowly and fixed the man with a look of withering contempt. 'Mary Magdalene was a prostitute, my son. And she was praised by the Lord for her kindness.'

'You stick to what you know from your books, Brother,' the sergeant said unabashed. 'Me, I'll stick to what I know. Moll was a nice enough girl, but she was still a whore and there's nothing more to be said.'

'Shut up,' Simon ordered, sickened both by the sight of the young woman and by this man's casual attitude towards her death. 'Where's the man who found her?'

The fellow from outside was brought in, and he

stood anxiously wringing his hands, seemingly looking all over the room except at Moll.

'Who are you?' Baldwin asked.

The man threw a nervous look over his shoulder. Then he seemed to sag as he recognized some faces. 'I'm called Peter from Sidmouth.'

Baldwin and Simon questioned him for some while, but he had witnesses who confirmed that he had been at a tavern with them. Before that, he had been at his stall in the market, and plenty of people vouched for his presence all morning and afternoon. It appeared he was innocent of any crime.

'There is no sign of the weapon,' Baldwin said. 'It must have been a heavy club of some sort. The killer took it away with him. Find that, and we've got a murderer.'

Simon nodded, then called, 'Did she have any special customers recently? It could have been a new gull did this to her.'

'I saw her with a new man,' a man said. He said his name was Jack, and his voice was quiet as he took in the sight of the ruined body. 'No one should do that to a maid!'

'Who was this new man?' Simon asked.

'I don't rightly know,' Jack admitted. 'He was in the Rache the other evening, and I saw him talking to her there, but I didn't think much of it. Why should I, knowing how she earned her crust? He was a tall bastard. Tall and rangy, dressed all in black. His cloak had seen better days. Oh, he had good black boots, too.'

'You remember him clearly, this man? Can you describe his face?'

'Easily done. Skinny face, like he'd lived in it a while. Dark eyes, very intense. You know, the sort that don't blink hardly at all? That was how he looked, like he was looking through you all the time, not bothering to see the outside. He was looking at your soul.'

Baldwin joined them, wiping bloodied hands on his tunic. 'You would say all that from a glimpse as you entered the tavern?'

'I caught sight of him, and you don't forget a man's face like that. His eyes were on me as soon as I was over the threshold. And anyway, I was looking about me carefully.'

'Why?' Simon asked.

'Well, that daft sod Will had left just before me, and I was going inside for a pot of ale when bloody Adam came out in a hurry and nearly knocked me down. Clumsy git. He was always like that, even before he left the city. He can't help it. I think he never realized that life is different when you get older. When he was a youngster he was always good with his fists, and as he grew up, his mind was set on using his fists or a dagger to resolve any problems.'

'Could he have killed a woman like this?' Simon asked.

Jack stared, gaping, but although his head shook slowly, his eyes were drawn back to the body on the floor, and his expression hardened. 'He knew her, certainly.'

There was an angry muttering from the doorway as the men watching realized what had been said, and the sergeant had to thump the butt of his staff on the ground and bellow to silence them all.

Baldwin thought. 'It is possible he had a part in this murder, and also the death outside Moll's door, too: Will's murder. Moll's death could have been committed to silence a witness.'

Simon glanced about the room. 'If she saw something, perhaps it was the man she was with in the tavern?'

Glancing at Jack, Baldwin considered. 'Jack? What do you say to that? When did Moll leave the tavern?'

'I don't know. A little while after me, I suppose. I saw her with the man at the corner of the tavern and when I left they'd gone. I don't know when they walked out – didn't seem important at the time.'

'Will had gone, and a short time later Adam hared off out. Perhaps that is the explanation,' Simon suggested. 'Maybe Adam killed Will, and then came here to kill off the only witness: Moll.'

'The killer surely returned to murder the witness,' Baldwin agreed. He looked at the sergeant in the doorway. 'But who killed Adam?'

'There was one other person I saw up here earlier,' the sergeant said with a frown on his face. 'That girl, Rob's friend, Annie. She was here.'

'Do you have any idea why she might have taken such an irrational hatred to this girl that she could do this?' Simon asked.

'Moll was a whore. She could have stolen Annie's lover.'

The man was already in a great deal of pain, but the jug of burned wine at his side was helping. His brow was very sweaty, but Joseph applied a cool cloth to ease his pain as best he might.

'It's my duty . . . must get it to the bishop . . .'

'What is the relic?' Joseph asked calmly.

John Mantravers sat up agitatedly. 'The relic! De Beaujeu's cursed relic! I have to take it to safety!'

'Be calm, my son, please – sit back, calm your-self,' Joseph pleaded.

'It's cursed! All who touch it will die! I must take it! My sin, ach, my crime! God, help me!'

It was very late by the time Baldwin and Simon returned to their inn, and although Simon dropped off to sleep quickly, Baldwin found himself reluctant to slumber. In his mind he kept seeing de Beaujeu fall.

Guillaume de Beaujeu had been a strong and intelligent leader. Skilled in politics, he was the only voice warning of the imminence of invasion in the months before the disaster, but he never complained. He told the people of the risk to the Holy Kingdom, but they scoffed, and most of them were to pay with their lives.

The treasure of the Templars was rescued. First Thibaud took it all to Sidon, and then to Cyprus, where he died. Soon Jacques de Molay was the Grand Master, and the relics and treasure were transported to the Paris Temple for safe-keeping. All the Templars knew that. Even Baldwin had heard of the shipments of gold and valuables.

Yet this one relic was in England. Was it some-thing to do with the parchments? De Beaujeu implied that it was his, or that there was some sort of responsibility placed upon him with this relic. There had been rumours that he had prayed on the night before his death, taking some of the relics and using them to enhance his pleas to God. Perhaps this was one such. Baldwin couldn't tell. In Acre he had not yet joined the Order. That came later, and he never had the chance to advance very far.

He prayed that he might at least learn the secret

of this relic. He felt that there was a duty on him to see to it that any debt de Beaujeu had incurred was paid back. If the Templars, or de Beaujeu himself, had cause to protect this specific relic, Baldwin would see to it that their wishes were honoured. He owed that to the Grand Master's memory.

With that thought, he closed his eyes and tried to sleep, but still it evaded him, and at last he gave up. In the early hours of the morning he rose and padded across to a window, leaning on the wall and watching as the light changed outside. He felt sad, and the pity of it was, he didn't know why.

Joseph was woken from a light doze some little while after dawn. The gates were routinely opened as soon as it was daylight, and now he heard the door open, and yawned as he peered short-sightedly at the figure entering.

'Who is that?' he demanded.

'I am this man's brother,' the man said. 'Is he well?'

'If he were, he'd scarcely be in here, would he?' Joseph said drily. He was not ready for foolish questions such a short while after being woken, and his sympathy for a soon-to-be-bereaved man was at a low ebb. He had not slept properly since the man had been brought in here and his temper was not improved by the lack.

'I'm sorry, Brother. I didn't know he was here, though.'

'We couldn't tell anyone, could we? He couldn't tell us who he was, after all,' Joseph said with a more tolerant tone. His good humour was returning. 'Who are you?'

The man licked his lips. 'I'm Rob. He's my brother Andrew. Will he live?'

'Oh, yes, I think so.' Joseph walked to the bed and stood over Andrew. He took a cold cloth from the dish on the table and cleaned Andrew's face and brow. To his delight, he saw that the face appeared to relax slightly. When he put his hand to Andrew's forehead, there was a significant diminution in temperature. 'My God! Yes, I think he's fast recovering now. With God's good grace, he will recover!'

He turned and smiled at the sight of Rob's face. 'It must be a terrible shock. Please, friend, sit and collect yourself. I have a little wine in my chamber. I shall fetch you some.'

'Tha . . . thanks.'

Rob watched as the man bustled about the place.

This was all wrong! He had thought Andrew was safely dead. He'd stabbed hard enough, feeling the hilt of his dagger slam into his brother's back, he'd thrust so determinedly. Damn his soul, he wanted Andrew dead and out of the way. He'd wanted that ever since he'd first realized that Annie loved him.

She had been all he had ever wanted. To him, Annie represented love, comfort, ease, a home. She was beautiful. He'd thought that on the very first day he'd seen her walking here from Tiverton. All he'd done since then, he'd done to make a new home and life for her. And in return all he hoped for was her acceptance.

But Andrew had taken it instead. It was dreadful to have a rival for her affections, but how much worse was it to know that his rival was his own brother? It tore at his heart, and yet he could see no alternative. If he was to have his woman, he would have to remove his brother.

He rose as though in a trance, his feet drawing him towards the bed even as his hand reached to his dagger, and he had already drawn the steel as the door to Joseph's chamber opened and the little man came out with a bowl of wine.

'Here we are. I hope you are feeling a little more . . . What are you doing there?'

Rob turned for a split second, and his momentary hesitation was long enough. 'I . . . I have to . . .'

'No! You mustn't hurt him,' Joseph shouted.

On the next bed, the outlaw had woken a few moments before. Now he turned his head to see the scruffy felon with the dagger in his hand. He recognized the man from the attack at Bishop's Clyst, and the sight was enough to stir him. His belly hurt abominably, but he had to protect the man whose life he was sworn to defend. He reached down to the pile of his clothes by the bed. There was his sword, and he pulled it free, then swung his legs to the floor.

'Christ!'

His legs all but collapsed when he put his weight on them. As he spoke, the felon looked at him, and appeared to recognize him too, and stepped back as though terrified by the sight.

Naked, grunting with the effort, the outlaw clenched his teeth. 'The relic: where is it?'

Rob saw him teeter as though about to collapse, and was about to lift his dagger to strike Andrew when the knight gritted his teeth with a supreme effort and stepped forward, the sword's point unwavering.

'Where is it?' he demanded.

It was like watching a corpse come to life. The scene was enough to destroy Rob's resolve. He stepped back, one step, then another, and turned to the door to flee.

Joseph understood nothing about their actions, but he knew that this man had been about to murder his own brother. He had no compunction, and brought the heavy dish down on Rob's head as he passed. There was a veritable fountain of red wine, and it smothered Joseph, making him blink, feeling a sudden shock.

Rob howled with the pain of the blow, but continued out, dripping with wine. He lurched, then ran across the small green to the gate.

'Porter! Stop that man! He tried to kill a patient!' Joseph cried. He saw the porter turn slowly.

The man gaped. As he later said, he could see Joseph covered in red, as though his throat had been cut, and Joseph's words made him act without a second thought. He had an old bill behind his door for defending the precinct, and now, as Rob ran towards him, a hand wiping the wine from his face, he grabbed it. An old warrior, he swung it once as Rob passed, and hamstrung him.

Rob collapsed like a poleaxed heifer. He couldn't comprehend what had happened at first, only that there had been a thud at the back of his knees, and a leg had stopped supporting him. Now he rose on his hands and one knee, but his left leg wouldn't do as he wanted. It flopped, useless. He stared at it, realizing that it was drenched in blood, and looked up in time to see the evil, spiked pole-arm approaching him.

Joseph was about to cry out when he saw the spike hit Rob. The body twitched for a few moments, one leg beating a percussive beat on the dirt of the roadway, but then it lay still as the porter struggled to free his pole-arm from the dead body's eye socket.

'He is very unwell,' Joseph said. 'I would not have him upset any further.'

Baldwin and Simon nodded as Jonathan set out his reeds and parchment on a trestle table.

It was Baldwin who walked to the outlaw's bed. 'I am Sir Baldwin de Furnshill. Who are you?'

'I am called Sir John Mantravers, from South Witham. I was born there five-and-forty years ago, served Lord Hugh de Courtenay here in the west, and then joined the noblest Order.' His voice was weak, but as he uttered the last words, it strengthened, and he looked at Baldwin defiantly. 'I was a Knight Templar.'

Baldwin nodded. 'What happened to you?'

'After the destruction of my Order, I escaped the tortures and the flames. I returned to England at last, and went to my old preceptory at South Witham. There I met an ancient comrade, Johel. He told me that there was a secret kept there.

'A relic, a piece of the True Cross, was stored in a small casket in the Church of the Holy Sepulchre during the first of the Crusades. It was in the care of an Arab named Barzac, but he was murdered by Sir Miles de Clermont during the slaughter following the fall of Jerusalem. Barzac cursed the relic and all who would hold it. A few days later it passed into the hands of Geoffrey Mappestone, who wrote a document attesting to its authenticity.

'Eventually it was brought to our country, and it has remained here for many years. Then Guillaume de Beaujeu learned of it, and he took it with him to the Holy Land when he became Grand Master of our Order. It killed him.'

Baldwin felt the breath stop in his throat. 'De Beaujeu was slain on the walls near the Accursed Tower in Acre.'

'The night before, I am told, he prayed for the city's deliverance, and he took out this relic and prayed with it. The next day he died. The relic killed him, just as it kills all who touch it.'

Baldwin saw Brother Joseph crossing himself, and pressed the wounded man. 'What then?'

'It was saved with other relics, and taken to France, but there it was decided that this thing was too perilous: it could pollute other treasures. In preference, it was sent back to England, and it remained there safely in South Witham in obscurity, until the degenerate and avaricious King of France sought the destruction of the Temple. Then Johel and a few other men sought to defend the thing and protect others from finding it. When the preceptory was ordered to be closed, I was asked to come here to Exeter with a companion to give it to the good Bishop Walter, who was known to be an honourable man.'

'But you were attacked?'

'Footpads ambushed us at a river. They caught my companion and murdered him. They tried to kill me, but I escaped them, and defended myself against the man there in the bed. He fought well, and almost knocked me from my horse while his comrades fled. Then he too ran, trying to take a path through a stand of low trees where I could not follow on horseback. I left him, and went to my friend, but poor Tom was dead and his package was stolen. It was a disaster, the failure of our embassy.

'So I continued alone. A short way beyond the little wood, I found this man. I would have killed him, but I needed to find the relic, and I thought he could tell me of its whereabouts. He agreed to tell me all he knew in return for my parole. If I protected him and brought him here, he would answer my questions.

'This man told me that a companion of his had tried to kill him. For that he felt that he owed his erstwhile colleagues no loyalty. So he told me of the girl Annie. He loved her, and he wanted her to know he was alive. I found her and told her about the attack on her man, and she was enraged. She helped me, telling me of the whore Moll, and telling me where Adam and Will lived so that I could ambush them and find the relic. So this I tried to do.

'The first night I went to the tavern and saw the men there. I tried to return to catch Will, but he escaped me in the dark. I remained up in Moll's room. In the middle of the night, the brother of this man appeared, horrified. He had found Will's body. I left then, determined to find the man and search his body.'

'This was the middle of the night?' Baldwin queried.

'Yes. Moll persuaded him that it would be better to leave Will there and report the murder in the morning. Will had had his throat cut, and I went through his clothes but could find nothing on him. No relic. In a rage, I slashed at his corpse. He'd killed my friend Tom and robbed him, and now I couldn't find Tom's goods. I was enraged.'

'You would have killed him.'

'No. I wanted the relic, and I wanted to question

him to learn where it was. I have no taste for
murder. In the same way I tried to capture Adam.
He was stronger than I expected, though, and
didn't fall when I struck him. In the fight, I had to
kill him . . . and I think he has killed me.'

'So we still don't know who killed Will,' Simon
said. 'Nor Moll, either.'

'I killed neither,' the injured knight said. 'Who
would kill Moll?'

Baldwin was silent for a moment. Then he bowed
over the dying man. 'You have done well, poor
fellow soldier.' He drew his sword, and showed the
man the blade. There, outlined in gold, was the
Templar cross. He had asked for it to be carved
there when he had the sword made, and never had
he been more proud.

Sir John de Mantravers peered closely, and then
looked up at Baldwin. 'Thank you, comrade.' He
kissed the cross and sank back with a grunt of pain.

'Come on, then, Baldwin. Who would have killed
Moll?' Simon asked.

'I have little doubt that it was Rob,' Baldwin said.
'I think he feared that she saw something on the
day that Will was killed.'

'So you think that Will was murdered by Rob?'
Jonathan asked.

They were near the Broad Gate, the great main
entranceway to the cathedral, and Baldwin stopped
here. 'We may never know, of course, but I think
that for our report we should assume that he was
responsible for that as well. Clearly we may not
enquire of him any longer, but who else would have
had the motive? His brother had been leader of the
band, and when his brother was stabbed, perhaps

he thought that Will would take over. Maybe he thought the gang was his own inheritance? For whatever reason, he killed Will and then stabbed Moll in case she had seen something. Perhaps he thought she was a witness and couldn't take the risk that she might report him?'

'I see.' Jonathan nodded. He gave the two men his thanks for their company, and walked in under the great gates. In a moment he was lost to sight.

Baldwin nodded to himself. 'A pleasant enough fellow.'

'And about as gullible as you could hope,' Simon said more caustically. 'So now, Baldwin, what really happened?'

'Think of it this way, Simon. What reason was there for someone to kill Will? He was no real threat to anyone in the band. He had the others under control. When Adam wanted to get the relic, he didn't fight with Will, but picked a fight with Tad instead. Adam himself recognized Will's leadership.'

'Rob could have killed him.'

'True enough. He was a weak, ineffectual man, yet he still managed to attempt to kill his own brother when he thought that Andrew might take his woman. He could have tried to kill Will – but was there the desire? I think that someone else had more of a desire to see him dead.'

'Who?'

'Annie, Andrew's woman. She loved him, from what Andrew said to Mantravers, and surely she would not have expected Andrew's own brother to murder him; when she heard that Andrew was attacked and presumed dead, who would she have blamed? I think the first person would be Will. So she laid a trap for him, waiting in the alley. When he came near, she pulled his neck back and cut his throat.'

'You think that she went back to kill Moll?'

'Moll was sure she knew who had killed Will. She told you she was safe, didn't she? That was because she felt sure that the killer was Robert or Adam, and she didn't feel threatened by either of them. But she was wrong. One of them was quite prepared to kill her.'

'Adam was a violent, dangerous man,' Simon said thoughtfully. Then he shook his head. 'Yet he didn't kill anyone. He wouldn't rise to fight Will when Will prevented him looking at the box, and we know that Robert was capable of murdering his own brother to keep his woman. It must have been him.'

'Yes. He thought Annie could have been seen, so he went back to Moll's house and killed her.'

'What would make him think that she was a threat to him?' Simon wondered.

Baldwin said nothing. His friend the bailiff was too dear to him for Baldwin to talk about the time when they had both been questioning Rob on that first day they had seen him, when Baldwin studied the pool of vomit and Simon went to the whore and spoke to her quietly. Baldwin could see the two of them now, young Moll looking at Simon with that saucy smile, every bit the practised wench; Simon himself grinning back and asking her who she might have seen or heard. A man as anxious as Rob would be sure to wonder whether that quiet conversation could have led to information being shared. No, Baldwin wouldn't tell his friend.

But Simon's mind was already on another matter. 'So if this woman Annie killed Will, do you think we should have her arrested?'

Baldwin grimaced and shook his head. 'What good would it do? She has managed to remove a felon from the streets. In fact her act of revenge for the stabbing of her man had the beneficial result that it removed four footpads from the roads about here. I think she deserves to be left to her own conscience.'

Exeter, January, 1324

The little graves were a sad reminder of those days, he thought, as he looked down at them. On one side was the plain, simple cross of a monk; on the other was the more showy affair with the special sign etched into it.

Joseph rose from his prayers for the two men with a grunt as his knee seemed to lock. The cold wintry weather always had this result: the right knee would freeze, like a rusted hinge, and he would find it difficult to get up from his devotions. Now he must use a stick to hobble from here back to his hospital.

The two men were bold enough, he supposed. It was good of the knight from Furnshill to pay for their gravestones, but perhaps it was the sort of charitable gift a man like him would be expected to donate. Looking after those who had been on a journey and were assaulted on their way. It was a little disturbing to see that cross symbol, though, the mark of the Templars. Their Order had been disbanded because they were heretical and recusants. To have their Order's cross carved upon the gravestone felt almost sacrilegious – and yet Joseph couldn't begrudge it. The man himself had seemed a good man. He had saved Andrew's life, too, and that itself meant he deserved being remembered in a kindly light.

'Come in, Brother.'

'Thank you, thank you.'

Joseph hobbled inside and glanced about him at the beds. 'No customers, thank God.'

Andrew smiled. He was still a little bent from the after-effects of his wound, and the pain, and the reserved inward-looking expression, would never leave him, but he was content. 'No. No more strays, Brother.'

Joseph watched him from narrowed eyes. Yes, the lad would make a good lay brother. It was a shame that his woman would have to find a new lover, but that was the way of things. Those whom God called, and so on.

And what more clear call could there be, than that he should make a man touch a cursed relic and never be able to leave it behind? The relic was still in its box in Andrew's custody, secure. There had been a time when Joseph wondered whether it should be given to the bishop, but something made him hesitate. He had spoken to Sir Baldwin at length, and both thought that it would be best to keep the thing secret.

In any case, Andrew had touched the thing once, so he was cursed to keep it. If he relinquished it, he would die.

That was why he was here. He could have left the hospital to marry Annie, but the weight of this burden was too much to lay upon her.

No, rather than blight her life too, he would live

here for the rest of his life. Because he knew that if he left the hospital and gave up the relic, he would die. As surely as Will and Adam had died.

At least here he was safe.

ACT FOUR

Cambridge, late July 1353

The old friar closed his eyes and muttered a
prayer of relief when he saw the cluster of towers
and rooftops jutting above the distant line of
trees. His legs ached with weariness, and there was
a bitter, gnawing pain in his back that had been
growing steadily worse since Christmas. The
summer had been unpleasant for travelling,
starting with unseasonable gales and heavy rain,
and now there was the exhausting, searing heat
that drained his meagre supplies of energy. The
sun blazed high in cloudless skies, and even
farmers, who usually delighted in dry summers,
complained that their crops burned and that the
soil was baked too dry and hard. The friar glanced
at his companion, an eager, doggedly loyal novice
who had agreed to postpone his studies and go
with him on his long pilgrimage from their priory
in Exeter.

'It is not much farther now, Father Andrew,'
said the youngster kindly, seeing his master's
exhaustion. 'We will find a small, quiet hostel,
where you can regain your strength. And while
you do, I shall attend the public lectures given by
the scholars here – if any survived the plague, that

is. I heard the Death struck the universities very hard.'

'It did, Urban,' replied Andrew, recalling the bleak months some three years before, when a foul contagion had swept across the civilized world, claiming more victims than could be properly buried. 'It took every one of the Cambridge Dominicans, God rest their souls.'

'Is this our final destination?' asked Urban keenly, sensing in his elder a rare willingness to talk, and determined to make the most of it. 'Is this the end of our quest? Surely I have earned your trust by now, and you can tell me why we left Exeter in the depths of night and have been travelling on little-used pathways for months?'

'I trust you, Urban,' replied Andrew, knowing it was time he was honest, but unwilling to impose such a dreary burden on his youthful companion. 'That is why I asked you to accompany me – you were the novice who best suited my needs. I had intended to end my journey in Norwich, but I grow weaker with each passing day, and I am not sure whether I possess the strength to finish what I began. I may have to ask you to do it.'

'I will, Father,' said Urban, supposing the old man was paying him a compliment of sorts. Andrew was not an easy master, and there were times when he felt as though nothing he did was satisfactory. He was always compared unfavourably with another student, who had been everything a novice should be, and Urban often wondered whether he would ever meet Andrew's exacting standards. 'I promised obedience, and I will do what is necessary.'

'It will mean your death,' said Andrew, watching

alarm and then puzzlement flash in the young man's hazel eyes. 'Do you remember the rumours about our Holy Blood relic – the one under the high altar? It is said to carry a curse.'

Urban was startled by the mention of so odd a topic, but struggled to mask his reaction: he could not bear Andrew to think him stupid or unworldly. 'We – the novices – tease each other about it. We take a splinter of wood and thrust it into someone's hands, telling him he will die now that his bare skin has touched a piece of the True Cross stained with Christ's blood. It is all nonsense, of course. None of us really believes the story about it being cursed.'

As soon the words were out, Urban regretted them; Andrew was humourless, and would certainly disapprove of jokes about a relic, even one that was tainted with such a dubious reputation. He was unable to suppress the thought that Andrew's saintly former student would not have made light of such a subject, and that once again he, Urban, would be found lacking. To his surprise, Andrew did not issue a stream of reprimands.

'I am sure you heard about the Exeter murders,' Andrew said after a few moments. 'About how a Keeper of the King's Peace called Baldwin de Furnshill and his friend Simon Puttock discovered that four robbers had taken hold of the relic? They turned on each other, and three died in horrible ways. Eventually, it came to our priory in Exeter, which was chosen because it lies within the city walls, where it will be safe from thieves.'

Urban nodded slowly, wary now and unwilling to commit himself. He did not want to be accused of listening to the gossip of laymen who said bad things about their priory's only relic. 'But I do not believe them.'

Andrew gave the kind of grimace that passed for a smile on his pinched, lined face. 'I was the fourth thief, the one who survived,' he said softly. 'I saw it all. Indeed, the vile events in Devonshire all those years ago were why I gave up my secular life and took the cowl. My brother Rob and I were felons – God save my soul from the shameful iniquities of my youth – and I was rough and feckless. But I came to know the relic's power, and I wanted to be near it, to ensure it stayed where it was put, and that no one ever tried to steal it for dark purposes.'

Urban gazed at him. Here was part of the story he had not heard before. He had known his master had once been wild – some of the novices even claimed he had been an outlaw – but he had not realized that Andrew had played such an active role in the relic's history. It certainly explained why he had always spent so much time near the high altar, where the relic was hidden.

'I see,' he said, knowing his response was inadequate, but unable to find better words to express himself.

'And you know what happened next. Prior William de Regny sent me away as a minor envoy to distant places – Hungary and the land of the Bohemian kings – and I even studied in foreign universities.' Andrew gave a short bark of humourless laughter. 'My dim-witted brother would not have credited that I – his uncouth, loutish sibling – would become a scholar and an emissary! I was a teacher, too, grooming my best student to take my place in the university's hierarchy, before he . . . well, you know what happened with him. I took the relic with me, but I was never easy about its safety in such distant places, and after some years I brought it back to Devonshire again, to our little priory.'

'Yes, Father,' said Urban dutifully, wondering where the discussion was leading.

Andrew's expression was distant. 'It is powerful – more powerful than you can imagine – and it is genuine. Besides what I witnessed thirty years ago, there are two ancient parchments that carry its seal of authenticity.'

'I heard there were documents, but I did not think it was true.'

'It is true,' said Andrew with a conviction that surprised his novice. 'The fragment of the True Cross is in a vial, and the parchments are wrapped around it. Anyone can hold the glass, but to touch the stained splinter inside is certain death.'

Urban swallowed, and the bright sun seemed to lose some of its warmth. When a magpie chattered in a tree above his head, he jumped and found that his hands were shaking. Slowly, a nasty, unworthy suspicion began to form in his mind. 'Our priory has been the relic's guardian for years now. It is still there . . .'

Andrew rummaged under his habit and removed the purse he carried around his neck. The cord that held it was old and frayed, while the bag itself was sewn from cheap purple cloth, stained and worn from the actions of restless fingers. 'It is here.'

Urban was almost speechless, and fought hard against the urge to back away, appalled by what Andrew had done. 'You took it? You *stole* it?' All manner of questions suddenly found answers: the reason for their moonlit flight, the secrecy and orders to tell no one they were leaving, Andrew's refusal to say where they were going, the preference for little-travelled paths when the highways would have been faster and safer.

'It was for the best. My days are coming to an end, and the relic would not have been safe with our new prior. My duty was clear: I must convey it to Norwich, where there is another Holy Blood relic, and where the Benedictine monks will know how to keep this one from harming others.'

Urban was not convinced. Stealing was a mortal sin, but stealing a relic from a priory was an unimaginably wicked crime, and now he, Urban, was implicated in it. And Father Andrew, whom he had idolized and whose grim piety he had sought to emulate, was no more than a common thief. His thoughts whirled in confusion, and he felt betrayed. Andrew read the unhappiness and bewilderment on his face and touched his arm gently.

'I did what was right. Do not ask me how I know – perhaps God planted the knowledge there, because I assure you I would rather have spent my last days at home than traipsing across England – but I feel it with my whole being. Prior John de Burgo is not a believer in the power of blood relics – few men in our Order are – and I was afraid one of the tasks he would perform as he took up his new office would be to rid his priory of the anathema the relic has become.'

'The Master-General of the Dominicans did just that,' acknowledged Urban. He glanced uneasily at the bundle his master still held. 'He said Holy Blood relics cannot possibly exist for complex theological reasons that I do not understand, and he has ordered the destruction of what he terms "heretical idols of veneration".'

'I do not want this relic consigned to the fires of ignorance: what God has seen fit to place in our hands is not for man to burn. It is not a common Holy Blood relic, anyway: it is different, because of the curse it carries.'

'The curse,' mused Urban. 'Is it true that a dragon bewitched it, in the days of King Arthur?'

'Do not be ridiculous,' replied Andrew curtly. 'Dragons cannot speak. The Knights Templar took the relic into their care, and I learned its history from one of them, a man named John Mantravers, of South Witham. He saved my life.'

'But the Knights Templar were suppressed, and their leaders executed years ago,' said Urban, uneasy with the notion that Andrew had cavorted with heretics.

'Some refused to renounce their Order, and Mantravers was one of them. He told me that this piece of the True Cross was once in the possession of an Arab called Barzak, whose duty it was to protect it from infidels. When our blessed Crusaders liberated the Holy City, Barzak uttered a violent curse when his family were considered enemies and slaughtered. But his curse was too strong, and it became the bane of good men, as well as bad. Prior John de Burgo is a case in point: he is not wicked, but if he had taken hold of the thing to "prove" it holds no power, it would have meant his death regardless.'

'So, you decided to take it to Norwich and give it to the Benedictines,' surmised Urban. 'They do not hate Holy Blood relics, and will treat it with the reverence it is due. You did the right thing, Father.'

Andrew nodded, relieved that the novice had been so easy to convince. He had anticipated all manner of recriminations – he was sure he himself would not have been so readily accepting, had their roles been reversed. 'Before I took it, I removed it from its vial, to make sure it was the same splinter that caused Mantravers all his trouble. It would have been a pity to arrive in Norwich and discover it had been exchanged at some point. I had to be sure.'

Urban gazed at him. 'But that means . . .' He trailed off, not liking to give voice to the awful conclusion.

Andrew nodded. 'It means I will die as soon as I relinquish it from my keeping. But I grow weaker with each passing day anyway, so it matters little now. However, I may be obliged to ask you to carry it for the last stage of its journey.'

'But if the relic's curse is genuine, then I may die, too.'

'Only if you remove the splinter from its vial.'

'Then I will not touch it,' said Urban, relieved. 'I will keep it wrapped up.'

Andrew stopped walking and opened the pouch, carefully removing the tiny box that held the small tube of glass, green and misty with age. Urban gazed at it in fascination, then stepped back sharply when Andrew removed the gilt stopper and slid the contents into his hand. The relic was not much to look at – just a rough piece of silvery-grey timber with a curious stain blackening one end.

Andrew held it up between thumb and forefinger. 'That will not be enough, Urban. Only if you truly believe in the relic's power will you see your quest through to the end. You must hold it in your hand and feel its strength. If you are not up to the task, then tell me, and I will recruit another servant. Cambridge has friaries and convents a-plenty, so it should not be too difficult to find a substitute.'

Urban was stung by the notion that he could be so easily discarded. 'Of course I shall do as you ask,' he cried. 'I vowed to carry out your wishes, and I will do so as long as there is breath in my body. *I* will not abandon you.'

This last comment was spiteful, and Urban was ashamed when he saw Andrew wince. The old friar's former favourite, on realizing he had learned all he could from Andrew, had left him for other, more knowledgeable masters, and Urban knew he had considered it a betrayal. It was unkind to have made such a remark, and he regretted it immediately.

Andrew rested his wrinkled hand on the younger man's shoulder, partly for support and partly as a gesture of affection. 'I know. I have every faith in you. Hold out your hand.'

Urban shuddered as Andrew moved the stained wood towards him.

Cambridge, a few days later

Brother Michael was blissfully unaware that his fine Benedictine habit would never be the same again. He held forth knowledgeably on all manner of subjects as he shared the Dominicans' excellent dinner, and did not notice that his audience was looking not at him, but at his right shoulder. His colleague, Matthew Bartholomew, had tried several times to draw his attention to the problem, but had been silenced by a dismissive wave of the monk's fat white hand. Michael did not like to be interrupted when he was of a mind to be erudite.

'So, to conclude my thesis,' he said pompously, revelling in the fact that no one had challenged his arguments for almost an hour, 'I concur with the great theologian Francis de Meyronnes. During the three days between our Lord's death and His resurrection, some of His blood became separated from His body and remained on Earth. Ergo, no relic containing Holy Blood is united to His divinity, just as it was not united to His divinity during the three days in the tomb. The blood of the mass, which *is* fully joined to His divinity, is thus far more worthy of veneration. However, this is not to say that Holy Blood relics are to be shunned – on the contrary, they are sacred and vital reminders of Christ's resurrection and man's subsequent redemption.'

He sat back, pleased with the elegance of his reasoning and certain that the Cambridge Dominicans would be unable to refute what he had said. He reached out with his knife and speared a roasted chicken, dragging it towards him and clearly intent on devouring the whole thing, despite the fact that the friars had already laid down their spoons and were waiting for the final grace. Michael was a large man, who used his position as the university's senior proctor to inveigle invitations to some of the finest meals in Cambridge. It had been several days since his last grand repast, however, and so he was enjoying himself more than usual.

He had been summoned to the Dominican priory that day because one of its student novices had been involved in a fight – as Senior Proctor, Michael was obliged to investigate all incidents of violence among the university's scholars. He had taken Bartholomew with him, anticipating that his friend's skills as Master of Medicine might be required. The novice's injuries were not serious, but Prior Morden was grateful for the physician's services nonetheless, and had invited them to dine before they returned to their own college of Michaelhouse. Bartholomew, who had other patients to tend, started to decline, but Michael knew that the Dominicans ate well, and had accepted the offer before he could speak; the monk was acutely aware that the Black Friars' supper would be far superior to anything on offer at Michaelhouse.

Prior Morden cleared his throat uncomfortably, and glanced at his assembled friars. He was a tiny man, so small he needed cushions on his chair to allow him to reach the table, and he had an odd habit of swinging his legs back and forth while he ate. It was fortunate they were short limbs, or his colleagues would have suffered cruelly from his vigorous kicks.

'Well,' he said eventually, his eyes straying from the monk's flushed, greasy face to the vicinity of his right shoulder. 'I see.'

Bartholomew could have told Michael he was wasting his time expounding to the Dominicans, who were known to be the least academically minded of the many religious orders that had gathered around the university in Cambridge. Morden had rashly mentioned an old chronicle in his library, however, which described an event in 1247: the third King Henry had presented Westminster

Abbey with a phial containing blood from Christ's passion. A violent debate was currently raging between Dominicans and Franciscans about the nature of Holy Blood, and whether it should or should not be venerated, and Michael had come down firmly on the side of the Franciscans. Bartholomew did not find the subject an especially engaging one, so kept what few thoughts he had on the issue to himself – there were far more fascinating topics to debate, and he felt it a waste to expend energy on a matter about which he was indifferent.

None of the Dominicans had spoken for some time, and the physician suspected they had understood very little of Michael's complex analysis. Technically, Prior Morden and his friars should have been hammering on the tables with their pewter goblets, shrieking that the monk had spoken heresy within their halls. It would be what their order expected of them. But most had been more interested in their food than the monk's erudite postulations, and Bartholomew sensed that they were bored by the monologue and wished their guest would talk about the murders he had solved or the disgraceful price of grain. Only one Black Friar looked as though he had followed what the monk had said, but he sat at that part of the table reserved for visitors, and was too polite to speak when he had not been invited to do so by his hosts.

Michael's eyes narrowed, and he paused with a chicken leg halfway to his mouth. 'Is that all you have to say? I think my assessment of the nature of Holy Blood warrants a more in-depth response than "I see". Do you not agree, Matt?'

'That theologian you kept citing,' said Morden, before Bartholomew could formulate a suitably non-committal answer. 'Meyronnes. I may be wrong, but I thought he was a Franciscan.'

Michael gazed at him, barely crediting that he should make such an observation when the name Meyronnes was on the lips of every scholar even remotely familiar with contemporary scholastic debate. Even Bartholomew, who was not at all interested in the controversy, knew its leading protagonists and the stances they had outlined. 'Yes,' he said warily. 'What of it?'

'Franciscans know nothing of theology,' said Morden matter-of-factly, sounding relieved that he had got something right. 'So, your thesis will be fatally flawed if you use *him* to prove your points.'

Michael sighed. Rivalry between the Orders was intense, particularly between Franciscans and Dominicans, and it was not unknown for scholars to dismiss entire schools of thought merely on the basis of who had proposed them. He saw, somewhat belatedly, that he would have to simplify his ideas if he wanted a sensible response from Morden and his slow-minded minions.

'The blood relics polemic challenges some of the most basic tenets of our faith,' he said, trying not to sound testy – he did not want to jeopardize future dining opportunities by revealing his disdain. 'It concerns whether samples of Holy Blood – the most famous of which can be found at Hailes and Ashridge – should be venerated. The Franciscans say they should, your Order claims they should not.'

'Well,' said Morden again, still looking puzzled.

His eyes dipped to Michael's shoulder, and he rubbed a hand across his mouth. 'We would of course say no, if the Franciscans say yes: it is only natural we should disagree. Christ's blood is *not* holy, then – none of it, not a drop.'

'But think, man!' said Michael, becoming exasperated, despite his best intentions. 'If you claim Holy Blood should not be venerated, then what does that say about the mass? You venerate the blood of Christ every day, so some of it must be sacred.'

'Oh,' said Morden, perplexed. 'Well, if you put it like that, then I suppose it must be all right to revere these blood relics. However, as you have just pointed out, there are very few of them in existence. Most cannot be authenticated, and only Hailes and Ashridge have real ones.'

'That is not true,' said Bartholomew. Even he, a disinterested listener, was unwilling to allow such a wildly inaccurate statement to pass unchallenged. 'There are flasks of Holy Blood in shrines all over the country. I hear some liquefy on special occasions, while others are associated with miracles.'

Michael's attention was fixed on the hapless prior. 'If you accept that blood relics *should* be venerated, then you are saying that the Franciscans are right and your own Order is wrong.'

'I am not,' said Morden, affronted. 'I would never say the Franciscans are right! You are twisting my words with this complex theology.'

'It is complex,' agreed the visiting friar, apparently unable to bear the savaging any longer. He, too, addressed his comments to the monk's shoulder, and the monk glanced behind him briefly, half expecting someone to be there. 'And

307

theologians from both Orders are proposing fascinating arguments.'

Morden remembered his manners and made
some introductions, waving a tiny hand towards the
visitor. 'This is Brother Tomas from the university
at Pécs. He says Pécs is near the Mediterranean
Sea, although I have never heard of it. He arrived
recently to read about angels.'

Tomas's southern origins explained his dark,
somewhat foreign looks and the lilting quality to
his Latin. Bartholomew smiled at him, intrigued to
meet a scholar who had travelled so far from home.
'I understand Pécs has an unrivalled collection of
Arabic texts on natural philosophy,' he said.

Tomas returned the smile. 'It has, and we—'

'Well, I am pleased you came,' interrupted
Michael, rubbing his hands together. 'Oxford is
making a name for itself with brilliant arguments
on the Holy Blood debate, but our own Franciscans
are sorely hampered by the fact that these
Dominicans rarely challenge their intellects. Now
you are here, we can enter the arena and show the
world the quality of our thinkers. Well, the quality
of some of them, at least,' he corrected himself,
shooting a disparaging glance at Morden.

'I would be woefully inadequate,' said Tomas
modestly. 'Especially since Master Witney of Grey
Hall in Oxford is studying in Cambridge this term
– he is one of the Franciscans' acknowledged
experts on blood relics, and I cannot compete with
him. He is staying at Bernard's Hostel, where I am
told the university houses its most auspicious
visiting scholars.'

While Michael reduced his chicken to a pile of
bones, Tomas began a careful refutation of the

monk's thesis, punctuated by the occasional and wholly unnecessary apology for his lack of understanding – he was a skilled disputant, and his knowledge of the material was detailed and sound. Despite the fact that he was restoring the Dominicans' intellectual honour, his brethren grew restless, and some shot meaningful glances to where the day was wasting outside. Morden kicked his legs in a way that suggested he was equally bored, and then his eyes dropped to Michael's right arm for the last time. He could stand it no more.

'Did you know there is a fish-head on your shoulder, Brother?' he asked. 'It is difficult to discuss theology when we have something like *that* leering at us.'

Michael glanced to one side, then leapt to his feet at the sight of dull piscine eyes staring at him from such close quarters. He flailed furiously at the offending object, sending it skittering across the table, where it dropped into Morden's lap. The prior, equally repelled, flicked it towards the floor, although one of his feet caught it as it fell and sent it cartwheeling towards Tomas. The visiting friar ducked with impressively quick reactions, and the missile sailed harmlessly over his head to slap into a wall before plummeting to the ground. Michael glowered at the servants behind him, who struggled to remain impassive. One was less adept at hiding his amusement than the others, and the monk rounded on him.

'I wondered why I was the only one to be served a trout whose head was missing. Now I know. You deliberately set out to embarrass me.'

'It was not deliberate,' objected the man,

attempting to appear chastened and failing miserably. Bartholomew was sure the tale would be told with relish at his favourite tavern that night.

'I am sure Roughe meant no harm,' said Tomas soothingly. 'Those trays are heavy, and supporting them with one hand and serving with the other cannot be easy.'

'Roughe,' said Michael, continuing to glare. 'Where have I heard that name before?'

'It was a man called Roughe who started the fight with Bulmer – the novice I have just tended for his swollen jaw,' replied Bartholomew.

'That was my brother,' said Roughe quickly. 'I am John, and it was Kip who punched Bulmer. That skirmish had nothing to do with me.'

'Perhaps,' said Michael coldly. 'But I—'

He stopped speaking at a sudden commotion outside. Someone was shouting, then came the sound of running footsteps. The door was flung open, and a friar stood there. He was extraordinarily ugly, with eyes that glided in different directions, a face deeply indented with pock marks, and oily hair that hung in unattractive wisps around his flaky scalp.

'Father Prior!' he yelled. 'News!'

Morden frowned. 'I have warned you before about making this sort of entry, Big Thomas. You are supposed to come in quietly, and whisper your message, so only I can hear it. You do not bellow it for the world at large. You are a friar now, and your days as a braying thatcher are over.'

'*Big* Thomas?' asked Bartholomew. The man was not particularly large.

'He is taller than our visitor from Pécs.' Morden lowered his voice. 'It is kinder than Handsome

Tomas and Ugly Thomas, which was how the brethren instantly started to differentiate between them.'

'News from St Bernard's Hostel,' shouted Big Thomas. 'A man there has been smothered by soot!'

Because St Bernard's Hostel was university property, a death within its walls came under the Senior Proctor's jurisdiction. Wiping his greasy lips on a piece of linen, Michael left the Dominicans and made his way to the High Street. Bartholomew walked at his side, wondering what grisly sight he would be assailed with this time. Michael often used him when he investigated deaths, and appreciated the insight he could offer when he inspected a corpse. It was not a duty he enjoyed, however, and he much preferred tending living patients to dead ones.

'Strange men, the Black Friars,' the monk mused. 'I enthral them with my incisive comments pertaining to the holiness – or otherwise – of blood relics, and all they do is point out that some of my ideas came from Franciscans. Still, Tomas of Pécs seemed a cut above the rest of them.'

Bartholomew agreed. 'I could tell from the expression on his face that he followed your arguments, and the speed of his reaction when that fish-head sailed towards him was very impressive. I suspect there is more to him than a mere student of angels, no matter what he would have us believe.'

'Perhaps he is here to spy on his fellows over the Holy Blood debate,' suggested Michael. 'It is becoming very heated in places like Spain, with accusations of heresy screeched from all quarters. After all, he *did* know all about the visiting Oxford Franciscan and his chosen subject of study.'

Bartholomew was thoughtful. 'Someone pointed out that Oxford friar – Witney – to me the other day. He is here with a companion, also from Grey Hall.'

'Why should Witney be singled out for comment and identification?'

'Because, at the time, he was engaged in a vicious and very public squabble outside King's Hall. Everyone was looking at him, and Chancellor Tynkell, who had cornered me for a remedy for indigestion, told me who he was. He said we are honoured to have him in Cambridge, although Witney's language during that particular quarrel could hardly be described as scholarly.'

'With whom was he arguing?' demanded Michael, peeved that the information had not been shared with him. He was Senior Proctor, and should have been the first to know about eminent academics arriving in his town.

'With Big Thomas, although it is an unlikely pairing – an eminent theologian and a one-time thatcher. Thomas and Witney were bawling at each other like fishmongers, and Witney's companion was powerless to stop them. Thomas seems to like screaming at people: he just hollered at Morden in much the same way.'

'Fighting in public places is against university rules,' said Michael angrily. 'You should have mentioned this sooner.'

'They were quarrelling, not fighting – about thatching, would you believe? But then Little

Tomas arrived, and he succeeded in quietening them. The incident ended peacefully enough.'

They arrived at St Bernard's, which stood opposite the recently founded Bene't College on the High Street. It comprised three houses that had been knocked into one, providing a hall with two teaching chambers on the ground floor, and several smaller rooms above in which visiting scholars were accommodated.

A servant answered the door, and ushered Michael and Bartholomew into the smaller of the two lower-floor rooms. It smelled of wood smoke and the oil that had been used to make benches and tables shine. At the far end, by the hearth, stood three men. As Bartholomew approached, he was immediately aware of a tension between them. One stood apart from the others. He was tall, his grey hair was neatly trimmed, and he wore the habit of a Franciscan. He held himself stiffly, clearly furious. He was Witney's companion, the man who had been unable to calm his colleague during the spat with the loud-mouthed thatcher.

The other two were a Carmelite and his apprentice. The White Friar was elderly and frail, and Bartholomew did not think he had ever seen more haunted eyes. His novice was burly and young, with thick yellow hair and the kind of face that did not seem made for priestly solemnity.

There was a fourth man in the room, too, whom Bartholomew had not immediately noticed, and who looked as though he was about to climb up inside the chimney. His head and shoulders were out of sight, while his body and legs, clad in the robes of a Franciscan, were stretched across the floor. It was Witney. As the physician drew closer, he saw soot had cascaded downward, leaving a dirty black residue over the fine wooden floor. Horrified, he hurried forward and grabbed the prone legs, hauling the body out of the fireplace. Dust billowed in all directions, causing the three onlookers and Michael to jump back, in order to avoid being coated in filth. The Oxford scholar became angrier still.

'Have a care!' he shouted, brushing himself down. 'You should have removed him gently, so you did not scatter grime over the rest of us.'

'He might have been alive,' objected Bartholomew, although he could see that Witney's rescue from the choking embrace of the hearth had come far too late. The open eyes were clotted with powder, which also clogged his nose and mouth. Blackened though the face was, Bartholomew could still make out an unnatural blueness there. He also noticed blood at the back of the skull, where something heavier than soot had landed on it.

'He would not have been alive,' said the novice. 'Not after what *he* did.'

'What do you mean?' asked Michael. 'And who are you, anyway?'

'Urban,' replied the youngster. He gestured to his elderly companion. 'And this is Father Andrew, my teacher. We travelled here from Devonshire.'

'Speak when you are asked,' said Andrew sharply. The novice's pained grimace indicated he was used to such admonitions but that he had not yet learned to bear them with grace. 'It is not for you to make introductions.'

'*My* name is John Seton and *I* am Master of Grey Hall in Oxford,' said the Franciscan, in the kind of voice that indicated he considered himself superior to mere Carmelites. He gestured to the body. 'And this is my colleague, Peter of Witney. He has been murdered.' His cool glance in Andrew's direction made it clear whom he considered his prime suspect.

'And *I* am the university's Senior Proctor,' said Michael coolly. 'It is for me and Dr Bartholomew to determine your colleague's cause of death.' He turned to Bartholomew. 'Has he been murdered? I see a cut on his head.'

'That was caused when this stone struck his skull,' replied Bartholomew, holding up the offending piece of masonry for the monk to see. He demonstrated how its square edge fitted perfectly into the jagged gash on the dead man's head, although neither Michael nor the other three paid close attention to the grisly illustration.

Seton pointed an accusing finger at Andrew. 'That stone was wielded by *him*. He has been hostile towards poor Witney ever since we arrived. It is clear what happened here, Brother. Arrest the Carmelite and let us make an end of this unhappy business.'

'There are questions I want answered first,' replied Michael, raising one hand to stall the litany of objections that started to burst from Urban. Andrew made no attempt to deny the accusations, and merely stood regarding the dead man dispassionately. 'This is Cambridge, not Oxford. We are rather more civilized here, and do not go around arresting men before we have properly examined the evidence. Matt: what can you tell me?'

'The stone probably dropped down the chimney,' replied Bartholomew, peering up the dark funnel and noting that it was not in good repair. 'But the injury is not serious enough to have killed him outright. I imagine he breathed his last inhaling the soot that came with it. In other words, he was stunned by the blow, and was insensible to the fact that the soot was choking him.'

'Someone did not hit him, then shove him *and* the stone up the chimney to make it look as though the death was an accident?' asked Michael.

Bartholomew shook his head. 'From the juxtaposition of stone, soot and body, there are only two possibilities: either Witney was looking up the chimney when it collapsed, or someone climbed on the roof and dropped the stone when he happened to be underneath. You will agree that it would have to be a very patient killer for the latter to be true.'

'Witney was not in the habit of peering up chimneys,' said Seton angrily. 'He was a scholar, like me. He was here to study, not to prod about inside hearths.'

'He was not always devoted to his studies,' said Andrew softly. 'He spent a lot of time walking around churches, looking at relics.'

'So?' demanded Seton, outraged by what sounded like an accusation. 'He was interested in them. It is not a crime.'

'Perhaps,' replied Andrew non-committally. 'But perhaps not.'

'Now you listen to me,' began Seton hotly. 'You cannot—'

'Wait for me in your chamber, Master Seton,' interrupted Michael. 'I will see your colleague is removed to St Botolph's Church and decently laid out. Then I will hear your complaints.'

Seton scowled at the Carmelites before snatching up his hat and stalking away.

Father Andrew smiled wanly after Seton had gone. 'Divide and conquer: that is one of the first lessons I learned when dealing with unruly lads – I once held a post similar to yours, Brother. Separate the factions and speak to them apart. Of course, sometimes it is wiser to let them argue, so that one may make a fatal slip and reveal himself a villain.'

'Is there a villain here?' asked Michael, raising his eyebrows. 'Or just a case of a man being in the wrong place at the wrong time?'

'There *is* a villain,' replied Andrew with considerable conviction. 'But it is not a man.' He fumbled with something tied around his neck with a leather thong. It was a pouch made of ancient purple cloth, and looked like the kind of amulet carried by peasants too superstitious to place their faith entirely in the Church. Thinking it was being proffered to him, Michael reached out to take it, but the friar drew back sharply.

'You must not touch it,' explained Urban. 'If you do, you will die – just as Witney has done. Father Andrew's relic is the reason for our long journey: we are taking it to the abbey at Norwich, where similar holy items are held.'

'Urban!' snapped Andrew. 'What have I told you about speaking before you are asked?'

Urban sighed, and pulled the kind of face that indicated he thought the story would be told sooner or later anyway, and that he had just saved everyone a good deal of trouble. He went to stand near the window, making Bartholomew wonder whether he craved distance from his difficult teacher or from the corpse that lay next to the hearth, eyes still gazing sightlessly at the ceiling.

'A relic?' asked Michael, regarding the pouch uneasily. 'You are wearing a relic around your neck? That is unwise: real ones do not like being used like charms.'

'You are right,' replied Andrew. 'And this is an especially powerful one that comes with a curse for all those who dare to lay hands on it.'

'Relics cannot be cursed,' said Bartholomew immediately. 'They are holy. A malediction would render yours *un*holy, which means it cannot be a relic. What you are saying is a theological impossibility.'

Andrew ignored him. 'An Arab called Barzak set the spell after the first of the Crusades. I saw its power thirty years ago in Devonshire, while Urban will tell you a story about a long-dead coroner called John de Wolfe and how death surrounded him when he encountered its power.'

'And there was Master Falconer, the Oxford philosopher,' added Urban eagerly. 'He saw it—' He fell silent as Andrew's stern gaze settled on him again.

The old man's glare shifted to Bartholomew, who was looking openly sceptical. 'Barzak's evil oath has been active for centuries, and anyone who touches the sacred wood contained in this vial will die.'

'You have touched it,' Michael pointed out, although he made no attempt to move closer to the friar. He was not a superstitious man, but it was not unknown for relics to be dangerous, and it seemed a pity to end a glorious university career for the want of a little caution. 'But you are not dead.'

'I will be,' replied Andrew calmly. 'As soon as it

leaves my possession – either when I deliver it to Norwich, or when I am obliged to entrust another man to take it there.' He gestured to Urban, to indicate that the novice could speak if he liked.

'Evil men are killed quickly,' elaborated Urban obligingly. Michael edged away, unsure of how he stood in respect of his virtue in the eyes of God and His saints. 'But good ones are permitted to carry it to a place where it will be safe. It has rested with Father Andrew for nigh on three decades, mostly in Exeter.'

'Then why choose now to move it?' demanded Michael. 'And why inflict it on Cambridge first?'

'It was not our intention to bring trouble to your town,' replied Andrew apologetically. 'And you are right to question my timing: I waited too long, and should have carried it to a safe place years ago. But I was happy in Exeter, and the relic was safe enough, lodged in the altar of a priory within the city's great walls, and it is difficult for a content man to decide to end his life.'

'But then a new prior was appointed,' continued Urban. 'And Father Andrew is afraid he might destroy it. We do not want it burned, and nor did we want Prior John de Burgo to die trying to demonstrate that it has no power.'

'I see,' said Michael flatly. 'This is quite a tale. And what is this relic, exactly? We had a lock of the Virgin's hair once, but it disappeared.'

'It is a fragment of the True Cross, stained with Holy Blood.' Andrew opened the pouch and withdrew two pieces of parchment. He proffered them to the monk, but Michael gripped his wrist and moved it into the light, taking great care not to touch the documents himself.

'This says it was found in Jerusalem,' he said, scanning the meagre contents of the first. 'In the Church of the Holy Sepulchre, and it is authenticated by Geoffrey Mappestone, Knight. The second is a warning by Guillaume de Beaujeu, who says the relic was bought with innocent blood and is utterly cursed. "Any man who touches the fragment of Holy Cross will die as soon as the relic is relinquished."'

'Guillaume de Beaujeu was a Grand Master of the Knights Templar,' said Bartholomew, recalling the sorry history of that order. 'It must be genuine, then.'

'It *is* genuine,' said Andrew quietly. 'I have an ancient wound that pains me, and I feel myself becoming weaker with every day that passes. I *must* leave for Norwich tomorrow. I do not want to press my burden on Urban.'

'I do not mind, Father,' said Urban bravely.

Bartholomew glanced at him, wondering whether he was a little too eager. Did he believe in Barzak's curse? Or did he see Andrew's weakness as a means to gain hold of something that was obviously valuable? Many abbeys and priories were willing to pay veritable fortunes for relics, and the crumbling parchments indicated that this one was as authentic as most. Even if it had not performed miracles when it was first purchased, he knew it was only a matter of time before unscrupulous or malleable men started to spread stories to the contrary. And then there would be pilgrims; pilgrims left donations, and they needed inns, food and clothes. Many people would grow rich once a relic had produced a few timely cures.

'I know, Urban,' said Andrew kindly. His expression became wistful. 'I had that honour in mind for another man, but he betrayed me years ago.'

Michael waited, expecting him to elaborate, but the Carmelite merely sat on a bench and began to put his relic away. The monk moved the discussion along, to mask the fact that he did not know what to think about the curious tale.

'All this is very interesting, but what does your relic have to do with Witney?'

'He tried to steal it,' replied Urban. 'He discovered what Father Andrew carries so close to his heart, and he was determined to have it for himself. He weaselled his way into our confidence, and when Father Andrew showed it to him, he tried to grab it.'

'He used a knife to slice through the thong,' explained Andrew, showing Michael a bright new cut across the dark leather strap. 'He was almost out of the door before Urban wrestled him to the ground. While they struggled, I managed to retrieve it. However, before I did, the stopper came loose and the relic fell out. It brushed Witney's arm when he and Urban were rolling across the floor.'

'Are you saying Witney died because he touched a relic?' asked Bartholomew, seeing the direction in which the explanation was heading. He had witnessed enough murder and mayhem since qualifying as a physician to know that people were capable of all manner of vile acts, and he was always sceptical when suspects tried to blame suspicious deaths on supernatural phenomena.

'Of course,' said Andrew. 'And now I must take it to Norwich before anyone else pays such a high price for his greed or his curiosity. You cannot arrest me – although I accept responsibility for

Witney's death – because more people will die if I do not fulfil my obligations.'

'No,' said Michael firmly. 'You will stay here until I am satisfied no crime took place. Perhaps this relic did take Witney's life because he dared lay profane fingers on it, but perhaps his sudden demise has a more earthly explanation. Either way, I intend to find out.'

'Why did Witney want it?' asked Bartholomew. 'To sell?'

'He is – was – a Franciscan, and if you know about the Holy Blood polemic, then you will be aware of the stance the Grey Friars have taken on the matter. No doubt he saw one in the hands of a poor Carmelite, and was afraid I would destroy it – or worse, give it to the Dominicans.'

'I do not think he believed us when we said we were taking it to the Benedictines for safe-keeping,' added Urban. 'Personally, I think he intended to sell it and keep the profit for himself. You can tell from his expensive habit that he was a worldly sort of man.'

'Where were you when he died?' asked Michael, turning to more practical matters. 'And where was Seton?'

'We were in our sleeping chamber on the floor above – my old wound was aching, and Urban was reading to me while I rested,' replied Andrew. 'Then we heard a hissing sound, followed by a thump. We came to investigate, but we were not surprised to find Witney dead. He had touched the relic, so it was only a matter of time before Barzak's curse claimed him.'

'He died from a lack of timely help,' countered Bartholomew tartly. 'If he had been pulled from the chimney immediately, he would not have choked.'

'Then *Seton* should have done it,' said Urban. 'He was here first. When we arrived, he was standing over Witney's body like a crow over carrion. Then he accused *us* of killing him, when it was God.'

'God,' mused Bartholomew. 'It is astonishing how often He is blamed for things men have done.'

Andrew ignored him, and turned to Michael, who represented a more sympathetic ear. 'I promise to do all I can to help with your investigation, Brother, although you will find no earthly cause for Witney's death. I will stay three days, but then I must go, or you will be adding more names to the list of those whom the relic has claimed.'

'The Carmelite and his novice are lying,' said Seton angrily, as he paced back and forth in the chamber he had shared with his Franciscan comrade. 'Witney *did* have an interest in relics, but it was an academic fascination – he is one of our order's leading proponents in the Holy Blood debate, so of course his curiosity was piqued when they claimed to possess such an object. But he would never have tried to steal one. Their story is preposterous.'

'So what do you think happened to him?' asked Michael.

Seton sighed. 'It is obvious. Urban and Andrew killed him, and now they have invented this outrageous tale about ancient curses to cover their tracks. You are an intelligent man, Brother. Surely you are not taken in by this nonsense?'

'I shall reserve judgement until I have all the

facts. Is that why Witney was here? To pick fine Cambridge minds about the Holy Blood polemic?'

Seton sneered. 'Hardly! There are none worth picking – on Holy Blood or anything else. Our visit has been a sad disappointment so far.'

Michael's expression was cold. He disliked outsiders denigrating his colleagues, although he did it himself regularly. 'Why are you here? To study what, exactly?'

'Angels – although I do not see what that has to do with my colleague's murder.'

'Angels,' mused Bartholomew thoughtfully. 'Brother Tomas of Pécs is here to investigate angels.'

'*He* is a Dominican,' replied Seton contemptuously.

'His knowledge about angels is lacking?' asked Bartholomew curiously. If that were true, then there would indeed be something odd about Tomas: he would know a good deal about the blood relic debate, but less about the subject in which he claimed to specialize.

Seton backed down. 'Perhaps I spoke hastily. He has studied different texts to me, which I suppose is not surprising, considering he hails from a foreign school.'

'Tell me what happened when you found Witney dead,' said Michael, more interested in the victim than in an irrelevant visiting scholar's academic skills.

'I was out – looking for Tomas, actually. He can often be found in St Andrew's Church at this time of day, and I was hoping to talk to him.'

'Why did you want to do that?' asked

Bartholomew. 'You have just implied you consider his intellect inferior.'

Seton regarded him as though he were lacking in wits himself. 'Of course he is inferior! He is a foreigner – not even from a civilized country like France or Spain – and a Dominican into the bargain. But I wanted to ask whether he knew where I might find a copy of Grosseteste's *De dotibus*. Although he has only been here a few days, he already knows his way around the libraries.'

'*De dotibus* is not about angels.' Bartholomew pounced. 'It is a short tract on the various aspects and qualities of resurrection.'

'You are a physician, not a theologian, so do not make assumptions about matters you cannot possibly understand,' snapped Seton, becoming nettled. 'Of course angels relate to issues pertaining to resurrection. Besides, it is none of your affair why I want a particular book.'

'And did you meet Tomas?' asked Michael, raising a hand to prevent Bartholomew from responding. The point was irrelevant to Witney's death, and he did not want to waste time on it.

'No, and when I returned, I found Andrew and Urban in that hall, and Witney was . . .' He trailed off with a shudder.

'You were out when Witney died?' asked Michael, to be sure.

'Why? Did that pair claim otherwise? You can check my story, because I was seen in St Andrew's Church by several people. I do not know their names, because I am a stranger here, but I spoke to an ink-seller and three Franciscans from the Cambridge friary. They will confirm I was out when Witney was murdered.'

'What did Andrew and Urban say when you found them with Witney's corpse?' asked Bartholomew, wondering which of them was lying – and someone was, because the stories conflicted. Seton was arrogant and overbearing, Andrew was deeply convinced of his own rectitude and Urban was blindly loyal. None of them could be trusted to tell the truth.

'They said nothing. When I saw it was Witney, I accused them of killing him – a servant must have heard us arguing and sent for you. What will you do, Brother? You cannot allow them to leave when it is clear they have committed a grave sin.'

'They can go nowhere without my permission,' replied Michael. 'So, you claim Witney never attacked Andrew and made a grab for his True Cross?'

'Of course not! Why would he do such a thing? And do not say to sell, because we are Franciscan friars, and not in the business of peddling relics. We leave that sort of thing to the Dominicans – when they do not destroy them in a frenzy of righteous bigotry, of course. But we are veering away from the point: those two Carmelites killed Witney. Urban could easily have climbed to the roof and made noises to attract Witney to the hearth. Then, when his head appeared, the stone was dropped that led to his stunning and subsequent suffocation.'

'You said he was not the kind of man to peer up chimneys,' Bartholomew pointed out.

Seton sighed. 'He would have investigated odd sounds. We all would. But he was a good, pious man, who has been brutally slain, and the angels will not rest until his death is avenged. I know angels and how they think.'

'I will not rest, either, if what you say is true,' promised Michael, not to be outdone by celestials. 'But why would Urban and Andrew want Witney dead? They have no motive.'

'They do,' countered Seton. 'Did they not tell you? He was about to expose them as charlatans – them and their so-called True Cross.'

'How so?'

'By logical analysis. He listened to their story – that the relic hailed from the Church of the Holy Sepulchre after the first of the Crusades, and that it was cursed by a Mohammedan called Barzak. But there is no written evidence that our Church has *ever* laid claim to a supply of Holy Blood from Jerusalem – if it had, then it would have been taken to Rome or Constantinople, years before the Crusades.'

'That is impossible to prove . . .' warned Michael, thinking the supposition unsound, to say the least.

'It is very simple to prove,' countered Seton. 'No blood – soaked into the True Cross or anything else – came from the Holy Sepulchre. It is a lie, perpetrated by greedy and unprincipled men. Did you see the parchments they claim authenticate the thing?'

Michael nodded. 'One was ancient, and bore the seal of a bishop.'

'It probably is old,' agreed Seton. 'It was signed by a knight named Geoffrey Mappestone, who then affixed the seal of the Bishop of Durham.'

'So?' asked Michael, not understanding the man's point.

Seton made a moue of impatience. 'So the Bishop of Durham at that time was *not* Mappestone, but a man named Ranulf Flambard.

Flambard never set foot in the Holy Land – we know about his life from ecclesiastical records – and so could *never* have set his seal on this document. And if the relic were real, do you not think it would have been venerated at Flambard's own cathedral at Durham? But no! Andrew's splinter has been hidden in an obscure priory in Exeter. If you view it with an unbiased, dispassionate mind, you will see the whole thing is ridiculous.'

Bartholomew thought he might well be right. There were enough 'genuine' pieces of the True Cross to crucify the King's entire army, and fragments could be bought for pennies, although to claim this one was stained with Holy Blood made it a little unusual. If Witney was about to expose Andrew and his acolyte as charlatans, however, – and perhaps deprive them of a handsome gift from a grateful Norwich abbey – then it was certainly a good motive for murder.

'That pair killed my colleague,' reiterated Seton firmly. He wrinkled his nose suddenly, and looked around him with disapproval. 'Ever since you arrived, I have been unable to get the stench of fish from my nose. Do you smell it, too?'

'No,' said Michael sharply, brushing his shoulder.

'What do you think, Matt?' asked Michael, as he and Bartholomew left St Bernard's Hostel and started to walk to Michaelhouse together. It was almost dark, although the western sky was still tinged pink by the summer sun.

Because it was summer, many folk had been labouring in the fields outside the town, harvesting grain before the fine weather broke. Too much sun meant it had been a poor year for crops, however;

granaries were half empty, and there would not be enough to see the poorer folk through the winter. The street along which they walked was baked as dry as fired clay, although the manure that carpeted it meant it was never really hard under foot. The river was unnaturally low, some brooks had run dry, and the entire town stank. Earlier that week, Bartholomew had gone to visit his sister in a nearby village, and when he had returned his eyes had stung and watered from the acrid stench of rotting sewage, festering entrails abandoned by the slaughterhouses, and the rank aroma of unsold fish on the quays. Living in the town, he had not realized how bad the reek had become.

'What do I think about the cursed – and potentially fraudulent – relic? Or what do I think about Seton's claim that Witney was murdered?' asked Bartholomew, glancing up to see the first of the stars begin to twinkle. A soft breeze blew from the south, although it was hot and arid, and did little to reduce the heat.

'Both. But take the relic first. Do you think it is real?'

'I have no idea, but I have been offered two fragments of the True Cross this week alone, and there is always someone trying to sell some sacred body part or item once owned by Christ and His saints. Why should Andrew's be different?'

'Because of Andrew himself,' replied Michael. 'I have been Senior Proctor long enough to gauge a man's character with reasonable accuracy, and I sense he is telling the truth.'

'Perhaps he is, but that is not what you asked – Andrew believing in the sanctity of his relic does not prove its case. But Seton was right about the

Bishop of Durham: the one who lived during the first of the crusades *was* called Ranulf Flambard and not Geoffrey Mappestone. I have been to Durham, and I was told about Flambard when I visited the cathedral. That is two suspicious things: the seal does not match the name on the document, and Flambard never went to Jerusalem. He was far too busy doing unpleasant things here and in Normandy.'

'Then we must agree to differ. I think you are wrong, and Andrew does hold something powerful and holy.' Michael hesitated, and his next words were blurted. 'I sensed it when I reached out to take it from him.'

Bartholomew was startled. 'I had not expected a pragmatic man like you to be convinced by something as ephemeral as a feeling.'

'Do not scoff at me,' snapped Michael. 'It is not easy admitting that I was assailed by a wave of reverence when I saw Andrew's blood relic, so do not make my discomfort worse. All I know is that I sensed something decent about Andrew, and something strong in his pouch.'

'That was because he did not let you touch it,' replied Bartholomew practically, supposing he had better nip Michael's uncertainties in the bud before they interfered with his investigation. 'Such tactics work on the feeble minded, but I am surprised you succumbed.'

'Seton was right,' retorted Michael irritably. 'You are a physician and know nothing of theology. But we should not argue when we are unlikely to agree. What do you think about Seton's claim that the Carmelites murdered Witney?'

Bartholomew considered the question for some

time. 'Urban seems a hot-headed lad, but I do not see him climbing on to a roof to dispatch his victim in so bizarre a manner – nor would Andrew condone it. As far as I am concerned, the evidence suggests that Witney was unlucky enough to be peering up a chimney when a piece of it fell. He was stunned and died inhaling soot. But . . .' He rubbed a hand through his hair and sighed deeply.

'But what?'

'It is too convenient. A Franciscan argues with two Carmelites and threatens to expose them as charlatans and, shortly afterwards, he is found dead in an accident that is unusual, to say the least. Urban and Andrew just happened to be in the house at the time, while Seton just happened to be out.'

'So Seton says. Andrew and Urban claim *he* was with the body when they arrived to investigate the strange sound. Someone is lying.'

'I am inclined to think it is Andrew.'

'I think it is Seton,' countered Michael. 'Urban is not clever enough to deceive someone of my intelligence – I would have caught him out in any inconsistency.'

'Not with his master ready to step in and help him,' argued Bartholomew. 'You prefer Andrew because he is reasonable, whereas Seton is aggressive, rude and arrogant. But character does not make a murderer or an innocent.'

'So,' concluded Michael as they reached Michaelhouse and hammered on the gate to be allowed in, 'you believe Witney threatened to expose the Carmelites' relic as a forgery, and they killed him before he could do so. Meanwhile, I think Witney and Seton had some sort of argument that left one of them dead. You say yourself that he squabbled with Big Thomas the other day, so he was clearly a quarrelsome sort of fellow – and he died as a result of it.'

'How? Did he wait obligingly with his head inside the hearth while Seton dropped a stone down the chimney?'

'Why not? It is what you envisage Urban doing.'

Bartholomew rubbed his chin, and nodded an absent greeting to the night porter who had opened the gate. 'It does not make sense, does it? You and I have our suspects, but the reality is that we cannot prove there *was* a murder. It is more likely – far more likely – that Witney died in an odd, freakish accident.'

Michael was unwilling to dismiss the case so soon. 'What do you think of Tomas? He seems to crop up with suspicious regularity in this case – he quells public quarrels between Witney and the ex-thatcher; he knows a good deal of blood relic theology, Witney's favourite subject; however, we are told that his knowledge of angels – Seton's speciality – is lacking.'

'I do not see why Tomas should be involved in Witney's death, Brother. He is intelligent, but not so obsessed with his studies that he cannot laugh, unlike most of these clerics. I am looking forward to knowing him better.'

Michael pursed his lips. 'You have just warned *me* against allowing amiability to colour my judgement, and now you are falling into the same trap. However, *I* think there is something unsettling about Tomas. He is a Dominican, whose Order believes blood relics should not be revered, just as the Franciscans propose they should be accorded the greatest respect.'

'You have uncovered one or two odd facts about him, and you are determined to see him guilty of some crime. As I have told you – twice – I do not think there *was* a crime. And nor do I think Tomas had anything to do with Witney's death.'

'How can you be sure?'

'Because he has an alibi: he was in the Dominican priory when Witney died – and you and I were with him.'

'So we were,' acknowledged Michael with poor grace. 'However, just because he did not physically scramble on the roof, hurling masonry atop the heads of rival Franciscans, does not mean he did not hire someone else to do it.' He was thoughtful for a moment. 'Did you say the argument he quelled between Witney and his namesake was about thatching?'

Bartholomew nodded. 'Big Thomas was a thatcher before he took the cowl.'

Michael's eyed gleamed. 'A thatcher is an expert on *roofs*. And Witney was killed when something dropped from a *roof*. I wonder whether that is significant.'

'It is not,' said Bartholomew firmly. 'It is far too tenuous a connection.'

Michael sighed. 'We will get nowhere with this tonight, so we should put it from our minds and see whether there is anything for supper. I am ravenous.'

Bartholomew stared at him. 'You ate enough at the Dominican priory to last most men a week.'

'I am not most men, Matt,' replied Michael comfortably. 'I am different. And that is why I shall prod about this peculiar death until I have answers.'

The next day, Bartholomew spent the morning teaching, then went with two of his senior students to visit a patient in the Carmelite friary. The victim was the prior, William de Lincolne, a large man with an oddly brushed tuft of hair that rose vertically from his forehead. He had been confined to his bed since the onset of an ague, and was more than willing to pass the time of day in idle chatter with his physician. Bartholomew found it hard to extricate himself, and it was some time before he escaped to his other duties.

It was another scorching day, and he sweltered under his woollen tabard. He longed to pull it off, but the university had decreed that all college scholars should wear liveries that were immediately identifiable, and he did not want to set a bad example to his students.

He was not the only one overheating. He was just walking past St Botolph's Church on the High Street when he saw a familiar figure. It was Father Andrew, sitting disconsolately on the wall that surrounded the graveyard, mopping his forehead with the sleeve of his habit.

'Can I fetch you some watered ale, Father?' asked Bartholomew solicitously, knowing that hot weather could take its toll on the elderly.

Andrew shook his head. 'It is not the heat that ails me – I have known far fiercer suns in the past. Ten years after I took holy orders, my prior dispatched me on a long, arduous mission in the lands of the Bohemians and Magyars.'

'Really?' asked Bartholomew, intrigued. It was

unusual to meet men who had journeyed to such exotic places. 'That must have been interesting.'

Andrew smiled. 'It *was* a stimulating interlude in my life. It allowed me to visit distant universities, and I was appointed as a law-keeper in one, a post rather like Brother Michael's. But I never really settled, and was glad to return to the peaceful Devonshire hills once my mission was completed.'

'What was your mission? To search for relics?'

Andrew grimaced. 'I was a minor political envoy, but Prior William's real purpose in sending me away was to cure me of what he perceived to be a dangerous obsession with my relic. However, during my absence, that prior departed and another replaced him. Master Hugh and his successors did not try to "cure" me; they left me to my own devices – until John de Burgo was elected, that is.'

'I see,' said Bartholomew. He was more interested in the man's journeys than in what had happened when he returned; even the name of the kingdoms of the east brought back memories of his own travels. 'How far did you go?'

But Andrew did not share his enthusiasm. 'Too far, and I was glad to be home.' He sighed, and wiped his head again.

'What ails you, if not the heat?' asked Bartholomew. 'Can I help?'

Andrew indicated Bartholomew's bored medical students, who waited at a discreet distance. 'I have nothing a physician can cure, and your boys are restless. Do not linger here, wasting time with old men, when you could be instructing them in the ways of virtue and goodness.'

'I teach them medicine. Goodness and virtue I leave to the priests.'

'You should take more care of them,' recommended Andrew. 'If you do not temper their learning with the teachings of the Church, they will make their own interpretations of what you tell them, and they will hurt you with betrayals.'

Bartholomew helped him to his feet and watched him hobble away, puzzled by the advice. His students immediately began a barrage of questions about the effects of the heat on elderly humours, and he was absorbed in answering them until one, Deynman, gave a yelp and raised his hand to his head. It came away bloody.

'A stone!' he cried indignantly, pointing across the road. 'He threw a stone!'

'Who?' asked Bartholomew. He could see no one.

'Kip Roughe,' shouted Deynman. 'He is the Dominicans' servant, and is always jibing us because we are not theologians. He hurled the rock: I saw him.'

'Why would he do that?' asked Bartholomew, leading him to the churchyard wall. The student was pale, and he did not want him to faint.

'He is just plain nasty,' replied Deynman, tilting his head so Bartholomew could inspect it. The wound was not serious, although, like many scalp injuries, it bled profusely. 'He has no reason to lob missiles at me. I have never even spoken to him, although I know who he is – everyone does, because he is a lout.'

'He even brawls with students from his own institution,' added his friend. 'Poor Bulmer has a sore face from one of his punches.'

Bartholomew recalled Bulmer's jaw – a nasty bruise that would make eating painful for weeks to come. He gave Deynman a clean dressing to hold to the cut and sent him home. He warned him not to retaliate to Roughe's assault, knowing how quickly such situations could escalate, and watched until he was out of sight. Then he marched towards St Botolph's Church and stamped inside.

The interior was cool and dark after the brilliance outside, and it took a moment for his eyes to become accustomed to the gloom. Then he saw two shadows easing silently along the south aisle, aiming for the priest's door in the chancel. He broke into a run and had Kip Roughe by the scruff of his neck before he could reach it. Kip was a burly fellow, with the kind of battered face that indicated he enjoyed a brawl, while his brother John was larger. It occurred to Bartholomew that it was unwise to tackle them when they could easily overpower him, but the grabbing was done and he knew it would be a mistake to reveal his unease.

'What did you think you were doing?' he demanded, not relinquishing his hold. 'You could have hit Deynman's eye, and blinded him.'

'It was an accident,' objected Kip. He tried to free himself, and looked angry when he found he could not. 'We were aiming at the pigeons.'

John stepped forward in a way that was threatening, so Bartholomew released his brother and pushed him hard, so they stumbled into each other. 'I will report this to Prior Morden,' he said coldly. 'He can decide what to do with you.'

'It will be your word against ours,' said John,

leaning against a pillar and removing his knife from his belt. 'Who will believe you?'

'Morden,' replied Bartholomew curtly. 'And the Senior Proctor.'

'Let's go, John,' said Kip sullenly. 'I am not staying here to be threatened.'

John pulled away from him. 'We are alone here. No one will—'

'People saw him chase us in here,' snapped Kip. He took a firm hold of his brother's arm and dragged him outside, leaving Bartholomew angry and unsettled.

Bartholomew sat for a while in the church, relishing the coolness of the stones after the heat of the day, and left only when scholars from the Hall of Valence Marie entered for their afternoon prayers. They were noisy, speaking loudly about a debate that had just ended, and shattered the peace with their strident voices. Bartholomew emerged into the sharp afternoon sunlight, and looked both ways along the street, wondering whether the Roughe brothers might still be there, ready to lob stones again. As he did so, he saw Michael outside St Bernard's Hostel. The monk was standing on the opposite side of the road, his eyes fixed on the roof. Bartholomew went to join him.

'Do you think you will understand how Witney died if you stare up there long enough?' he asked, amused by the monk's intense interest.

Michael did not smile back. 'Look at the chimney and tell me what you see.'

'Stone tiles, Brother,' said Bartholomew, not sure what the monk wanted him to say. 'This is an old building, so some are probably worn.'

'I must know for certain,' said Michael. 'I want you to go up there and look.'

Bartholomew laughed at his audacity. 'Do you, indeed! Well, you can go and do it yourself.'

'I cannot. I am too heavy – do not deny it, because you are always telling me to eat less – but you are fit and agile. It will only take a moment.'

'And how do I get up there?' asked Bartholomew, who had no intention of doing anything so perilous. 'Fly?'

'I suggest you use a ladder, like everyone else. Bene't College has a long one; I will fetch it for you.'

Before the physician could object, he was gone, and Bartholomew was left alone at the side of the street doing much what the monk had been doing just moments before. He saw Andrew and Urban pass by on the opposite side of the road, the teacher deep in a monologue and his student straining to appear interested. Andrew looked ill and tired, and Bartholomew was concerned by how heavily he leaned on Urban's arm.

'I heard what happened,' came a voice close enough to make him jump.

'Tomas!' exclaimed Bartholomew, regaining his composure, and smiling a greeting. The Dominican stood next to him, gazing up at the roof.

'The word is that Witney was crushed by a chance stone that fell down the chimney,' said Tomas. 'I have also been told he died because he touched a sacred relic – a cursed sacred relic. Did Father Andrew mention this to you?'

Bartholomew nodded. 'Why should he not?'

Tomas shrugged. 'I thought he might try to keep

it a secret, lest the Chancellor demand he hand the thing over to a higher authority. He is old and frail, and may not have the strength to refuse.'

'He *is* concerned that someone might take it. He claimed Witney tried.'

'Witney was a Franciscan, and his Order is determined to preserve blood relics. Perhaps he was trying to make sure it was kept safe.'

It was a possibility Bartholomew had already considered, but it was interesting to hear it from another quarter. 'Did Witney follow his Order's teaching or did he have his own opinion?'

Tomas shrugged. 'I have no idea: we never shared personal reflections on that debate. He did tell me he was horrified Andrew carried such a thing around his neck, and it is possible a misunderstanding arose – that Andrew mistook a well-meaning gesture for something else.'

'You knew Witney,' said Bartholomew, recalling him singing the Franciscan's praises at the Dominican priory the previous day.

Tomas nodded. 'His main interest was the Holy Blood debate, and he was deeply involved in the question of whether it is possible for Christ's blood to exist as a sacred form outside His body – if His body was fully raised from the dead, then His blood would have been resurrected with him. He expressed some very powerful theories, all very well phrased, and his logic could not be faulted.'

'Was he firm enough in his beliefs to make someone want to kill him?'

Tomas gazed at him, and answered with a question of his own. 'Are you saying his death was not an accident? It was not the relic's curse that killed him, but some jealous mortal?'

Bartholomew made no attempt to keep the scepticism from his face. 'I do not believe a relic – cursed or otherwise – can bring about a man's death.'

Tomas raised his eyebrows. 'Do you not? But Seton told me you have been appraised of this relic's history. Are you not suspicious of the amount of blood in its history? Personally, I err on the side of caution: I do not know whether such things can manifest themselves, but I treat them with respect lest they do. It is a policy that has served me well for many years.'

Bartholomew was surprised that Tomas, a Dominican friar, should adopt such a stance, but supposed Michael had done as much, too, despite his customary scorn for superstition. 'You did not answer my question. Was Witney the kind of man whose strong opinions caused offence?'

Tomas considered, then nodded. 'It is possible. However, although he was not easy to like, I do not think having an objectionable character is a good motive for murder.'

'He was objectionable?'

'He was not always pleasant, and I sensed a certain dishonesty – that some of the ideas he expounded were not his own.'

'A theory thief?'

Tomas shuffled uncomfortably. 'I should not have been so blunt, but yes. A few of his ideas actually came from Meyronnes, the Franciscan theologian. Witney was a brilliant logician, and few could best him in an argument, but he was not an original thinker.'

'And Seton?'

'His theories about angelic manifestations are all

his own. However, since Witney did not "borrow" ideas from Cambridge men, I do not see how plagiarism is relevant to his death. Are Michael and the Roughe brothers carrying a ladder?'

'He wants me to inspect the roof,' said Bartholomew resentfully, scowling at monk and servants as they approached. Kip and John did not acknowledge him.

'That is a good idea, especially since Seton is watching – he will see you taking his accusations seriously, and even if you find nothing, he will know the Senior Proctor did everything possible to investigate the death of his colleague. Do you want me to help?'

'No,' said Bartholomew. Then he saw the Roughe brothers lean the ladder against the wall in a way that was precarious, and changed his mind. 'You can hold the bottom. It looks unstable.'

'It is unstable,' said Tomas, elbowing the servants out of the way while he set the steps in a more secure position. Bartholomew could not but help notice the unreadable glance that passed between Kip and John. Had they wanted him to fall? He took Michael to one side.

'Did you ask Kip about his fight with Bulmer?'

Michael nodded. 'While we were waiting to borrow the ladder. It was all Bulmer's fault, of course: Kip was innocently drinking ale when Bulmer attacked him. Bulmer is a troublemaker, and Kip knows that – without independent witnesses, it will be impossible to prove who started the fracas.'

Given his own recent experiences with the sullen servants, Bartholomew was not so sure. 'Did you ask what they were quarrelling about?'

Michael waved a dismissive hand. 'I did not, but it will be over poorly cleaned shoes, or whether Bulmer paid Kip enough for making his bed. It will be nothing of consequence.'

'Ask him,' suggested Bartholomew.

Michael sighed, but did as he suggested.

'Bulmer was spying,' came the unexpected reply. Kip was simultaneously indignant and sanctimonious, neither expressions that sat well on his pugilistic features. 'Prior Morden does not approve of behaviour that brings Dominicans into disrepute, so I suggested Bulmer should stop. He refused, and we fought. He threw the first punch, though, as I told you earlier, Brother.'

Michael scratched his chin. 'And whom was Bulmer spying on?'

'He was lurking outside St Andrew's Church, where the whores display their wares. It was even more reason to send him back to his prior.'

'Right,' said Michael flatly. 'And your sole intention was to protect the Dominicans' reputation?'

Bartholomew grabbed his arm and tugged him out of earshot. 'Several prostitutes *do* work near that church, and Bulmer *is* the kind of novice to forget his vow of celibacy and hire one now and again. But Seton mentioned that Tomas also visits St Andrew's Church – as does Seton himself, and perhaps Witney, too. I think you should interview Bulmer and find out *exactly* what he was doing when he was caught by his friary's servants.'

With Michael and the Roughe brothers holding the bottom of the ladder, Bartholomew climbed to the top, expecting at every step that a rung would break and send him tumbling to the ground below. Then he became aware of Tomas behind him.

'What are you doing?' he demanded, grasping the rungs tightly.

'It is much safer with two,' replied Tomas. 'Brother Michael declined to oblige, and I do not think Kip or John would be much help, so I came myself.'

Bartholomew nodded his thanks, and stepped on to the roof, clutching one of the bands that held the thatch in place. As he did so, and while his balance was at its most precarious, the ladder jerked to one side.

'Hey!' came Michael's angry voice as Bartholomew scrabbled to gain a handhold. 'Be careful!'

'I am sorry,' said John, not sounding at all repentant. 'My hand slipped.'

'Then do not let it slip again,' called Tomas, shocked. Bartholomew glanced at him and saw that his face was white. 'Bartholomew almost fell, and so did I.'

'You might topple to your dooms yet,' called Kip carelessly. 'I had to climb on the friary thatch a few weeks ago, and it was very slippery. Men who poke about on roofs are asking for accidents.'

While Bartholomew pondered what sounded ominously like a threat, he became aware that the ladder was moving again, as Tomas clambered up next to him.

'Do not stand there,' advised Tomas. 'Go to your right.'

'Why?' demanded Bartholomew, declining to comply. He did not feel comfortable so far above the ground, and disliked the way his legs were shaking.

'Big Thomas was a thatcher, and knows a lot about roofs. He told me never to stand where you are now, because that is the part most vulnerable to decay and instability.'

Hastily, Bartholomew followed the advice, and together he and the Dominican made their way towards the chimney. At one point he started to slide, but Tomas caught his wrist and held it until he had regained his footing. He smiled his gratitude weakly, wanting the examination over so that he could descend to the ground again. When they reached the chimney, Bartholomew stopped in surprise, and exchanged a startled glance with Tomas. There was a harness fastened around it, as though someone else had been there and had wanted to make sure he would not take a tumble.

'Is this from last year?' Bartholomew wondered. 'When the roof was repaired?'

Tomas shook his head. 'It is recent – the rope is almost new.'

Bartholomew grabbed the chimney in a rough embrace and squinted down it, praying someone would not choose that moment to light a fire. There was a narrow ledge just inside, and several broken tiles had been placed on it.

'Missiles,' mused Tomas thoughtfully, lifting one out to inspect. 'It looks as though someone intended to drop them down the chimney. They have not been here long, because they would be more covered in soot if they had.'

Bartholomew stared at him. 'You know rather a lot about this kind of thing.'

'I was a proctor – or its equivalent – at Pécs, and

investigated far more deaths than would be considered decent by my order. I became quite adept at it.'

Bartholomew returned his friendly smile, trying to hide the clamouring thought that would not be silenced: had Brother Tomas learned enough from solving murders to be skilled at committing one himself?

Bartholomew felt considerably happier once his feet were back on firm ground. He told Michael what he had seen, and added in an undertone that the monk was not the only one with experience as a proctor who was interested in Witney's death. Michael was troubled by both revelations. He watched Tomas remove the ladder from the wall and issue the Roughe brothers with instructions for returning it to its owners. The pair picked it up reluctantly, as though they were troubled not only by the weight, but because they had hoped to learn what had been discovered on the roof. After a moment, Tomas decided to go with them, apparently thinking they could not be trusted to carry out his orders unsupervised. They were slovenly and insolent, and Bartholomew thought he was right to be watchful – long ladders were expensive, and the Dominicans would be obliged to pay for another if their servants left Bene't's somewhere it could be stolen.

'When I am rich, I am going to buy one of these,' muttered John, as they made their way down the street. 'If I charge a penny each time someone wants it, I will make a fortune.'

'Peterhouse paid to use this one *three* times last week,' agreed Kip. 'And the Gilbertines borrowed it four, because of pigeons. Witney had it once or twice for pigeons, too. Remember Urban knocking that nest down for him? Feathers everywhere!'

'So, Seton was right after all,' mused Michael unhappily as their chattering voices receded. 'He said Witney had been murdered, and now you discover evidence that someone harnessed himself to the roof with a pile of missiles at the ready. Obviously, Seton would not have insisted on an investigation if he was the killer.' He considered for a moment, unwilling to dismiss his prime suspect too readily. 'Or was he calling our bluff – hoping the very act of ordering us to look into the matter would annoy us into doing the opposite?'

'I doubt it, Brother,' replied Bartholomew. 'It is too risky. Besides, he was in St Andrew's Church with independent alibis at the time of Witney's murder. I was right in my original assumption: the Carmelites are the villains. I doubt Andrew is agile enough to scale roofs, so we must look to Urban.'

But Michael shook his head. 'You are wrong; they are not killers. A powerful relic, like the one they carry, would not allow itself to be toted by evil hands.'

Bartholomew regarded him askance, thinking about the many acts of wickedness they had witnessed in the past, when sacred objects had suffered all manner of indignities in the hands of wicked men. 'Do you really believe that?'

Michael rubbed his eyes. 'I do not know what to think. However, there *is* something about that particular relic . . . but my thoughts are irrelevant. Our duty is to assess the evidence you found and draw rational conclusions from it. Are you sure about this chimney? Is it possible *Tomas* put the harness and stones there, to confound us for some reason? There is something about him I do not trust – and now he admits to expertise in murder investigations.'

Bartholomew smiled. 'And this "something about him I do not trust" is a dispassionate analysis of the evidence, is it? But I suppose it is possible he placed the rope and masonry by the chimney for us to find, although I cannot imagine why. He was very helpful when we were up there – he saved me from falling.'

Michael grimaced. 'We are destined to agree about nothing in this case, Matt. You believe the Carmelites are our best suspects, while I remain suspicious of Seton. You consider the relic nothing special, while I feel there is something unique about it. And you admire Tomas, while all my senses clamour at me to be wary of him. I do not like the way he seems to feature in the various strands of our investigation – and just chances to stroll by when you need help on the roof. But tell me again about what you found. What do the harness and stones mean?'

'That someone really did kill Witney, and made it appear as though the stone fell on him by accident. It is an unusual way to kill, and not one without difficulties: what if the perpetrator killed the wrong man; how could he be sure his victim would oblig-ingly stick his head up the chimney at the right time . . .?'

'Perhaps he did not kill the right man,' suggested Michael. 'Witney is dead, but that does not mean he was the intended victim. All you would see from the top of a chimney would be a head-shaped silhouette. Perhaps our killer failed in his objective, and even now is stalking his real victim. I should tell Andrew as soon as possible, and ensure he takes proper precautions.'

He broke off the discussion when Tomas returned. The Dominican made straight for the harness they had retrieved and began to inspect it. Michael assumed an expression of friendly interest as he walked towards him, and Bartholomew knew from experience that an interrogation was about to take place.

'I understand you and I have shared similar experiences,' said Michael. 'I did not know you were a proctor.'

Tomas returned his smile. He had a pleasant face, and dark eyes that twinkled when he laughed. 'Keeping law and order in Pécs took so much time that my studies suffered, and I was obliged to resign. It was an interesting life, but not nearly as fascinating as angels.'

'But you are intrigued by this particular case,' said Michael, and the smile turned cold. 'It was not safe to climb on that roof, yet you did so willingly. Why?'

'To help your colleague,' said Tomas, sounding surprised the monk should ask. 'You are right: it *was* dangerous, and it was unfair to send him up there alone. You should have gone with him yourself.'

Michael glared, although Bartholomew thought he had a point. It was not the first time the monk had merrily ordered his friend to do something risky because he did not fancy doing it himself.

'What conclusion have you drawn from your discoveries?' asked the monk icily.

'That you have a murderer to catch. It is clear

someone wanted to kill someone else – whether
Witney or another man. Also, your villain tried to
conceal the unlawful killing – he used the chimney
in the hope that you would see Witney's death as an
unfortunate accident. Perhaps he wanted you to
believe the cursed relic was responsible.'

Michael looked superior. 'We have already
reasoned this ourselves.'

'Not about the relic,' said Bartholomew, earning
himself a weary glower.

'I suspect the killer wanted you to see Witney's
death as divine intervention, an angry saint, or
Barzac's malediction,' Tomas went on. 'He will be
angry when he learns his ruse did not work.'

'You seem very familiar with Andrew's relic,' said
Michael, his voice dripping with suspicion. 'I was
under the impression that he tells very few people
about it.'

Bartholomew did not agree. He had not noticed
much reluctance on the elderly friar's part to
discuss the 'burden' he carried. And if he had willingly shared the information with Michael, then in
whom else had he confided?

'Father Andrew did *not* tell me about it,' replied
Tomas. 'Indeed, I have never spoken to the man. It
was Witney who obliged. He was intrigued by it,
and asked me to go with him to various libraries, to
help research the validity of the accompanying
letters of authentication. He had learned that a
bishop of Durham's seal was used, but that the man
who signed it was no bishop.'

'Why did he ask *you* to help him?' asked Michael.
'And why did you agree?'

'He asked because I am a Dominican and he was
a Franciscan. Our Orders disagree about blood

relics, as you know: you expounded on the matter only yesterday. Witney said he wanted a man from the opposing side of the argument to be with him as he investigated, in case Andrew's relic transpired to be important – I would be an independent witness who would substantiate his findings without prejudice. I agreed, because I have an interest in the Holy Blood debate myself.'

Michael narrowed his eyes. 'And where did Witney stand in the polemic? Did he follow his Order's teachings, and declare blood relics worthy of veneration? Or was he swayed by the arguments of the Dominicans, and believed such items to be anathema, to be destroyed as heretical idols of veneration?'

'I imagine he was an adherent of his own Order's theology,' replied Tomas, unperturbed by the monk's hostility. 'We discussed the issue at length, but neither of us injected personal opinions into the discourse – we argued purely along theosophical lines. To do otherwise would have been highly unprofessional.'

Bartholomew grinned. The previous day, Michael had been unable to resist adding his own views – some of them emotive and unsupported by logical deduction – to the thesis he had outlined.

Michael pursed his lips. 'So, you cannot tell me whether Witney's obsession with Andrew's relic was because he wanted it revered or wanted it destroyed?'

'No,' replied Tomas. 'He never told me, and I did not know him well enough to ask. It is easy for a Benedictine, like you, to state his mind freely, because your Order has not taken a dogmatic stance on the matter. However, to enquire of a

Dominican or a Franciscan whether he accepts his Order's teaching is a different matter entirely. You are asking him whether he is loyal or perfidious.'

Michael rubbed his chin. 'Now we have issues of fidelity to consider when we explore the circumstances of Witney's death. Was our victim true to his Order's beliefs, or did he think them erroneous? And, since you do not know the answer, we must ask his friend Seton.'

Michael was to be disappointed when he went to interview Seton, because the Oxford academic was not at home. Bartholomew refused to wait until he returned, on the grounds that the man could be gone all day, listening to lectures or reading in one of the college libraries, and opted to visit the Dominican priory instead: he wanted to see the injured Bulmer, and examine his swollen jaw. Michael offered to accompany him. His investigation was at a standstill until he could interview Seton, but there were other proctorial duties awaiting, one of which was determining whether the Dominican novice had been ogling prostitutes when Kip Roughe had fought him. If that were true, then Michael would impose a hefty fine as a way of warning him – and his friends – not to do it again.

He and Bartholomew left the High Street and made their way through the maze of alleys to the marshes on which the Dominican priory stood. The sun was blazing in another clear blue sky, and Bartholomew felt sweat trickling between his shoulder blades. He wiped his face with his sleeve, and stepped over a dog that lay panting in the road, too hot to move away from trampling feet.

Another lapped greedily at a bowl of water placed for strays by some thoughtful person. By the time they reached the friary, Bartholomew was sticky and uncomfortable, and Michael's flabby face was flushed red. The gate was opened by Big Thomas, who demanded to know their business.

'I want to speak to Prior Morden,' said Michael, starting to push his way inside.

Big Thomas barred it. 'What about?'

Michael gazed at him in disbelief. 'Nothing I am prepared to share with a gatekeeper. Tell Morden immediately that I am here to see him.'

Big Thomas scowled. 'I hate gate duty! If I ask too many questions, visitors accuse me of being nosy; and if I ask too few, I am berated for letting just anyone inside. I never get it right. I should never have abandoned thatching to take the cowl – there is too much thinking involved.'

Michael sniggered as the man went to fetch his master. 'He is lucky he chose the Dominicans, then. They think less than any Order in Cambridge.'

'What is this about thinking?' asked tiny Prior Morden, hurrying to greet them. 'Too much of that goes on in this town, and no good will come of it. A prime example is this aggravation pertaining to Holy Blood, which you were holding forth about yesterday, Brother. I did not understand a word – I still do not, even though Little Tomas spent hours explaining it to me last night.'

'I do not suppose you discussed blood relics with Seton and Witney from St Bernard's Hostel, did you? They had views on just this issue.'

'I most certainly did not,' replied Morden indignantly. 'They are Franciscans.'

353

'Are you sure you never spoke to them?' probed Michael. 'You did not cross swords, even briefly?'

Morden pursed his lips. 'Well, there was an occasion a couple of days ago, when Witney sidled up to me and asked whether I had been to Hailes or Ashridge. But I am not stupid, Brother, and I know perfectly well what those two places are famous for: blood relics. I told him I had not and left without further ado.'

'And your friars?' pressed Michael. 'Are they equally astute when it comes to dealing with sly Franciscans, who try to make them discuss contentious subjects against their will?'

'They are,' declared Morden. 'None would hold forth on such a dangerous topic with Grey Friars, especially ones who hail from that pit of devils, Oxford.'

'Is that so?' asked Michael mildly. 'Then perhaps you will explain why Little Tomas has just admitted to helping Witney investigate the validity of one particular Holy Blood relic.'

'Did he?' asked Morden unhappily. 'I know nothing about that, but he is a guest, not one of my own friars. I tend to leave visitors to their own devices, especially ones who come here to study: if I try to regulate them, they become testy and claim I interfere with the progress of their education. I have learned to let them get on with it. So, Little Tomas has benefited from my leniency, although I cannot imagine what a decent man like him would find to say to Franciscans, especially that pair: Seton is arrogant and Witney is – was – a fanatic.'

'A fanatic?' echoed Michael.

'About blood relics.' Morden sighed. 'He spoke in confidence, but I suppose it does not matter now he is dead. When he asked me about Hailes and Ashridge – before I walked away – he told me that all such relics must be destroyed, because otherwise ignorant people will venerate them and stain their souls. However, as long as prayers are headed in the right direction, I do not think it matters whether they are directed through Holy Blood, the mass, the saints or anything else.'

'Be careful, Father Prior,' warned Michael, amused to hear such a tolerant attitude from a member of so vehement an Order. 'That is close to heresy, and your Master-General is very particular about that sort of thing.'

Morden grimaced. 'Yes, you told me yesterday that, as a Dominican, I am supposed to denounce blood relics. I imagine that was why Witney approached me: as the highest-ranking Black Friar, he expected me to concur with his views.'

'Views which run contrary to those of his own Order,' mused Bartholomew. 'So, now we know where he stood – we do not need to ask Seton about him.'

'Do you know what Little Tomas thinks?' asked Michael. 'Does he follow your Order's guidelines, or is he, like Witney, the kind of man to take against them?'

'I have no idea,' replied Morden. 'We have discussed the polemic, but he has never honoured me with his own opinions. Do you think he might have been sent by the Master-General, to ferret out heretics and rebels among us?' His elfin features creased into an expression of alarm.

'It is possible,' said Michael spitefully.

'No,' said Bartholomew at the same time.

Morden looked unhappier still as he snapped his fingers at a passing servant. It was John Roughe, who was ordered to convey the visitors to the dormitory Bulmer shared with the other novices. On the way, Roughe did his best to engage them in conversation and find out what they wanted to ask Bulmer. He was clearly unconvinced by Bartholomew's claim that he was there in a professional capacity, and looked meaningfully at the bulky presence of the Senior Proctor.

'It was Bulmer who started that fight,' John asserted, abandoning his ingratiating manner when he saw it would not work. 'Not my brother Kip. If Bulmer tells you otherwise, then he is a liar. He was at the church, after whores.'

'Is that so?' replied Bartholomew, not much caring what the novice was doing. It was not his affair.

'Yes,' stated Roughe angrily. They were in a narrow corridor, and he stepped forward smartly to block their way. 'And he does not need the services of a physician, so you might as well save your time and go home.'

Bartholomew was unmoved. 'I am a better judge of that than you. Stand aside.'

'I will not—' But Michael's bulk loomed, and Roughe's words died in his throat. With a silent and infinitely resentful gesture, he indicated that the room they wanted was straight ahead.

'He does not like us being here,' mused Michael, watching him slouch away. 'We are *personae non gratae* wherever we go these days.'

'You have the power to fine his brother for attacking Bulmer – and from what I saw of Kip earlier today, I would not be surprised to learn that he was the aggressor. It is an odd tale anyway. Why should a lout like Kip take exception to Bulmer eyeing prostitutes? Is it because he has a favourite lady, and he does not want to share her with members of the university?'

He opened the dormitory door and entered the long chamber. Bulmer was sitting in the end bed with a cooling poultice pushed to his swollen face. He looked a good deal worse than he had the day before, because the swelling had come out, although he was no longer reeling and stupid. He scowled as they approached.

'I told you yesterday,' he began without preamble. 'Kip Roughe punched me.'

'It is a strange wound to be caused by a punch,' said Bartholomew, inspecting the bruising closely. 'He must have caught you at an odd angle.'

'It hurt, I know that,' said Bulmer ruefully. 'But, being a peace-loving man, I have no knowledge about what constitutes the right or wrong angles for blows.'

Bartholomew raised his eyebrows, knowing perfectly well that Bulmer was an accomplished and experienced brawler, and that he knew exactly how to hit people.

'It is difficult to find the truth when there are no independent witnesses and both protagonists claim the other is at fault,' said Michael, watching Bartholomew sit on the bed and gently probe the swelling.

'I have told you what happened,' objected Bulmer, pushing the physician away. 'I will take final vows soon, and I am not given to lying. The Roughe brothers are, though; they steal, too.'

'Can you prove dishonesty?' asked Michael. 'I will prosecute them, if so.'

Bulmer looked sheepish. 'I am repeating what others have told me. *They* may be too timid to take on the Roughes, but I am not.'

'Where did the altercation happen?' asked Michael.

'Outside St Andrew's.'

'What were you doing there?'

Bulmer was surprised by the question. 'It is the nearest church to the friary, and I often go there to pray. Many Dominicans do. Our own chapel can be noisy in the daytime, and some of us crave a quieter place for our devotions.'

Bartholomew struggled to keep the incredulity from his face, although Michael had no such qualms, and his expression was openly sceptical. 'You are not a pious lad, Bulmer, so do not pretend you are. Your skills and merits lie in other areas – equally valuable to your Order, I am sure – but do not try to deceive me.'

'Very well,' said Bulmer stiffly. 'I was watching someone.'

'I see. Does Prior Morden know you spend your time ogling whores?'

'That is *not* what I was doing!' cried Bulmer, shocked. 'I only ever watch them at night, and the incident with Roughe happened in daylight.'

'Who were you watching?' asked Michael curiously.

Bulmer was uneasy. 'I would rather not say.'

Michael followed his nervous glance towards the door. 'Do not worry about being overheard. Matt will stand guard and make sure no one is eavesdropping.'

Bartholomew obliged, and the novice began to speak. 'I was watching Little Tomas. I do not like him.'

'Why not?' asked Bartholomew.

'I am not sure,' admitted Bulmer. 'I am not given to flights of fancy, being a practical fellow, but my feelings about him are strong, and I felt the need to act. Prior Morden is a good man, but overly inclined to see the good in people. I do not want him harmed because of the likes of Little Tomas.'

'Can you be more specific?' asked Michael, raising his hand when Bartholomew started to point out that the suspicion probably arose from the fact that Tomas was a foreigner, and such men often excited negative emotions in English towns.

Bulmer played with the compress against his injured face. 'He says he is from a university called Pécs, but I have never heard of it, and I do not believe it exists. I am afraid he is here to spy on us, to see where we stand over this Holy Blood business. None of us really understands the wretched affair, and Prior Morden is too open for his own good – I think he may even believe the Franciscans are right, and might confide in the wrong people. I do not want the Cambridge community excommunicated when I am about to take my final vows – I should like to be a prior one day, and that will not happen if I am deemed a heretic.'

'Is that all?' asked Michael. 'You do not like Tomas because he is from an unknown university and you think he may be part of an inquisition?'

Bulmer nodded. 'And because he asks questions. I detest Kip Roughe, as you know, but even he is uncomfortable with Tomas, and *that* is why we fought. I was watching Tomas, but it was Kip who was about to thrust a knife between his shoulder blades. I cannot condone murder, not even of someone like Tomas. I ordered him to put down his weapon, and he punched me.'

Michael's eyebrows shot up. 'Why not mention this sooner? We assumed you were gawking at prostitutes, but now it seems you averted a crime. Why did you keep your noble actions to yourself?'

'Because I would have had to admit to following Tomas,' replied Bulmer resentfully. 'Although I suspect he probably already knows – as I said, he is clever. Besides, this is not the first time Kip and John have tried to kill him, but he is too cunning to be dispatched by mere servants. It is the Roughes who will die if they continue to stalk him, not Little Tomas.'

As soon as he emerged from the Dominican priory, Bartholomew was summoned by the Carmelites, whose prior had taken a turn for the worse, obliging the physician to spend the rest of the day with him. By the time he returned to Michaelhouse, it was too late to speak to Michael and the lights in almost every room were doused. Exhausted, he slept soundly, despite the stifling heat, and woke only when the bell chimed for prime. He waylaid the monk before breakfast, and learned that Kip Roughe had confirmed Bulmer's tale – and had been proud that he had raised the courage to take a stand against a man of Tomas's obvious wickedness. Michael had warned him not to do it again, and fined him heavily to make his point.

Both scholars spent the morning teaching, and it was well past noon before they were able to meet again. Michael, whose classes were smaller and less demanding, had gone a second time to warn the Roughe brothers against murder, only to learn that neither had been seen since the previous evening. Both Bulmer and Morden informed him that it was not an uncommon occurrence for the pair to disappear on business of their own, and neither seemed concerned about their untimely absence.

'I am worried, Matt,' said Michael as they walked towards the High Street. He wanted to visit Seton. 'I do not want the Roughe brothers dead at Tomas's hand.'

'It is they who are trying to dispatch him, not the other way around. And if they are killed, Tomas can quite legitimately claim self-defence. I do not know why they have taken against him: he has done nothing wrong, other than to be an intelligent foreigner.'

Michael was not so sure, but did not want to argue when he knew they would not agree, while Bartholomew also dropped the matter and looked across the road to where two men in Carmelite habits walked, deep in conversation – or rather, Andrew talked while Urban listened. Bartholomew could not be certain, but he thought Urban was sobbing, and supposed the master was admonishing him for some infraction. His own, albeit brief, observations had told him that Andrew was a hard and exacting taskmaster, difficult to please. He recalled him mentioning a previous novice, who had been all a master could desire, but who had 'betrayed' him by seeking more knowledgeable teachers. He supposed Urban was lacking in comparison, and felt sorry for the lad: competing with ghosts was a grim and unrewarding business.

Michael knocked briskly on the door to St Bernard's, and paced back and forth while he waited for it to be answered. Bartholomew watched Andrew sink gratefully on to the low wall surrounding the churchyard opposite, while Urban perched next to him. The old man was weary, eager for rest, while Urban appeared to be unsettled and restless. When a greasy scullion arrived to ask Michael's business, the monk did not reply; he pushed past the man and strode inside, aiming for the smaller of the two chambers on the ground floor, where Seton was enjoying a solitary meal.

'You are alone?' asked Michael. 'Where are the Carmelites?'

'Out,' said Seton, before Bartholomew could say they were sitting in the sun outside. 'They have been gone much of the day, which suits me. I am here to study, and it is difficult to read when they chatter all the time.'

'They talk a lot?' enquired Michael, helping himself to bread.

'Andrew does,' replied Seton, grimacing when Michael took the last piece of chicken. 'He is always telling that stupid novice something he will forget within an hour. Carmelites accept anyone into their ranks, and more often than not their wits are inferior. I am afraid the same is also true of my own Order. Still, at least the Franciscans have men like *me* to present an intelligent face to the world. Witney did so, too, before that pair murdered him.'

'Witney was interested in Andrew's Holy Blood relic,' began Michael. 'Are you sure he did not try to take it from him? Your Order is intent on preserving such items from destruction by the

Dominicans. Perhaps he tried to seize it in a misguided attempt to protect it – to take it from a feeble old man who would be unable to repel the determined advances of single-minded Black Friars.'

Seton sighed. 'I was not going to bother you with irrelevant detail, but Witney was *not* an adherent of my Order's teachings – he did not accept the validity of such relics. But why do you ask? Have you come around to my way of thinking: the Carmelites killed him?'

'Did you like Witney?' asked Michael, declining to reply.

Seton was taken aback. 'I have known kinder, more gracious men, but *I* did not kill him, if that is what you are asking. I heard what you found on the roof, but I am not a man to scramble up buildings, Brother. That sort of agility is for the likes of young Urban.'

'Did you see Urban by the chimney?' asked Bartholomew. 'Or covered in bits of thatching to suggest he had been climbing?'

'No,' admitted Seton. 'But I paid little attention to him or his master, because I considered them beneath my dignity. It was Witney who engaged them in conversation. But, now I think of it, Urban *did* climb a ladder at one point. There was a pigeon's nest near our window, and the constant coos and flaps were disturbing Witney, so Urban offered to knock it down for him. There! I have proved your case, Brother: Urban is an experienced user of ladders and happy on roofs.'

'I hardly think—' began Bartholomew, but Seton was not to be deterred.

'And whoever murdered Witney was a man with

exactly those skills. Urban is the villain, just as I predicted.'

It was clear they would learn no more from Seton, so Bartholomew and Michael took their leave.

Bartholomew followed Michael out of the hostel into the intense glare of the afternoon sun. Michael gasped at the sudden heat, then insisted they visit the Brazen George for cool ale while they discussed what they had learned. Although scholars were not permitted in taverns, Bartholomew felt the humidity was unpleasant enough to warrant some rule-breaking. He followed the monk into a peaceful room at the back of the inn, where they were served ale that had come directly from one of the deeper cellars. It was clear, cold and refreshing, and he began to feel somewhat revived. The same could not be said for their progress on the case, however, and although they discussed it at length, neither had anything new to add. They were staring disconsolately into the dregs of their ale when the door opened, and Little Tomas walked in.

'Your beadles said I might find you here,' he said pleasantly. 'I understand you have been looking for me – to ask about the fact that the Roughe brothers have been trying to kill me.'

If Michael was disconcerted by the bald pronouncement, he masked it. 'Yes,' he replied. 'You are aware of what Kip and John have been doing?'

Tomas smiled as he took a seat. 'It is difficult not to notice a crossbow bolt that misses you by the length of a finger, or a horse that tries to ride you down. They also shook the ladder when I climbed it yesterday – endangering Bartholomew into the bargain. Of course I have noticed.'

'And what have you done about it?' demanded Michael.

'Nothing. Their attempts are clumsy, and I am never in real danger – although the crossbow bolt was a little close for comfort.'

'Why are you so sanguine about it?' asked Bartholomew. 'Most men would confront their would-be assassins and demand to know what they are about.'

'I do not need to ask; I know exactly why they have taken against me. None of the other Cambridge Dominicans is a scholar, and neither they nor their servants understand why I devote my life to books. Also, I am from a university in a country they have never heard of, and I look, speak and behave differently from them. I am a stranger, a foreigner, and therefore suspect. Their dislike of me is simple ignorance, no more and no less.'

Bulmer had admitted as much and so had the Roughe brothers, and Bartholomew supposed that, even in a university town, it was possible for advanced scholarship to be considered an unnatural vice. Also, the Black Friars tended to be local – even Welsh and Irish scholars were regarded as aliens, so someone from the mysterious-sounding Pécs would be an obvious target for their petty hatreds. Michael was not content with Tomas's explanation, however.

'They think you are an inquisitor. Are you?'

'There are Dominican inquisitors who report incidents of heresy to our Master-General, but they are Englishmen, who blend in with the host community. They are not foreigners whom no one will trust. Such a ploy would be pointless.'

'Is that a yes or a no?' pressed Michael.

'It is a no,' replied Tomas, a little impatiently. 'I am just a scholar and a priest.'

Michael was about to ask him more about his interest in Witney's death – and *his* stance on Holy Blood relics – but there was a knock on the door and one of Michael's beadles entered.

'You are asked to go to the river, near the quays, Brother,' he said breathlessly. 'There has been an accident, and the dead man is said to have been staying in St Bernard's Hostel.'

Bartholomew jumped to his feet. 'Who? Seton?'

The beadle shook his head. 'An old man wearing a White Friar's habit.'

'Do you mean Father Andrew?' asked Tomas in an appalled whisper. 'Dead?'

Bartholomew glanced at him, startled by his sudden pallor. Afraid he might swoon, he leaned forward to take his arm. Tomas did not notice, and fixed his dark, intense eyes on the beadle as he waited for a reply.

'I did hear his name was Andrew,' acknowledged the beadle.

'God save us!' breathed Tomas. When he raised his hand to cross himself, it shook so much that he was barely able to complete the motion.

'What is the matter?' asked Bartholomew, certain there was more to his shock than hearing about the death of a man he had, by his own admission, never met. As proctor of Pécs, he would have seen death on a daily basis – assuming he had been telling the truth about his previous vocation, of course.

'I have not been entirely honest with you,' said

Tomas, accepting the remains of Bartholomew's ale and taking a tentative sip. 'You were right: I do have more than a passing interest in this case. I am one of many Dominicans scattered across the country whose task it is to listen for information about Holy Blood relics and their movements. And Andrew's sounded particularly important.'

'An inquisitor?' demanded Michael angrily. 'You just denied that.'

'Not an inquisitor,' said Tomas. 'An *observer*. It is not the same thing.'

'It is,' declared Michael. 'Remember that fish-head John Roughe left on me at your priory? It sat on my shoulder without my knowledge and surveyed us all with its flat, watchful eyes. Well, that is what your kind is like, Tomas. A fish-head perched on the shoulders of honest men.'

Bartholomew and Michael hurried towards the quays with Tomas at their heels. Michael had tried to dissuade the Dominican from coming with them, but the man was insistent. His face was grim as they walked, leading Bartholomew to wonder whether they had learned all there was to know about his connection to the relic and its carriers.

Because it was the end of a market day, the streets were choked with carts, and people and animals were everywhere. Cattle lowed as they were driven towards Slaughterhouse Row, while chickens flapped and geese strutted in hissing gaggles. A dog barked furiously at a herd of sheep, and a donkey brayed its displeasure at the cacophony. The smell of animal dung and urine was overpowering, so strong under the baking summer sun that

THE MEDIEVAL MURDERERS

Bartholomew felt himself become breathless from want of clean air.

It took some time to make their way through the crowds and reach the riverside quays. These were a series of ramshackle piers, used to unload goods brought on the flat-bottomed boats that traversed the fens. The active ones in the southern part of the town were in better repair than the disused ones behind Michaelhouse, and it was to the dilapidated set that the beadle led them. The jetty Michaelhouse owned was among those that were virtually derelict, and anyone venturing on to it was taking his life in his hands. The area surrounding it was seedy and abandoned.

Tomas looked around. 'I do not like this place. It feels eerie.'

'Only because it is quiet after the hubbub of the main roads,' said Bartholomew, who was used to it. 'It can be quite pleasant on a balmy summer evening.'

'Well, it is not pleasant now,' retorted Tomas sharply. 'On a blazing afternoon with the sun at its hottest and more flies than leaves on the trees.'

Because July had been so dry, the river was considerably lower than usual. Stripes of dried black slime on the jetty's legs showed it was down by half the height of a man. The beadle pointed, and Bartholomew saw someone standing in the chest-high water at the end of the pier. The figure was leaning forward, so its head was just below the surface. A group of people had gathered to gawk at the spectacle, and Bartholomew saw Urban among them, sitting on a discarded barrel with his head in his hands. He appeared to be crying.

'We left the body where it was, so you could see for yourself,' said the beadle to Michael. He frowned. 'It is an odd way to die. If he had stood up straight, his head would have been above the water, and all he would have had to do was call for help. There was no need for him to drown.'

Before the monk could reply, Tomas darted forward and began to wade towards the corpse. The river shelved quickly, and water soon reached his waist. In his haste, he stumbled and disappeared completely. Bartholomew tensed, half expecting to be looking for a second body. The river was not deep, but its bottom was foul, and it was not unknown for a man's legs to become entangled in weeds or mud and for him to find himself unable to reach air again. But Tomas burst spluttering to the surface, and continued to make his way to the pathetic figure that bobbed up and down in the waves he created.

Bartholomew inched his way along the pier, aware that the boards had become very much more rotten since he had last ventured on to them. He warned Michael to stay where he was, suspecting the whole thing might collapse if too much weight was placed on it. When he reached the end, he knelt, noting that some of the planks had recently snapped off. The new breaks were bright, contrasting starkly with the dark green of the weathered ones. Tomas was just below him, struggling to lift Andrew's face above the surface. It was already far too late, but Tomas urged him to breathe anyway.

'There is nothing you can do,' said Bartholomew, leaning down to touch his shoulder. 'He has been dead too long.'

'His feet are stuck,' said Tomas in a voice that held a hint of panic. 'I cannot pull him out.'

'Mud,' explained Bartholomew. 'It is notoriously sticky in this part of the river, which is why no one is swimming here, even though the day is hot. Folk know to bathe elsewhere.'

'Andrew was a stranger,' said Tomas bitterly. 'He did not know to avoid this stretch of water. Besides, the mud is not as thick as you think. I am standing next to him, but I can still extricate my feet.'

Bartholomew regarded him intently. 'What are you saying? That something else is holding him there?'

Tomas rubbed a shaking hand over his eyes. 'I do not know. However, I can tell you one thing: the pouch containing his relic has gone.'

'Perhaps it was washed off during his death struggles. He told us Witney had damaged the cord that held it around his neck.'

'He would not have been that careless – not when he knew its loss would mean his death.'

'Give me his hands,' instructed Bartholomew. He saw where the Dominican was going with his assumptions, but was loath to accept that the relic had claimed another victim. 'I will pull him up.'

Tomas obliged, and Bartholomew took the frail arms and braced himself to haul. It was harder than he had imagined, and he was beginning to think he might have to enlist help when the river finally yielded its prize with a sticky plop and a gurgle of thick, black mud. He pulled the body on to the pier and knelt to examine it.

There was little to see. There was no wound on Andrew's head to indicate he might have been stunned before he entered the water, and no marks on hands or arms to suggest he had been involved in a struggle. He leaned on the old man's chest and watched frothy bubbles emerge from his mouth, leading him to suspect drowning as the cause of death. The only odd thing was that Andrew's pupils had contracted to tiny points, no larger than the hole made by a needle. While Tomas waded out of the river, Bartholomew carried the old man to the bank, where Urban was waiting. Michael took Bartholomew's arm and tugged him to one side.

'I have just spoken to Urban. He tells me Andrew was ill last night, and was beginning to accept that he might not have the strength to carry his True Cross to Norwich. He said he went out this morning, and when he returned, he no longer had the relic.'

'He lost it?' asked Bartholomew, slow to understand.

'He gave it to someone,' explained Michael. 'Someone who would take it north. Then he told Urban that he would die today, and, sure enough . . .'

'I thought his plan was to pass the thing to Urban,' interrupted Bartholomew, refusing to accept that some ancient curse was the cause of the old man's death.

'So did Urban.'

'I saw them earlier today,' said Bartholomew, struggling to recall whether the pouch had been around Andrew's neck at the time. He decided it was not, and concluded that Andrew must have just returned from passing it to his elected carrier. The old man had been tired, and the physician recalled his relief as he had sat on the churchyard wall. Urban, perching next to him, had been weeping – perhaps because he had just been told that he was not to be trusted with his master's quest. Had the novice been sufficiently hurt by the lack of trust to kill his master?

Bartholomew stared at Andrew's pale, water-logged features and wondered whether he had believed so strongly that he would die once the True Cross was out of his possession that he had jumped into the river of his own accord. The mind exerted a powerful force on the body, and it would not be the first time a man had willed himself to death.

Because Andrew was a visitor to Cambridge, and Urban seemed incapable of dealing with his master's body, it was Michael who arranged for it to be taken to St Botolph's Church. Bartholomew, Tomas and Urban carried the sad burden, and when they arrived Tomas took Urban to pray in the chancel, while Bartholomew manhandled Andrew into the parish coffin and Michael hunted for candles. When they had completed their sorry duties, Bartholomew studied Urban. His face was tear-streaked, and his shoulders slumped, as though he had been deprived of something very dear to him. The physician could not decide whether the loss related to his teacher, or to the fact that the relic was gone and he was no longer obliged to play a part in its journey.

'Tomas is interrogating him,' said Michael, watching. 'Except *his* enquiries sound rather more desperate and meaningful than did mine.'

Bartholomew watched the Dominican, and conceded that Michael was right. The expression on Tomas's face was more agonized than an informal discussion warranted, and it was clear that Andrew's death – or perhaps the disappearance of the relic – had grieved him as deeply as it had Urban. He walked over to them, wanting to hear what was said for himself. While Tomas's reaction to Andrew's sudden demise was odd, he still liked the man, and did not want Michael to draw all the conclusions regarding his behaviour.

'I thought he trusted me,' Urban was saying, scrubbing his face with his sleeve. 'I could not believe it when he said he had asked someone else to take it. I promised *I* would do it. I even offered to touch it, to prove my sincerity.'

'You did?' asked Tomas uneasily. 'When?'

'The day we arrived.' Urban sniffed. 'I would have done anything he asked!'

'I am sure he knew,' said Tomas kindly. 'I imagine he had grown fond of you, and did not want to load you with such a heavy burden.'

'Barzak's curse,' said Urban numbly. 'He was right – he said he would die the day the relic left his care. When he handed it to me, I hesitated. Perhaps that gave him second thoughts. I was a coward, when I should have been bold.'

'Being wary of handling holy relics shows good common sense, lad,' said Michael. 'Only a fool seizes them up as one might grab marchpanes at a feast. I doubt your caution reduced your standing in his eyes. But before we explore his death further, there is something I would like to ask. Have you ever been on the roof of St Bernard's Hostel?'

'No,' replied Urban miserably. 'Yes.'

Michael, who had joined them, regarded him with raised eyebrows. 'Well, which is it?'

'I did not go as far as the roof, only to the gables

on the upper floor. There was a pigeon's nest outside Witney's window, and he said the noise was driving him to distraction. I found him trying to climb a ladder one day, but he was a danger to himself, even on the lower rungs, so I went up instead. He gave me a penny, which I considered insulting.'

'Because you wanted more?' asked Michael.

Urban glared at him. 'Because I am a friar, and helping other people is part of my vocation. I do not require to be paid for acts of kindness, and I was offended that he thought I did.'

'Andrew,' prompted Tomas, more interested in the Carmelite than in Urban's sensitivities. 'What happened to bring him to this vile end today?'

Urban took a deep, shuddering breath. 'After he told me he had given the relic to someone else, he asked me to walk with him by the river. I was angry and distressed – refused to listen to him – and he wandered alone to the end of that pier, probably to avoid my stupid, prideful sulks. Then, before I could do anything to stop it, the boards snapped and he plunged into the river, feet first.'

'Feet first?' asked Bartholomew. 'He did not crumple or flail as he fell?'

'He went in as straight as an arrow. It was almost as if he knew the planks would break and he was ready for them. I tried to reach him, but I cannot swim and was afraid to venture too far from the bank.'

'The water is shallow at the moment, and the currents are weak,' said Michael. 'You could have reached him by wading, just as Tomas did.'

The novice regarded him with an agonized

expression. 'You mean I could have saved him, if I had had the courage to wade into the water?'

'No,' said Bartholomew before the monk could make matters worse. 'Even if you had reached him, you could not have prevented his death – for three reasons. First, it is obvious the pier's planks are rotten, especially at the far end, and I suspect Andrew knew exactly what he was doing when he trod on them. Second, your description of his fall sounds as though he intended to force himself deep into the water – to drown; his feet were certainly very firmly embedded in the mud. And third, he could have held his face above the surface of the water had he been so inclined. But he did not.'

'He is right,' agreed Tomas. 'Andrew believed he was going to die, and he willingly embraced his fate. There was nothing you could have done to save him. But did he tell you why he had elected to choose another man in your stead?'

'He said I was too young.'

'Did he tell you to whom he gave the relic?' asked Bartholomew.

Urban nodded. 'But he made me promise, on peril of my immortal soul, that I would never reveal the information. And I shall not, no matter what you do to me.' He thrust out his chin defiantly.

'Do not worry, lad; no one will force you to break your oath,' said Michael gently. He turned to Bartholomew. 'Are you *certain* his death was a combination of accident and self-murder? You do not think someone encouraged him out on to the pier, knowing it would collapse?'

'*I* did at first,' said Tomas, speaking before Bartholomew could reply. 'But not any more. I saw from Bartholomew's examination that there was nothing to suggest a struggle. Andrew allowed himself to die. I thought he would fight it.'

'How would *you* know what he might do?' demanded Urban. 'You do not know him. He was with me the whole time we have been in Cambridge – except this morning – and he never met you. How would a stranger know what he was like?'

'Is that so?' asked Michael mildly, eyeing Tomas's neck to see whether he wore a purple pouch. 'And where were you this morning, Tomas?'

'Andrew did not give me the relic,' said Tomas, understanding exactly what the monk was asking. 'I only wish he had.'

'He would never give it to a *Dominican*,' said Urban bitterly and rather accusingly. 'They would destroy it, claiming it heretical.'

'Many would,' admitted Tomas.

'Would you?' demanded Michael. 'You have been very coy about where you stand in the debate. Do you follow the teachings of your order, or are you of a more independent mind?'

'What I think is irrelevant . . .'

'You *did* know Andrew,' said Bartholomew, regarding the Dominican intently as certain facts became clear in his mind. 'Your reaction to his death has been one of distress. An ex-proctor, used to violence, would not have shown grief for a stranger – or for a man of brief and recent acquaintance. Ergo, you knew each other at some point in the past.'

Tomas bowed his head, and when he spoke his voice was so soft as to be almost inaudible. 'I knew

Andrew, although I took care not to let him see me here. I was once under his tuition.'

'You cannot have been,' said Urban unsteadily. 'You are a Dominican, and he is a Carmelite. He would have nothing to do with a Black Friar.'

'Andrew travelled when he was younger,' said Bartholomew. 'His prior sent him to Hungary, which is where Pécs is located. You met him there.'

Tomas nodded. 'I studied with him, but we disagreed on too many issues.'

'I do not believe you,' said Urban unhappily. 'We are *Carmelites*, and he would not have studied with a Dominican. Or did you come with the express intention of killing him and taking his relic?'

'A good question,' said Michael.

'It is coincidence that brought us to Cambridge at the same time,' replied Tomas. 'I never expected to see him again, and I did not make myself known when I spotted him in the street. I did not want my presence here to distress him.'

'But he knew you were here regardless,' said Bartholomew, thinking about what he had reasoned. 'He thought you did not see him, just as you thought he did not see you. But he did. He told me about you in a roundabout way – twice.'

Tomas stared at him. 'He did?'

'He said there was a student to whom he had hoped to entrust the relic, but the fellow proved unacceptable. He also said he had once held a post similar to that of proctor. So did you.'

'Yes,' admitted Tomas. 'I learned my skills from him.'

'He warned me about letting my own students have too much freedom of thought. He gave you too much, and you turned against him.'

Tomas hung his head. 'We grew apart as I read more, and he disliked me for it. We parted, and I never expected to see him again. I knew he had returned to England – to his beloved Devonshire – but that was all. It was a shock to see him here, so far from his home. But I loved him, and I would have taken his relic to Norwich, no matter what the cost.'

'He did not give it to you?' pressed Michael. 'It would make sense if he had. He would probably far rather send you – the traitor – to your death, than the boy of whom he was fond.'

Tomas winced. 'I wish now that I *had* made myself known to him, and that he had asked me to take the relic. But he did not.'

'You have far too many secrets, Tomas,' said Michael gravely. 'Is there anything else about you that I should know? If so, then tell me now. If I learn it from other sources, I shall arrest you and charge you with murder.'

'Whose murder?' demanded Tomas. 'Not Andrew's, because you have just concluded that his death was a suicide. And not Witney's, because I was with you when *he* died.'

'I shall make up my own mind about Andrew, and I will not allow your or Matt's interpretation of the "facts" to confuse me. So, I ask you again: is there anything else I should know?'

'No,' said Tomas. 'Not about me.' He looked at Urban, who glowered at him in the kind of way that suggested he intended the Dominican serious harm.

'Andrew's death is *your* fault,' Urban declared angrily. 'It was seeing you here that made him decide to accept an early death. If you had not appeared, none of this would have happened.'

'That is unfair,' said Bartholomew quietly. 'Besides, you should bear some responsibility for what has happened, because you have not been truthful, either.'

'What do you mean?' cried Urban.

'I mean you are no White Friar. I have been tending William de Lincolne, the Carmelite prior, for a fever of late. He is well acquainted with his order's foundations, and he tells me there is no Carmelite friary inside Exeter's walls – and Andrew was very specific about the positioning of his priory, because he felt its fortified location rendered his relic safe. In fact, Lincolne says there are only two friaries which match Andrew's description in Exeter, and they are Dominican and Franciscan. I strongly suspect you belong to one of these.'

Urban started to cry. 'I knew we would be found out sooner or later. I *knew* one of us would make a mistake that would see us exposed, especially in a place like this, where there are so many well-travelled mendicants.'

'Your real Order – the Dominicans – does not approve of blood relics,' continued Bartholomew. 'Your prior in Exeter – a man you called John de Burgo, although I am told there is no high-ranking Carmelite of that name – was newly elected, and you were afraid he might destroy the relic, acting boldly, as men freshly appointed often do in an attempt to make a mark.'

Urban nodded miserably. 'There is no point in denial now, and my role in the affair is over. Andrew and I *are* Dominicans, but he did not agree with our Order's stance on Holy Blood. He did not want his relic destroyed in a wave of religious bigotry, and that is why he did what he did.'

'Very noble,' said Michael dryly.

'People lie to me on a regular basis,' said Michael, as he and Bartholomew walked away from St Botolph's Church. 'But I do not think I have ever encountered quite so many untruths in such a short period of time as I have in this case.'

'Most are not lies, but omissions. Tomas neglected to mention his relationship with Andrew – as did Andrew himself – and Andrew and Urban told no one they were saving the relic from their own Order. And I have lied, too, I am afraid.'

Michael laughed. 'You? I do not think so! You are the worst dissembler I know, and I would have seen through you in an instant.'

'You did not this time, thankfully. I lied about Andrew. I do not think he jumped into the water of his own volition, for two reasons. First, the pupils in his eyes were severely contracted, which often means some sort of medicine or poison has been ingested; and second, it is not easy to stick your head under the surface and expect to drown – the instinct to lift it up again is too strong.'

Michael stared at him. 'Are you sure?'

'Not completely – mine is an inexact science – but there was a tiny pink-coloured phial in Andrew's scrip when I searched his body. The stopper was out and it was full of water, so I shall never be able to tell you what it originally contained. However, I cannot help but wonder whether he was given something to swallow – perhaps to calm him over giving up the relic – and it robbed him of the use of his limbs or made him lethargic. It would explain why he did not lift his head to breathe.'

'And you did not say this in front of Tomas and Urban because . . .?'

'Because one of them might have given it to him.'

'Interesting. You have always been more positive towards Tomas than I, but now you hesitate when it comes to sharing information with him. Why?'

'Because I had already suspected a prior connection between him and Andrew, and I did not know what it meant. They parted on bitter terms. Do you think he might have seen his former master and decided to avenge some ancient grievance?'

Michael nodded, pleased his friend was finally coming around to his way of thinking. 'However, it is equally possible that Urban might have avenged a more recent one. He is furious that Andrew gave the relic to someone else. Hurt. He may have fed him this substance, then shoved him in the water. They were alone, after all. But now I have two murders to investigate.'

'Andrew and Witney. I wonder whether they were claimed by the same hand. Whoever it is, the culprit is clever. Both deaths could easily be seen as accidents.'

'But not by us,' said Michael comfortably. 'We are clever, too. Let us consider Witney for a moment. You said he might not have been the intended victim. Perhaps Andrew was the target, because he stole a blood relic from his Order, and Witney's head happened to be in the wrong place at the wrong time.'

'Very wrong,' agreed Bartholomew. 'Perhaps the culprit is the current holder of the relic. However,

I doubt we will ever know, because he will be long gone with the thing, if he has any sense.'

'Where? To Norwich? Or to some Franciscan foundation that will pay handsomely for it?'

'He will die when he parts with it, if Andrew was to be believed, although I do not believe in such nonsense.'

'I wish Urban would tell us to whom Andrew entrusted it,' said Michael. 'Can we be sure it was not Tomas, his old student and a man he once loved? Urban is a solid, reliable lad, but he is not of Tomas's mettle. Urban would be very much a second choice.'

'Perhaps it was Seton. He is a Franciscan, who adheres to his Order's tenet that Holy Blood relics are worthy of veneration, unlike Witney. Or perhaps it was someone from the Dominican priory – Andrew preferred the Franciscan stance to that of his own Order, and he was not alone in rebelling. Morden admitted as much, after a fashion.'

'Morden never leaves Cambridge, and I cannot see Andrew passing such a valuable thing to a man who looks like an elf – or to one who barely knows what the Holy Blood debate entails. It will not be Morden, and it will not be his friars, either. They are all the same – likeable, but inveterately stupid.'

'What about the servants? Kip and John Roughe?'

'They are more intelligent than the men they serve,' agreed Michael. 'But they are untrustworthy. I do not see Andrew putting his faith in such low fellows.'

It was already past dusk, and Bartholomew was tired from a day of teaching, seeing patients, scrambling over roofs and inspecting bodies. He was ready for bed, and did not want to wake himself up by speculating further on the mysteries. When they reached Michaelhouse, he went to his chamber. He removed his tabard and boots in the gathering darkness, rinsed his hands in a bowl of fresh water, and lay on his bed, expecting sleep to claim him immediately.

The room was stifling, so he rose to open the window. After he had lain down again, he found he was too hot in shirt and leggings, so stood to remove them. By the time he was comfortable, the Franciscans in the room opposite had embarked on a noisy debate, and their strident voices roused him from the edge of a doze. He climbed to his feet a third time, to close the window. But the friars' discussion was an intense one, and their clamour carried on the still night air. They were just loud enough for him to make out some of the words, so he knew they were arguing about the Holy Blood and its place in the mass. He returned to his bed but found himself straining to catch what they were saying, so pulled the blanket over his head to block out the sound. But the hot night made many scholars restless. There was a constant procession across the yard for drinks or visits to the latrines, and someone was playing a lute. Bartholomew slept fitfully, and by the morning he felt wearier than when he had retired.

He joined his colleagues in the yard as they assembled to process to the church, breathing in deeply the slightly cooler air that whispered in from the east. After the mass, he remembered that it was Saturday, and that he had arranged for his students to study with another master, which meant he was free. Normally he used any spare time to write the treatise on fevers that took most of his free hours, but he could not settle to it that day. He was not sure whether the problem was the heat or the odd business surrounding the relic.

Since there was no point in staring at blank parchment all morning, waiting for inspiration, he went in search of Michael, who was enjoying an illicit second breakfast in the kitchens. The monk waved to a stool, inviting the physician to join him in a small repast comprising oatcakes smeared in white grease and heavily sprinkled with salt. Bartholomew declined, knowing they would only make him thirsty. The monk had just started to outline again some of the facts they had uncovered about the deaths of Andrew and Witney when there was a tap on the door and one of his beadles sidled into the room.

'You are needed, Brother,' he said, eyeing the oatcakes longingly. 'You too, Doctor.'

'Is it Prior Lincolne of the Carmelites?' asked Bartholomew. 'I thought his fever was over.'

'It is Urban, the novice. Hurry, though. I am no physician, but I can tell he does not have long for this world.'

'Where?' demanded Michael, making for the door.

'St Andrew's Church,' replied the beadle, standing aside to let the senior proctor go first, so he could steal an oatcake before he followed.

Bartholomew and Michael hurried along the streets in the early morning light. Carts and people were already out, indicating that few were sleeping long when the heat was so intense. Even before the sun had fully risen, the town was sticky and humid, and Bartholomew felt himself become breathless as he walked, as though there were not enough air to go around. Michael panted next to him, complaining vociferously about the wretched furnace of a sun.

Urban had been stricken in the churchyard, and he lay in the long grass near the porch. Both scholars stopped dead when they saw they were not the first to arrive: Tomas was there, kneeling next to the novice and giving him last rites. Bartholomew was aware of Michael's tense anger, but he could hardly object to a friar's prayers for a dying soul, and so was obliged to hold his tongue until the ritual was finished. It was some time before Tomas packed away the chrism and the stole he wore around his neck; the Dominican took his duties seriously.

'What happened?' asked Michael in a whisper to Bartholomew while they waited. 'Can you see?'

'It looks as though Urban has fallen on top of something,' replied Bartholomew. 'I can see a spike protruding from his stomach, and he is lying awkwardly.'

'Fell or was pushed?' asked Michael.

Bartholomew shrugged. 'It is impossible to say – not from this distance and without having inspected the wound, and probably not even then. You will have to ask him. Tomas has finished now.'

Bartholomew dropped to his knees, assessing the young man's injury, but making no attempt to touch it. As he had surmised, Urban had toppled on to a metal spike that had pierced him clean through. It was an ugly wound, but Urban did not seem to be in pain, although his hands were stained red with his own blood. Bartholomew suspected it had damaged his spine and deprived him of feeling. There was nothing he could do to save him, and there was no point in moving him when it would only cause him discomfort in his last few moments.

While Michael spoke gently, identifying himself and telling Urban what he needed to know, Bartholomew studied the object that had killed the lad. At first, he saw only that it was an unusual shape and seemed to be attached to the ground. Eventually, he realized that it was the shoe-scraper that stood outside many churches, so parishioners could remove the worst of the muck from their feet before entering. Urban had dropped, fallen or been pushed on top of one that was particularly ornate, and it had speared him like a fish.

'Dr Bartholomew is here,' said Michael softly, when the lad's eyes seemed to focus on him at last. 'Do you want anything to ease the pain?'

'There is no pain,' whispered Urban. 'Only cold.'

Bartholomew removed his tabard and laid it over him, although he doubted it would make much difference. Without a moment's hesitation, Tomas hauled off his habit and wrapped it around the lad's legs, revealing a light shift that was unusually clean for a garment that was probably never seen by anyone else.

'Did Andrew take any medicines?' asked Bartholomew. 'Perhaps something for the ache in his back – his old wound?'

'Poppy syrup – but only when it became very bad,' replied Urban. He gave a sudden, heart-broken sob. 'I cannot believe he so suddenly decided he would not complete his journey. I would have helped him, no matter what the cost. I lied for him, too. Seton was not in St Bernard's Hostel when Witney died. We said he was with the body when we found it, because we knew *he* was going to accuse *us* of the crime, and it was the only way to make sure you knew we were innocent.'

'Never mind that,' said Michael softly. 'Did someone push you on to that spike? Tell me his name.'

Urban shook his head. 'No one pushed me. I am dying because of Barzak's curse. I touched the relic, you see.'

'I thought you hesitated,' said Bartholomew, not sure he wanted to hear about another death for which the relic was deemed responsible. 'And that Andrew had second thoughts about your—'

Michael silenced him with a glare. 'We believe your master may have been murdered,' he said, as gently as such grim news could be imparted. 'It is possible that the man to whom he gave the relic was also the villain who killed him. As far as I am concerned, this releases you from your promise to Andrew. You are dying, but I will avenge you and him if you tell me this fellow's name.'

'Thomas,' said Urban in a whisper. Bartholomew could tell by the glazed look in his eyes that he could no longer see Michael.

'Thomas?' asked Michael, looking up at the friar, who appeared to be astonished by the claim.

'Andrew took it to the Dominican priory, and gave it to Kip Roughe with orders that he was to pass it to Thomas,' breathed Urban. 'He put it in a box, so Roughe would not touch it and become a victim of Barzak's curse, too. He was careful. I touched it, though, when Roughe gave it to the wrong Thomas.'

'What do you mean?' pressed Michael, confused by the disjointed explanation.

Urban swallowed. 'Andrew told me he had arranged for the relic to go to his old student, but it was clear that had not happened yesterday: Tomas did not have it. I was jealous at first, but then I came to my senses – if that was what Andrew wanted, then it was my duty to see his wishes fulfilled. I asked Roughe about the box, and I realized why it was not in Tomas's possession.'

'Because Roughe had stolen it for himself?' guessed Michael.

'Because he had given it to Big Thomas, not Tomas of Pécs,' said Bartholomew, quicker on the uptake. 'Andrew is a stranger here: he did not know that there is more than one Thomas at the Dominican priory.'

Urban nodded. 'I had to put matters right. I persuaded Big Thomas to give it back – told him it was cursed and he yielded it eventually . . .' He trailed off with a weak cough that brought blood to his lips.

Michael waited until Bartholomew had wiped the boy's face. 'Then what? Did Big Thomas change his mind and demand it back, so he would not die from this curse, too?'

Urban did not seem to hear. 'I wanted to give it to Tomas secretly, without anyone else seeing. So I hid among those bushes, and waited for him to attend prime. Roughe said Tomas keeps all his religious offices – Andrew taught him well. When I was safely hidden from prying eyes, I opened the box to make sure the splinter was inside its vial. But the night was dark and I could not see, so I was obliged to identify it by touch.' His eyes became dreamy. 'It it so small. It should be bigger, after all the lives it has claimed.'

'What happened next?' urged Michael as Urban's eyes closed. 'Did you fall?'

'I dropped it,' said Urban in an agonized whisper. 'The hot wind blew dust in my eye. It hurt, and the relic slipped from my hand as I tried to rub it out.'

'Lord!' muttered Michael, leaping up and lifting his feet to make sure he was not treading on it. 'Are you saying that it is here somewhere?'

Urban shook his head. 'I put it back in the box, and hid again. But . . .'

'Yes?' asked Michael urgently. 'But what?'

'Someone came . . . he tripped me,' said Urban weakly. He became agitated. 'Where is it now? Did I give it to the right Thomas? I cannot recall.'

'I have it,' said Tomas, kneeling next to the lad, while Bartholomew held his head and soothed him by stroking his hair. 'It is safe, so do not despair. You have done your duty to Andrew and to Christ's Holy Blood.'

'Thank God,' breathed Urban. And then he died.

'Do you have the relic?' asked Michel, watching Tomas don his habit, while Bartholomew covered Urban's face with his tabard. 'Where is it?'

'I do not,' said Tomas, indicating that there was nowhere for it to be. There was nothing but a wooden cross around his neck, while he carried no purse or scrip at his side. 'The boy was distraught, so I told him what he needed to hear in order to die in peace. I lied, Brother, although doing so gave me no pleasure. It was simply the right thing to do.'

'Lying to dying men is right?' asked Bartholomew doubtfully.

'On occasion,' said Tomas. 'What good could have come from telling him he had sacrificed his life for nothing?'

'Who tripped him? Who forced him on to that scraper?' Michael was looking at Tomas in a way that made it clear he was the prime suspect.

'I attended prime with several other Dominicans,' said Tomas. 'I did not see Urban when we arrived – although I confess I did not look in the bushes – and he was lying here when we came out. You must look elsewhere for your murderer, Brother – and for your thief, too.'

'Have you searched for the relic?' asked Bartholomew. 'Perhaps it flew from Urban's fingers as he fell, and it is still here.'

'Your beadles did that after I raised the alarm and told them what had happened,' replied Tomas. 'I did not, because I was absolving a dying boy. Besides, I have no wish to take possession of something so dangerous. If Andrew had asked me to take it, then it would have been hard for me to refuse him, a man to whom I owe a great deal. But I would not have accepted it from Urban.'

'Why not?' asked Michael. 'You are a Dominican, and they renounce the efficacy of relics containing Holy Blood.'

'Perhaps we do, but there is no need to ignore the warnings of centuries,' said Tomas tartly. 'The cold fact is that people who touch this thing die –

whether from accidents, murder or just driven to take their own lives. I want none of it.'

'Very courageous,' remarked Michael.

'Would *you* touch it?' demanded Tomas, finally angry. 'If I found it here, in the churchyard, and handed it to you, would you take it?' Michael had no reply. 'No! I did not think so.'

'This is not the place for such a debate,' said Bartholomew. 'One of you needs to anoint Urban, and then we can carry him inside.'

'Forgive me,' said Tomas, glaring at Michael as he knelt again. 'I became distracted with earthly concerns when I should have been performing my priestly duties.'

Michael moved away, pulling Bartholomew with him, and assessed the Dominican through narrowed eyes. 'I cannot make him out, Matt. However, I do not like the fact that he was here when a grisly murder took place – and one most certainly did. You heard Urban say someone tripped him and flung him down on to that sharp implement.'

'I heard him say he was tripped,' corrected Bartholomew. 'He did not say it was to fling him to his death. There is a big difference.'

'Really? Then where is the relic, if the objective was not to kill him and steal what he possessed? You are too willing to protect that priest, and I am tired of it.'

'You are exasperated because you have no evidence,' said Bartholomew, knowing the real cause of the monk's anger. 'And you are appalled that people are dying and you have no idea why or how. It is nothing to do with Tomas.'

'Perhaps,' said Michael, sounding weary. 'But I

do not like his connections to our three victims – Andrew, his old master; Urban, who took his place; Witney, with whom he discussed the Holy Blood polemic.'

'Do not forget the Roughe brothers,' said Bartholomew. 'They had possession of the relic, albeit briefly, when they passed it to the wrong Thomas. Andrew might have put it in a box to protect them, but I am willing to wager anything you like that they looked inside it before they did as they were asked.'

'And probably touched it. So, we may be looking for two more corpses.'

Bartholomew was not so sure. 'They are missing, but I do not think they are dead – yet. However, we must not forget Big Thomas, either. He may have looked at the relic, too.'

Michael groaned. 'We shall visit him today and ask about it. But look at Tomas, kneeling and praying so diligently over a lad who may be his latest victim. I do not believe his presence here is coincidence, Matt. I really do not.'

When they arrived at the Dominican priory to ask Big Thomas about the missing relic, Prior Morden hurried to greet them, his elfin face creased with worry.

'Little Tomas told me what happened this morning,' he began, wringing his hands as he stared up at Michael's monstrous bulk. 'It is a dreadful business, but I hope you do not think a Dominican brought about this death. A number of friars – and some were Franciscans, so you can be certain *they* would not lie in our favour – were with Tomas when Urban met his end, so he is not your culprit.'

'It is not Tomas I want to see, but his namesake,' said Michael.

'He did not dispatch Urban, either,' squeaked Morden in alarm. 'And you must not make that accusation publicly. Can you imagine how it will look, to have one of our Order accused of killing a Carmelite?'

Michael shrugged. 'If he has done nothing wrong, he has nothing to worry about. Where is he?'

'Unwell,' replied Morden. 'He was unable to attend church this morning.'

Bartholomew felt a pang of unease. Was Barzak's malediction working its ugly magic on Big Thomas, too? Or was he allowing an overactive imagination to run away with him? He had heard so many people say the curse was real that he was slowly beginning to believe it. 'What is wrong with him?'

'We do not know. Some ailment brought on by the heat, perhaps.'

Without further ado, Morden led them to the dormitory where his friars slept. It was larger than the one used by the novices, but it was a more pleasant chamber. Large windows flooded it with light and it boasted immaculately polished floorboards, spotless walls and cobweb-free window sills. Several friars were there, sitting in companionable silence as they read or knelt in quiet contemplation. Tomas of Pécs was on the pallet nearest the door, but was engrossed in a psalter and did not look up as Morden trotted to the far end of the hall, where Big Thomas lay. Bartholomew advanced cautiously, aware that even if the ailment was something within his powers to treat, he might die regardless: the mind held a powerful sway over the body.

'Here is Dr Bartholomew to tend you, Brother,' said Morden loudly, as if he thought illness rendered the sufferer hard of hearing, too. 'Sit up, so he can make his examination and calculate a horoscope for your recovery.'

'No!' shouted Thomas, making several men jump. 'Make him go away.'

'Why?' asked Morden, startled. 'He is here to help you.'

'He cannot,' cried Thomas. 'No one can. Go away.'

So, the relic's curse would work yet again, thought Bartholomew unhappily. Thomas would die simply because he believed he was beyond earthly help, and there was nothing a mere physician could do to prevent it.

'You look well enough to me,' said Morden. His eyes narrowed. 'Are you telling the truth? You have not fabricated this illness as an excuse to stay in bed?'

Big Thomas looked furtive. 'No,' he said, clutching the blanket to his chin.

'Perhaps we could speak alone,' said Bartholomew. 'A physical consultation is a very private thing, and I do not usually conduct them with an audience.'

'Very well,' said Morden, ignoring Thomas's furious protestations as he retreated with Michael to the other end of the room. The monk watched sullenly, resentful that he had been excluded. His irritation did not focus on Bartholomew for long, however. Tomas had been distracted from his text by his namesake's yells, and the monk homed in on him, to ask more questions about his movements during the time that Urban met with his unpleasant death.

'You are not ill,' said Bartholomew to the ugly friar. 'And *that* is why you say no one can help you – they cannot, because you do not need a cure. Prior Morden is right: you feigned sickness because you want to remain indoors today. Why?'

Thomas rubbed calloused hands over his face. 'Damn Prior Morden! Why did he have to fetch *me* a physician, when I told him all I needed was rest and good food? It is not fair! He does not foist physicians on other friars, when *they* decide to take a day off from their labours.'

'You are malingering because you do not want to work?'

'Gate duty,' explained Thomas bitterly. 'I *hate* it. Why can they not use me as a thatcher, which is where my skills lie? Have you seen the state of the roof here? It is in desperate need of repair.' He sighed. 'Now you will tell him I am shamming, and I will be forced to do gate duty for the next month, as penance.'

'I will not tell him – but only if you answer my questions,' said Bartholomew. 'Kip Roughe brought you a box recently.'

'He said it contained a relic – a gift from a Carmelite,' replied Big Thomas, transparently keen to be helpful. He frowned. 'It was odd, actually, because I do not know this Carmelite. No one ever brings me presents, and to be frank, I did not like the look of this one.'

'Did you open it? To see what was inside?'

'I was going to, but I have been talking to Tomas, and he mentioned a blood relic that kills anyone who touches it. He said it was missing, so I decided to be cautious, and let someone else open it instead.'

'Who?' asked Bartholomew uneasily. 'Did Tomas look on your behalf?'

'I did not trust him not to steal it, so I took it to Kip Roughe instead. Do you *promise* not to tell Prior Morden any of this? He will be angry if he finds out – and that would not be fair, because I gained nothing from it.'

'I promise,' said Bartholomew reluctantly. 'But what have you done?'

'When Kip heard what the box held, he suggested I sell it to an abbey. He looked inside – he said we needed to be sure what it contained before we acted – and there was a small glass bottle. It was the relic right enough: we were going to be rich! I hid the box under my bed, but then Urban came to see me and repeated everything Little Tomas said – only *he* told me what had happened in Devonshire thirty years ago, when his master was witness. He said the relic had come to me by mistake, and offered to risk his life by returning it to its rightful carrier.'

'And you handed it over?'

'I did – the boy was very persuasive, and I am not ready to die yet. Kip was furious, of course, but that is too bad. I know my Order claims Holy Blood relics have no divinity, but I am not so sure. Urban's master died from being around this one, and so did that Oxford man who tried to steal it from him – Witney. Urban told me *he* would die, too, as soon as he had delivered it to Norwich. These things are beyond the ken of us mortals, and I am inclined to leave such matters to those who think they know what they are doing.'

'Very wise,' said Bartholomew. 'Where is Kip now?'

'I have not seen him since we argued. Perhaps he is dead – he did touch the relic, after all. Do you think the curse can pass through wood, Doctor? Will I die, because I held that damned box?'

'No,' said Bartholomew, as firmly as he could. 'You will not die. However, your prior may have other ideas if you malinger. You do not look ill, so I would not try to fool him, if I were you.'

Thomas grinned in a conspiratorial manner that made Bartholomew feel guilty. He took his leave and went to where Michael was standing over Little Tomas. Immediately, he sensed something was wrong. Several friars had gathered in a quiet block behind their prior, and Tomas was kneeling on the floor, an expression of shock on his dark features.

'You are just in time, Matt,' said Michael grimly, as Bartholomew approached. 'I want you to see this.'

'I do not know how that came to be here,' said Tomas in the kind of voice that suggested he had said as much before and had not been believed. 'I have no use for poppy syrup.'

'I have witnessed *one* use of late,' said Michael. He held several pots in his hand, all labelled as containing a powerful soporific. 'It can be fed to elderly friars, so they drown when they are pushed in the river.'

Tomas's face was white. 'You think *I* brought about Andrew's death? I was not even there, as Urban will tell you. I was with you – you watched me try to save him.'

'We cannot ask Urban, as you well know,' said

Michael coolly. 'He is dead – murdered attempting to give *you* the missing relic.'

'That had nothing to do with me,' protested Tomas. 'Many friars saw me—'

'You are clever,' interrupted Michael. 'It is not beyond your talents to arrange witnesses to "prove" your innocence. However, no one else has strong soporifics in his possession, and a substance like this contributed to Andrew's death.'

Tomas's shoulders sagged in defeat. 'Is there nothing I can say to make you believe me?'

Michael's expression was harsh. 'You had an ancient quarrel with Andrew, while Urban had something you wanted. You did not have to kill the boy – he was going to give you the relic anyway.'

Meanwhile, Morden had been searching the rest of the friar's possessions. He held something up for the monk to see. 'What is this? It looks like a diagram, but I cannot tell of what.'

Michael took it from him, and when he looked at Tomas, his eyes were accusing. 'It is a picture of the chimney at Bernard's Hostel, and a map showing the safest way across the roof towards it. Now I see why you were prepared to risk your life to climb up there with Matt. We thought you were trying to help, but your intention was to make sure he interpreted the harness and the pile of missiles in a way that suited you. So, you killed Witney, too.'

'No!' cried Tomas, appalled. 'I have killed no one!'

'The evidence is too strong to ignore,' said Michael gravely, gazing at the stunned faces that surrounded him. 'I have always been suspicious of you, Tomas, and now I see I was right. You have lied to us from the start – about the fact that you were once Andrew's student, and about your true purpose here.'

'To study angels,' began Morden, appalled at what was happening.

'To spy for your Master-General,' said Michael harshly. 'To find out what honest Dominican friars think of the Holy Blood debate, and to report these findings to powerful men.' He pointed a finger at Tomas. '*You* are our killer – and I am arresting you on three counts of murder.'

Tomas was led from the Dominican priory and marched through the town to be placed in a cell near the church of St Mary the Great. He said nothing more in his defence, but declined to provide Michael with details of his various crimes. Bartholomew walked behind him, feeling angry and rather guilty. He had liked Tomas, and had defended him against Michael's accusations, but he had been wrong, and he was unsettled to think he may have influenced the monk in a way that had seen a murderer left free to take another two victims – Andrew and Urban.

'I cannot make you speak to me,' said Michael as he prepared to abandon the Dominican in the proctors' prison. 'But it would be helpful if you would tell me where you have hidden the relic. Holy Blood is potent, and should be treated with respect. I would like it put somewhere safe, where it will do no more harm.'

'Against the teachings of my Order, I am inclined to agree with your assessment,' replied Tomas. 'Holy Blood is powerful *and* divine. But I cannot tell you where it is, because I do not know.'

'Urban gave it to you before he died,' pressed Michael.

Tomas sighed softly. 'The only words we exchanged pertained to his absolution. I knew he did not have many moments to live, and I thought the fate of his immortal soul was of greater importance than this tainted relic. He tried to talk about it – he said it dropped from his hand when he fell on the shoe-scraper – but I urged him to make his final confession instead.'

'I will find it,' vowed Michael. 'I will dig up the churchyard if I have to, but I will recover it.'

'Good,' said Tomas with a smile that lacked humour. 'It is a comfort to know that it will soon be in your able hands.'

Bartholomew regarded him uneasily. His comment sounded like a threat. He decided to go with the monk when he began his search, and ensure he was very careful before he laid hands on anything that looked like a splinter in an ancient glass vial. He rubbed a hand through his hair, realizing that he, too, was becoming certain there was something sinister about the relic – beginning to accept that it could do great harm to those unfortunate enough to come into contact with it.

'It will go better for you if you tell me where it is,' said Michael, trying for the last time.

'I know,' said Tomas tiredly. 'But I cannot tell what I do not know.'

Michael locked the door to Tomas's cell, and walked into the sunlight, heaving a sigh of relief. 'The case is solved. The diagram of the hostel's roof proves he planned mischief up there, and I imagine his intended victim was Andrew.

Unfortunately, it was Witney who went to investigate odd noises coming from the chimney and he paid the ultimate price for his curiosity.'

Bartholomew nodded, feeling chilled, despite the warmth of the sun. 'Tomas mentioned a discussion he had had with his namesake about roofs. On its own, it means nothing, but it is suspicious in the light of Witney's peculiar death.'

Michael nodded, eyes gleaming as details of the case began to come together in a way that made sense. 'He was taking advantage of Big Thomas's expertise. But his cunning ploy failed. Still determined to kill Andrew, he fed him a powerful dose of poppy syrup to render him helpless, and encouraged him to walk on to the rotten jetty. And we know how he killed Urban.'

Bartholomew frowned. Michael's explanation was too simple, and did not take into account some of the facts. 'I am not sure about this. First, Urban did not mention Tomas giving Andrew potent medicine, or being present when the old man trod on the pier. He said they were alone. Second, I saw Andrew and Urban not long before Andrew died, and Tomas was not with them. And third, we know Urban was killed while Tomas was praying inside the church – we have independent witnesses who will attest to that.'

Michael did not seem discomfited that his carefully constructed explanation had several glaring inconsistencies. He shrugged. 'As I keep saying, Tomas is clever. Perhaps he will answer these questions when I interview him again later, but perhaps he will not, and we will never know.'

'Are you certain of his guilt? Sure enough to see him hang?'

Michael raised his hands, palms upward. 'That is for a jury to decide. But the diagram and the hidden soporifics are damning, Matt. Even you must see that. And do not forget we are still missing Kip Roughe. It would not surprise me if his corpse were to appear sooner or later, too.'

'Then you are going to be disappointed,' said Bartholomew, pointing across the street. 'Because there he is, and his brother John is with him.'

Michael shot across the road to apprehend the servants. The pair looked distinctly uneasy when they saw the monk bearing down on them and, for a moment, looked as though they might run. But they held their ground, and waited until he reached them.

'You have been missing,' said Michael without preamble. 'We were afraid something untoward had happened to you.'

'Something did,' replied Kip harshly. 'Tomas.'

'What do you mean?' asked Bartholomew. 'Did he try to harm you?'

'Several times,' replied John. 'He shot a crossbow at us one night, as we were leaving a tavern. It was a good thing Kip had not swallowed as much ale as me, or I would not be talking to you now – he pushed me to safety. Then Tomas rode a horse at us, aiming to crush us under its hoofs. He is a dangerous man, Brother, and I am relieved you have him under lock and key.'

'We heard the good news a few moments ago,' elaborated Kip. 'We have been hiding in a cousin's house, terrified that he might try again.'

'Why did you not tell me this sooner?' demanded Michael.

'Would you have believed two servants over a

friar?' asked Kip scornfully. 'Of course not! He would have told you that *we* attacked *him*, and then it would have been *us* at the gibbet. Still, we hear you have proper evidence against him now.'

'We do,' acknowledged Michael.

Bartholomew was not so sure. 'Bulmer said it was you who were trying to kill Tomas, not the other way around – *you* shot the arrow and rode the horse. He said you and he were suspicious of Tomas, and were stalking him together.'

'When we learned Bulmer felt the same way as us, we offered to combine forces,' admitted John. 'But Bulmer proved too hot headed. He intended to murder Tomas, while all we wanted was to watch him and see what he did. We were arguing about it when the horse crashed into him.'

'Bulmer's jaw,' said Bartholomew, remembering. 'I said at the time that it did not look like an injury from a punch. He was hit by a horse?'

'A horse ridden by Tomas.' John nodded. 'We said Bulmer should tell Morden what had happened, but he was afraid Tomas would smother him in his sickbed.'

'All this is most interesting,' said Michael. 'And I shall ask you to repeat it in front of a jury when Tomas is brought to trial. But we are still missing the relic. Do you know where it is?'

'Tomas must have it,' said John. 'Was it not among his belongings?'

'Not that I saw.'

'He has hidden it, then,' declared Kip. His face dissolved into an expression of fury. 'I detest that man and his sly ways. He came here to spy, you know. He intended to take tales to the Master-General about the Cambridge priory, and have it closed down over this Holy Blood nonsense. He *says* he is from Pécs, but old Father Andrew once lived in Pécs and *he* said Tomas was never there. I imagine that is why Tomas made an end of him.'

Bartholomew knew he was lying. 'Andrew would have said no such thing – he had no reason to deny his former student's existence, especially to servants. Besides, Tomas did not have the relic when he gave Urban last rites, but Urban definitely had it with him in the graveyard, because he told us so.'

'Andrew's relic is just a splinter,' said Kip, eyeing him angrily. 'Tomas could have hidden it anywhere on his person.'

'No, he could not,' argued Bartholomew. 'He removed his habit to cover Urban, and he has no purse.'

'He wears a shift, though,' persisted John. 'It could have been there, in some secret fold. He probably took off his habit just to "prove" he had not stolen the relic. As we said, he is cunning – he never does anything without some sinister motive.'

'How do you know the relic is a splinter?' asked Bartholomew. 'Have you seen it out of its vial?'

'Oh, yes,' replied Kit carelessly. 'Big Thomas asked us to open the box – before Urban asked for it back again – and I took it out then. It is nothing to look at – just a bit of wood, stained black at one end.'

'You touched it?' asked Bartholomew uneasily.

'Only for a moment.' Kip had the grace to look sheepish. 'Big Thomas was going to sell it to an abbey, and share the profits with us, but Urban took it away before we could damn our souls. I expect the curse led us to be tempted by the Devil.'

'You touched it?' asked Bartholomew again.

Kip regarded him sombrely. 'For the shortest of moments. But do not be concerned: Barzak's curse will not affect me. Even Little Tomas admits it only kills the wicked.'

'I have some excellent French wine in my room,' said Michael, watching the two servants swagger away. 'We should share it, to celebrate our success.'

'I do not want to celebrate,' said Bartholomew. 'I want to think. There are too many people telling me what I should and should not believe – and nearly all of it is contradictory. None of the tales fit together. Tomas said Kip and John attacked him with a crossbow – and so did Bulmer – but now the brothers say it was the other way around.'

'Tomas is a killer, Matt,' said Michael patiently. 'He will say anything to shift the blame away from himself, and it has worked admirably until now.'

'I want to visit St Bernard's Hostel,' said Bartholomew. The hostel was only a few steps along High Street. 'I need to examine the place where Witney died again.'

Michael sighed. 'It is too hot to go on fools' errands. I accept there are loose ends and questions that have not been answered, but we have been in this position before. It is no good looking for logical explanations when you have a clever man like Tomas as your culprit.'

'There *is*, Brother,' insisted Bartholomew, knocking at the hostel door. 'Tomas is a theologian and a scholar – he lives by logic. Of course we should look for logic in any crimes he is accused of committing.'

The door was opened by a servant who had the

heavy-eyed gaze of someone who had enjoyed too much ale with his midday meal. Bartholomew pushed past him and made his way to the chamber in which Witney had died. The servant did not seem to care, and returned to the kitchen to resume his post-prandial nap. When Bartholomew and Michael reached the hall, Seton was there, sitting in a window seat and nodding drowsily over a religious tract which lay open on his knees.

'I hear you arrested Witney's murderer,' he said. 'It is a pity you did not catch him before he claimed another two lives. I did not like Andrew and Urban, but it is unfortunate they had to die before the case was resolved.'

'It was,' replied Michael coldly, disliking the implication that his inefficiency had resulted in additional victims.

Seton saw that his barb had hit its mark and smiled nastily. Then he gestured to a corner, where two packs had been carelessly stuffed with various items of clothing. 'Since there was no one else to do it, I gathered up what belonged to them. Perhaps you could arrange for it to be collected?'

Bartholomew inspected the scruffy bags. 'This is everything?'

'They did not own much.'

'What is this?' asked Bartholomew, prising a glass container from a pouch that had been sewn inside the older of the two packs. 'Medicine?'

'Andrew told me it was poppy syrup, which eased the pain of an old wound and allowed him to sleep. I saw him swallow most of what he had left the morning he died.'

Bartholomew raised the phial to his nose and smelled the dregs: poppy syrup. 'You have a problem, Brother. This phial is virtually identical to the one I found with Andrew's body. However, it is considerably smaller than the ones you discovered under Tomas's bed.'

'So what?' demanded Michael.

'I only ever saw Andrew drink from that kind of container,' said Seton. 'They all have a strange pinkish colour; I remember them well.'

'I suspect we were right about Andrew's death in the first place,' said Bartholomew, sitting on a bench with the bottle in his hand. 'Andrew was in pain, and regularly swallowed poppy syrup as a palliative. Now we have Seton telling us he imbibed a hefty dose – all his remaining supply – before he died, which explains the contracted pupils. I think Andrew took his own life, just as we thought. He jumped into the river – hard and straight, as Urban described – and he drowned because he was unable to raise his head. But Tomas had nothing to do with it.'

'Perhaps,' said Michael, reluctantly. 'But he still killed Witney and Urban.'

Bartholomew was thoughtful. 'Do you still have that diagram?'

Michael rummaged in his scrip, and produced it with a flourish.

'Where did you get that?' demanded Seton, trying to snatch it away from him. His eyes narrowed. 'Big Thomas!'

Several facts came together in Bartholomew's mind. 'Unless I am very much mistaken, this picture belonged to Witney.'

'What if it did?' demanded Seton angrily. 'What business is it of yours?'

'It is very much our business,' said Bartholomew

softly. 'It proves Witney had more than a passing interest in that chimney. The picture was among Tomas's possessions, but he was astonished when you found it, Brother. I think someone else put it there – just as someone else left the wrongly sized, wrongly coloured medicine phials for you to discover.'

Michael narrowed his eyes. 'Are you saying someone placed evidence in a way that was deliberately intended to mislead me?'

Bartholomew nodded. 'Tomas is an easy target, because he is a foreigner, and everyone is suspicious of outsiders. No one was surprised when he was revealed to be the killer – shocked, but not surprised. However, he is innocent.'

'I do not see how you can claim all this from a drawing,' said Michael. 'It—'

'I see exactly what happened now. Witney was planning to do something untoward on the roof. The harness and the pile of missiles were his, not Tomas's – just as this diagram was his. And his interest in the chimney explains why he was found dead with his head sticking up it.'

'You are wrong,' said Seton, although his voice lacked conviction. 'Witney was not interested in the chimney because he wanted to kill someone, but because a savage draught whistled down it. He told me so when I found him poking about up it once.'

'Then you are not the only one who caught him doing something odd involving the roof,' mused Bartholomew. 'So did Urban, although he did not understand its significance. He found Witney with a ladder, and Witney fabricated some tale about a pigeon's nest. But the reality was that he was about to ascend to the roof to set his lethal trap with stones. He pretended to be inept at climbing when Urban saw him – the boy ended up knocking down the nest himself. But do you remember what Kip Roughe said about the people who had recently borrowed Bene't's long ladder, Brother?'

'That Witney had done so *once or twice*,' said Michael. 'If his purpose had been just to rid himself of a noisy pigeon, once would have sufficed.' He turned to Seton with considerable anger. 'Why did you not tell us about his interest in the chimney before? Surely, you must have seen it was pertinent to my enquiries?'

'It was irrelevant,' snapped Seton. 'The poor man was *murdered*!'

'I am not so sure about that,' said Bartholomew. 'You and Urban both noticed his fascination with the roof – and with the relic. Andrew said he had tried to take it by force, and I think he was telling the truth. Witney was a fanatic, passionate about the Holy Blood debate and, contrary to his Order's teachings, believed blood relics should be destroyed. He took it upon himself to oblige, but first, he had to dispatch its owner.'

Seton rubbed his eyes tiredly. 'I did see him covered in thatching once. He told me he had been looking for pigeon eggs as a surprise for my supper. But then he was murdered, and . . .'

'He was *not* murdered,' said Bartholomew. 'He set his trap with loose masonry in the chimney, and then came to see if it would work. Perhaps it was a freak gust of wind, or perhaps it really was Barzac's curse, but a stone fell just as he happened to look up it. The rock did not kill him, but the soot that tumbled down with it did. It was an accident and

Tomas had nothing to do with it. Someone else hid the diagram among his possessions, to mislead Michael.'

'Big Thomas,' said Seton heavily. 'Witney gave the diagram to Big Thomas before he died.'

'Big Thomas was a thatcher,' said Bartholomew. 'He knows about roofs, and I heard Witney arguing with him about thatching in the High Street. I imagine the picture was central to that row?'

Seton looked as though he would continue to deny the allegations, but a glance at Michael's stern, forbidding expression convinced him to prevaricate no longer. 'Witney was rash enough to show it to Big Thomas – he told him he was going to pay for St Bernard's roof to be replaced, but that he needed the opinion of a professional thatcher before he parted with money. However, Big Thomas claimed the scale was wrong or some such stupid thing. He would not listen when Witney said scale was unimportant, and was determined to have his say. We might still be there, forced to listen to his deranged ranting about angles and pitch, if Tomas of Pécs had not rescued us.'

'Poor Tomas,' said Bartholomew. 'Witney's death was an accident, Andrew killed himself and Tomas has an alibi for Urban's demise. You should let him go, Brother: he had nothing to do with any of it.'

'But there are still loose ends,' complained Michael, as they walked towards the proctors' prison to release the hapless Dominican.

'You said that did not matter when we arrested Tomas,' said Bartholomew. 'So, logic dictates that it should not matter now he is innocent.'

Michael shot him a black look. 'You can show

that no one killed Andrew and Witney, but Urban is another matter. He told us on his deathbed that someone tripped him with the sole intention of forcing him on to the shoe-scraper.'

'Someone tripped him,' agreed Bartholomew. 'But I think his ending up pierced was an accident, too. It must be Barzak's malediction. He did touch that damned relic, after all.'

'You believe that?' asked Michael, startled. 'I thought you had dismissed it as superstition, and I was the one convinced of its power. Now, *you* claim that these horrible deaths were brought about by this wicked curse, and it is *me* telling *you* that there may be a human hand involved.'

Bartholomew shrugged sheepishly. 'Two days ago, I would have insisted that the relic was irrelevant to all that has happened, but Witney's death is unusual, and Andrew could have saved himself when he jumped into the water. And then there is Urban. All three touched the thing. Perhaps I was wrong to be dismissive of matters I did not – do not – understand.'

'Kip Roughe touched it, too,' Michael pointed out. 'But he is still alive.'

'He said he only touched it briefly,' said Bartholomew.

'I do not think the length of time matters to the heavenly hosts. You either die when you handle it, or you do not. If you believe in Barzak's spell, then you must expect Kip to meet with a grisly end, too. We had better warn him.'

Bartholomew hesitated. 'The mind has considerable power over the body. If you tell him he will die, it is possible he may will himself to do so. I think you should say nothing.'

Michael smiled. 'You are not completely convinced about the curse, or you would not believe Kip has a chance of life. However, I would not mind another word with him, anyway. I am not sure that he and his brother were telling the truth when they said they did not know what happened to the relic.'

Tomas said nothing when Michael unlocked the door and indicated he was free. He stepped out of the cell and spent a few moments gazing up at the deep blue sky, as if he had not expected to see it again. He gave Bartholomew a shy smile.

'Brother Michael says I owe my release to you – that you were the one who reassessed the evidence and found it lacking. Thank you.'

'We are going to visit the Roughe brothers,' said Bartholomew. 'Bulmer told us they are inveterate liars and we have caught them in at least two untruths – about you trying to kill them, and about it being Big Thomas's idea to sell the relic to an abbey. Thomas is not clever enough to invent such a plan – but they are.'

'If they lie about one thing, they will lie about another,' said Michael. 'And someone placed that "evidence" among your possessions for me to find. They have access to all parts of the friary, and they had the opportunity – and the wits – to leave phials and diagrams to mislead a lowly proctor.'

'You are not lowly, Brother,' said Tomas charitably. 'Cambridge is lucky to have you.'

'Generally, you are right,' agreed Michael immodestly. 'But in this case, I have been wrong at every turn. Will you come to see the Roughes? The sight of you may encourage them to say something they might otherwise keep to themselves.'

Tomas gave a rather wolfish grin, obviously keen to avenge himself on two men who might have seen him hanged. He led the way to the Dominican priory, where the door was opened by a sullen Big Thomas, back at his duties on the gate. Bartholomew paused.

'Witney and Seton asked you about St Bernard's roof,' he said.

Big Thomas nodded. 'Witney said he was going to pay for it to be replaced, but I suggested he give his money to Prior Morden for the one here instead. I told him that I expect to see a tragedy every time a brother bends to poke the hearth, what with loose stones tumbling down our chimneys from want of repair.'

'You said that?' asked Bartholomew, thinking that inspiration could come from the least likely of sources.

Big Thomas nodded a second time. 'And then, in a strange coincidence, Witney himself died exactly that way just days later! He had drawn a plan of Bernard's roof, which he asked me to look over – he valued my opinion as a thatcher, you see. It was terrible, and he got angry with me when I told him how wrong it was.'

'In the end, I suggested you take it home and redraw it,' said Tomas, frowning as he recalled the incident. 'He was becoming overly aggressive, and I did not want a squabble to end in a fight – and you to be blamed for starting it.'

'I spent ages making it right, but he never did see it,' said Big Thomas in disgust, as though Witney had died specifically to inconvenience him. 'I was complaining about the waste to Kip, and he kindly gave me a penny for it. He said such a picture might come in useful, although he did not say for what.'

Michael raised his eyebrows. 'I doubt he was motivated by kindness. Do you know that he is telling everyone that it was your idea to sell the relic to an abbey?'

Thomas was affronted. 'It was not! Besides, I have come to think my Order is right about this Holy Blood debate. These blood-soaked relics should be destroyed – not because they are unworthy of veneration, but because some of them are evil, and capable of causing great harm.'

'Where are John and Kip?' asked Michael, thinking about more harm that might be waiting to happen.

'In the kitchens.' Thomas grimaced. 'And you can tell them that I do not take kindly to lies spread about me. It was *their* idea to sell that relic, and I am glad I had nothing to do with their nasty plans.'

The Dominicans' kitchen was a large room in a separate block, to reduce the risk of fire. It was dominated by a massive hearth, over which hung an extensive rack of knives and ladles. The rack was worked by a pulley, which could be raised or lowered, depending on whether the utensils were needed at hand or stowed out of the way. John was chopping onions on the table, while Kip was stirring something in a pot over the fire, tasting it every few moments. It was obvious he was fishing out the best bits as he did so.

'You have some explaining to do,' said Michael, as he entered, Bartholomew and Tomas at his heels. 'You placed pots of strong medicine and a drawing among Tomas's possessions for me – or perhaps Morden – to find, but you made two mistakes. First, the phials were the wrong kind. And second, Big Thomas has just confided that he gave Witney's diagram to *you*.'

'Tomas took it from us,' replied Kip coolly, eyeing the friar with dislike. 'We warned you about him, but he has already convinced you to let him out of gaol.'

'Why do you want him hanged for murder?' asked Bartholomew. 'What is it about him that you do not like?'

'He is a liar,' said Kip, angry when he saw that his stories were not believed. 'He is *not* here to study angels, but to spy on his brethren and their faithful servants. Then he will tell the Master-General that Prior Morden is prepared to revere Holy Blood, and this friary will be suppressed. We have worked here for ten years now. Where will we find other employment if he succeeds?'

'So, you tried to kill Tomas to ensure that would not happen – first with a crossbow and then with a horse,' surmised Bartholomew. 'The horse missed Tomas, but it almost broke Bulmer's jaw.'

The brothers exchanged an uncertain glance as they saw the net closing around them. 'All right,' said John. 'We admit we tried to dispatch a man who is evil, but we were protecting the friars whom we have served faithfully for a decade. I shook the ladder the other day, too, although you were the one who almost fell. And we left the phials and the picture for Brother Michael to find, but only because we wanted to see justice done.'

'Hanging an innocent man is not justice,' said Michael sharply.

'You are still lying,' said Bartholomew. 'You threw

a stone at me on the High Street – it injured Deynman, but it was aimed at me – because Michael and I were investigating matters that were coming too close to your activities for comfort. I imagine you would have tried to harm Michael, too, in time.'

'For the good of our Dominican employers . . .' said John in a bleat.

Michael was unmoved. 'You are killers, thieves and liars, so do not pretend your motives are honourable.'

'Killers?' squawked John, appalled. 'We are not killers!'

'You murdered Urban,' said Michael. 'You knew he had reclaimed the relic from Big Thomas, because Big Thomas told you so. You were angry to be deprived of a potential fortune, and followed him to the churchyard. You hurled him on to that spike . . .'

'It was an accident,' cried John. 'He would not listen to what I had to say, so I chased him and Kip stuck out his foot . . .'

'Shut up!' hissed Kip. 'Tell them nothing. They have no proof.'

'Urban said it was not our fault,' shouted John, eyes wild in his white face. 'As he lay there, with that point through his middle, he said it was not us who killed him. We should have stayed, but we were afraid, and we ran away. We knew Tomas would help him when he came out . . .'

'Enough!' roared Kip furiously. 'We have done nothing wrong, except tell one or two untruths for the benefit of the priory. Do not say anything else.'

But his brother was unstoppable. 'It was the relic. The relic killed Urban, because he touched it.'

'Rot,' said Kip firmly. 'I touched it, and I am perfectly healthy.'

'Where is it?' demanded Michael.

Then everything happened quickly. Kip made a quick, darting lunge, and all of a sudden he had snatched two knives from the rack above his head. Bartholomew ducked behind a table, but Tomas and Michael were slow to react, and only gazed in horror as Kip prepared to throw the first one.

'No, Kip!' cried John, horrified. 'Do not make matters worse.'

'I can kill two men with these,' said Kip, calmly assessing his situation. 'First, I will spear the monk for not believing us over Tomas, and then I will kill Tomas himself. Bartholomew is nothing – it does not matter if he lives or dies.'

He drew back his arm. Tomas shot towards the wall and Michael dived to the floor, which meant Kip was obliged to clamber on to the table in order to gain a clear view of his first victim. He raised his arm to take aim, but there was a tremendous groan as first one half of the iron rack, and then the other, descended towards the servant's unprotected head. Bartholomew saw Kip's mouth open in an expression of horror before he was lost among crashing utensils and the heavy thump of the rack itself. He leapt forward to haul it away, but the load had fallen in such a way as to break Kip's back.

'He cut the rope that held the rack with his own knife,' explained Tomas, holding the severed twine for Michael to inspect. 'As he lifted his hand to hurl the weapon, his blade scored through the rope. The cook keeps them very sharp.'

'Barzak's curse!' cried John in horror. 'Kip

touched the relic so was doomed, just as Urban and Andrew said.'

'I will not die,' muttered Kip, although it was obvious to everyone that he had but moments to live.

'Make your confession,' Tomas urged. 'Before it is too late.'

'And tell me the location of the relic,' added Michael. 'I do not want anyone else to die because they inadvertently handle the thing.'

Kip snarled a refusal, but John scrabbled at his brother's neck to reveal a purple pouch. 'There,' he said. 'Take it.'

Michael regarded it warily, and made no attempt to oblige, while Bartholomew certainly had no intention of doing so and Tomas was more concerned with the dying man's soul. Kip ignored the friar's exhortations to confess his sins, and his groping fingers found the purse and began to open it, each movement slow and laboured.

'Is that it?' asked Michael, watching cautiously. 'It is not a decoy? You have not hidden the real one elsewhere?'

'Why not look?' suggested Kip tauntingly, waving a small splinter in the monk's face. He smiled when the monk leapt backward. 'To be certain.'

They were his final words. He closed his eyes and, after a few moments, his breathing slowed then stopped, although the splinter remained firmly clutched in his fingers. Tomas began to intone a final absolution. At the sound of the Dominican's voice, Kip's eyes flew open and he hurled the relic from him. It hit the startled friar square in the middle of his chest. His prayers faltered and Kip went limp for the last time.

'Lord!' whispered Michael in horror. 'Tomas has touched it.'

'I do not think we have ever made so many mistakes and erroneous assumptions with a case before,' said Michael the following day, as he sat with Bartholomew in the little orchard at the back of their college. 'We thought we had three murders, but there were only three accidents – four, if we count Kip. First, there was Witney, a fanatical hater of Holy Blood relics, who would stop at nothing to destroy one. He died when the trap he had set for Andrew sprung early, and stones dropped down the chimney to stun him and then smother him with soot.'

'Witney's death may have been accidental, but Andrew's and Urban's had a human component. John insists Kip did not mean to kill Urban when he tripped him, and I think he is telling the truth, but Kip was responsible for the death nonetheless. Meanwhile, Andrew's demise was a clear case of self-murder.'

'He deliberately walked on to the unstable pier, and he had dosed himself with a sedative to ensure he would not swim. There is also the way Urban says he fell – with his legs rigid and straight, as though he intended to plunge as deep as possible. He probably thought he would never rise.'

'But there is a drought, and the river is low,' mused Bartholomew. 'Fortunately for him, the syrup did its work, and he simply slipped into unconsciousness and drowned. I think he staged his suicide to be perceived as an accident, because he wanted to make a point to Tomas. He knew he would not live long anyway, and decided to use his death to ensure Tomas took Barzak's curse seriously.'

'And fulfil his last wishes. All friars are trained to obey their masters, and Tomas would be no different, despite their rift. I wonder why he elected to use Tomas, rather than Urban. Was it because he was fond of Urban, and hoped to spare him an early death?'

'I can think of no other reason,' said Bartholomew. 'Urban had hesitated when he was offered the relic earlier, and Andrew saw that, for all his protestations of loyalty, Urban was not ready to die. But Andrew should not have killed himself before making sure that the relic was in Tomas's hands, and that Tomas agreed to do what he asked. All manner of things could have gone wrong – did go wrong.'

'Not really. I have just told you that Tomas would obey his former master's dying wish – and that is exactly what he is doing. He left Cambridge this morning, with the relic around his neck. It will be in Norwich in a week. You were right about him, and I was wrong. It is a pity he will die, because the Dominican Order needs more men like him – open minded, mild, tolerant. '

'I do not think he will die,' said Bartholomew. 'And I was not right about him: you were.'

'What do you mean?'

'Tomas killed Kip.'

Michael stared at him. 'No – Kip killed Kip. Tomas pointed out the severed twine that held the rack to the ceiling, remember?'

'I remember that is what he said. However, when Kip snatched the knife from the ceiling, Tomas grabbed one from the table. Then he flew across to the wall, where the rope holding the rack was secured to a hook. The rack dropping on Kip looked like divine vengeance, but it was just Tomas, cutting the rope that held the pulley. Besides, the situation Tomas described – with Kip slicing the twine as he took aim at you – is quite implausible.'

Michael gazed at him. 'Are you sure?'

Bartholomew nodded. 'I saw exactly what happened.'

'Then why did you say nothing?'

'Because he saved you, and I was grateful to him. But he is a liar. He lied about his real purpose in visiting Cambridge – gaining the trust of good men like Prior Morden in an attempt to discover treachery in the Holy Blood debate is hardly an honourable duty – and he was not honest with us about his former acquaintance with Andrew.'

Michael continued to stare. 'Then perhaps it is just as well he has gone.'

'It is,' agreed Bartholomew. 'You compared him to the fish-head John Roughe left on your shoulder at the Dominican priory, before we had ever heard of this relic. You were right: he *is* the kind to sit unseen, waiting for others to harm themselves with their own careless tongues.'

'A stinking, malevolent presence with all-seeing eyes,' said Michael with a shudder. 'Like Barzak's curse.'

Tomas had been travelling since dawn, when he had taken his leave of Prior Morden and the Cambridge Dominicans, promising to deliver the relic to Norwich as Andrew had requested. He glanced at the man who sat in the cart next to him, and they exchanged yet another grin of satisfaction.

'The monk and the physician were so easily fooled,' crowed Seton. 'They believed it was the real relic Kip hurled at you. They all did.'

'I might have been dead if it were,' said Tomas. 'It was fortunate you were to hand when Urban died, to find it and hide it until we could spirit it away.'

'Our Minister-General will be pleased,' said Seton, delighted with his success, 'although it is a pity Witney grew impatient and tried to act too soon.'

Tomas nodded. 'I am sorry he died.'

'This venerable object does not belong with Benedictines in Norwich, but in the hands of the Order that is making a stand for the sanctity of Holy Blood against the vile ravages of fanatical Dominicans. It belongs with us Franciscans – true believers, like you and me.'

Tomas smiled. 'It will be a relief to don the habit of a Grey Friar again. I hate the Dominican garb – I have done ever since I changed my allegiance after hearing Andrew's flawed ramblings in Pécs all those years ago. I owe him a great deal – it was his inadequate grasp of theology which convinced me I was in the wrong Order.'

Seton laughed. 'You played your part well – perhaps too well. Brother Michael still believes you are a Dominican inquisitor, and did not suspect for a moment that we had been watching Andrew all the way from Exeter, waiting for an opportunity to wrest his treasure away from him. But you should not have played with Michael. It was not kind.'

'I was bored among all those dull-witted Dominicans, and needed something to amuse me.' Tomas fingered the pouch at his neck.

Seton glanced at it uneasily. 'I will be glad when we pass that to our Minister-General. What do you think he will do with it? Display it, so common folk can come and pay homage? Or will he keep it in a secure vault, to ensure the Dominicans never seize it for their pyres?'

'It is worth a fortune,' replied Tomas. 'And London is the place where fortunes are made.'

Seton gazed at him in alarm. 'You mean he will sell it? But it might fall into the hands of someone unscrupulous!'

Tomas nonchalantly drew a knife from his belt and hugged Seton to him as he slipped the blade into his companion's stomach. Seton's eyes bulged, and he struggled for a moment before going limp. The friar shoved him off the cart and watched the body bounce into a ditch.

'You will never know what happens to it,' he murmured. 'And neither will your Minister-General.'

Historical Note

Blood relics were controversial items throughout the Middle Ages, and they gave rise to a complex scholastic debate. This concerned not only whether such relics could exist and, if so, whether they should be venerated, but also touched upon such topics as the definitions of death and resurrection, transubstantiation and the mass, and the precise nature of the kind of blood that may or may not have been involved. Since contemporary medical science was of the belief that there were several kinds of blood in the human body, the specific type alleged to have been contained in blood relics, such as the ones at Hailes or

Ashridge, was extremely contentious, and had all manner of theological implications.

There were two peaks in the polemic. One occurred in the 1350s, when the Franciscan Francis Bajulus of Barcelona declared that the blood of Christ's Passion had become separated from His divinity; he based his claim on the writings of the Provençal Franciscan Francis de Meyronnes (died c.1325). The claim might not sound particularly significant today, but in the 1350s it created an uproar. The implication was that if blood and body had indeed become separated, then the blood was unworthy of veneration – which raised questions about the veneration of Christ's blood in the mass. This in turn had profound implications for fundamental tenets of Christian orthodoxy. Bajulus's theory was referred to the nearest Dominican inquisitor, and it is no surprise to learn that it was deemed heresy. Thus began yet another chapter in the long series of disagreements between White and Black friars.

The second peak in the debate came a century later, with the Franciscans vociferously arguing that Holy Blood relics were sacred, and the Dominicans furiously seeking to suppress the claims. The battle lines between the two Orders over these issues remained in place until well into the seventeenth century.

Norwich Cathedral was one of several English foundations said to possess a portion of Holy Blood. It came from Fécamp in the 1170s, and may have been an attempt to attract pilgrims who might otherwise have gone to the shrine of Thomas á Becket in Canterbury. It was still there in 1247, and may explain why it was the Bishop of Norwich who was invited to give the sermon when Henry III gave his portion of Holy Blood to Westminster in that year. Norwich Cathedral was ravaged by fire in 1272 and, despite attempts to save it, the crystal vase in which the blood was kept cracked and the reliquary was damaged by flames. The blood was removed from the split vessel, and the monks were amazed by the 'miraculous' suspension of most of the blood in the upper part of the vase (it had probably dried).

Adherence to one or other side of the argument can be seen in the world of Renaissance art: the slab on which the dead Jesus lay was either painted red, showing an affinity with the Franciscans' beliefs, or grey, indicating a preference for the Dominicans'. Presumably, a multi-coloured one indicates a hedging of bets.

ACT FIVE

London, 16??

Although the interior of the tent was dim, making it difficult to see clearly, there could be no doubt about it. The man was dead. Ulysses Hatch, publisher and dealer in books, was lying flat on his back. His arms and legs were splayed out and his eyes stared sightlessly at the faded stripes of the tent fabric overhead. He was a large man and the hummock of his belly almost reached to our knees. There wasn't much doubt either that he'd died by violence. A great splotch spread out like a bloody flag across the incline between his triple chins and his chest.

The dead man and his lumber took up so much space there wasn't much room for the three of us who were still alive and upright. All around was the clutter of his trade, piles of books, bundles of pamphlets. There were in addition a couple of trunks, stuffed with bolts of cloth, with parcel-gilt plates and goblets and other things, for Ulysses Hatch had not restricted himself to bookselling. I knew this because barely an hour earlier I'd been gazing at the interior of the smaller trunk while Master Hatch carefully withdrew from it a little box that was swaddled in coarse woollen cloth and jumbled, apparently carelessly, among other items.

When he told me what the box contained, my vision swam and my legs almost gave way. Moments later, the wooden box was once again tucked among the jumble inside the trunk, which was in turn padlocked by its owner. Now the lid of this same trunk lay open while Ulysses Hatch was spreadeagled on the ground near by. I hadn't checked yet but I would have bet half a year's pay that the little box had gone.

The interior of the tent was generously proportioned but a heavy brown curtain almost divided it in two, cutting off the area by the entrance where the book vendor had set out his table and making a private chamber behind. At that moment I was very thankful for that thick fustian curtain. Beyond it, the sounds of the fair proceeded as though nothing had happened. Against the background hum of the crowd, we could hear the cries of ballad singers and confectioners and horse coursers. Within the tent the only sounds were the buzzing of a pair of flies and the slow-drawn breath of three baffled and frightened stage players. The smells that I'd been aware of on my first visit to the tent – the smell of summer's end and of musty fabric and unwanted paper – were now overlaid by a bitter, burnt odour.

Not one of us had bargained on this development. And it had seemed such a straightforward errand. I was only doing a favour for a man whom I was proud to consider my friend, and the others were here to keep me company. Early that morning we'd been in good spirits. And now look at us, standing over the corpse of a fat publisher and wondering what to do next . . .

*   *   *

They say that Saint Bartholomew's Fair is the biggest in the whole world, and who am I to contradict them? Certainly it sometimes seems as though the whole world flocks to the fair for a few days in August, all for the pleasure of being crammed into a couple of acres of land in Smithfield.

It was a hot morning at the back end of summer. Behind us the London walls were visible above a jumble of rooftops while before us the fair was bubbling away like a cooking pot. The hazy air was filled with the cries of the traders and balladmongers and the smell of roasting flesh. Smithfield is the place where animals are sold for slaughter, and it's hard to avoid the idea that the same fate awaits plenty of the Bartholomew visitors. Not slaughter maybe but a good fleecing. At least, that's what might occur to your average Londoner as he surveys the simple country folk picking their way across the green fields of Hoxton and Islington.

I don't know whether this thought was in the minds of my two companions as we watched the crowds flowing towards the encampment of stands and booths, each flying their banners and signs like an army before battle. Maybe my friends were preoccupied with less cynical notions: a sort of London pride that we lived in a place that was great enough to bring the world to its door. And a sort of London pity for those unfortunate enough to have to dwell somewhere else.

Needless to say, neither my two friends nor I were Londoners by birth.

A word about the three of us.

We – Abel Glaze, Jack Wilson and I, Nicholas Revill – are members of the King's Men, formerly the Chamberlain's Men, based at the Globe theatre in Southwark. We are players, at your service. Or at the service of King James I, to be precise. Jack Wilson was the longest-serving player among us three and Abel Glaze the most recent, but we'd all notched up a good few years by now with London's premier acting company.

Jack and I had set our hearts on playing from quite early days, but Abel had joined us by an odd route. He had once made a good living – a very good living, much better than the wages he earned on the stage of the Globe playhouse – by trickery. As a counterfeit crank, he had regularly tumbled down in the public highway, foaming at the mouth (the foam produced by a sliver of soap tucked into his gob) and with eyeballs rolling upward in his head. The outskirts of a town were the best place, he said. Abel would wait until the road was clear and a well-dressed party was picking its way along. Younger women were the softest marks and sometimes middle-aged men, he claimed, because girls were naturally tender hearted (unless they were very well dressed) and prosperous middle-aged men generally had something to atone for. Abel once defended this practice to me by saying that, when he'd succeeded in parting these gullible spirits from their money, he was sure that they went on their way with a lighter heart than his own. His practices were an incentive to charity, weren't they? But now Abel Glaze had gone straight, or as straight as a life in the playhouse would permit.

At the moment I could see Abel's tapering nose almost quivering while he gazed across the crowd milling round the stalls of Bartholomew Fair.

'Looking for likely marks, Abel?' I said.

'Those days are well behind me, Nick.'

'Smell that,' said Jack Wilson. 'That is Ursula's smell if I'm not mistaken.'

He sniffed appreciatively and gestured towards the source of the smell, a nearby stall which was advertising its wares with a pig's head stuck on a pole. I couldn't help recalling the traitors' heads which are displayed at the southern end of London Bridge. But those blackened, wizened objects looked less human than that of the pig on the pole, which to my eyes had something beseeching about it. Beneath it was a sign saying: 'HERE BE THE BEST PIGS. THE PIG'S HEAD SPEAKS IT'.

I'd had breakfast not so many hours earlier but I felt a sudden hunger at the sweet, crisp aroma of roasting pig. Later, I promised myself, we would visit Ursula's stall for a taste of her wares. Later, after we'd concluded our business at Bartholomew Fair.

'And look there,' said Abel. 'You mentioned marks, Nick . . . there's a whole crowd of 'em.'

From our position by the railings that edged the fair, I looked. On an open patch of ground was standing a handsome ballad singer with fair, curled hair surmounted by a red cap. He'd just finished a song and was nodding and smiling at a little gaggle of spectators who, by their own smiling and scattered applause, showed that they appreciated him almost as much as he appreciated himself. He raised his hands placatingly as if they were compelling him to offer one more number. Oh, very well . . . if you insist. He tossed his red-capped head like a frisky colt before bending once more over the lute that was strung round his neck.

'I've seen him before,' said Abel. 'He calls

himself Ben Nightingale. You could say it's his stage name. But Ben Magpie would be more fitting.'

After a few moments' fiddling with his instrument, all done to heighten audience expectation, the singer called Nightingale struck up to his own accompaniment. He had a pleasant voice which carried clearly through the other shouts and cries in the area. The words were distinct.

> *My masters and ladies, good people draw near,*
> *And take to your hearts these words you do hear,*
> *Look well to your purses, of robbers beware,*
> *At 'tholomew Fair, Bartholomew Fair.*
>
> *Cling fast to your goods and tight hold your purse,*
> *Or else you had better been starved by your nurse.*
> *Here are bad men a-plenty, all worthy the noose,*
> *But none, say I, worse than Master Cutpurse.*

And so he wound on with his execrable verses. But the bystanders seemed to be enjoying it, nodding in agreement with the sentiments or laughing at the foolishness of those who allowed themselves to become victims of 'Master Cutpurse'.

'*He* should be hanged . . .' I said.

'A bit severe,' said Jack.

' . . . for rhyming "noose" and "purse".'

'This piece of his is called "A Warning against Cutpurses",' said Abel.

'Very public spirited of the singer,' said Jack.

'Oh, very,' said Abel. 'But see the individual at the edge. That one there. His name is Peter Perkin.'

Slightly to one side of the group there stood a short man, his head bent sideways to scoop up the singer's words. He was squinting as if to concentrate the better on the sound. But I noticed that, beneath half-closed lids, his eyes were darting to and fro. He was dressed as though he'd just come in from the country for the day. There were even a few stems of straw sticking to his rustic hat. Aha, I thought, I bet I know what those straws are for . . .

All the time the red-capped singer was running through half a dozen stanzas, each of them reflecting on the iniquity of cutpurses and the need for honest citizens to be on their guard, Perkin kept his head down. And as the singer thrummed on the lute strings to signal the end of his piece and the audience's hands hovered over their pockets and pouches, the short fellow's eyes flickered ever more rapidly. When Nightingale concluded with a flourish, this bystander was foremost in the applause. I noticed, however, that he didn't dive for his own purse.

The singer removed his cap and moved among the audience, smiling in the way that all performers smile at the end of the show. To judge by his expression, each coin dropped into the upturned cap appeared to come as a genuine surprise. Why, it seemed to say, you mean that I am to be paid for what is purely my pleasure! As the little audience began to disperse and he was tipping the coins with a practised movement into his own purse, I saw him motion very slightly with his head to his confederate, Peter Perkin. You wouldn't have guessed that there was anything to connect the two of them if it hadn't been for that briefest of gestures. This second gentleman casually took himself off in pursuit of a couple of well-padded dames. No doubt, once he'd relieved them of what they were carrying, he would track down others whose fat purses he'd noted while he was pretending to listen to Nightingale.

You had to admire the slickness of the operation. The singer drew the crowds and took their honest tribute once he had rounded off his session with a song against the cutting of purses. Meantime his associate kept watch on where those purses were stashed. It saved time later on if he knew exactly which part of the body to target. Even some bumpkin clinging for dear life to his wordly wealth wouldn't be secure. It's wonderful how a straw gently tickled in the ear will cause anyone to let go of what they're clutching, and our friend in the rustic hat had his armoury of straws.

A cruder pair of thieves would have robbed the spectators there and then while they were listening. But there was a double disadvantage to this: the singer wouldn't have been paid for his pains if their purses had gone missing and so a little profit would have been forfeit, and – perhaps more important – some suspicion might have been directed at him for distracting the crowd. This way, Ben Nightingale was free to set himself up in another quarter of the fair. It was a trick which he and his accomplice might play two or three times that day, depending on how greedy they were.

There was a court of justice which sat within the precincts of Bartholomew Fair for the duration. It was called Pie-Powder Court. Even though its business was mostly restricted to trading matters (short measures in the ale-tents, coltsfoot mixed in with the tobacco), common thievery and cutpursing certainly fell within its jurisdiction. So we might have marched boldly up to the justices in Pie-

Powder and alerted them to these rogues who had the temerity to sing a warning about the very crimes they were about to commit. And yet not one of us – not Jack nor Abel nor I – was going to do anything about it. Every man (and woman) is responsible for his own property. As the old proverb has it: 'Fast bind, fast find'. And hadn't Ben Nightingale sung an explicit warning to his patrons, *Look well to your purses, of robbers beware*? We had quite enough to do to look to ourselves. Besides, we had other business at Bartholomew Fair.

We were searching for a relic.

At least, that was how WS had described it to me. A 'relic'.

I liked to think of William Shakespeare as my friend. He'd shown kindness to me from the moment I joined the King's Men when they were still called the Chamberlain's. Some of the other Globe shareholders held themselves a little apart from the run-of-the-mill members of the company. Whether it was because of their age or their temperaments or the heavy responsibilities they bore, the Burbage brothers, John Heminges and the others tended to be aloof. But WS had been ready to talk from the first, to give advice and even to make confidences. Or so it seemed at the time to this junior player. And there had been occasions when he had rescued me from the consequences of my own folly or rashness.

Because I'd been grateful to him and because I had a high esteem for the man, I was always prepared to listen when WS asked me to do something, even regarding any request as a privilege. But this was an especially odd request.

At the end of the play the previous day, WS and I had fallen into conversation. We'd been performing in a piece called *Love's Triumph* by the playwright William Hordle. The *Triumph* had lived up to its name and the audience at the Globe clapped and cheered at the end while we did our jig. When we came offstage we were running with sweat – it was a muggy afternoon – but more than content with our reception. I was looking forward to a drink in the Goat and Monkey once I'd got out of my costume in the tiring-house.

Our costume man is Bartholomew Ridd, a fussy fellow as those in charge of stage clothes tend to be, I've noticed. Like others of his trade, he seems to think that the purpose of plays is to display his finery. Actors are no more than clothes-horses. He's very hot on damage, ready to rebuke anybody whose outfit catches on a nail or is accidentally sullied with a spillage of beer. For some reason Master Ridd is particularly suspicious of me and always takes a personal interest in the condition of my costume when I've come offstage. I used to get annoyed with this but now I try to humour him. Anyway, all this meant that, as usual, I was one of the last to leave the tiring-house.

In the dim passageway outside I almost collided with William Shakespeare. We walked together towards the side door that gave on to the alley known as Brend's Rents. I couldn't have explained why, but I had the sense that he'd been waiting for me.

'Off to the Goat and Monkey, Nick?' he said when we were outside in the alley.

'Just for a quick one – or a quick two,' I said, wondering whether he wanted to accompany me there. The Goat, not a very salubrious alehouse perhaps but the players' local, wasn't the sort of place usually frequented by the shareholders. We walked in its direction. There were a few other people around. It was that stage of the day when business is more or less done but the evening's pleasures have yet to begin.

William Shakespeare and I had to proceed carefully at certain points in the walk. This area of Southwark around the Globe playhouse and the bear garden is criss-crossed by channels and ditches that feed into the river. Bridges carry one over the dirty streams. They are often little more than a single warped plank, and to cross them requires concentration.

'Hot work onstage this afternoon,' said Shakespeare.

'But enjoyable.'

'Oh yes, enjoyable.'

I glanced at my companion. He hadn't taken a part in *Love's Triumph* – indeed, WS took little part in playing these days – but he generally spent his mornings and afternoons at the Globe. The mornings were given over to rehearsals and (for the shareholders) business matters while the afternoons were for performances. Even though his acting days were mostly done with, WS liked to be in attendance at performances, ready to offer a word of advice or encouragement. I sometimes wondered when WS actually *wrote* his plays. I visualized him sitting up late into the night in his lodgings in Mugwell Street north of the river, covering the paper by candlelight, his hand flowing smoothly across the blank sheets. Unlike some other writers I've known he never came to work with inky hands.

'A good writer is that William Hordle,' said WS.

'We've already done his . . . let me see, his *Love's Diversion* and *Love's Despair* and now there's been his *Love's Triumph*,' I said, asking myself where this conversation was headed.

'With every play he grows better – and William Hordle was good to begin with,' said WS, who was generous in his assessment of other men's work. 'He skipped the rough apprentice stage. Hordle jumped over that *hurdle*, you might say.'

Experience had taught me to ignore WS's puns, which varied from the passable to the terrible. Instead I said, 'Like you, William? You never were an apprentice?'

'Why do you say so?'

'It is reported that you never blotched a line.'

Now it was WS's turn to glance at me. The sun was in our faces. His eyes were shaded by his hat and I couldn't read his expression. But then, he was a man who was always hard to read. We came to one of the narrow bridges spanning a channel which we had to cross single file. The smell of the river is never agreeable in high summer but the aroma of a Southwark ditch is enough to flatten a fishwife. If you fell in – and people did fall in from time to time on their way to the bear pit or from the tavern – you'd be unlucky to drown in the couple of inches of sludge that adhered to the bottom but you'd quite likely be smothered by the stench.

When we were safely across, WS stopped and took me by the arm.

'Those reports are wrong,' he said. 'I had my rough apprenticeship, when I bodged and blotched with the best of them.'

This talk of apprenticeship was interesting. I'd always been curious about Shakespeare's early life in London. But WS wasn't talking now to satisfy my curiosity. Just as I'd sensed that our encounter outside the tiring-house hadn't been accidental, so I realized that we had now come to the nub of the matter. I couldn't imagine what he wanted to tell me, though. That Shakespeare could have made mistakes like any other tyro playwright was hardly surprising, for all his reputation now. But what did this have to do with the man who was famed as the creator of Falstaff and Prince Hamlet?

'Nick, enough of this beating about the bush. I have a request to make. You've been to St Bartholomew's Fair?'

'Not this season.'

'Maybe you are intending to go?'

'Maybe,' I said. I had been meaning to wander through the fair, as it happened, but was slightly reluctant to confess this to WS for fear that he might consider me a gawping provincial. The traders at Bartholomew are Londoners while those who come to buy (or to be fleeced) tend to come from outside town, for this is a fair that draws people from all over the kingdom.

'Well, if you should happen to find yourself in the region of Smithfield . . .'

He paused, waiting to see whether I would flat out deny this possibility. When I said nothing, Shakespeare continued, 'If you were to visit Smithfield, I say, I would be most obliged if you could call on a certain gentleman who is set up at the fair. A book vendor.'

'Of course, but why?' I said this with genuine

curiosity. I'd no objection to being asked to do my friend a favour but was unable to see why he couldn't cross the short distance to Smithfield and call on the bookseller himself. In addition, there was a trace of discomfort in his voice, something very unusual in WS.

'I want you to recover what one might call a – ah – relic,' said the playwright.

'A relic?'

'I shall explain.'

And so he did, as we paced slowly in the direction of the Goat and Monkey alehouse.

It turned out that in his very early days in London, William Shakespeare had penned a journeyman drama about Domitian, one of the mad emperors of the Romans. Not liking the work – which was packed with rape and dismembered limbs and written in three days to catch a public fashion for sensational drama – he'd put it to one side and forgotten about it.

'Don't mistake me, Nick,' said WS. 'It wasn't the subject matter of my *Domitian* which I rejected. Shortly afterwards I wrote a thing called *Titus Andronicus*. That had more than its fair share of horrors and was accounted a success.'

'I've heard of *Titus*,' I said.

'It was simply that the piece about Domitian was rough in the wrong way. Crude, crude . . . I should have destroyed it there and then. Put it in the fire. Sometimes flame is the author's best friend. But I didn't destroy it. And at some point in my shift from one set of lodgings to another, *Domitian* went missing. I don't suppose I've thought of it more than twice in the last fifteen years. You see why I call it a relic of my early days. Now I hear that a book vendor has somehow acquired my foul papers.'

(Don't get the wrong idea about 'foul papers', by the way. This is simply the earliest stage of the writer's finished composition before the material is sent to a scrivener to make fair copies. As the expression suggests, a foul paper is likely to be full of blotches and crossings-out.)

'Are you sure that it's in the hands of this book dealer?' I said. 'After all, if you haven't seen it for the past fifteen years . . .'

'I have it on good authority,' said WS. 'Yes, I'm sure he has my *Domitian*.'

'I suppose he's going to sell it,' I said.

'Sell it to you, I hope,' said WS, quickly adding, 'I want you to buy it, Nick. I don't want this thing falling into the wrong hands, one of our rival companies, for example, like Henslowe's. Hatch would go a long way to embarrass me.'

'Hatch?'

'This book vendor rejoices in the name of Ulysses Hatch. For the most part he's a dealer in scurrilous ballads and scald rhymes rather than books. In fact, he will trade in anything that turns a profit. A long time ago he and I had a falling-out over . . . something. Even after all these years he wouldn't miss an opportunity to get back at me.'

I didn't ask WS why this oddly named gent wanted to get back at him. Instead I said, 'Does it matter if this piece of yours is sold elsewhere? After all, you have such a reputation . . .'

An eavesdropper might have thought that I was flattering Shakespeare but I was speaking no more than the truth. Nor did he waste our time with false modesty. 'Yes, I have a reputation now,' he said, 'yet I might be struck down tomorrow. No man can see the future. I would be unhappy if I knew that a ragged piece about a mad emperor was resurrected after my death to be staged and laughed at – for the wrong reasons. It was journeyman work, I tell you. Would you like to be remembered for your earliest, halting attempts to speak verse on the stage?'

'Well, no, I wouldn't . . .'

I was about to say that there was no comparison between an obscure actor and the most famous playwright in London. But I stayed silent, slightly surprised – but also touched – that even so notable a man as WS should be concerned about his posthumous reputation. Until quite recently, he'd been seemingly indifferent, and given to statements such as 'Let them sort it out after we are all dead'. Maybe it was age which was causing him to change his tune.

By this time we'd arrived at the Goat and Monkey. Absorbed in listening to Shakespeare's story I'd almost forgotten my thirst. But not quite. We paused by the door of the alehouse.

'I cannot go and see Master Ulysses Hatch myself,' said WS. 'We know each other too well, fat Hatch and I. He would most likely refuse to sell it to me out of sheer spite.'

'But the foul papers are yours,' I said. 'You never sold them but mislaid them.'

'Proving title to a piece is very difficult,' said WS. 'He could claim to have come by them honestly, and for all I know he did. Bought them from a landlord perhaps.'

'What about sending one of the shareholders?' I said, instinctively reluctant to undertake this task.

'He would recognize any of my fellows. He is familiar with the stage world.'

'But he wouldn't recognize an obscure player?'

'Obscure? Do not say so. Bitterness isn't in your repertoire, Nick, for all that you're a good player. One day, perhaps, a fine player.'

'Then why me?' I said. 'Why are you asking me to recover your old play?'

'Because you are a straightforward person,' said WS. 'No one will suspect you of double dealing.'

In another man one might have suspected flattery, but with WS I chose not to. Instead I strove to hide my smile in the glaring sun of early evening and, almost before I knew it, agreed to visit St Bartholomew's Fair the following morning. Agreed to track down Ulysses Hatch and, without revealing who had sent me, to obtain the foul-paper manuscript of a play entitled *Domitian*, if it was in his possession. WS authorized me to offer up to to five pounds for the play. This was a hefty price and, if questioned, I was to insinuate that I was a member of a rival company to the King's Men – one of Henslowe's men, say – interested in getting hold of an early work by the tyro Shakespeare.

So it was that on this fine morning I found myself at St Bartholomew's Fair with Jack Wilson and Abel Glaze. I'd met my friends in the Goat and Monkey the previous evening and outlined Shakespeare's request. I'd no hesitation in doing this since WS himself had suggested I might take some company to give 'colour' to the enterprise, as he put it. He gave no other instructions on how to go about getting hold of his *Domitian* foul papers, merely leaving it to my 'discretion' and 'good sense'. Perhaps he was a flatterer after all.

The three of us threaded among the crowds and between the confectioners and horse dealers, the barbers and the pin-makers. At one point Abel said, 'Isn't that Tom Gally?'

Crossing the path ahead of us was an individual with unkempt black hair. The man certainly looked like Gally, who acted as a kind of unofficial agent for Philip Henslowe, the owner and promoter of playhouses, bear pits and much else besides. I knew Tom Gally and distrusted him. His long, soft hair was reminiscent of a sheep's fleece but there was a wolf beneath. I wondered what was his business at St Bartholomew's Fair and whether he was after the *Domitian* foul papers too.

We came to a relatively quiet little quarter of the fairground, one given over to the vendors of books and pamphlets and printed ballads. We weren't long in finding our objective. Among the stalls was a more elaborate yellow-and-white-striped tent with its flaps folded back on one side. Hanging from a crossbar above a trestle table scattered with sheets and tatty volumes was a sign announcing the presence of *Ulysses Hatch, Publisher*. Many booksellers are also publishers and prefer to advertise themselves as such. There was no one to be seen at the mouth of the tent.

Like the browsers we were, we idly cast our eyes over Master Hatch's wares on the table-top. I glanced into the interior of the tent. The sunlight made it difficult to see much of the inside. In any case, there was a curtain slung near the entrance which shielded the interior. The curtain quivered and I had the feeling that we were being observed, probably through some small slit or spyhole. Confirmation that the tent was occupied came from indistinct sounds of talking within.

'This seller seems to specialize in cony-catching and thief detection,' said Abel Glaze, picking up a handful of the pamphlets. They were headed by titles such as *A Manifest Detection of Dice-play* or *A Notable Discovery of Cozenage*, this latter adorned with a picture of a rabbit or cony holding up a playing card in each paw.

'Not altogether,' said Jack Wilson, pointing to a pile whose topmost title read *The Quickest Way to Heaven*. 'This should be more up Nick's street, eh?'

Jack was in the habit of pretending that, since I was a parson's son, I must have devout tastes. I ignored him and picked up a volume I recognized. It was by a playwright I'd once known, a man called Richard Milford, and this was a piece of his entitled *The World's Diseas'd*, a play that was performed and published posthumously, as it happened. I knew it well, for I had played the character of Vindice the revenger. Now this book, which couldn't have been more than three or four years old, looked forlorn and dusty in the summer sun. I already owned a copy but, if I hadn't, I might have bought it for the sake of Milford's memory. I hefted the book in my hand. Who else would remember him in a few years' time? Before I could start on a melancholy train of thought about memory and reputation (the thing that William Shakespeare was so concerned with), my attention was caught by a definite stirring behind the curtain in the tent's interior.

A man came out from the shadows. If anyone, I expected it to be Ulysses Hatch, proprietor, publisher and bookseller. I'd never seen him before and knew nothing about him, except that he'd once had a falling-out with WS and that he was fat. But the individual who came into the space by the mouth of the tent was small and slight. Furthermore I did recognize him. So did Abel and Jack, for it was the nip or cutpurse who'd been standing near Ben Nightingale the ballad singer. Peter Perkin was still wearing his rustic hat with the tickling straws. With the merest glance at us and the tiniest inclination of his head, he edged round the trestle table and walked off into the crowd.

I was surprised to encounter him. What was *he* doing inside a bookseller's tent? The last we'd seen of this gent, only a few minutes earlier, he'd been in pursuit of a couple of the more prosperous-looking members of Nightingale's audience. True, he might have carried out a fistful of thefts in that time (nips can be as quick as lightning), but surely his place was at the ballad singer's heels, prospecting for new victims? Abel and Jack and I looked at each other, queries on our faces. I put down the volume I was holding.

'Can I help you, gentlemen?'

Distracted by the appearance of the cutpurse, we hadn't noticed another man emerging from the tent. He stood behind the table. Or rather he leaned against it, his belly flopping on to the surface as though it was a further object for sale. Ulysses Hatch was one of the fattest men I'd ever seen. Just as the pig's head on a stake had reminded me of the traitors' heads on London Bridge, so now Hatch's visage reminded me of the pig's. His cheeks bulged, his chin drooped and his eyes were small and reddened. There was a fringe of white hair round his head like a garland of dirty snow. He breathed heavily and there was sweat on his brow as though he'd been running to get to his present position behind the trestle table.

'Only looking,' said Jack.

'I've got something stronger back there,' said the pig-faced seller, peering at the three of us and indicating the inside of the tent with a plump hand. 'Spicier wares. *The Widow's Solace*, you know the ballad? Or *Venus Pleasure*? It tells you what Mars did with Venus. There are pictures with that one. I publish them myself so quality is guaranteed.'

We all shrugged or grimaced as if to say 'no thanks', but I suspect that if any of us had been by himself he might have permitted the bookseller to show off some of his spicier wares. From the sounds of conversation emanating from the tent, there were others already in there.

'Shut your gob!'

I started. The voice came from the tent. Ulysses Hatch smiled and jerked his head.

'Hark at him,' he said, then, seeing my expression, added 'Don't worry, sir. That wasn't directed at you.'

As if to prove his words, a woman's voice said something in altercation only to be answered with another 'Shut your gob!' in the same tone as before.

Jack was perusing a pamphlet called *Kemp's Nine Days' Wonder*. On the front was a picture of a dancing man in motley, with a drummer in the background. Like *The World's Diseas'd*, this item I was also familiar with, since Will Kemp had been a clown in the Chamberlain's Men, though before my time. Kemp's career had dwindled after he'd quit the company, and his most notable feat had been to jig all the way from London to Norwich in nine days. Afterwards he wrote an account of his journey.

'Ah, Will Kemp,' said Ulysses Hatch. 'Those were the glory days. He was a man of rare parts.'

Now, I'm pretty sure that Jack Wilson had known Kemp personally, since he'd been playing onstage longer than either of us. And indeed, both Abel Glaze and I had met the clown once when he was retired, and sick and listless in lodgings in Dow-gate. Nevertheless, our faces gave nothing away. For some reason, we were all on our guard.

'They were fools to replace Kemp with Bob Armin,' said Hatch.

Robert Armin was the current clown of the company and *they* were the King's Men – us, or the shareholders to be precise. I had the sense that this fat man was probing us, testing us. Certainly he was familiar with the big names of the playing companies. None of us responded to his comment about the clowns.

'Now our stage grows refined,' continued the bookseller. 'Audiences want a roof over their heads and carriages to convey them to the playhouse. They want polite clowns. They want cushions under their bums.'

'You're in the right there,' said Abel.

'You gentlemen are connected to the theatre, then?' said Hatch, shifting his piggy head from side to side.

'In a manner of speaking,' I said.

'And what manner might that be?'

I shrugged. This wasn't going how I'd planned it. Or rather I hadn't planned anything, relying instead on the 'discretion' and 'good sense' that WS had credited me with. He'd also called me 'straightforward', so now I decided that an honest approach might be best. Nevertheless, I paused before I spoke and glanced around. The business and pleasure of Bartholomew Fair trickled past us, rather sluggish in this backwater. No one was paying attention to three men standing at the door of a bookseller's tent. If anyone had noticed us, they'd most likely assume we were in search of Hatch's spicy wares.

'You have found us out, sir,' I said. 'We are to do with the playhouse.'

'Which playhouse?'

'Any one that will have us,' I said.

'Not Shakespeare's.'

I shook my head almost imperceptibly, no spoken lie. The others said nothing.

'As long as you're not from Shakeshaft's lot,' said Hatch. 'But I thought you were players. I can smell you over a distance.'

'Then I hope we smell sweet,' said Abel.

Hatch's expression suggested otherwise. Once more he looked from one to the other of us. A kind of calculation entered his gaze. He seemed to come to some decision. If his face was easy enough to read, his next words were obscure. 'I was not expecting three of you.'

Not expecting three of us? How could he be expecting us at all, since he didn't know we were visiting Bartholomew Fair, did he? And Shakespeare certainly wouldn't have gone about broadcasting our mission. But Hatch's remark indicated that he was expecting *someone*. I thought of the cutpurse man with the straws in his hat, but it couldn't be him because he'd already been and gone.

I blundered forward, feeling more and more unsure of my ground. After denying that we were part of WS's playing company, I now tried relative honesty. 'I have been, ah, commissioned to come to your stall, Master Hatch, to retrieve something . . . to pay a fair price for a . . . for an . . .'

I dithered. What was I to say? A journeyman play by Shakespeare? A piece about a mad Roman emperor? Then the author's own phrase floated into my head. 'You might say we're looking for a relic,' I said.

'Not so loud,' said Ulysses Hatch, although I had been speaking quietly enough and there was no one in our immediate neighbourhood. He reached across with a plump hand and gripped me hard by the shoulder.

'What is your name?'

'Nick Revill.'

No recognition at all showed on his face and for once I could be glad. Hadn't I described myself to WS as an obscure player? Here was the proof of that.

'You alone can see the item,' he said. 'Your friends must remain outside.'

I felt baffled. It was as if this fat man had divined straight away what I was searching for. And, more than baffled, I felt a little alarmed. Still, what was there to fear from this large, sweating individual? Or the others who were in his tent? I raised my eyebrows at Abel Glaze and Jack Wilson and, skirting the table, followed Hatch into his striped tent. He pulled aside the hanging curtain and ushered me into his inner sanctum.

After the brightness of the day outside, the interior was dim. Flies buzzed and Hatch wheezed. The place smelt musty, as if shut up for years, yet Hatch's tent could have stood on this spot only for a couple of days. There were books and pamphlets stacked in casual piles and scattered on the ground, as well as a couple of trunks. A woman was sitting on one of the trunks. She looked me up and down. She might have been handsome not so long ago but the features in her large face were on the point of melting, as if she'd been left out in the sun too long. Her hair, which was unbonneted, straggled over dark shiny eyes. She had a leathern flask in one hand. She raised it to her lips, after giving me the once-over.

'Shut your gob!'

I jumped. The voice came from over my shoulder. I looked up to see a raven sitting on a perch. It repeated itself and then cocked its head on one side as if to estimate the effect of its words on me. There was an unpleasant glint in its diamond eye.

'Master Revill,' said Ulysses Hatch, 'let me introduce you to Hold-fast. I call him that because once's he's got something in his grip he doesn't let go. Oh no, he doesn't let go.'

'Oh no. Hold-fast doesn't let go,' said the raven. 'Jump to it. Shut your gob!'

'You wouldn't think it but he's an old boy,' said Hatch. 'He was old when he adopted me for his own.'

The raven looked ageless to me. It seemed odd to talk about an animal, a bird, adopting a man rather than the other way about, but perhaps that's how it is with ravens. I glanced at the woman sitting on the trunk.

'What about me?' she said. 'Aren't you going to introduce me to this nice young man?'

Master Hatch made a little bow, or at least bent as far as his bulk would allow.

'May I also present Wapping Doll.'

'I used to live south of the river,' I said.

'Oh, good for you,' said the woman, her speech slightly slurred. 'But what's that got to do with anything?'

'Ha ha. He thinks you come from Wapping,' said Ulysses Hatch. 'But let me tell you, Nick Revill, that for this good lady Wapping isn't a *place* – it's what she used to do with her time. It's what she did for a living. You know. She wapped, she knocked and she banged.'

'Still do, for a living,' said Doll, rolling her eyes. They were like ripe blackberries, glossy, squashy.

'Alas, sir, her price has fallen of late. Who'd have her?'

'You can shog off, Ulysses Hatch,' said the woman, lifting up her flask once more but pausing before she stuffed it in her mouth. 'Who'd have *you* anyway, you great bag of guts?'

'You would. You *did* have me, yesterday morning,' said Hatch.

'Apart from me nobody'd touch you, you bombard of sack.'

'Go ask at the pig stall,' said Hatch with what sounded like genuine indignation.

'Shog off,' said the raven.

I coughed to remind them all of my presence and the bookseller seemed to remember why he'd summoned me inside his tent.

'Get your fat arse off that chest,' said Ulysses Hatch to his doxy. 'Come to think of it, get your fat arse out of this place altogether.'

The woman hoisted herself to her feet.

'Oh, Ulysses, oh, Yew-lee, you'd not banish your Doll, would you? Banish your Wapping Doll?'

She spoke somewhere between earnest and jest, and pouted her lips in a similar spirit. She winked at me.

'This gentleman and I have a matter to discuss. *You* know, the item.'

Hatch gestured towards the other trunk. I didn't know what he was talking about but from the expression on Wapping Doll's face, she did. Her good humour disappeared and she said, 'Not again, Ulysses. That item brings me out all over goose bumps.'

Hatch swung one of his hands and whacked her on the arse, but it was an affectionate blow as far as I could see, and she exited from the tent, still clutching her leathern flask.

Then he got down on his hams, an awkward manoeuvre given his size, and retrieved a key from his doublet. He fiddled with the padlock of the trunk, not the one recently vacated by Wapping Doll but the other. Suddenly he looked up at me. The raven's coal-black head flicked with deep suspicion between his kneeling master and me, yet any time I looked at the bird he pretended indifference.

'What are you after, Master Revill?'

'I . . . have already said it,' I said, uncertain what reply he wanted, for I had not yet named the item that I was in pursuit of, the foul papers of Shakespeare's unperformed play, *Domitian*.

'You spoke of a relic.'

'I did,' I said, wondering why he fastened on this word so.

'Then behold,' he said.

Hatch pushed at the lid of the trunk. It swung open. Inside, I glimpsed bolts of cloth and what looked like items of plate. Quite delicately he moved these objects aside. In the middle of the collection was something wrapped up in a dark, coarse cloth. With what seemed to me exaggerated care, Ulysses Hatch lifted it from the trunk and laid it on a clear patch of ground. He knelt in front of this anonymous little bundle, then began to unfold the woollen wrapping.

I was abruptly conscious of my surrounding. The dusty light that filtered through the yellow fabric of the tent. The buzz of the flies, lazy, as if they knew that summer was near its end. The heavy breathing of the bookseller. The raven shuffling on his perch.

I was curious and puzzled, and not a little apprehensive. Whatever was going to emerge from this dumb-show would not be WS's manuscript – for one thing, the shape of the bundle was wrong – but something altogether different.

What did emerge was, at first sight, disappointing. A small oblong wooden box with a hinged lid that had an inlaid pattern of a star. Hatch opened it. Without raising the box from the ground, he beckoned me to look more closely. Inside was a glass vial, a little more than a finger's length, with a faded gilt stopper. Treating the vial as warily as he might the contents of Pandora's box, Ulysses Hatch lifted it out and cradled it in a pudgy palm.

'Look near,' he said. 'What do you see inside?'

'I see a bit of wood.'

THE MEDIEVAL MURDERERS

'Yes, and . . .?'

'Jump to it,' said the raven.

'The wood is grey and stained in places,' I said, attempting to ignore the bird.

'Just so.'

I made to reach out my hand to take the glass vial with its unremarkable contents for a closer examination, but Hatch snatched it towards him and began wrapping it up once more inside the woollen cloth.

'You would not want to touch what's in here, master,' he said. 'This is what gives Wapping Doll the goose bumps.'

What in God's name was he talking about? I was on the point of saying that this was not the item I'd come in search of when Hatch raised a hand to silence me. He was still kneeling on the ground, and when he looked up again there was an odd mixture of fear and calculation on his sweaty face.

'You *are* working for Philip Henslowe, aren't you?' he said.

Just as I'd earlier nodded to deny that we were with 'Shakespeare's lot', so I now gave a rueful smile to indicate that he'd got this right too. I felt happier not delivering an outright lie, yet not altogether happy.

'I knew it!' said the bookseller. 'That man has got his hand in plenty of plackets. Playhouses, bear pits, pick-hatches, you name it, and Philip Henslowe will be there, turning a penny. But let me tell you, Nicholas Revill, your employer should beware of this item.'

He gestured at the wooden box. Now it was his turn to read my face. What he read was confusion.

'You don't know what it is, do you? Old

Henslowe's sent you to purchase something without telling you what it is.'

'No, I don't know what it is,' I said, 'and that's no more than the truth.'

'Why, man, this object which is secure in its glass case ... is a fragment of the True Cross. It is marked with the blood of Our Lord.'

At first I thought I'd misheard him or that he was joking. Then I studied Ulysses Hatch's expression more carefully and understood that it was no jest. My eyes swam and my legs almost gave way beneath me.

Of course, like everyone, I have a glancing acquaintance with the business of relics. I've heard of the vial of Christ's blood which they keep in Walsingham, and of saints' bones that are stored elsewhere. Yet in these latter days such items are somewhat discredited as being associated with the old religion. My parson father, for example, would refer to them as popish gewgaws. He'd say that those who looked for salvation from old bones would do better to seek God's grace directly rather than gawp at what were most likely the remains of sheep and swine. But it's one thing to hear this from the pulpit and quite another to be confronted with such an object in the flesh, as it were.

Perhaps the bookseller didn't believe he had done enough to convince me, for he once again unwrapped the wooden box, opened it and extracted not the glass vial but a strip of folded parchment. This he handed to me, telling me to take care.

There was some lettering on the parchment, but very faded. The skin was also so torn and frayed that I feared it might crumble in my hand. In the uncertain light of the tent I struggled to read the words but was able to make out only a handful, which appeared to be in Latin, among them *sanguis* and *sancta*. There was what looked to be a signature underneath, although I could not decipher any more than isolated letters, together with a small raised area like a scab, the remains of a seal perhaps. All this time Hold-fast the raven paid close attention to what we were doing, as if he were capable of reading better than either of us.

After a moment I returned the parchment to Hatch.

'I have this in English,' said the publisher and bookseller. 'It confirms the wood in the vial to be a piece of the True Cross, rescued from the Church of the Holy Sepulchre in Jerusalem. It is signed and sealed by Geoffrey Mappestone, Knight. It is very old.'

'How . . . how did you come by it?'

'They say that a friar had it in the old days. It passed from his hands to others – and so to mine.'

He made it sound like a natural process, but I would bet a week's wages that he had acquired it less than honestly.

'You are willing to sell this thing?'

'It is not to the seller's advantage to say it, but I will be glad to be rid of this "thing", as you call it,' said Hatch. 'What Master Henslowe does with it is his business, but I've had enough of it. Good fortune does not follow the possessor, though I did not know that until after I'd . . . obtained it. They say that to touch it is death.'

This might have been so much seller's talk, perversely heightening the attraction of something by drawing attention to its dangers, but I felt the nape of my neck crawl.

'You might give it away.' I paused and chose my next words with care. 'There must be many who would be glad to receive such an object.'

'Give it away? I have a living to make, Master Revill. Why shouldn't I turn an honest penny? No one will get their hands on this unless they have first paid me an honest price.'

And also from the trunk he produced a battered pistol. It was a rusty old gun, with a bulbous handle and a blunt muzzle.

'I keep this primed and ready,' said Ulysses Hatch, toying with the flint-arm. 'The world is full of rogues.'

'Master Hatch,' I said, tired of this and not a little frightened by the sight of the pistol. 'It's time to get one or two things straight. It's true that I have been sent here to obtain something from you but not . . . whatever is contained in that vial. I know nothing of any cross, true or otherwise.'

At this Hatch replaced the box inside the trunk, which he fastened with the padlock. The pistol, however, he did not replace, but positioned it carefully on top of the chest, as though he might want to use it at any moment. Everything he did, he did slowly, but I had the impression that he was taking even longer over this sequence of small actions so as to give himself time to think. I glanced at the bird on the perch. Hold-fast was now so interested in the proceedings that he was pretending to be looking in the opposite direction.

'Then you're not a player?' said Hatch eventually.

'I'm a player all right. And I'm here about

playing matters. In brief, I have heard that you possess the foul papers of a play by William Shakespeare which is called *Domitian*. I have been commissioned to buy them off you.'

By now Ulysses Hatch had struggled to his feet. The mixture of expressions that had played across his fat features while we were discussing the relic – fear and calculation – had been replaced by a guarded look.

'By Henslowe?'

'I never *said* so, whatever you may have thought,' I said, growing hotter and more uncomfortable, then moving rapidly on before he could rebuke me for misleading him. 'I can offer a fair price for these foul papers of WS. William Shakespeare, I mean.'

'Shakespeare, pah!' He almost spat out the word. Then added, more calmly, 'The foul papers of *Domitian*? I may have what you are after. What do you mean by a fair price?'

'Three pounds, shall we say?'

'Let us say six pounds.'

'Four.'

'Five.'

'Done,' I said.

For the first time a smile broke out across Hatch's face. 'You'll never make a buyer and seller, Master Revill, agreeing so quick. Come back in an hour. The item you require I have somewhere among other papers but I need time to hunt it down. Five pounds, now. No going back.'

'No going back,' I said.

'You may give me a pound now as an earnest of your good intentions.'

I reached for my purse and extracted two angels, part of the money that WS had given me when we'd talked the previous evening. Altogether it was a large sum – I don't think I'd ever had so much in my purse at one time – and it was a mark of his trust that he should hand it over. Still, I told myself, the Globe shareholders were prosperous men (certainly in comparison to mere players). When the bookseller had hold of the money, his attitude changed. He smiled again. I took advantage of his change of mood.

'Give me one thing in exchange for the coins, an earnest of *your* good intentions,' I said. 'A piece of information.'

'That depends.'

'Why do you dislike Shakespeare so?'

'Jump to it!' said Hold-fast the raven.

Ulysses Hatch sighed. Then he glanced at the trunk where Wapping Doll had been seated.

'We had a falling-out over her once.'

'Over *her*?'

'Why so amazed, Master Revill? She was a fine piece of goods in her day, even if she's somewhat price-fallen now.'

There must have been some surprise still showing on my face for Hatch said, 'Oh, you regard Master William Shakespeare now as a fine upstanding fellow, ever so respectable. But let me tell you, when he first came to this city of ours, he was young and hardy and full of fire. That was a long time ago. Why, I was thin in those days. It was just the time when Hold-fast adopted me. The raven looks no older but I have grown somewhat.'

'And after all these years, Master Hatch, why do you still . . . ?' I said.

'Still what?'

'Feel resentful?'

'Some things that happen in youth you don't forget – or forgive,' said Hatch. 'Shakespeare won my Doll with words. She opened her ears to him and his words.'

'So now you are in possession of some of his words,' I said, guessing at the hidden truth. 'You like having hold of his foul papers.'

'You may be right.'

'Yet you are willing to sell them.'

'I'll sell anything to anyone at the right price.'

'Even a piece of the cross?'

'Our first talk you should forget,' said Hatch, looking uneasy and gesturing over his shoulder at the other trunk and its strange contents. 'Tell no one of that item.'

'Shut your gob!' said Hold-fast.

'The bird knows best,' said Hatch. 'I expect it's a fake. There are many such sham objects.'

This was absolutely at odds with his tone and manner while he'd been describing the cross fragment, but I said nothing, only too glad to have the chance to escape from the stuffy tent, and glad above all to escape the company of the raven.

When I was outside, I looked around for Abel and Jack but there was no sign of them. No doubt they'd grown tired of waiting and gone off to taste the other delights of Bartholomew Fair. As I went in search of them, I debated whether to tell them about what Hatch had shown me, despite his warning. And other questions came to mind too. Was that a real fragment of Christ's cross? With the instinct of the canny salesman, Hatch had permitted only the briefest glimpse of the thing. I was not so gullible as to trust Ulysses Hatch without some additional proof, and it was quite likely he didn't believe his own words either. Why, there must be enough pieces of the 'true' cross in existence to rebuild Noah's Ark!

But Hatch was evidently expecting someone to come and purchase the item, and so had assumed I was that person. I suddenly remembered the glimpse of Tom Gally just after we'd arrived at the fair. Now, it was well known that Philip Henslowe employed Gally as a go-between for enterprises that were dubious or underhand. Wasn't it possible that Henslowe had dispatched his agent to collect the relic? If so, what could he possibly want with it? Even as I asked myself this, Hatch's own description of Henslowe suggested an answer. Henslowe had his finger in many pies. He put money into playhouses and bear-baiting and, less respectably, into houses of pleasure. He was a businessman, none too scrupulous about how and where he made his wealth. It might well be that he'd regard the relic as a good investment, perhaps a long-term investment to be sold on when the market was right. Or perhaps he would treat it as a kind of talisman, to give him power or bring him luck. Yet hadn't the bookseller claimed that the fragment brought ill fortune?

Anyway, it was nothing to do with me. All that was necessary for me was to return to Hatch's tent in an hour, collect the *Domitian* foul papers, and hand over the rest of the money.

I felt rather than saw someone keeping company with me on my left hand. I looked round. It was Tom Gally. When he saw I'd observed him, he screwed his head sideways and smiled. His black hair hung unkempt and tangled. I didn't particularly want to talk to him and so walked faster.

'Master Revill, I hope I find you in good health,' said Gally, keeping pace with me.

'Well enough,' I said. I nearly added that I would be even better without his company.

'You have business at Bartholomew Fair?'

'Just looking.'

'I noticed you visiting Master Hatch's emporium.'

'That's a grand word for a tent,' I said, wondering what the man was after.

'He has some ... interesting wares,' said Tom Gally. He had a disconcerting habit of pointing with his forefinger at the person he was addressing and squinting down the finger as if taking aim with a pistol. Even as we were walking side by side, he sighted at me when he said 'interesting wares'.

'I dare say,' I said.

'Odds and ends he has. Books and papers ...'

'Well, he's a bookseller.'

' ... and other stuff.'

I stopped and faced Tom Gally. I had learned from experience that the best way to deal with him was to be direct.

'Master Gally, if you have anything to say to me then say it straight out. Otherwise, I have business to pursue at the fair.'

'Business? I thought you were "just looking", Master Revill.'

Seeing the expression on my face, he quickly added, 'I was merely going to ask if you had seen some of Master Hatch's more, ah, specialized wares.' He pointed his finger-gun at me and smirked. 'Hatch has a book called *Venus Pleasure* –

with pictures. Or *The Wanton Wife.* That's a good one. And another called *Rape of the Sabine Women.* I thought that a youngish man like you might appreciate such salty items.'

'I expect I am less in need of them than you are, Master Gally.'

'As you please. I will leave you to your business at the fair, or to your pleasure.'

He walked off. Feeling a bit priggish, I watched his black fleece bouncing on his shoulders. He'd obviously been concerned to discover what I was doing with Ulysses Hatch, the comment about the bookseller's salty items being a blind. I remembered WS saying that Henslowe would be glad to get his hands on the *Domitian* foul papers. Was it those which Gally was after? Or was he interested in the relic of the True Cross, as I'd thought a moment before?

Only half aware of the direction I was going in, I found myself heading towards the stall selling roasted pork. Perhaps I was following my nose. But as I drew closer I saw that there was more exciting fare on offer than cooked meat. A crowd of people was gathering to watch an argument that was threatening – or promising – to tip into a fight. Furthermore it was between two women, always an attraction. They were standing close to the roast-pig stall. The pig's head was looking on discreetly. I recognized one of the women, since it was Wapping Doll, the person from Hatch's tent. The other woman was her equal for size. Were all the inhabitants of St Bartholomew's Fair so large? She was brandishing a greasy roasting-spit like a sword. This fact, together with her red, greasy countenance, caused me to think that she might be Ursula the pig woman. This was no great deduction. From her look, she was a cook, and it is well known that all those who work in kitchens are short tempered and usually foul mouthed. It's the fires which do it, you know.

On the other side, Wapping Doll had no weapon, although she held out the leathern drinking flask as if she might do damage with it. But my money was on the roasting-spit.

At that moment the women were happy enough exchanging insults and gestures. 'Turd in your teeth' and the Spanish fig and so on. The crowd was split between urging them on to better things and glancing round to see whether any constable from the Pie-Powder Court was about to intervene. I might have known that Abel Glaze and Jack Wilson would be among the watchers.

'What's this all about, lads?' I asked.

'What do women ever fight about?' said Jack. 'They are as ready to go to blows over men as we are to go to blows over women.'

'I wish someone would fight over me,' said Abel, who was not lucky in love.

And suddenly it came to me. Hadn't Ulysses Hatch said to his doxy when they were bantering in the tent, *Go ask at the pig stall*? Was it possible that these two were scrapping over the publisher of spicy wares?

Wapping Doll and Ursula – if it was indeed the pig woman – circled each other like two dogs, one jabbing with the roasting-spit and the other flapping her flask, but each reluctant to make the first move. The crowd kept quiet, unwilling to break the spell. But before the women could get down to fighting, a pair of constables pushed their way through the throng and, in a practised manoeuvre, placed their staffs of office on the ground. These were long heavy poles, intimidating in appearance and tough enough to break an arm or crack a skull. If they'd been dealing with men they might have employed the staffs. But, with women, they preferred a more personal touch.

They laid hands on the pair. They were big fellows with beetling brows, a regular Gog and Magog. One wrapped his arms round Ursula while the other seized hold of Wapping Doll's flask. For an instant it looked as though the women were going to turn their fury on the constables, but I also sensed a kind of relief in the pair, as though they'd been honourably relieved of the requirement to fight it out.

Then, as a late arrival on the scene, there appeared a diminutive man with a trim beard. By chance I recognized him. He was an alderman and a justice, Walter Farnaby by name. A year or more earlier I'd witnessed him sealing up a plague house in Kentish Street. He was a precise individual, not to be gainsaid. He was evidently acting as the St Bartholomew's Fair Justice. A number of the crowd recognized him too, to judge by their groans and whispers. At Farnaby's gesture, the two constables released their charges. The men obeyed but they looked as though they might have enjoyed grappling with the women for a few moments longer. I don't know what the Justice said to the two women – he went to each and spoke softly in her ear – but it was enough to cause them to turn round and go off in separate directions, Ursula back to her pig stall and Wapping

Doll towards the area of the fair where I'd just come from.

There was general disappointment at the Justice's intervention. I heard some comment about the authorities interfering with people's innocent amusements while proper criminals roamed free about the place. Thinking of Nightingale the ballad singer and his accomplice, I couldn't help agreeing.

Jack and Abel were curious to know what had happened with the bookseller. I stayed quiet about the relic, saying only that Ulysses Hatch claimed to be in possession of Shakespeare's foul papers but that he'd needed time to search for them. I added that there was some old enmity between Shakespeare and Hatch and that the bookseller kept some odd company, which included, as well as the woman we'd just seen, a talking raven called Hold-fast. I also told them of my encounter with Tom Gally.

While we were waiting to return to Ulysses Hatch's lair we occupied the period wandering round the fair, stopping to sample some ale and being propositioned by the sellers of horseflesh, human flesh and other gewgaws. As smart Londoners, however, we were resistant to pretty well every temptation.

Eventually, after we'd judged that enough time had passed, we found ourselves once more at the mouth of the bookseller's tent in that quiet quarter of the fair. It was odd that Master Hatch should set up here out of the run of things. Maybe his customers liked to visit him discreet and unseen on account of his spicy wares. The books and pamphlets lay undisturbed on the trestle table. The flaps of the tent were open and, once again, I had the sense of being spied on through the curtain that hung across the interior. Perhaps it was the raven with his diamond eye. I'd have preferred a human gaze.

I called out for Master Hatch. No reply. Called more loudly. Half expected Hold-fast to tell me to jump to it. Or shut my gob. I glanced at the others and indicated that we should go inside. Hatch could have no objection, surely. A simple transaction, no more. Hand over the four pounds and depart with the *Domitian* papers. And, on a future occasion, show myself a little less ready to undertake errands on behalf of William Shakespeare.

We filed into the tent. I slipped round the curtain.

Inside, it was dim and stuffy and smelly. But the smell was different this time, burnt and bitter.

You know what we found next.

'My God, Nick, what shall we do?' said Abel Glaze.

'I don't know.'

'We should go to the Justice,' said Jack Wilson. 'This is murder plain and simple.'

'He's been shot,' said Abel, looking at the dark hole in the man's upper chest and the bloody flag surrounding it. In his very young days, before he turned to confidence trickery, Abel had served time in the Netherlands campaign, and so knew more about war and wounds than I ever hoped to know.

'With his own pistol, it must have been,' I said. 'He showed it me when he was showing me ... something else.'

Jack and Abel looked at me. Perhaps they were

wondering what the 'something else' was. I pointed to the murder weapon, which lay in a corner of the tent, as if the perpetrator had flung it there in panic before his exit. Or her exit. For a pistol can be discharged by a man or a woman.

'That's a snaphaunce,' said Abel. 'They were much used in the Low Countries.'

Neither of us responded to this piece of professional information.

'We can just walk out,' said Abel after a moment. 'We don't have to report this to anyone. Not a soul knows we've been here.'

'*You* can walk out,' I said. 'But I've been seen already in this place.'

I was remembering Wapping Doll. I also recalled the individual with the straws in his hat who'd slipped out as we arrived at the tent for the first time.

'Then we must go to the Pie-Powder Court,' said Jack. 'This isn't some case of a cutpurse and a ballad singer.'

'Yes, you're right, we must go to the court,' I said, looking round. 'Where's the bird?'

'Bird?'

'Hold-fast, the raven I told you of.'

'Blast the raven,' said Jack. 'We have a dead man on our hands.'

'Wait a moment,' I said, bending down to examine a pile of paper which I'd just noticed lodged beneath Ulysses Hatch's bulk. I eased it from under the body. The sheets were old and crumpled and blood-smeared but a glance was sufficient to show that they were WS's unperformed play of *Domitian*. It said as much on a handwritten title page. Hatch had found it after all. The last thing he did, perhaps. Well, I thought, as I tucked the creased sheets into my doublet, I've saved my master four whole pounds. It's odd how these trivial thoughts come at the direst moments.

Seeing that I'd obtained what we'd come for, the others made to leave, but I lingered for an instant, curiosity overcoming fear and revulsion. I glanced inside the open trunk then rummaged among the cloth and plate. I'd been right. There was no little box, nestling among folds of cloth. No glass vial, no sacred fragment of wood.

'He said it was cursed,' I said.

'Who said it was cursed? What was cursed?'

'What are you talking about, Nick?'

There was exasperation as well as alarm in my friends' voices.

'It'll take too long to tell now,' I said.

'Then tell it to the Justice,' said Jack. 'Let's get out of here, for Christ's sake.'

But it was too late. We should have quit the tent the moment that we'd seen what it contained. All at once the crowded space – three living players in the company of one dead publisher and bookseller – was filled with two more figures. Big fellows they were, the ones with beetling brows. Justice Farnaby's constables. We'd seen the easy way they dealt with large Ursula the pig woman and the equally large Wapping Doll. Three slender players were no match for them.

They indicated in their rough-and-ready fashion that they'd been alerted by reports of a pistol shot. Now we were to accompany them to Justice Farnaby. Obviously, we stammered out our innocence and ignorance. But equally obviously we had questions to answer. Jack and Abel and I were left with no choice but to go quietly to the Pie-Powder Court. We exited the tent, leaving the body on the ground. The constables hadn't quite placed us under arrest. Yet, if we had tried to flee, not only would it have suggested guilt but we would most certainly have been brought down by their long staffs of office.

The only crumb of comfort in all this was that the makeshift court was situated in part of what had once been St Bartholomew's Priory – a tent or stall obviously being an undignified place for the administration of justice – and that the old monastic buildings lay in this quarter of the fair. As I've already mentioned, it was a comparatively quiet spot, and so we didn't attract too many gawpers while we were being escorted there. We tried to put on an air of innocence, as though we were simply out for a stroll with this pair of hulking figures. But then innocence is the air assumed by every guilty man, isn't it?

The grounds and buildings of Bartholomew Fair are owned by the Rich family (never was a family better named) and, at some time in the past, one of them had caused parts of the priory to be restored, not for pious reasons but so that he could swell his coffers by leasing them out. So we found ourselves shoved into a room that might once have been a monk's cell and was now used for holding malefactors caught at the fair. The constables searched us in a rudimentary fashion. We had nothing of interest about our persons. The pile of paper that I'd retrieved from under Hatch's body and tucked into my shirt, the foul papers of Shakespeare's *Domitian*, were riffled through. I doubted that either man could read, and even if he could, what was there to see? A load of paper which its creator considered worthless and wished to see destroyed.

It crossed my mind to attempt to bribe our gaolers with the money that WS had given me, and indeed they were reluctant to hand back the coins once they'd tipped them out of my purse. But the very fact that they did return them indicated that they were principled. Either that or they were more fearful of Justice Farnaby than they were eager to be corrupted into letting us go. Our search over, they turned the key in the door. There was nowhere to sit in the cell. A small barred window let in a few dusty strings of light and the distant sounds of people enjoying themselves.

Jack Wilson and Abel Glaze looked at me. They didn't have to say a word. This was my fault, wasn't it? What had I got them into? Nevertheless we were innocent. Cling to that fact. Rely on English justice and fair play. A few words with Justice Farnaby should be enough to clear up the confusion. Or so I thought.

'Nick,' said Abel, 'have you told us everything?'

'Yes. No. Not exactly,' I said.

'Maybe you had better tell us everything,' said Jack, 'before we find ourselves going to Heaven in a string.'

Jack's reference to a Tyburn execution was casual enough, but it made me feel cold in spite of the stuffy cell.

'There's not much to say,' I said. 'But Ulysses Hatch wasn't only in the business of selling Shakespeare's foul papers . . .'

And so I explained how the bookseller had mistakenly assumed I'd come in quest of the relic, how he'd shown it to me and how – when it was evident that I knew nothing of it – he had hastily hidden it away again in the chest, with instructions to keep mum. The revelation about the relic took them aback, but I could see that they believed me. If I was going to invent a story it wouldn't have been as far fetched as this one.

'That's what you were looking in the trunk for?' said Abel. 'A fragment of the True Cross? Can it really be so?'

'Real or sham, the item has gone.'

'Taken by whoever murdered Hatch?' said Jack.

'It looks like it.'

'Then it's easy,' said Abel. 'We find the person who's in possession of this so-called fragment and get him arrested.'

'And how are *we* going to find this individual when we're locked up in here?' said Jack. 'Besides, if he's any sense he'll be miles away by now.'

'It may be that we're looking for a dead man,' I said. 'Ulysses Hatch told me that to touch the relic was death. It seems to have worked in *his* case.'

Like the remark about the Tyburn string, this added to the general discomfort of the cell.

'Tom Gally is at the fair,' said Jack. 'From what you said, Nick, he was after something.'

'It might have been the foul papers or the piece of the cross – but perhaps he wasn't after anything particular. Gally's the kind of person who sniffs around by instinct. Like a dog. Though it may be that he . . .'

'What?'

'He noticed me leaving Hatch's tent. Perhaps he'd already arranged to buy the relic – or the foul papers – and got worried when he saw me.

Thought I was trying to get my hands on them and stepped in to prevent it.'

'But why should he kill Hatch?' said Jack. 'He'd simply offer him more money than you did. Henslowe's got deep pockets.'

This was true enough and I could think of no reply. After a time, Abel said,

'There were those two women about to fight over Hatch, weren't there? The pig woman and what's her name . . . ?'

'Wapping Doll.'

'Either of them looks as though she'd be capable of felling a man with her bare hands. Where did Wapping Doll go after the Justice broke up the fight? Back to the tent to confront Master Hatch?'

Abel was so excited by this possibility that he couldn't resist throwing us another suspect. 'And don't forget we saw Nightingale's accomplice – that nip called Peter Perkin – coming out of Hatch's tent just as we got there.'

'Hatch was alive then,' I said. 'And afterwards.'

'Perkin could have gone back later.'

'Someone went back later.'

'You said that there was bad feeling between William Shakespeare and Ulysses Hatch?' said Abel.

'Yes. It's one reason why he wasn't willing to deal with the bookseller himself,' I confirmed. 'And before you go any further, Abel, I don't think WS slipped into Hatch's tent and killed him with his own pistol. Have you seen him around this fair? I haven't.'

'Master Shakespeare is good at passing unnoticed,' said Jack.

It was true that WS had the knack of slipping into places and out again without drawing attention to himself, but for some reason the comment irritated me.

'Don't forget he's killed many – in his imagination,' said Abel.

This irritated me even more and I said, 'Well, so have I killed many, and so has everyone, apart from the purest nun.'

'Leaving aside William, we have at least three people who might have done this murder,' said Jack. 'Two of them possibly because they wished to get their hands on the relic, that's Tom Gally and Peter Perkin. And then we have this Wapping Doll, who is apparently jealous of Hatch's success with the pig woman. Perhaps she headed back to the tent when the fight was stopped. Her blood was up and she decided to have it out with him.'

I recalled the scene between Wapping Doll and Ulysses Hatch in the tent. There'd been a kind of ribald affection there. They might strike each other, just as she might swap blows with a woman. But to seize a pistol and shoot him . . . ? And why should she take the so-called relic away with her? She was frightened of it. I didn't think so. I shook my head, and noticed that the others were shaking theirs at the same time.

'It doesn't work, Nick,' said Jack. 'I know Tom Gally a little better than either of you since I've been with the playhouses longer. He's a nasty piece of work, ready to spread lies and slander and not above a spot of pilfering. But that's a distance away from being a murderer.'

'It's the same with Peter Perkin,' said Abel. 'I don't *know* him or Ben Nightingale except by reputation. But nips and foists rely on their wits and the speed of their hands. I have kept company with a few of them in the past. They don't kill people. Why, their proudest boast is to rob you without you noticing it for the next five hours.'

'I was thinking the same about Wapping Doll,' I said. 'She's not a murderer surely. So . . . if we exclude them, who does that leave?'

'It leaves *us*,' said Abel.

'You mean, it leaves *me*,' I said.

My friends didn't reply but I realized that this was exactly what they did mean. I had been summoned into the tent by Ulysses Hatch while they had been left outside, only to drift out of earshot after a few minutes. The bookseller and I had been talking for half an hour perhaps. In all probability, I had been the last person to see him alive apart from his murderer. Of course, Jack and Abel couldn't really think I was guilty of shooting him, could they? If so, why would I have urged them to accompany me on my second visit to Hatch's tent? Besides, if I'd really killed Hatch I would be halfway across the Surrey Downs by now.

These were gloomy thoughts. We lapsed into silence, slouching against the cell walls or sitting with our backs to them. The dusty rays of sunlight inched up the far wall. For all that there was nothing *so* alarming about our present predicament, my confidence that this was a simple confusion which would be cleared up after a few words with Justice Farnaby began to dwindle. I'd been in gaol before, under a false accusation. So had Jack Wilson, come to that, since he'd served a few days in one of the Clink prisons following a youthful affray. And I didn't doubt that Abel was familiar with the inside of a cell or two. Nevertheless, it is not pleasant to be locked up, even for an hour or so. And there's something incongruous about being confined in the midst of a fair while everyone else is so free and easy. When the noises of it – the shouts and the cries and songs – come distantly to your ears you feel like a child, punished and shut out from some treat.

I may have been quietly fearful but, sitting against the rough-cast wall, I fell into a kind of daydream in which the figure of Tom Gally pursued me, trying to sell copies of a pamphlet called *The Wanton Wife* complete with salty pictures. Over Gally's head hovered a raven shrieking 'Jump to it!' Then I visualized a youthful William Shakespeare – more hair in those days – whispering compliments into the ear of an equally youthful Wapping Doll, as fine a piece of goods as Ulysses Hatch had claimed. Suddenly I was woken by the sound of the key turning in the cell door. Jack and Abel also jerked to attention.

The beetle-browed constables stood at the door. By gestures rather than words they indicated that we were to follow them. They escorted us down a flagged passage and into a pillared chamber that had probably been the monks' refectory. At the far end, seated in an oak chair that could have belonged to a prior, was Justice Walter Farnaby, neatly bearded and precise. There were a handful of other individuals standing or sitting near by, including a couple more constables and an elderly clerk positioned behind a table with pen and paper. This was Pie-Powder Court. I don't know the origins of this strange name but I do know that it's not empowered to hear serious cases, only instances of trading without licence or cheating or petty theft. Nevertheless, Justice Farnaby had the authority to arraign any man and to cause him to be taken before a more severe court. We lined up before him, flanked by the constables. To judge by the way he was looking at us, if we weren't quite prisoners we were definitely not free men.

There was a sudden shriek of 'That's him!' from one of the bystanders. This was unnerving. More unnerving still was to discover that it was Wapping Doll. She was pointing at me. Her face was distorted with rage or grief. 'I saw him with my Yew-lee. I left them alone together. He killed Ulysses Hatch!'

'Be silent, woman,' said Justice Farnaby. 'You don't know what you're saying.'

His voice was low but commanding. Wapping Doll gaped but said nothing more.Farnaby requested that we identify ourselves by name and occupation. It was for the record only, since I'd have bet a week's wages he already knew who we were.

'Gentlemen,' said Justice Farnaby to us when this process was complete, 'a man has been murdered. This is too grave a matter for Pie-Powder Court. I have given orders that Hatch's tent is to be guarded before the body is removed. Nevertheless, preliminary statements will be taken here and, if the evidence is persuasive, indictments will follow. I have already heard accounts from several of those who recently saw Master Hatch alive, like that lady there. But you were the first to find him dead. Your stories, if you please.'

Jack and Abel turned to me. This public hearing seemed a slightly irregular way of going about evidence-gathering but I supposed that the Bartholomew Fair court was a more provisional affair, one in which matters had to be settled quickly. As briefly as I could, I outlined the circumstances that had brought the three of us to the fair, my commission from WS, the conversation with the bookseller, the arrangement to return when he'd found the item in question, our discovery of Hatch's body. The elderly clerk took notes of all this, snuffling and clearing his throat in a distracting way.

The only details I omitted were probably the most important ones, to do with the relic. Even though the theft of the fragment provided a motive for murder I didn't want to complicate matters. As it turned out, not mentioning this was a mistake since Farnaby already knew of it.

'Master Hatch showed you nothing else?' he said.

'I am not sure what you mean, sir,' I replied.

'There was no other item of value?'

'I do not recall so.'

'Yet you are carrying four pounds in your purse, are you not? As if you came here with the wherewithal to purchase something of value.'

'That was the sum which Master Shakespeare had given me to buy back his foul papers.'

'The money was not to buy a piece of wood which purported to come from the cross of our Lord and which is no longer to be found anywhere on Master Hatch's premises?'

There was a gasp from someone in the makeshift court at this. I felt myself grow red like a child.

'Wood from the cross?'

'Just so. Did Master Hatch mention such an item?'

'He may have done. I do not take much account of such popish gewgaws but yes, I think he did mention it – now I come to think of it, sir.'

'. . . now you come to think of it, Master Revill. Yet we have testimony that Ulysses Hatch intended to sell this "popish gewgaw", as you call it, and sell it to the players.'

'Not to us, sir,' I said, realizing that such testimony could only have come from Wapping Doll. 'As I said, my business at the fair was simply to buy the foul papers of an early play by William Shakespeare. My friends can confirm this.'

Jack and Abel nodded away but Farnaby no longer seemed very interested.

I became conscious of the wad of papers stowed under my shirt. I rather wished now that I had let them lie under Hatch's body. The Justice's words also cleared up the mystery of why Tom Gally was at the fair. Hatch had intended to sell the 'item' to the players, as reported to Farnaby by Wapping Doll. So Gally had not come in pursuit of the *Domitian* text after all, was perhaps unaware of it. Instead he was on commission from Henslowe to purchase the fragment of the cross. I was considering whether I should name Master Gally when Farnaby put another question to me.

'Did Master Hatch show you a pistol when you were in his tent on the first occasion?'

'Yes, sir. He kept it primed . . .'

'Why?'

'Because the world is full of rogues. They were his words.'

'He's right enough there,' said Justice Farnaby. 'This is the pistol?'

With a flourish he produced the weapon from

the ground beside his chair. It had a bulbous handle and a blunt muzzle. I hadn't noticed it before. Perhaps Farnaby was intending to shock me into a display of guilt.

'I . . . I think so, sir,' I said. 'It's a snaphaunce.'

'Ah, you know your weapons, Master Revill,' said the Justice.

Never handled one, I wanted to say, but it was too late now. I realized that, while the three of us had been stuck in our cell, there'd been plenty of coming and going between the court and the dead man's tent, as well as the taking of witness statements. None of this put us in a good light.

'What happened to the bird?' said Farnaby.

The question, coming abruptly, took me by surprise.

'You mean the raven?'

'Yes. I have testimony that Hatch kept a bird which went by the name of Hold-fast.'

'I do not know what happened to it, sir. The raven was in the tent earlier. When I returned with my friends he had gone. Perhaps he took fright, with his master dead.'

There was a sob from the sidelines. Wapping Doll had her hands to her face in grief.

'Very well,' said Farnaby. 'Have you two associates of Master Revill anything to add to his story?'

When Jack and Abel indicated that they hadn't, Farnaby said, 'This is enough for the present. You may go.'

This sudden dismissal was surprising, but I caught a glance that passed from the Justice to one of the constables. I wondered just how far we would be permitted to go. Outside St Bartholomew's Priory, we debated what to do next. It was afternoon by now. The sun hung in the sky, hot and heavy. Earlier I'd felt hungry, but now I had no appetite left. Abel was for quitting St Bartholomew's Fair and the Smithfield neighbourhood straight away, but Jack said doing that would make us look like guilty men. Out of the corner of my vision I caught sight of one of the beetle-browed constables, undoubtedly ordered by Farnaby to keep an eye on us.

I gestured over my shoulder.

'We've got Gog or Magog on our tail,' I said.

'Gog? Magog?' said Jack.

'My name for the constables,' I said. 'Those hulking fellows who took us in just now. They look like the wooden statues outside the Guildhall, big and ugly brutes.'

Jack looked dubiously at me.

'They didn't find the box or the glass vial or the piece of the cross when they searched us, so they think we must have deposited them somewhere about the fair. They're waiting to see if we go in search of them.'

'As I said, we should get out now,' said Abel.

'No we shouldn't,' I said. 'Look over there. On second thoughts, don't look. Pretend to talk instead.'

In the shadow of the priory, half hidden behind a crumbling buttress, stood two men. Like the seasoned professionals they were, my friends didn't falter but at once entered into an energetic 'conversation' of the sort we often pretended to have on the Globe stage. Meanwhile, between their shoulders, I watched Ben Nightingale the ballad singer and his accomplice, the little man with the rustic hat who went by the name of Peter Perkin.

They must have thought themselves quite unobserved for they were occupied with their business. Their real business, which was the lifting of purses and the division of the spoils. I'd no doubt that was what they were doing now.

The ballad singer had laid aside his lute in favour of his loot, you might say. In his outspread palm he was counting out some items that Perkin had just spilled into it, coins or trinkets presumably, the fruit of the latter's nipping and foisting. Meantime Perkin had picked up Nightingale's lute and was fiddling with it. I wondered that they were so bold to do this out in the open and close to Pie-Powder Court, but they were in a secluded spot and the day's successful labour had perhaps made them careless.

But it wasn't the sight of a couple of thieves counting out their money which interested me. Rather, it was the fact that Perkin, having put down the singer's lute, had suddenly produced from somewhere about his person the wooden box that I'd last seen in Ulysses Hatch's tent. The box with the lid and the star-shaped pattern. The box that had contained the fragment of the cross. So Peter Perkin had been the thief all along! And not just the thief but the murderer too, for whoever had stolen the cross fragment had surely shot Hatch into the bargain. Despite Abel's earlier claim, Perkin the cutpurse was capable of murder after all.

As I watched surreptitiously, Perkin drew the box out into the open and showed it to Nightingale, at the same time shaking his head. As if to prove the honesty of his gesture, he opened the box and held it upside down. Nothing fell out. It was truly empty. Perkin said something else and Nightingale replied. The stiff postures of each man indicated an imminent argument.

If the two men hadn't been so wrapped up in their dialogue they might have noticed me. As it was, Nightingale uttered some more sharp words – which weren't audible – and shook his head so violently that his little red cap almost fell off. For answer Perkin passed him the box. Go on, his whole manner said, if you don't believe me, take a look for yourself. There's nothing inside, it's truly empty.

The ballad singer seized the box and raised it to his eyes as if to give it further scrutiny. Perkin grew more determined to make his point, and he gesticulated and flapped his arms about. Nightingale's mouth gaped, giving a good impression of surprise or disbelief. I couldn't understand what they were on about. Once again the singer examined the interior of the box. Then he looked over the rim and saw me staring at him. And immediately his eyes flicked over my shoulder and I saw them widen in surprise or fear. I glanced round. Approaching us was the constable whom I'd christened Gog (or maybe it was Magog).

After that a couple of things happened simultaneously.

I decided that the only way to prove my – or our – absolute innocence in the matter of Hatch's murder was to lay hands on Peter Perkin the cutpurse and Ben Nightingale the ballad singer *and* on the box, which, empty or not, would be proof of their complicity in theft. I say 'decided' but of course it was an instinctive move. Yelling something to my friends, I started off towards the shadowy spot where the two men were standing.

But, already alarmed by the appearance of Magog (or Gog), Nightingale snatched up his lute with one hand and, still holding on to the wooden box with the other, slipped round the buttress and took to his heels. His accomplice was a second or so behind him, but he too was away before I got within twenty yards.

Nightingale and Perkin would have done better to have stood still and tried to brazen it out. Running was a sign of guilt. And even someone as dense as the constable could react to a running man, as a hound reacts to a hare. I sensed rather than saw him lumbering after us.

The ballad singer and the cutpurse would also have done better to separate so as to divide pursuit, but Perkin stuck close to Nightingale's track. The priory lay on the north side of Smithfield and the edge of the Bartholomew ground. Indeed, this point really marked the ragged fringe of London. There were a few people about but most of the crowd was still at the heart of the fair.

Given their head start and likely practice in running, it was quite possible that the thieves might have outpaced us and made their getaway among the lanes and ditches that fanned out into the open fields of Hoxton or Islington. But suddenly, from behind the wall of an outbuilding, there sprang the other constable, Gog (or Magog). Whether he acted by instinct or whether he was more quick-thinking than I'd credited either of them with being, he stuck out his long staff so that it tangled up in Ben Nightingale's legs. The singer, impeded by what he was carrying, stumbled and fell. His red cap flew off while his lute somersaulted into the air before crashing to the ground with an unmusical clatter. Then the constable gave him a clout over the head.

Perkin the cutpurse almost collided with his fallen companion, although he jumped to one side at the last moment and drew off to the left. But he'd lost precious seconds by the manoeuvre and, with four individuals on his tail, he didn't stand much of a chance. Small fellow that he was, he was soon overwhelmed by all our attentions.

I left it to the others to deal with Perkin and went in search of the box, which Nightingale had also dropped as he fell. I found it on its side a few yards off. It wasn't quite empty for, wedged in a corner, was the strip of parchment that Ulysses Hatch had claimed showed the authenticity of the fragment of the cross. The parchment was so faded, however, and the words so hard to decipher, that, by itself, this would prove little. Nevertheless, I carefully nestled the box under my arm and joined the others. Ben Nightingale was on his feet but looked as though he scarcely knew where he was – or indeed who he was. He was holding his bare head where the constable had thwacked it.

Gog and Magog looked gratified to have apprehended two more villains who had demonstrated their turpitude by fleeing. When I indicated that we should all return to Pie-Powder Court and Justice Farnaby, they seemed happy enough to fall in with the idea. On our way there, I noticed Abel pick up Nightingale's fractured lute. For his part, the singer was still not sure what was going on and staggered forward clutching his head. Peter Perkin, meanwhile, looked crestfallen.

'This is the singer's means of trade,' said Abel, cradling the lute in his arms. The neck of the instrument was splintered and the strings tangled.

'Singer? He's a thief – or worse,' I said, full of righteousness that we had tracked down the individuals responsible for Hatch's demise.

'It will be a long time before he makes enough money to buy another of these,' said Abel, gazing on the lute as though it were a sickly baby.

'Then he can always steal one,' I said, wondering at Abel's softness. I suppose it was because he had once earned his living by trickery that he had a sneaking sympathy with unreformed cony-catchers.

We returned to the priory and to the hall where Justice Farnaby was still sitting on his oak chair, as if waiting for more malefactors to be produced. I was eager to explain that we'd come back with proof, of a sort, as to the real identity of the thieves and probable murderers of Ulysses Hatch. Wapping Doll was still there. To her especially I was eager to show that I was no murderer. I handed over the box to the Justice, describing how this was the very object I'd first seen in Hatch's hands and then in Perkin's possession before it was seized by Nightingale. The cutpurse looked indignant but it was for form's sake only. Gog and Magog could add their testimony to the effect that I was telling the truth, I said, appealing to the constables.

Farnaby opened the box and took out the fragile strip of parchment. He glanced at it for an instant then shut the box once more. He looked at Nightingale, who was still clutching his battered noddle, and at Perkin. He considered, for a long period he considered.

'Wait in there with your friends, Master Revill,' he said, gesturing towards a door at the side of the hall. 'Let me hear what these individuals have to say for themselves.'

Jack and Abel and I filed into a room that must have been the kitchen to the refectory. There was an open fireplace with a roasting-spit operated by a small treadmill. A dog would have turned the treadmill in the monks' time. The equipment was old and rusted. The kitchen door was firmly closed on us. Again, if we weren't quite prisoners we weren't free men either. My confidence that justice was about to be done dwindled slightly.

'Where's this bit of the "true" cross, then?' said Jack. 'All that Perkin had was the box which you said it was in.'

'That's only what he showed Nightingale, the empty box,' I said. 'Most likely he'd already taken it for himself. Maybe he was planning to sell it on his own account.'

'If it ever existed,' said Jack. In his irritation he tried to spin the treadmill, which was connected to the spit by a sagging chain. It creaked like some ancient implement of torture.

'I saw it, I tell you, I saw it in Ulysses Hatch's own hands.'

'Well, *he* can't testify any longer, can he? And now it's vanished into thin air.'

'Nick's not the only one to know of it,' said Abel, coming to my rescue. 'Justice Farnaby mentioned it. Someone must have informed *him*.'

'Wapping Doll,' I said. 'She knew about the cross, said it brought her out in goose bumps.'

'Then her bumps can be brought in evidence,' said Jack. 'Until such time we shall have to say that the cross has gone.'

'Perhaps this can be repaired,' said Abel, changing the subject. 'I'm not an expert, mind . . .'

Abel was still holding Nightingale's damaged lute. And, watching him, an ingenious idea flashed into my mind. I recalled the scene of the two thieves standing in the shadow of the buttress. The way in which Perkin had been fiddling with the instrument while his friend was counting out the coins in his hand. Suppose that Perkin had got the bit of sacred wood after all and did plan to keep it for himself. Suppose the plan had come to him at the very instant the two men were counting out their money in the shade of the buttress. Perkin is holding the wooden box containing the item. He's about to surrender it to the singer when greed gets the better of him. He palms the glass vial and, almost before he's aware of what he's doing, slips it into a convenient hiding place instead of handing it over. Then he shows Nightingale the empty box, pretending ignorance of its contents. Meantime the glass vial and the relic are somewhere else altogether.

'Give me the lute, Abel. I've got an idea.'

Abel passed me the broken instrument. The neck was cracked and splintered and some of the strings had snapped. I shook the thing. Something rattled within. I dug my hand through the sound-hole and rummaged about the interior of the lute. With mounting certainty, I grasped hold of an elongated object. It didn't feel like glass but wood. Too late I remembered Ulysses Hatch's warning, *They say that to touch it is death.* But I'd already seized the wooden piece and was easing it out of the sound-hole. The thrill of being proved right banished fears of an old wives' curse. Like a magician, I uncurled my palm and showed Jack and Abel what it contained.

'See! I told you!'

'Yes, I see it,' said Jack. 'So what?'

Only now did I glance down at the item in my palm. It was a shaped sliver of wood all right, but it wasn't a piece of the True Cross. For one thing, the wood was new and unscarred.

'That is a sound-post, Nick,' said Abel. 'Every lute has them. They're put inside to strengthen the frame.'

'So what exactly was your idea, Nicholas?' said Jack. 'That the cutpurse might have slipped what you're searching for inside the lute?'

'Stranger things have happened,' I said.

I could see from the expression on Jack's face that he was undecided whether to laugh or curl his lip in scorn. Abel merely looked baffled.

Luckily, at that moment the kitchen door opened and once again Gog (or Magog) ushered us into Justice Farnaby's presence. The scene was much as we'd left it. Peter Perkin, still crestfallen, stood before the oak chair. Ben Nightingale was sitting on a bench, looking dazed. The aged clerk's pen was poised above a pile of paper. The only change was in the expression on Farnaby's face. Instead of looking grave and precise, he looked rather as Jack had done just now, somewhere between amused and scornful.

'They say truth will out, don't they,' he said, half to himself. 'Well, Master Revill, it appears as though you at least were telling the truth. The trouble is that a grain of truth is wrapped up in a tissue of lies.'

I nodded, though I hadn't the slightest notion what he was talking about.

'This person here,' continued Farnaby, indicating Perkin the cutpurse, 'has made a deposition to Pie-Powder Court. My clerk here will read out the salient features of it.'

The clerk, elderly, with grey hair straggling from under his cap, bent his head to the topmost sheet of paper and cleared his throat in a way that might have been thought excessive onstage.

'Witness Perkin deposes ... let me see ... deposes that he is in the habit of attending Bartholomew Fair, sometimes in company with his good friend Benjamin Nightingale, ballad singer of Tooley Street ... because he enjoys the honey tones of his friend's voice when he sings ... witness deposes that his mother, that is Ben Nightingale's mother, knew what she was about when she married a man called Nightingale and that she must have had foreknowledge that her son would grow into a fine—'

'Never mind all that nonsense,' said Farnaby. 'Get to the quick of the matter.'

Put out, the clerk snuffled. He coughed to clear his throat and moved his pen down the page.

' ... er ... witness Perkin acknowledges that he is a dealer in small items ... he calls himself a, er, "snapper-up of trifles" ... this is his sole trade ... Perkin says that he went to the tent of one Ulysses Hatch, publisher and bookseller, because he had purchased items from the aforesaid Hatch on other occasions. Once in the tent, Perkin was shown a box which contained a glass tube which contained, in turn, a piece of wood which the aforesaid Hatch claimed to be a fragment from the cross of the Lord Jesus Christ. Witness states that he enquired as to the price of the item but then left the tent because his pockets were not deep enough for the item in question. Asked to explain this, he said that he didn't have the cash. Furthermore, he said, he was somewhat alarmed by the presence of a talking raven in the tent. Outside the tent witness saw three gentlemen who from their shifty expressions he judged to be players . . .'

We stiffened at this but Justice Farnaby shot us a warning glance.

'Perkin deposes that he later thought better of his rejection of the item and, after consulting with his good friend Nightingale, returned to the tent to make another offer to Ulysses Hatch, publisher and bookseller . . .'

At this point the clerk was overcome by a fit of coughing and lost his place in the text. Farnaby looked on with pursed lips. Presumably what we were listening to was what the Justice had recently referred to as a tissue of lies. Perkin as a snapper-up of trifles, eh? Well, that was one way of describing a cutpurse. The only accurate parts of the statement related to Perkin's account of his two visits to Hatch's tent. Whether he was there by chance on the first occasion or whether he was on the lookout for what he could filch, he'd been shown the glass vial. Hatch had obviously been as prepared to sell it to the cutpurse as to Tom Gally. Hadn't he said he'd sell to anyone if the price was right? Perkin had left the tent, bumping into us on the way out. With or without consulting Nightingale, he'd gone back in an attempt to steal the relic. Perhaps he'd sneaked into the tent somehow, been surprised by Hatch and a struggle had followed. Perkin had wrested the pistol from Hatch's grasp . . . so that it detonated at close quarters . . . but if that was so, surely he'd be covered in burns or scorch marks?

The clerk gave a final cough, expelling a bolus of phlegm into a filthy handkerchief. Then he resumed his, or rather Perkin's, account.

' . . . witness deposes that he entered Master Hatch's tent to negotiate over the sale of the relic. There was a pistol lying to one side on top of a chest. Witness says he does not know whether he was more alarmed by the sight of the pistol or by the presence of the raven which told him to, er, jump to it. For a second time, the aforesaid Hatch produced the box which contained the glass vial which contained, in turn, a piece—'

'Oh, get on with it, man,' said Farnaby. 'We know what it contained. To the quick of the matter.'

'Yes, sir . . . witness Perkin states that the next thing which happened was . . . was that . . .'

But we were never destined to learn what happened next from the clerk's own mouth for he was again seized by a coughing fit. His thin frame shook and he unfolded the filthy handkerchief again preparatory to expelling whole flights of phlegm.

Justice Farnaby, despairing of his clerk, had to speak up loudly to drown out the sounds of hawking and spitting. 'In short, witness Perkin here claims that he is quite innocent of the murder of Ulysses Hatch, publisher and bookseller. He says that the real killler is—'

'Shut your gob!'

As it happened, the clerk's titanic throat-clearing ceased at the very moment that these heretical words rang out in Pie-Powder Court. Or rather, the words didn't so much ring out as squawk out. Another oddity was that the words were delivered not from ground level, where a man might have been standing, but from many feet above our heads. The refectory was criss-crossed by beams.

We all looked up. On a beam almost directly above Justice Farnaby was perched a bird that I recognized. So did Peter Perkin. He held out a trembling arm.

'That's him,' he said. 'That's the bird that killed his master. He jumped on the pistol as it was lying there and the thing fell sideways and got discharged somehow and shot Master Hatch in the throat.'

'Shut your gob!' said Hold-fast, and then for good measure, 'Jump to it!'

The raven bent his head downward, assessing the effect of his instructions to the court. Nobody spoke. The Justice was silent. Even the clerk stopped examining the contents of his handkerchief to raise his head.

For some reason I straight away believed what Perkin had said. It was too ridiculous not to be true. Who could make up such a tale? I'd seen for myself the primed pistol and the way in which Hatch laid it carelessly to one side when we were talking. It was quite plausible that the bird had landed – clumsily, accidentally, even intentionally perhaps (for who can tell what was going on inside that dark little head) – on the thing and had set it off. Men are always shooting at birds. Why shouldn't it happen the other way about, and a bird shoot a man? Even with a bird that had adopted a man and might be presumed to be his special friend.

Hold-fast wasn't planning to submit to questions from anybody. He seemed to duck out of sight. But he was only gone for an instant. Next, with a flap of his black wings, he was down at ground level, although careful to keep out of the reach of all of us. He paraded up and down a stretch of flag-stoned floor, more cocksure than any Justice you've ever seen. Mind you, he looked a bit ragged. Even at a distance his plumage did not seem as glossy as it had earlier in the day. His feathers were, literally, ruffled. There were smudges around his head. Exactly the sort of marks you might expect to see if a pistol had exploded somewhere in his vicinity.

What gave added credence to Perkin's tale was the fact that Hold-fast was not talking now. No commands to 'shut up' or to 'jump to it' issued from his mouth. He wasn't speaking because he couldn't. Tucked athwart his beak was a glass tube, which he must have temporarily deposited up aloft so as to give us the benefit of his voice. It was, for certain, the vial, which contained a piece of . . . well, you know what it contained. It was as if he'd brought this item to Pie-Powder Court for proof and waited up in the roof until the right moment came. Then he'd flown down from the beam to show us precisely what he'd done.

And, having shown us, Hold-fast flapped aloft once more and resumed his perch on the cross-beam. Still clutching the vial, he waddled sideways towards the point where the beam joined the wall. Being a monastic building, the refectory was well supplied with windows. In the old days, before the suppression, they were probably filled with fine coloured glass. Now they were mostly unglazed so that the winter winds and the airs of summer could come and go freely through them. On a hot August day it was pleasant to have unglazed windows. Useful too for Hold-fast, who wanted to make his exit as easily as he must have made his entrance. Reaching the end of the beam, and with one final cock of his head in the direction of his human audience, he slipped over the lintel of a window and apparently vanished into the afternoon. I've seen well-known players, especially the clowns among us, make their exits in just that way. With a knowing nod towards the crowd and a kind of aren't-I-the-very-Devil air to their departure.

Nobody spoke. Nobody moved for an instant. I'm not sure that everyone understood what had just happened. Gog and Magog and the other constables stared as if the appearance of a guilty raven was an everyday occurrence in Pie-Powder Court. Poor old Ben Nightingale was still recovering from being struck by a constable's staff. The aged clerk resumed his throat-clearing. But the quicker-witted among us – Perkin, Justice Farnaby, us players and even Wapping Doll – realized that we'd witnessed something very peculiar.

'Well, go after it,' said Walter Farnaby to no one in particular.

And, as if that was our cue, we rushed out of St Bartholomew's Priory in the forlorn hope of laying hands on Hold-fast. Outside, the sun had slipped down a notch or two. The sounds of the fair – the cries and the songs and the raucous laughter – filled the heavy air.

Instinctively I looked up at the flank of the

building, where we'd seen the raven make his exit.
It was as if he'd been waiting for us to emerge, I
swear, because at that moment Hold-fast lifted off
from the window ledge. He must have been
wanting one last glimpse of his pursuers, to taunt
them finally. As he extended his wings, I observed
a certain raggedness to one of them. Perhaps it was
just his age (*he's an old boy*, Hatch had said) or
perhaps it was the result of standing too close to an
exploding pistol. And as Hold-fast flapped away,
the sun glinted off what he held in his beak. Hold-
fast was a good name for him. He'd not let go of
that object before he had good cause.

'And you followed him?' said WS.
'Not so much followed him,' I said, 'but we saw
the general direction he was going in. He was
heading for the river, flying south. Perhaps he was
going to deliver it to Henslowe.'
'A raven won't deliver anything to anyone,' said
WS. 'He is his own man.'
I was sitting in Shakespeare's lodgings in
Mugwell Street. They were good lodgings. We were
drinking wine. It was good wine, fitting for one of
the Globe shareholders. WS was all concern and
solicitousness. He'd been appalled to hear of the
trouble and to-do which Jack and Abel and I had
tumbled into the previous day on his behalf and in
pursuit of his *Domitian* foul papers. Although some
of his concern was purely rhetorical, I knew WS
well enough to recognize that he was being sincere,
mostly.
The rescued foul papers now lay on a table
beside their creator, an untidy little pile. He'd
hardly glanced at them. The paper was old and

yellow. The sheets were streaked red with Hatch's blood, and they were creased from where they'd been nestling under my shirt the previous day. Nevertheless, all's well that ends well . . . as it says somewhere.

'According to Ulysses Hatch, there was a legend attached to the cross fragment,' I said. 'It was cursed. Whoever touched it would die. It seemed to work in his case.'

'I've heard such stories before,' said WS. 'Also that the last person to possess such an item will perish when he parts from it. I wonder if the raven will let it drop from his beak now . . . ?'

I visualized Hold-fast letting go of the glass vial, perhaps because (bright and shiny though it was) he could see no ultimate purpose for it. I visualized him dropping it somewhere on the remote wastes of the Thames foreshore, the vial landing in the soft mud or in the water.

'So you think that Tom Gally was out to purchase the relic on Henslowe's behalf?' said WS.

'That's what it looked like. The story was that Hatch intended to sell it to some "players". Gally made himself pretty scarce. There was no sign of him at the fair later on.'

'He probably got wind of what happened to Hatch. And as for those other two, Nightingale and—'

'Peter Perkin. I think they just blundered into the situation by chance. In fact, I don't believe the ballad singer had much to do with it. He was the singing attraction, he just stood there and warbled while Perkin picked out the marks. Perkin was the cutpurse. He'd probably gone to Hatch's tent to purchase some of his spicy wares. While he was there Hatch saw a selling opportunity. He told me he'd sell anything if the price was right. It wouldn't matter if he'd already promised the item to Henslowe. And when Perkin glimpsed the relic, he must have thought he was going to make some easy money. His story was true enough. He was negotiating with Hatch for a second time when the bird hopped down and dislodged the gun, setting it off.'

'Can that happen?' said WS.

'Abel Glaze has some knowledge of these things,' I said. 'Once when he was in the Low Countries he saw a fellow whose pistol dropped from his belt by accident. It hit the ground and went off, killing him stone dead.'

'And so Ulysses Hatch died by his own weapon.'

'Perkin claimed he was deafened and terrified. He fled from the tent, clutching the empty box. Later on he met up with Nightingale and they divided the day's takings. He was showing him the empty box and telling him the story of what happened, flapping his arms like a bird. I don't think Nightgingale believed him. Who would?'

'Until the bird himself appeared to give evidence,' said WS. 'Naturally the raven picked up the glass vial. Bright and shiny and valuable.'

'Then he must have waddled out of the tent,' I said.

'Did Justice Farnaby bring the humans to account for their thieving?'

'He did not, William. I think that he was so . . . surprised by the turn of events that he had no appetite for relatively trivial offences. Besides, there wasn't any evidence against Perkin or Nightingale. No one saw them stealing anything. The money they had *could* have been their own, honestly earned. No, they got off scot-free. And Hatch's death is accounted a strange misadventure.'

WS turned to one side and picked up the sheaf of paper from the table. He crossed to the fireplace and deposited the sheets there. He struck a flint and set the flame to the paper.

'There,' he said as he watched the fire catch hold and the sheets curl and blacken. 'Sometimes flame is the author's best friend. No one will ever see or hear of my *Domitian* again. You have done me no small favour, Nick.'

'In return, I shall ask for some information.'

'If I can give it.'

'You were once familiar with someone called Doll. Wapping Doll?'

WS had been crouching on his hams supervising the destruction of his script. Now he levered himself to his feet once more, groaning slightly and making some time-filling comment about old bones.

'Wapping Doll? No, I don't think so.'

'Ulysses Hatch said differently.'

'Did he now?'

'Said that you and he had once had a falling- out over her.'

'Never contradict a dead man,' said WS.

'Was he right?'

'Why so insistent, Nick?'

Now it was my turn to feel uncomfortable.

'Do you mean to ask,' said WS, 'whether I was once young and energetic and far from home in this great city, as you were yourself not so long ago? And glad of company?'

'I suppose so,' I said.

'Young ravens must have food, you know. However, your question is a fair one, considering what you've done for me. I've never told you of my early years in London, have I?'

'Not much,' I said.

'Then I shall tell you now.'

And he did.

EPILOGUE

Greenwich, London, 2005

The turbid waters of the Thames swirled around the bend in the river, like dirty cocoa in some gigantic drainpipe. Half a dozen workmen in their yellow hard hats fussed over the unloading of steel girders from a barge that was moored to a landing stage on the south shore. A telescopic crane mounted on the back of a huge truck was swinging the two-ton girders around in a wide arc to deposit them on the ground behind the wharf. The Millennium Dome was undergoing yet another facelift to try to establish some enterprise that might at last allow the place to start making a profit.

The foreman looked back at the unlovely hemisphere as he took out a narrow tin to roll himself a skinny cigarette. 'Waste of time, this job. The bloody place is cursed!' he muttered pessimistically.

Yelling 'Take five!' to the other men, he gestured to the crane driver. Stefan Kozlowski locked his controls and left a girder swaying gently twenty feet above the ground. Clambering down, he gratefully arched his aching back and, lighting a cigarette, ambled along the debris-strewn foreshore beyond the landing stage to stretch his legs. After he had walked a few yards, a glint of yellow caught his eye, and he bent to pick up what he hoped was a gold coin.

It was embedded in the old mud well above the high-tide mark, and when he pulled it, a small glass tube slid reluctantly from the filth with a sucking sound. When he wiped the top, it glistened, but when he scratched it with a fingernail, Stefan saw that what shone in the sunlight was just the peeling remains of gold leaf.

Idly, he pulled out the tight-fitting bung from the mud-smeared tube and shook out what was inside. To his disgust, it was just a piece of rotted wood, sodden and crumbling. He poked it around his palm with a finger, then shrugged and put it back in the vial. Just above him on the bank was one of the large rubbish skips that dotted the construction site around the Dome, and with an overarm toss that would have done credit to a Test cricketer, he sent the disappointing object sailing up into the skip.

Soon there was another yell from the foreman, ordering everyone back to work, and with a sigh Stefan trudged back towards his crane. He didn't much like his job, but it was better than being unemployed in Cracow. As he passed under the load he had left suspended, disdaining all those stupid British Health and Safety Regulations, there was another frantic scream from his foreman.

Later, when the ambulances, the police cars and the duty undertaker's van had left, a battered truck came to remove the skip, taking its load of hard core to add to the foundations of a new Church of the Holy Cross which was being built in Bromley.

The End

SIMON & SCHUSTER

The Medieval Murderers
Sword of Shame

Five enthralling interlinked mysteries from Michael Jecks, Susanna Gregory, Bernard Knight, Ian Morson and Philip Gooden.

Qui falsitate vivit, animam occidit. Falsus in ore, caret honore.
The Latin inscription carved on the gleaming blade read:
He who lives in falsehood slays his soul; he who lies, his honour.
If only they had known how true those words would prove
to be . . .

Lovingly crafted by a Saxon swordsmith shortly before the
Norman invasion, treachery and deceit are the Sword of
Shame's constant companions. From the Norman
conquest of 1066 to the murder of Thomas à Becket,
from an attempted coup against Richard the Lionheart to
the bloodstained battle of Poitiers: at the heart of every
treasonous plot, murder and betrayal lies the malign
influence of the cursed sword. As it passes from owner to
owner in this intriguing series of interlinked mysteries, ill
fortune and disgrace befall all who wield its glittering but
deadly blade.

Sword of Shame is the second series of gripping medieval
mysteries from the acclaimed authors of *The Tainted Relic*.

ISBN 0 7432 8545 X
PRICE £10.99

POCKET
BOOKS

This book and other **Simon & Schuster and Pocket Books** titles are available from your local bookshop or can be ordered direct from the publisher.

074328545X	**Sword of Shame**	£10.99
0743492153	**The Elixir of Death**	£6.99
0743492145	**Figure of Hate**	£6.99
0743449894	**The Witch Hunter**	£6.99
0743449908	**Fear in the Forest**	£6.99
0671029673	**The Grim Reaper**	£6.99
0671029665	**The Tinner's Corpse**	£6.99

Please send cheque or postal order for the value of the book, free postage and packing within the UK; OVERSEAS including Republic of Ireland £1 per book.

OR: Please debit this amount from my
VISA/ACCESS/MASTERCARD..
CARD NO:..
EXPIRY DATE...
AMOUNT £...
NAME...
ADDRESS...
....
SIGNATURE...

Send orders to SIMON & SCHUSTER CASH SALES
PO Box 29, Douglas Isle of Man, IM99 1BQ
Tel: 01624 836000, Fax: 01624 670923
www.bookpost.co.uk
Please allow 14 days for delivery. Prices and availability
subject to change without notice